CHRIS HART

Gravity
of the
Divine

The Future depends on what we do in the present.

Mahatma Ghandi

Nitere Publishing: ISBN 978-1-9993194-5-8
Worldwide Copyright © Chris Hart 2021
All rights reserved.
Cover Design by Chris Hart

First Edition

This is a work of fiction. Names, characters, places and incidents either are the product of the author's imagination or, if real, are used fictitiously.
No part of this book may be reproduced, transmitted, stored in an information retrieval system in any form or using any means, graphic, electronic, chemical, biological, optical or mechanical, including photocopying, digitising, taping and recording, without prior written permission from the author.

*For my wife, my girls
and my mentors of Science Fiction who inspired me
to write.*

1: PRAGUE 2258 CE 5
2: ARRIVAL 2275 CE 28
3: PLANS 57
4: POWER 65
5: BUSINESS 79
6: MURDER 88
7: KINSHIP 97
8: WEAPON 108
9: BELIEF 115
10: APPREHENSION 131
11: GAMES 145
12: BLOOD 169
13: DEFENCE 186
14: SHOWDOWN 198
15: ATTACK 218
16: DISCOVERY 258
17: RAID 276
18: SUCCESSION 290
19: ULTIMATUM 311
20: ALLIANCES 324
21: SURVIVAL 350

1: Prague 2258 CE

"To the left!" Trent shouted a warning. Cole threw himself to the floor and twisted, releasing a salvo of plasma pellets from his compact rifle toward the indicated target. Bricks exploded from the ruined walls in front of the enemy bunker.

Trent stepped forward, there was no cover for the World Gov soldiers, caught in the middle of the wide pedestrianised causeway of the ancient city. He sighted along his rifle and lined up his shot. A hail of bullets ran across the pavement and up his leg. Trent cursed as his knee buckled with the impact and he rolled to the ground. His armoured nano-suit had not been penetrated by the mass of hot lead, but his reaction had drawn jeers from the rebels as both soldiers now lay in the street, their integrated suit helmets darkened now from pale green to dark blue as the full armour setting activated, obscuring their features.

"I've had enough of this!" Cole was angry. He knelt upright and swung his pack from his back, ignoring the hail of lead surrounding him. Withdrawing a weapon slightly wider and clumsier than his pistol; he stood up and took aim. The gun whined for a few seconds then discharged a piercing blue flame as the white spherical projectile ejected. The plasma shell moved as if lobbed by a child, toward the concealed bunker protecting their enemy.

Trent witnessed the weapon choice from a few metres away and realised he was too close. He scrambled behind Cole for safety. The explosion sent a tremor through the ancient city centre. It ripped the air from the street, replacing it with the dust of the bunker, the buildings and the last of the enemy. The world fell silent.

"That was our only plasma shell. The next bunker will be..." complained Trent.

"Come on, I'm tired." Cole was in no mood to listen to Trent complain. "Break out the coffee."

They moved to a dismal ruined building across the street. Once a petite street-café, only its front wall remained standing. The door was locked. Discarded iron street furniture was heaped before it, the building behind, gone.

"Coffee's bitter." It was a simple statement of fact. The two young men resumed their comfortable silence and stared along the debris strewn avenue flanked on either side by the newly ruined ancient buildings. They sat at a reasonably undamaged iron table extracted from the pile of twisted metal; they had scavenged two serviceable chairs and despite the destruction around them, had even found some chipped, but otherwise intact crockery. The brown air choked the view and the silence leant an unrealistic fugue to the tableau.

"Looks like rain!" Cole's remark was a peace offering. They both relaxed at the comment and the tension broke; it hadn't rained in Europe for twenty years.

"I checked the label, your armour's waterproof." Camaraderie restored.

"These suits are a lot better than the old ones." It sounded like a complement. Trent wasn't gulled, he waited for the 'but' that usually followed his friend's remarks. "But... it could do with a bit more padding around..." He indicated the area in contact with his rusty wrought iron seat.

The war had made most of the cities uninhabitable, poisoning the world with a legacy of fine yellow dust that settled everywhere. Even two hundred years later, the suffocating properties of the dust had preserved the ruins of an earlier age. While the seats were sturdy, the intricate filigree design had almost disappeared as time continued to win minor battles to reclaim details of the past.

An intimidating six-wheeled armoured vehicle glided silently to a halt beside them. Each wheel was as tall as a man. The dark presence unmarred except for the insignia of the World Gov, the pseudo religious power, publicly intent on reunification and reparation of the world at any cost. No windows were visible and they had no idea who was contained within.

Trent stared at the logo almost hypnotised. The black circle containing the red cross sitting in a pool of flame and considered his ministry training.

"The cross indicates compassion," his tutor had said, "The black circle is the abyss from which we pull the world and the purification of flame indicates our divine right to purge the heretics who prevent us from doing God's will." Trent hated it.

"Just a thought," Trent decided to voice his discontent. "If the black is the 'Abyss', then why do they dress us in black. The helmet's black, the guns are black, that vehicle is black..."

"Armour Grey." Interrupted his friend.

"Sorry?"

"I saw a tin of it once, when I was doing a stint in logistics. It's called Armour Grey."

Trent considered this new information. His momentary passion spent, the men resumed their silence and sipped their coffee. Sparks played across the energy fields that provided their faceplates; the pale green colour indicating filter mode. Simple adjustments to power and frequency enabled the faceplates to allow clean air through or keep bullets out.

The two salvaged ceramic cups from the detritus of the once quaint café had each been given a cursory wipe, knowing that when passed through the glowing barrier, any residual dust would be eliminated along with poisonous airborne particles, protecting their bodies and their pure air supply.

When lifted to their lips the energy screen analysed the contents and removed all contaminants from the beverage leaving behind a pristine white wedge of disinfected ceramic where the cup passed through. The coffee as dark as the marks beneath their eyes, became tepid and bland as the filter did its work.

The vehicle remained unmoving, unreactive, seemingly content to eavesdrop on their conversation.

"Probably the tech team," suggested Trent, "waiting for us to 'liberate' that power plant. Come on Cole, break over." The young man stood. Placing his hands on the back of his head, he bent and stretched to loosen his body. It had been a tiring three days in Prague. One last objective before they could rest.

Synchronised to his movement, a personal drone evaluated his intention and lifted silently from behind a nearby pile of rubble. Its chrome body and flashing blue light indicating the absence of detected threats; the device assumed its vigilant position above him.

Cole gently replaced the cups in their saucers and stood. The razed city around him and the total destruction of the ancient café itself, did not lessen his need to tidy the table before he left. His own accompanying drone took its guardian station above his shoulder. Each soldier twisted and bent, stretching emphatically to relieve their stiff joints as they retrieved their weapons and packs.

Without another word they started down the wide avenue heading east toward a decrepit bridge over the now dried bed of a once important river. In another time their stroll would have been construed as leisure, even romance, but beyond their visible line of sight lay the enemy stronghold.

A harsh escape of pressure signalled activity from the vehicle. The men stopped and turned to see what was happening. Exiting the vehicle, a World Gov officer sporting black armour trimmed with the red insignia of technician had approached the table and was scanning the cups with a hand-held device.

"Take care," the voice on their comms was female. The men smiled at the pleasantry, "If you damage that reactor, I'll skin both of you alive." She held up the DNA scanner, "...and I know who you are." There was a trace of humour, but no joy in the words. The two men resumed their daylight promenade toward the target.

"I wish someone would shoot me," Cole broke the silence with yet another moan. "My suit's down to seventy-two percent."

"I told you to keep it off full-armour mode unless you need it. It eats through the power." Trent had modified his own suit with extra power packs, but Cole had a habit of leaving his basic issue suit on armour mode hours after a fire-fight. "Can't charge it out here."

An imposing square grey building marred the ornate parkland around it. The trees a hundred years dead, their ossified limbs parodying a winters afternoon; their bark blackened with age. The branches powdered in the ubiquitous fine yellow radioactive dust that settled everywhere in the old city; a poor substitute for the fabled snow seen only in children's storybooks. Forty percent sterile earth, thirty percent sulphur and thirty percent... God only knows. Man's gift of death to the planet.

"Who's in there?" Trent stood looking at the square featureless reactor building. The scorched earth around its perimeter evidence of the initial bombardment last night; wiping out all external defences. The twisted metal remnants of defence emplacements providing a firm statement of the current tenants' desire to resist eviction.

"Russian mafia... according to control." Cole read the screen hovering in front of his faceplate.

"Well, I bet your suit comes out with more power than you've got now." Trent held his hand out to seal the wager.

"No bet." Cole's face clouded over. "Damn Russians, don't know how to die."

"Could be worse, could be the Tongs. Much better weapons than the Russian's."

"I thought they'd been taken over by the Yakuza..."

"Both working together now. Can't remember what they call themselves, seem to have a new leader every week." Trent's voice became lighter, "Hey, look at the bright side, at least we brought together a couple of ancient enemies; 'Working together in peace toward a common goal'." He couldn't keep a straight face and chortled as he quoted one of the many propaganda slogans used freely by the World Gov.

"Our destruction... hardly a goal to celebrate." Cole was distracted, something was wrong.

The drones gave a shriek and engaged their camouflage, removing themselves from visibility. The ground opened up ahead of them, falling away to form a ramp down into the ground. Four armour clad bodies advanced from the revealed subterranean bunkers, guns blazing. Cole responded with a return of fire and put one down, though the recumbent target continued to fire.

Trent instantly set his visor to full armour mode and dived to the floor; he sighted carefully and took out a second. The body fell and ceased to move.

"Old suits, external armour; they're not moving fast," crowed Cole. His shots pierced the suits of the criminals. Armour plates shattered and flew from their bodies, useless under the onslaught of modern World Gov plasma weapons. Each energy pellet ripping asunder the atomic bonds of the material it hit.

***

Within the reactor building, sat in a dark conference room behind a flimsy plastic table, a well-groomed muscular man in a modern red nano-armour suit sipped a clear liquid from a shot glass. He smacked his lips appreciatively and stared at the holo screens before him.

A young soldier barged through the door excitedly, "World Gov soldiers are here!" His ragged breath and excited tone betrayed his eagerness for confrontation. "Do you want us to arm the Synths?"

The old man looked at his young cousin in his bulky patched enviro-suit and frowned, fewer men these days spoke the mother tongue.

"No, they are not ready." His thick Russian accent clouded his response, but his tone of authority sobered the excited man.

The young recruit became distracted, entranced by the glowing monitors, he stood awaiting orders. He stared at the strange flickering images. It was not the first time he'd seen them. Once before the strange images had spoken, when the 'liberators' had arrived to 'purify' his village. They'd seemed like magic.

"Set the fuses, if we can't have it neither can they." The leader nodded to himself mentally ticking off a list of things to do. "Instruct the synthetic humans... we'll take them with us through the tunnels. Do not arm them!" He raised his voice to underline the importance of his last order.

The young man excited by the screens, watched in horrified fascination as the World Gov weapons easily shattered and stripped the added armour plating he'd help weld to the suits of his friends.

Disappointed with his instructions, he turned away from his boss and the video carnage. Reluctantly, the man swallowed his hatred and frustration, relaying his superior's orders through his suit comms. Obedience meant survival.

"Dmitri, Kai, Set charges, five minutes. Everyone else retreat. Repeat, retreat. Exit four!" He left, slamming the door behind him.

***

"Get down, you fool!" Trent admonished his partner. Cole stood, enacting the macabre ragdoll dance of death as the automatic fire from a 12mm ultra-gun raked his suit. The hot metallic bullets failed to penetrate, but the bruising would be real. He fell to the floor and groaned, slowly rolling over to face Trent.

"Ninety-six percent," he gave an impudent smile. The kinetic energy from the bullet impacts had recharged his suit. "They've only got slug-chuckers." He winced as he prided himself on his analysis of the threat.

Trent shot the last assailant and stood to meet the next wave of five guards emerging from a camouflaged bunker beside the Power Station's main entrance. Held low, his gun sprayed plasma charges at 40 per cent power toward the aggressors and chunks of armour encased flesh leapt from their bodies. Mentally he worked out the effect of reducing the power of his charges further, calculating the energy saved and the extra efficiency from each magazine. The screams of the enemy were tearing at his mind, he needed the disassociation from the carnage he was inflicting.

Cole knelt and made each shot count, the pain from his bruising mollified by automatically administered chemical medication, courtesy of his suit diagnostics.

An explosion shook the ground and the two soldiers were showered with shrapnel. Someone had detected a defensive gun emplacement upon the roof of the building and decided to render it harmless before it could be used against them.

"Was that you?" enquired Cole without breaking his shot pattern.

"Nope! I think the Techs are bored. Come on they're waiting for us." Trent checked his comms panel, worried they were not progressing fast enough.

The Tech team would be angry and the council could be harsh if it thought they were failing to uphold the standards of the World Gov. Causing unnecessary delay was as close to heresy as you could get without public execution.

'Don't think, act. You are worthy of divine protection.' The mantra rolled unbidden across his thoughts.

Cole stood and side by side the pair advanced through the hail of bullets, acting more like pest controllers than soldiers. Their cloaked drones had advanced into the reactor, scouting for further enemies and other obstacles. A map of the building was overlayed upon Trent's head-up display. It grew line by line as the drones penetrated the structure, scanning each corridor and room. Occasionally red dots appeared as the enemy were discovered.

Trent noticed a change in the guards before him. A wave of relief seemed to run through them. It was hard to describe; their demeanour changed and an edge of harsh red that seemed to colour their ancient suits faded to beige.

He'd been able to see aura's since he was a little boy, but the gift was sporadic and he wasn't sure what the colours meant anyway. His father knew he had the gift and had sworn him to secrecy. The World Gov didn't like anything they didn't understand or couldn't control.

It was now obvious the guards had been warned of their indomitable approach; armed resistance ceased and the defenders fled.

The drones located their next challenge; armed explosive caches. Their communications range was severely limited by the structure of the building and the machines concluded the need to return to their operators, but halted when a secondary comms channel appeared with high level World Gov access.

A quiet, calm female voice intruded upon Trent's reverie, "Your drones have found explosives. Two charges, both set and activated. Looks like a five-minute timer. One on the uranium pile, one on the coolant drainage valve." The tech observer's voice was devoid of emotion.

Simple facts, thought Trent, that's all we are trained to deal with. Keep it professional, keep it short, no emotion, facts only.

"You take the coolant valve," shouted Cole.

"No," Trent thumped his chest. "This has better radiation shielding than yours. You take the valve I'll sort the pile." The men ran toward the danger.

Entering together, the two World Gov agents soon split up to deal with their respective problems. The power had been tripped and they were in the dark, relying on their suit's night vision feed. Overlay maps provided highlighted routes on their screens, leading them unerringly through the green shadowy world to their targets deep within the structure.

Voices within his helmet provided a disjointed narrative for Trent's silent journey.

"Enemy have abandoned their posts travelling north, subterranean." There was a slight pause in the commentary, "Dammit, lost them." The Tech was frustrated by their escape.

"Simple tremblers and a timer," reported Cole. "Powerful, but straightforward."

"I see mine," whispered Trent.

Hovering silently above the device, his personal drone was now coloured red and blinking amber lights, while a white beam pierced the gloom of the unlit room highlighting the source of its distress.

"Force field protection," but as he spoke the words, his personal suit modifications analysed the obstacle and disrupted the weak field. The tremblers were quickly fused by the plasma welder in the back of his right glove and he took a deep breath before disconnecting the timer wires the old-fashioned way, with a pair of snips from his belt kit.

He dismantled the explosive and retrieved the detonator for later study. The building's internal lights had been restored, probably by the Tech, and he confidently followed his gleaming chrome drone out of the building to rendezvous with Cole.

"I win, mine's at six seconds," laughed Cole, ridiculing the one minute forty-three showing on Trent's device.

Walking along the deserted avenue, each carrying an identical explosive device they compared the timers. Like children comparing new toys, they passed them around and inspected them from all angles. Cole tossed his into the air with an offer to juggle them both, laughing as much with relief as bravado.

Cole's drone emitted an alarm, "Radioactive Explosive Device. Warning! Immediate disposal required."

Reluctantly, Cole withdrew a silver shielding bag from his belt. The Drone's logs would be inspected upon their return. No doubt someone behind a desk would feel it necessary to punish his exuberant behaviour.

He dropped his trophy without ceremony into the disposal bag and offered it to Trent. Carefully, the second device was placed into the sack and Cole secured it.

"Turn around," he instructed his younger partner. He busied himself with Trent's pack, stowing the explosives for later disposal.

"Must be nice having your own Sherpa!" Trent sighed as he shifted the weight. They'd saved each other too many times to keep count of who's turn it was.

The Tech's armoured vehicle had gone and their table outside the ruined café was set with clean cups and a cracked, ceramic vase of dead twigs, alongside which stood a tall steel flask.

Trent retrieved the flask and a holographic message was triggered. An attractive young woman in her late teens appeared upon the lid, dressed in a Senior Tech uniform. "Thank you, gentlemen. Real Columbian roast, enjoy." The image blew a kiss and tilted her head. The message flickered off.

"Have you ever noticed how there doesn't seem to be any old people in the service anymore?" Trent observed. "Present company excepted."

Cole had taken the flask from his partner and poured the coffee. "Four years of extra skill and knowledge," he replied, passing a cup to eighteen-year-old Trent. "If you want 'old', just look at the ruling council. Two hundred of the oldest crumbliest humans left alive."

"Shush! They hear everything." Trent was paranoid because he understood the way the system worked. His father had warned him and when out in public continually cautioned him, forcing him to understand the negative aspects of a worldwide governing, non-elected body. Fascist dictatorship didn't do it justice.

His mother had thought the whole thing was very exciting and had joined the local group when it was still a 'community protest movement'; a polite way of describing a fledgling cult. She'd been thoroughly committed to 'Saving the Planet'. The strapline used to draw in the weak minded who thought the poisoned Earth could be saved through meetings, fiery speeches from charismatic young people and free illegal alcohol; unshackling both mental and carnal repression.

"Anyway, how's the bruising?" Trent quickly changed the subject.

"Not too bad, but you'd have lost your bet. Suit's at thirty-two percent."

Trent was shocked. He was one of the few people on the planet who understood how the suits worked. Cole rotated his utility belt to show his colleague the external power pack. A bullet had passed through the secondary battery container, rupturing several cells.

Not part of the original suits, the enhanced power pack was essential for using the plasma guns, but the idiot World Gov engineers had tied the power stores together, placing the resultant power supply outside the suit's protection field, weakening the design.

The fatigued soldiers sat and savoured the gentle roast from their appreciative benefactor and silently took stock of the three-day operation. Darkness fell and washed away the yellow stain of the poisoned Earth.

"Come on, I've got a spare cell-pack back at base."

"Isn't it the Ambassador's party tonight?" groaned Cole. Sat on the age worn wrought iron chair, his pain relief had abated and every inch of his body was complaining about his reckless stunt to charge the suit.

"Tuxedo's, dancing and fine wine... it'll be hell, but I suppose we'll endure. We always do." Trent helped his friend up. "Two klicks to the car, come on."

"I wish we'd parked closer," Cole moaned forcing his battered body to walk.

"Sorry, this avenue is pedestrianised." Trent indicated ancient damaged signs lying in the rubble and moved to support his friend, offering his shoulder as a crutch. Their two drones, now embellished with highly specular chrome, seemed to hover closer, listening while sparkling in the threat free environment; drawn to the only conversation for miles.

The full moon cast an eerie green light upon the grand ruins either side of the wide avenue.

"That's where we need to be," Cole whispered looking at the bright green lunar body. "No enemy, no war..."

"No water, no air and little gravity." Trent dismissed the idea. "Who'd want to be up there?"

"It's the only place we'll ever get away from the fighting... from the World Gov." he sighed. "People have lived there before. They used to go there for holidays... once."

Trent stared at the moon in wonder. Could they really escape the violence? It was just a dream; there were too many problems... but Trent's brain betrayed him, it had already started working through the solutions, listing the possibilities.

"From there," he mused, "we could go anywhere."

"I'd like to think we could start again," whispered Cole.

***

"Well done, gentlemen." A quiet word from a heavily set, medal bedecked General was about as good as their congratulations would get. They nodded their thanks and mustered tired smiles, only marginally slowing their pace as they entered the historic gold and marble reception hall.

By force of habit, they assessed the room, scanning the entry and exit points, looking over the guests milling around the central dance floor and analysed the threat levels of clustered groups, busily talking loudly upon the ornate balconies, placed according to rank upon elevated levels. Reminding themselves this was a friendly country working with the World Gov, they straightened up and marched into the room, smiling at everyone, resplendent in their newly issued formal attire.

On the raised stage at the front of the reception hall, the Ambassador stood beside two people dressed as though they'd just stepped out of a romantic holo-vid. A man in a bright blue military style uniform whose face was dominated by an excessive caricature of a moustache, stood next to a young woman who looked uncomfortable with her place upon the pedestal.

She was wearing an old-style ball gown, widely flared, resplendent in colours of fire. Flames of green, blue and orange flickered as she moved. Trent recognised the girl from the hologram she'd left on the coffee flask. The Senior Tech was being publicly congratulated for her 'diligent work' in securing the power station; publicly acclaimed and applauded for her work in returning this opulence to the elite.

The uniformed man took centre stage behind a thin plastic lectern and coughed twice for attention. The room heavily stocked with sycophants, instantly hushed.

"Thank you, World Gov." He paused for applause. "You have literally saved our lives." The formally dressed Ambassador, pulled an ornate lever, a prop strategically placed by a faceless guard and the room became dark. Moments later a blue-white light from the newly constructed environmental dome, soaked through the decaying fabric of the long drapes covering the dust ingrained windows. Each rip and fray rent by lancing light, piercing the room with an intensity that dazzled those within.

The light surrounded the building, descending like a curtain from above, enclosing, protecting, banishing the night. The unsustainable energy field providing shelter until the permanent physical dome was completed.

Yet another city had begun ecological shielding, to cleanse the planet and remove the need for protective suits and constant decontamination regimes. Loud cheering from the crowd subsided into orchestrated clapping as the lights were turned back on. Joyous music began, signalling the end of the applause.

Several members of the World Gov council, magnificent in their jet-black uniforms adorned with gold braid and medals for ill-defined merit, were present within the hall, busily engaged in the onerous task of absorbing praise from the notable members of

Prague's high society. No-one spoke to the two soldiers who'd spent three days wiping out the criminal organisation that had controlled the city for the last year.

"Here, take this." Cole passed Trent a champagne flute filled with a sparkling, coloured drink. "Sorry, the real stuff hasn't arrived yet. The council members are livid."

Trent rolled his eyes in response to Cole's remark. He'd never tasted alcohol; he didn't understand its attraction. It was banned even before he was born. Half of the places he'd raided had barrels of it, but his job had been destruction not sampling.

Prohibition wasn't a bad thing, surely. Only the criminal's seemed to have it and if the World Gov needed to control their base behaviour by destroying it... well that seemed, logical. He was staring out of the window, watching the automatic clean-up machines as they swarmed over the grounds removing everything in their path.

"Tomorrow it will be fertile. A new city with new homes and a new purpose!" Cole recited the World Gov propaganda with a begrudged sense of pride.

"The domes can only be sustained by constant power; they don't generate water. They can't sustain life unless they're fed. That'll be the Russian's next target." Trent was treading on dangerous ground. It was unwise to voice your opinions. Cole looked around nervously. A place like this was bound to be tapped. Every word recorded; every thought analysed and judged.

"We need a better, self-sufficient solution." Trent was unhappy, he felt his current role was holding him back, stifling his true potential. He was a creator, an inventor, not a killer.

"I hear their having problems in America. We're being sent out there next week." Cole tried to inject some life into Trent. He figured work was a safer subject to discuss.

"What for?" It was conversation, but Trent wasn't particularly interested.

"Some psycho, slicing people up. Thinks he's an old-time gangster. Calls himself 'The Butcher'."

"That's not our problem. Let local crime deal with it."

"He's got an army and he's butchered several towns and somehow taken a World Gov base." Cole observed the flicker of interest as it invaded Trent's mind.

"How did he come by his suits?" Trent, ever practical, knew an unarmoured force couldn't take a World Gov squad, let alone a base.

"That's what we have to find out."

"Are they sure it's this guy, The Butcher."

"Published his own holo-vid. Sliced them all up, and their families. Quite proud of his work."

"But North America is desolate, a radiation zone. Where's he based?" Trent knew the worlds habitational zones were diminishing daily due to the historic damage inflicted by earlier generations. The nuclear barrages just joined the dots and filled in many countries with deadly radiation.

"Relatively untouched island called Puerto Rico. He's renamed it 'New Chicago'. It's tolerable, but the locals are all dead."

"Not that safe then."

"Genocide. Dead at the hand of The Butcher." Cole seemed to have a begrudging respect for the vicious criminal. Trent sipped his drink and watched as an automated machine removed ancient brittle trees outside.

"We need to plan our recovery," Trent spoke in little more than a whisper. "Give the place a rest."

"Are you ill?"

"Not me, the world, humanity; this... this is useless." He waved to indicate the stripping of soil and destruction of buildings, scarring the grounds outside. We move on, the Russians will be back in a few months. There's got to be somewhere we can gain a new foothold. You said it yourself."

"Hey, don't bring me into this." Cole laughed to break his friend's melancholy. Who could blame him after the past few days of non-stop killing?

The band had slowed and the music was dismal. Speeches were made and bad jokes endured. In a bid to divert his morose friend, Cole stole a tray of impressively decorated sweet-meats from a serving machine and the two men moved to an ornate recessed window at the far side of the hall for a little more privacy.

"We've been here all night; can we go yet?" Trent was tired, he sat upon the soft cushions covering the wide sill. Unlike Cole, he didn't use stimulants. He felt they did him more harm than good.

"Wait a moment... come here." Cole had spotted something interesting. He had that mischievous lilt in his voice. As Trent reluctantly followed his friend back to the throng, Cole stepped quickly to the side and shoved him gently to his right.

"What...?" Trent collided with the most beautiful and probably, at that moment, the most angry Tech on the planet. The collision had spilled her drink down her dress and several panels had lost their colour. Trent went from complaining to Cole, who'd miraculously disappeared, to apologising to the young lady in front of him in less than a second.

"What the... I'm so sorry, I... tripped." The excuse was lame and he coloured in embarrassment.

"Four panels, not the end of the world." Although angry, there was something that immediately brought out her sympathy for the awkward soldier in front of her. His tuxedo was pristine, still slightly creased, fresh from the packet, and she noticed he still wore a full armour suit beneath the thin dress coverall.

"I can probably repair it, if that would help," he offered.

She laughed, "Second sentence and you're inviting me to undress. You boys work fast."

Trent was mortified. He replayed his words in his head and cringed. Unexpectedly, Cole came to his rescue.

"They've cleared eight blocks. We've been allocated rooms away from the base. Come on." Cole sounded excited, but his face was full of devilment, "Come on," he urged his reluctant friend, "fresh air and real beds."

The mention of 'real beds' caused a fresh wave of colour to flood Trent's face.

"Congratulations on your success," he managed, ignoring Cole's lascivious innuendo.

"Oh please, don't. I didn't drive out the criminals holed up in there, all I did was set the machines to work and brought the output up to serviceable levels." She smiled and for Trent, the room dimmed. He was entranced.

Cole pulled at him, eager to leave, as Trent stared at her pure white aura, he swore he could make out fleeting sparkles of colour. Her emotions were unique.

"I think you have to go," she smirked, as Cole heaved theatrically, pulling his friend away from their conversation.

Trent was still struggling as he left the dance floor. "Thanks for the coffee," he shouted over the music, "Colombian is my favourite."

Her face fell as the realisation struck home. She stood, swamped by well-wishers who had filled the space left vacant by the men, unable to respond to the soldiers who'd delivered her glory. She was jostled and lost sight of Trent, her vision now filled with faceless social climbers eager to associate with the heroine who saved their city.

2: Arrival 2275 CE

The roar of the massive engines shook the vessel to its core. The 'Lady Mabel' was a sleek craft, penetrating the heavily polluted sky with ease. Fifteen, flame erupting engines ringed the dart shaped body which, at take-off, had its smooth symmetric beauty marred by the four booster rockets supplying the main thrust for escape velocity. Each was now exhausted and the empty programmable nano-metal tubes had successfully transformed into rigid spears of polished metal. Now, they melded seamlessly with the outer body to reinforce the hull of the sleek craft punching through the final hold of the planet's gravitic grasp.

Belying the pristine exterior, the rock-solid cockpit had seen better days. The panels were equipped with short lines of vertical green lights indicating each system's worthiness, attesting their serviceability in accordance with handwritten labels. Inset control screens, cracked and dead were covered in a mosaic of trivial notes; the intricate visual systems no longer serving any purpose other than to hold scrawled reminders of mechanical limitations, continually referenced by two pairs of anxious eyes. The tiny lights pinned to lengths of wood and plastic held in place by thin wires that burrowed through the control surface like rampant weeds.

With no supply of spares and no technological maintenance ability, anything that failed had to be worked around.

The control centre was lit by three fist-sized cone-shaped lights, clipped to exposed wires above the pilot's seats. They were powered by a repurposed battery pack, tied with string to an extruded pipe on the port side, emerging from a scrap of insulation material before plunging back into a maelstrom of components.

Breaking through the atmosphere, the seated pilots stared in awe through three circular forward-facing portholes providing a glimpse of the eternal darkness. The fragile green ribbon of atmosphere was left far behind. Their old ferry had once again achieved the required height above the planet and the two pilots industrially flicked switches, took readings and monitored their cargo through a grainy video link displayed on a re-purposed, hand-sized screen.

"Two minutes," announced the senior of the two pilots, his silver hair testament to the years of dedicated service to his craft. The faded gold bars on his clean white shirt, along with the frayed collar and cuffs, illustrated the struggles the business had endured due to the war and the ongoing troubles.

He reached past an old creased photograph of two youngsters cutting a tall cake at an archaic ceremony, smiling as he saw his wife's youthful image between the console switches.

"This is your pilot speaking. We have reached our destination and will soon be deploying your ship for the next leg of its journey. We hope you have a pleasant trip and that you will consider our service for your next planned escape." The pilot felt satisfaction delivering the traditional message he'd quoted over a thousand times before, many years ago.

"Where are they going?" asked his co-pilot, a much younger man wearing a garish tee-shirt that was definitely not company issue.

"They're off to that new 'Moon Base' holiday camp. Big players, with big ideas. Idiots!" He dismissed his passengers with contempt. "All the other platforms are dead now." He wistfully remembered the time when ten orbiting Space Hotels offered fun and adventure to anyone brave enough to leave the planet. They were halcyon days.

"Wish I could go on holiday somewhere like that," the younger lad whined a little.

"Not for the likes of you and me, Jeff." The older man considered his co-pilot's mood. "Look at it this way, after the last war no-one ever thought anyone would get back into space. My grandfather hid this baby and patched her up to keep her space worthy. Everyone said he was a fool. Now look at us, our books are full. We're the only commercial carrier left. No-one else saves all that cost of those big engines for satellites and cargo and as long as we keep our noses clean, we'll be left alone. Shuttles are fine, but they can't work like us," he beamed proudly and winked, trying to cheer up his despondent colleague. "Come on, give me a hand with the split."

***

"Another day, another million," Trent, resplendent in his beige suit, grinned at the seated man in the blue lunar guard uniform. The octagonal emblem proudly displayed on his arm in no way resembling the World

Gov badges. The holo-graphic screens floated above the dark desk in the utilitarian grey office, showing the docking bays where the first shuttles would be dispensing the lifeblood of his new lunar complex.

The guard looked uncomfortable behind his desk. His boss had a way of looking at you, or more precisely through you. It was rumoured that his gaze saw more than your nano-suit. He assessed the mood of his boss, remembering how convivial they'd been at the interview, two years ago and felt safe to reply casually, "First full day, Sir. We've been looking forward to this."

The remark was redundant and the freshly promoted guard fidgeted nervously. Trent looked him over with a scrutiny one might use when finding a strange metal tube with a wire protruding from one end whilst walking in enemy territory. The gold trim of the guards new rank insignia proudly shone and his badge glowed, displaying his name and increased security level, 'Martin B. 04'.

Trent nodded, the earlier advance guests had been handpicked technical and scientific people, allowed to bring their families for free as a reward for service to his project. They'd been the guinea pigs and after four weeks of constant drills he had gained a high level of confidence in his staff and his base operating procedures.

Martin knew he was less polished than usual, with a creased orange sash across his blue one-piece nano-armour suit, but two hours in, it had already been a long shift and he'd be damned if he was going to scrub up for the scum arriving today. A streak of rebellious anger appeared from nowhere and he struggled not to let it show.

Trent mentally flicked over to his Cybernetic implants. He linked to the internal security system and selected the guard's profile. He was good at faces, not so reliable with names. 'B' for Bailey, no... sounds like a prison; I'll stick to first names he thought.

"Relax Martin. Today will be a challenge for everyone. You'll be fine." The tall, dark haired man spoke and his personal charm shone through, instantly relieving the nerves of the new guard captain. Only then did Trent realise the guards power monitor shone upon his arm, indicating the full capacity charge of his nano-suit. Not a good idea. Usually, suits never exceeded eighty-five percent to allow for environmental charging. It was a pain for everyone when a suit had to flare off unwanted excess energy.

Martin's hand went to his ear and he dropped his head responding unintelligibly to the person on his intercom, he stood and straightened, acknowledging his boss with a curt "Sir!" then moved quickly away from the desk to answer his summons.

"Oh, and Martin," Trent called to his new Captain as he reached the door," Make sure you flare that suit... away from the guests." His genuine smile defused any tension Martin may have felt at the minor rebuke.

"Yes, sir!" Martin scolded himself for not noticing the energy build-up and stepped quickly out of the office.

Trent had a gift for picking the right people for the job. Some said it was down to his shrewd business sense, others claimed he had in-depth files beyond the limit of data laws, while competitors simply believed he was lucky. The truth was stranger and far more dangerous.

His father had told him many years ago, "Be nice to people, you'll be surprised."

Some people left devastation in their wake; Trent left a trail of friendship.

The baggage retrieval area was quiet, the machines at rest. Gentle music played to a hall, empty except for one solitary figure in blue.

"Ivor?" Martin hailed his opposite number, as he entered, "I thought your watch finished an hour ago?" Martin queried his friend with mock suspicion.

"It did," Ivor relaxed, genuinely pleased to see his friend. He looked resplendent in his clean, well pressed matching uniform, his arm patch colourful, but not glowing, despite the fact he'd just completed a twelve-hour watch, "...but I couldn't let you take on today, all on your own," he laughed at the jovial insult. "I couldn't have you wrecking the place on day one as the new early shift Captain." Ivor tapped the new badge insignia on Martin's arm and nodded toward the retreating Trent whose beige suit, emblazoned with two vibrant orange stripes, looked out of place in the austere white concourse. "What was all that about?"

"Oh, he was just checking the schedule, and the new guy..., me, ...probably. He's alright." Martin considered the brief exchange. "Hardly seen him since the interview back on earth, but he remembered me." He returned his friends smile and the two men walked to a desk at the end of the hall to check their plans. "Does this mean you're going to be late back on tonight?" Martin asked suspiciously.

Ivor had been a shift Captain for years, ever since the rebuild began. He'd shown Martin the ropes assuming the role of mentor, since he'd arrived at the Lunar Complex during the second phase of the build, once the place was airtight. Now, officially the two men were equals, but in Martin's mind Ivor would always take the lead.

"Nah!" Ivor teased his protégé, "I'll only stay for the first couple of shuttles, just to make sure you know what you're doing, then I'll be off." He grinned with devilment at the expression of disbelief on Martin's face and the two men got down to the business of discussing the planned bay assignments and timings.

"First private shuttle is due in ten minutes." Martin summarised.

"Whose is it?"

"Believe me," the smile had left Martin's face and his voice dropped, "you don't want to know."

***

The shining dart hung in space, to all appearance motionless above the turquoise planet. The fifteen engines, no longer standing proud upon rings around the fuselage, had been retracted and now huddled tight against the skin of the vessel. Without a sound the whole ship opened like a book, split from nose to tail along the spine. The pilot's cockpit was revealed as a glass bubble behind the armoured nose cone, allowing full visibility of the payload. A long brown unlit octagonal column lay within the hold.

"It's ugly," observed Jeff. "Anyone important?"

The Captain focussed on a flashing bulb. He moved to a scuffed pressure gauge, unhappy with the trembling needle. "Invoice signed by the World Gov, probably just a supply drop for the Lunar Base. Probably no-one inside." He reached for a thin sheaf of papers, retrieving the pen clipped to them and proceeded to gently tap the gauge with it. "Yeah, Khonsu supply," he read. Satisfied, he kept an eye on the needle until it settled, then moved back to his seat. The light now shone steadily.

"Why's it called Khonsu?" Jeff asked.

"Got to call it something, I suppose. Knowing this lot, it'll be named after some blood-thirsty General." He retrieved his microphone from the console and flicked a sequence of stiff switches.

"Clear to launch!" instructed the ferry pilot. There was no reply. The dull shape lifted slowly away from the carcass of the open ferry as invisible gas jets erupted between the vessels. Similar jets on the exterior of the ferry erupted in synchronicity, to counter the force, allowing the ferry to remain on station.

Slowly, the inner craft rose, monitored by a simple distance meter in the cabin, reminiscent of a personal thermometer. A repetitive beep slowed as the craft increased its distance, until a tinny metallic voice repeated the words, 'Payload Clear' three times. Twelve low power engines deployed from the brown octagonal shape, three chrome rings of four white engines against the dull brown lifeless shape. The rings emerged from the payload vessel, equidistant along the column.

"You're clear!" reported the ferry pilot. With no response, the engines on the commercial transport rotated slowly into position and glowed with a green flame. The two pilots observed the flames silently change, becoming tinged with blue as the emitted motive force increased and the ship smoothly accelerated away. The orbital ferry pilots watched in silence as the space ship disappeared into the blackness.

"Put her back together, Jeff. I'm going to grab a sandwich." Captain Sams unbuckled and floated gracefully from his seat to the improvised galley at the rear of the cockpit. "Want one?"

"No thanks. Aren't we going fishing?" Jeff looked shocked. Usually on a trip this short, they would spend an hour or so gathering the carcasses of destroyed satellites. The scrap was plentiful and worth a good bonus from the World Gov.

"Nah! Not today. It's Mabel's birthday," he nodded at the picture. "Let's just head home."

The chrome dart slowly resumed its former glory. A minor green light illuminated on the pilot's panel indicating the structural integrity of the reformed ship. Jeff looked out of the window and headed back to base. It's expensive, intelligent hull shrugged off the effects of the atmosphere as it plunged steeply through the layers of green air and pollution covering the planet, in a hurry to get home. Only as it landed, descending gently, vertically settling down upon the full length of the ancient runway, did the massive scale of the orbital ferry become apparent.

***

Trent stopped at the propaganda poster adorning the wall of the stark customs hall and shuddered. It was an anachronism based on a two-hundred-year-old idea of state control. A stylised sun shone down on a smiling family at play whilst behind them stood an image of an oversized ghostly young soldier in his divine armour, gun held ready to protect those in his care. The fascists had done their homework.

Trent's above average height and gentle demeanour accompanied by his witty banter, was underpinned by the gift of empathy. This meant he was generally an upbeat happy guy to be around, but this poster disturbed him. If he could remove it, he would, but his masters had certain expectations.

Growing up after the war, Trent had inherited his height and his gift of empathy from his father. Though a gentle unassuming man, his father had been a full empath and suffered for making his gift known to his superstitious wife.

There had been little love lost between his parents. She was a motivated supporter of the World-Gov, at a time when it was ridiculed as little more than a cult-based gang of fanatics. His father, on the other hand, had been a successful tailor and clothes designer. He was totally neutral in politics.

"Life is difficult enough, son" he would say, "without looking for more minefields to walk through."

His inventiveness and his success were the cause of his downfall. While working with a new nano-fabric he'd developed for robust outdoor wear, he successfully created the first working nano-suit material and with it, unwittingly, paved the way to success for his wife's fascist cadre.

While his father had travelled the world selling his invention and his ideas to anyone who'd listen, Trent's mother had become enamoured with the charismatic leader of the local World Gov movement. Their message was altruistic, but his mother disappeared for days on end, leaving young Trent to fend for himself from the age of seven. When she did return, she would be hungover, drunk or stoned on the latest street craze. Angry, demanding and dismissive of both he and his father, Trent learned quickly that his mother was not invested in their family. When his father found out about her neglect, he stopped his travels and stayed at home to care for his son. They learned together and worked together and Trent found the loving parent he needed.

Normally, Trent's moods were only influenced by the people around him, but this poster was... wrong. There was something intrinsically disturbing about its perverse message.

"What's the problem now?" Martin had already been involved in one incident at the Docking Bay since coming on duty this morning and he was angry at being summoned to return. He showed his exasperation as he entered the control cabin. A single dock worker monitored the desk. His name badge declared him to be, 'Rhet W. 06', a high clearance for ancillary staff, but Martin hadn't met him before today and their earlier meeting hadn't gone well. The man was a zealot.

"Ships are due any time," Martin láid down the law, "this Bay needs to be clear."

"It's plate three, the gravity is all over the place." Rhet produced a holo-screen above his desk and pointed out the anomaly. "If they don't get it sorted, this hangar's off limits and your schedule..."

"Have you reported it to Control?" asked Martin, his tone somewhat mollified, dismayed his hours of logistical preparation would be wasted, but a little happier now that he knew why the tower of crates had fallen on him earlier. Up until now, the only other variable in the bay had been Rhet. Naturally, Martin had blamed his ineptitude for the collapsing storage column that had fallen on him during his first inspection. Though not hurt, the incident had overcharged his suit and creased his presentation sash minutes into his first shift as a Guard Captain.

"They say it's a gremlin in the power feed. They're fixing it their end." The Logistics operator moved his attention to a different screen showing a long white cylindrical shuttle lit against a featureless black backdrop.

"Wow! Six boosters," Martin was in awe, like a child who'd seen his first hover bike up close. "Expensive...!" he whispered.

"You should see what's coming in tonight." Rhet had seen it all before; the super sleek behemoth with triple standard thrust was just a toy compared to some of the private liners due in later.

"It makes you wonder, doesn't it... how many more of these there'd be if the planet wasn't dying." Martin was tuned in to a mindset of peace and prosperity, and his unguarded thoughts were dangerously close to blasphemy.

"Careful, man! You know the World Gov hears everything. They're fixing it... as we speak." Rhet's voice assumed an almost narrative quality as he spouted the party line, just in case. "In five years, the climate will be sorted and the deserts returned to fertile gardens," he quoted. After reaffirming his purity to whoever might be listening, he returned to the console, and studied the screens. He noticed a new report from Control. "Gravitic plate three now serviceable," he read aloud.

Martin was still transfixed watching the shuttle approach. He gave no response to the good news.

"Are you all right, man?" asked Rhet. "You took quite a blow from those crates you know." Rhet was unable to appreciate the excitement generated by the vehicle on the screen. To him it was just another ship to secure, unload and service when it arrived.

"Yeah, I'm fine. These things," he indicated his blue security suit, "are a bit better than the old ones like yours." He gave Rhet a smile, which was meant to convey an element of apology for blaming him for the earlier incident. "I've got to get back to customs."

"No problem, Captain." Rhet returned the smile with a mock salute.

As he entered the office safety air-lock, Martin turned to Rhet and said "Thanks." He didn't really know what he was thanking the man for, but he'd felt privileged watching the craft approach, and he supposed Rhet was busy enough, without some security guy like him getting in the way, double checking basic protocols were being observed.

***

Officially, Trent was a World Gov Officer, privately he hated everything they stood for. He'd used them as they'd used his father and, at least for the time being, he was the Base Commander of the rescued and rebuilt Lunar Complex. Renamed 'Khonsu', for luck, apparently. To him the base was just 'The Base' or at a stretch the 'Lunar Complex'. If you called it the Khonsu then you were referring to the tourist trap he'd built to fund it. Khonsu was actually the name given to the Casino. What better name than the Egyptian God of the Moon, renowned for his love of gambling.

Originally, the Science Research Complex, was commissioned before the last war as a military base, then, in the euphoria of peace that followed, it was repurposed as a holiday destination by forward thinking ultra-rich dreamers. But as the World Gov took control and their subversive tactics destroyed long established governments, economies failed, the planet clean-up faltered and the population dwindled. The Lunar Base fell into ruin and was abandoned.

The now mandatory one-piece nano-suits had been designed by Trent's father, to manipulate the forces applied to them, converting and saving kinetic forces to usable energy. They were developed to protect emergency workers in the harshest of conditions. Any impacts or other extreme exposure to energy, heat, pressure or radiation was absorbed, converted and held in special power packs. This energy was used to power the true genius of the suits, the intelligent community of nano-bots contained within one layer of the fabric. Capable of creating microscopic force shields within the material bonds, forming a complete net of protection. The simple artificial intelligence maintained environmental controls designed to comfort and protect the wearer. But the altruistic invention had a dark side. After a few minor modifications the suit had rendered all current projectile weapons, knives and explosives redundant.

When the World Gov got their hands on them, it wasn't long before there were other options available to utilise all that stored energy and artificial intelligence.

The nano-suits were the ultimate in protection and so war became a game with almost no military death toll. Of course, you could still destroy property, infrastructure and homes. Civilians would die of starvation, thirst and disease, economies would crash, but the soldiers inside the suits would not be harmed.

Many quick-thinking criminal gangs exploited their potential. Using terrorist tactics on a wholesale genocidal scale, without the need for covert actions. The African warlords were particularly ruthless.

Declaring themselves as deities and destroying all opposition by self-imposed divine right, through assimilation of beliefs and the template used by the World Gov throughout Europe.

Africa became one country, but the death toll was horrendous. The surviving gangs used the nano-suits to govern a regime of starvation and disease, reducing the population from twenty-seven million survivors of the war, to only four million, by 'genetic purification' and personal whim in the years that followed. Life was cheap and the laws of morality ceased to apply.

The abundance of these 'easy' targets meant only established governments could lose. Rebel guerrilla forces could destroy with impunity.

Support for the traditional entrenched political defenders evaporated as systems and services were wiped out, sending the populace back to the stone-age.

Officially, it wasn't war. It was many things, liberation, unification, protection and in some cases education, but it was never war.

With this unique armour the World Gov movement spread across the planet; their claims of divine protection shown on the increasingly rare, public vid-screens daily. Initially they seemed intent on only destroying 'out of favour' despots and criminals. Then they were 'invited' to help oppressed countries repel insurgent forces looking to steal vital resources, until, eventually, the movement's cry for a unified world had unparalleled support. Of course, they would be the unifiers... they would control and dictate the assimilation of others.

Soon, the ubiquitous propaganda of the World Gov movement recruited a global membership, sizeable enough to empower them to oppose the world's greatest nations. Through clever manipulation of resources and their presence in so many strategic places, while continuing to 'help' the less fortunate, they were able to introduce global transport taxation; the World Gov fascists undermined the established economies. Teasing, goading, and even openly inviting military conflict; always portraying the traditional patriots bound by ancient borders, as the 'enemy of the people'.

It was amazing how many countries became 'oppressed' by 'rogue nations', requiring the World Gov's help, while still producing the planet's most highly prized resources. As the countries suffered, the cult continued to preach love and tolerance. Propaganda was the real weapon.

The movement was riddled with corruption. Short term intervention forces, could not be assigned national responsibilities; World Gov were simply helping out, the blame was always someone else's. Usually the scape-goats were those with the loudest voices telling the truth about the World Gov's true agenda. Medieval justice was commonly dispensed to the people they 'protected', after all you can't appeal against the divine will of God. Meanwhile, the World Gov forces and their elite sponsors were privy to the most advanced technologies and none of it was being used to clean up the planet.

Those who did not buy into the movement daubed slogans on walls, 'Just enough food to serve', was the most truthful of these. Banding together in communal groups people sought to escape, to live away from the tyranny and perverse rhetoric. But the poisoned planet limited the places they could run. The zealots pursued them and cast them in the role of usurpers, heretics and demons. Lies and hate were integral to their cause.

Earth was once again a war zone. Those who opposed the World Gov were godless demons, enemies of the planet; while those who supported the righteous had the privilege of all the comfort technology could afford, but in return were fitted with a tight leash. The wolves held at bay, while the rest were sheep to be herded.

The poster triggered a suppressed memory. Trent's anger rose as he remembered seeing it in the ramshackle old church hall, he and his father had visited to obtain a free hot meal. Somehow, unmarked by flame, it nestled beside the razed buildings of his youth. Their own home confiscated, their possessions stolen or destroyed, as he and his father were turned out onto the street until their 'purity' could be established. He tasted the dust and smelled again the sickly-sweet aroma of charcoaled bodies piled high in the street, purportedly a gift from the 'heretic oppressors' the night before.

"Dad," he'd asked. "Why do they want us to watch this man die?" Trent, no more than eight years old, remembered the day in the hall with his father by his side. In his pocket his only toy, a floppy puppy with oversized eyes, rescued by his father as they were bundled out of the house by soldiers. His father's jacket tied in place around him with a brown belt to keep out the chill, while deep in the pocket his hand held onto it tightly for reassurance.

The execution of a "Godless Demon" was broadcast over all the video channels as a warning. The soldiers projected screens upon the walls and made sure everyone looked on as a firing squad marched smartly into place to a soundtrack of cheering crowds.

"Is he an enemy soldier?" he whispered.

"No son, he's just a mechanic. A man with a family. They say he claims to see the truth." His father looked into his son's eyes and an understanding passed between them. A soldier stepped briskly towards their table, frightening young Trent.

"What did you say?" he growled.

"I told my son that the man claims to see the truth," his father held the soldier's gaze. He was exceptionally calm and the soldier eventually retreated a few steps, unable to maintain his aggressive countenance while looking upon his father's honest face.

"It's all in the eyes, son." His father turned to him and smiled again in his memory. "It's all in the eyes."

Licking his dry lips and massaging the weapon in his hands, the soldier scanned the downtrodden victims seeking shelter inside the decrepit sanctified building. Recovering his anger, he shouted at the screen,

"He's a heretic and demon possessed. Execution's too good for him, he should be burned alive. Purified before God!" The soldier gave an evil grin, satisfied he'd regained some moral authority and strode across the packed room to abuse another refugee who'd dared to look away from the screen.

Two weeks later his father had replaced the demon possessed heretic and suffered the same public fate and the young boy had been reunited with his dispassionate duplicitous mother.

Trent had grown up in fear, keeping his gift quiet, even from his mother. After seeing what they did to his father, he never revealed his ability to read people. He saw no reason for anyone to be threatened by his talent. He couldn't remember ever talking to the devil or one of his demons and try as he might, he couldn't see why the occasional sight of an aura, showing someone's feelings, could be anything he could exploit as a weapon; at least, not until he began working at the ministry.

At the age of twelve his mother removed him from his fearful grey school, where each week the quiet students seemed to simply fade into the background. Students often left; nobody ever talked about the missing.

She inserted him into the World-Gov intern program, where he was exposed to a curriculum of brainwashing and servitude. It was the last time he'd spoken to her. He hadn't thanked her.

Petty jealousies, unrequited desires, timid leaders with secret fears and their occasional crisis of confidence, all helped Trent climb high. His mother's loyalty to the cause, the personal sacrifice she'd so publicly made and her many associations with the powerful, had seen her rise to the ruling elite. She became one of the Two-Hundred. No-one remembered his father, except maybe as the price of her ascension.

He never forgave her for betraying his father and ensuring the World Gov were the only people to benefit from the perverse use of his father's beneficent invention.

Trent tutted quietly and shook his head in disbelief as he recalled the last brief memory of his mother. She was there when he announced his grand scheme. She'd been sat with the less important figures around the fringes of the gilded presentation room when he'd delivered his pitch to the executive committee. It had taken him almost a year to achieve a hearing, reluctant to pass details of his idea lest the enemy were warned. Eventually, he stood in the mock opulence of the World Gov offices, a shining resplendent jewel nestled in the ash covered ruins of old Vancouver.

"I will convert the abandoned Lunar Research Complex into the shining star of World Gov success," he confidently boasted. "Each night the children of the world will look up and know the power of the divine World Gov." The party members remained stoic. They had not come to listen to a sycophant brainwashed by their own schooling. Trent continued in a more salacious manner. "And in doing so create a new way of taxing the evasive criminal elite." The crowd murmured its approval.

"They foil our attempts at direct punishment," feigning anger he raised his voice. "They cost us time and money. They avoid taxation and publicly ridicule us. We know they must have agents in our midst, how else could they retain their independence." This prompted disapproving gasps. Was this impertinent youngster casting doubts upon their integrity?

"So, why not let them spend their ill-gotten gains on false dreams and deny them their wealth on our terms? Get them to lose control through debauchery and record their plans. Turn their own vices against them. Make them work for us." Trent revealed an image of a four-towered luxurious hotel surrounding a huge three domed casino complex. The building looked impressive until the animated overlay showed most of it would be beneath the lunar surface.

"This is outrageous!" announced one elderly representative of the board. He was dressed in a general's uniform adorned with a multitude of medal ribbons.

In Trent's heightened emotional state his gift had intruded upon his vision. The General's aura betrayed him, his opposition was not based on reason, but fear; it glowed bright red.

A double agent so high in the ranks, thought Trent and as usual he read the man correctly.

"Why not tell it as it is?" demanded the General, "Extortion, blackmail, fraud! Are you proposing the glorious army of the Lord become charlatans and con-men?" The General huffed in disdain almost believing his own propaganda.

"I prefer..." Trent paused, many members of the board were more interested in how this young pretender was about to handle himself, rather than his defence against the accusation. He continued in a soft almost condescending voice, "...to think of it as simply a change in tactics, General Parker." Trent noticed how the pride in his title reduced the man's level of fear. "It's called, beating them at their own game." He sneered at the frustrated general and noticed the old man's fear rise as positive murmuring travelled around the room.

Once the presentation reached estimated costs, timescales and return on investment, interest waned until finally, the ruse was laid bare, "...and we will get the underworld to pay for the whole thing!" He paused noting their rekindled interest. Almost conspiratorially, he continued manipulating their ego's.

"Our agents will convince them that they will be senior shareholders in the most lucrative opportunity of the age. We will feed them what they want to hear. We'll say the project is being used to ostracise inefficient or troublesome members of our own party." He cast a glance at his mother, "Look at me! My father was a traitor." The words burned deep into his soul and he hated himself for saying it, but the room was behind him now.

"We can mine the space between Earth and the Moon, retrieving rare metals from what is now just space junk that litters our skies. We can move out to resources beyond our own planet, to truly heal the world. We have everything we need to secure our future and we'll let the criminals pay for it."

"We'll promise old redundant technology as a prize worth fighting for and we'll expose their petty dreams and bring down their empires." Laughter rang out in the room. He noticed his mother leave during the standing ovation, unwilling to praise her own prodigy, unwilling even to meet his gaze.

***

In a secret, poorly lit room, two men wearing impressive gold trimmed World Gov uniforms, spoke quietly. The weak grey light struggled to escape from the bare plastered walls and the lack of furniture and damp stale air, exuded a perception of conspiracy and lies.

"Impressive idea," commented the first.

"Bright lad, just like his father," agreed the other.

"It would be a tremendous asset... for us."

"Agreed!"

"His mother wasn't impressed..."

"Who cares, she's old news."

"...neither was 'Hellfire' Parker. That could be a problem." The man was concerned and it showed in the narrowing of his eyes.

"Code 4?" suggested his co-conspirator. It was a logical solution and betrayed no emotional judgement. In the silence there was a suggestion of acquiescence. He touched his ear and issued the command.

"HQ, Code 4, Parker." The order conveyed the location, target, severity and timing required; no warning would be passed to those outside the meeting. General Parker's usefulness, as a known underworld informer, had come to an end.

"Is Trent... like his father?" the tone of the question was darker and accompanied by an undercurrent of fear.

"No, I'd have seen it by now. He's bright, but he's just normal."

"Someone should watch him!" The voice was shy of panic, but the urgency was conveyed.

"I've got it in hand." The man who seemed to gravitate to leadership smirked in the dark, dismissing the comment. He turned to the wall and activated an ancient internal monitor close to the doorway, casting a blue-grey light upon his companion, but he didn't bother to look. His hair glistened, reflecting the grainy illumination while a surreptitious flash of green and gold upon his uniform hinted at his medical status. The monitor confirmed the hallway was clear. "You go up, I'll go down." The meeting was terminated.

The leader watched his colleague go then exited the dark room through the same hidden door in the wall. Stepping out into the empty corridor, he straightened his uniform giving himself a moment to watch the door silently close behind him assuming invisibility. Good craftsmanship was always safer than unexplained power use. The corridor was fed by four others and two stairways, with strategically placed cameras that always reported empty passageways to the main security monitors.

A vocal General Parker left the meeting berating his fellow officers for voting in favour of the project. Escorted by two fawning supportive security officers, he suffered a fatal heart attack before he could leave the building. It was described in the pathology report as, 'Natural Causes: Heart Failure exacerbated by his agitated state and advanced years'.

Whispers and accusations quickly spread through the ministry building and Trent realised, he wasn't the only one in the organisation with a hidden talent.

Trent's 'Lunar Casino Project', officially branded 'Moon Complex WG-1', was approved as the first off-world, World Gov endeavour and at the age of twenty-nine, Trent had a direct line to the World Gov ruling body.

***

"Trent, my friend," an overly familiar voice with an ancient American accent pulled him from his reverie.

"Mr Garvy," replied Trent in a subdued tone. He produced a smile as the man approached, but there was no joy behind it. "Good flight?" he asked the criminal overlord. He took the offered hand and returned the greeting, his eyes fixed on Garvy's strange white headgear.

"Fantastic! So, this is our baby?" Garvy spun around to indicate his surroundings. His white linen jacket, loosely draped over his one-piece dark-blue armour, freely billowed out in the artificial gravity set just below earth standard.

"No, this is just the customs area at your shuttle bay. We have twelve of these." Trent could see the man's childish demeanour was born of simple innocent adventure. A trip to the moon, a lifelong ambition achieved.

"And you came to welcome me? I feel honoured." Garvy chuckled as he looked down, his feet seemed to be testing the floor. "I thought I might be floating," he explained. He removed his archaic hat, wiping his brow with a magically produced handkerchief. "And you brought friends," he nodded indicating the two red suited armed guards loitering at the entrance to the customs area behind Trent.

"Don't mind them, World Gov protocol; I must have baby-sitters wherever I go. Frankly, it's a pain." Trent wasn't lying, it was not something he enjoyed, but his overlords insisted. He knew he was under constant observation.

"I know, I understand, I've got two myself, but where are they when you need them? The useless..." he mumbled something and glanced behind, but no-one else had emerged from the baggage hall.

"I hope you will join us tonight for a little diversion in our leisure centre." Trent began. "We'd like to introduce you to our facilities, help you relax, meet the other shareholders and hopefully unwind from your journey. Maybe a small wager in the Khonsu Casino and a drink with friends." Trent's welcome speech had been rehearsed and he was prepared to give it to all of the key investors as they arrived.

"You wouldn't be trying to set me up, Mr Trent? Gambling is illegal, in the eyes of the World Gov." Garvy's eyes narrowed, though his manner was still jovial. He was never far away from suspicion.

"I've told you before, Mr Garvy," the honorific did not sit well with Trent, "we are not on the world below. We...!" The word was emphasised as Trent raised himself to his full height. Garvy comprehended the distaste in Trent's words, he'd seen it in his own men often enough.

"We...are not World Gov." Trent's anger at the suggestion, illustrated by the tightening of his smile was not feigned, even though it was supposed to be the truth. Trent forced himself to relax a little. "If gambling was good enough for Khonsu, the God of the Moon, then I'm sure we can always claim 'provincial religious observance'." Trent sniggered at his misuse of the official World Gov clause for excusing wealthy collaborators.

Ever since Jan, his Chief Tech Officer, had suggested the Casino name and explained the story of Khonsu, Trent had taken the idea to heart. Besides, 'Khonsu Casino', the alliteration was catchy.

"Now, if you'll excuse me? Sadly, this complex doesn't run itself." A trace of a bow followed by a wide grin, disarmed Garvy enough to prevent any further conversation.

As Trent walked away, he took a deep breath to steady his anger at Garvy's accusation, touched his ear and spoke quietly, "Garvy's in seven. Who's next?"

"Madam Ling Rong-Yu is docking at Bay Eleven and General Een-Eer is due to arrive thirty minutes later at Bay Four." Jan's cool informed voice always calmed Trent and his good humour returned.

"Bay Four? That's across the base, can you make sure there's a pod available to get me across in time." His request was more to continue his conversation than anything else, after all there was hardly anyone here yet. Until the World Gov decided to make good its threat of despatching a 'protection' force, who else could stress the internal transit system?

The main cross-complex transport system was essentially two horizontal elevators that were only available to staff with a security clearance of four and above. They went from East to West, from one set of Docking Bays to the other with only two stops available between; beneath the Khonsu Casino at the centre of the complex and at the Main Security building. Guests were encouraged to use provided electric vehicles to transfer to and from the hotel. Once there, everything was within a two-minute walk from their reception.

"Not a problem," Jan humoured him. "You know, we could fit four shuttles in each bay," she continued.

"Only if you want a blood bath," his face relaxed into a gentle smile as he entertained an evil thought. Maybe that would ultimately solve his problems, but that wasn't his plan, that was the ultimate plan of the World Gov. "Just dock them as planned, Jan." He touched his ear and signed off.

Garvy silently cursed himself for his enthusiasm. His excitement had got the better of him and as he replaced his white panama hat, his demeanour changed returning to one of hate and distrust of everything and everyone around him.

"Where are my cases?" He yelled at his two bodyguards as they emerged from the customs hall, laden with luggage.

3: Plans

"So, we take this gem." Sat in the closed booth with his entourage, Garvy announced his intention. The thin green glistening null-field around them prevented any sound escaping from their meeting. Beyond that, dark curtains had been drawn for privacy. One bodyguard sat next to him; two others stood outside the booth creating a wider visible cordon. A show of strength to any passer-by.

"Do we want it?" A female voice tried to reason with the plan. "If we take the whole Base, we're gonna have to defend it. Can't see the end of that. Better to just take what they've got. Pick their pockets, come back later."

"They're not armed," reported a thin faced man bearing an angry red scar above his right eye. He slowly caressed his own polished weapon, his voice thick with an improvised accent. Cutter relished the idea of being a 'true' Chicago gangster and while his accent and dress were taken from ancient vids, his psychopathic sadism and murderous impulses were entirely his own.

"Yeah, Cutter, but we are," guffawed a muscular man with short brown curly hair. He reached across the table to investigate a decorated silver bowl. Reaching in he withdrew a handful of peanuts, a luxury he'd never seen on the planet below.

The gangsters wore simple belts over their one-piece grey nano-suits, but were otherwise bare of accessories. The armour was a health and safety requirement while on the station. It was issued to everyone, but those with influence who enjoyed the finer things in life, never passed up an opportunity to display their status. Each had brought their own tailored protection.

The suits had to be worn everywhere, except in bed. Each *en suite* lunar bedroom was a self-contained armoured cell that would withstand massive impact energy from rogue meteors and protect against rare radiation flares. With the rooms hundreds of metres below the lunar surface the danger was minimal.

The whole complex was surrounded by force shields unheard of on Earth, but in the old days, despite the shields, micro-meteors had been known to penetrate the walls. The large area energy shields, developed in the early days of the last 'great war', were only effective in space. Essentially, they absorbed and repelled any excessive energy applied, but basic physics meant they were useless within any atmosphere where the constant movement of heavy gases disrupted their operation.

Today, the chance of a structure breach was as likely as being eaten by a shark while swimming in your bath, but old fears die hard and safety in the hostile environment of space was never taken lightly.

"Weapons are no-good here," observed the pale skinned woman with short black hair and piercing green eyes. Her jet-black suit differed from the other gangsters as it was adorned with reinforced faux suede patches on the right shoulder and at both elbows. It looked like an affectation. An announcement of the violence she carried with her, but on closer examination bulges and ripples would lead an observer to suspect the patches were more than just decoration. "They're not stupid. They saw what we had with us. They simply don't care." She leant forward and retrieved her drink from the table, sipping thoughtfully.

"Carney's right," affirmed Garvy. "Cutter, we need no stupidity. We want information not carnage. It's probably a trap, but no-one dies...yet. I want to know how this place ticks." He looked at the worried faces of his entourage. "And keep the shuttle ready to go."

"Right boss," acknowledged the thin faced man. He put his gun away.

"Harvey!" The big man looked up, from studying his now empty hand. "Manpower, energy, supplies; got it?" Garvy issued his instructions.

"Got it, boss." He scraped another handful of the complimentary snack from the bowl in front of him and tossed another peanut into his mouth. "What about, you know... the competition?" He spat chewed nuts as he spoke and Carney was not impressed.

"Stay clear, work in pairs. No violence here." Garvy was earnest. He knew his orders would be obeyed. "Trent's holding out on us, I can feel it. If he's offering us a dollar, you can bet he's found fifty. We find out what's worth taking, we liberate it and we go. We can always come back later, for the rest." The suggested plan was now the one he'd always had. He stretched across the table and retrieved the miniature flashing green scrambler device that enabled further privacy of their speech from any electronic eavesdroppers. He closed it and tossed it to Cutter who secreted it in a sealed side pocket under his arm. The green null-screen faltered, flickered and disappeared.

"Now... whose round is it?"

In a similar booth across the floor of the casino lounge another gossamer green field sparkled behind drawn curtains. General Eer Een was listening as his orders were relayed through his first lieutenant, Skabenga. Again, on the table, an electronic green privacy device was flashing.

"We do the thing," Skabenga instructed a gang of attentive men, chosen for their enhanced muscles, not their intelligence. To the right of both him and his leader sat two tall women of an uncertain age, silent and unmoving. The women had smooth ebony skin, the intense amber eyes of an eagle and were identical in every way. As one of the men moved, uncomfortable in his strange attire, the women tensed.

Skabenga pointed to his eyes and his wrist then used his open hand to indicate the man responsible. He then pointed to his nose and held his neck with three fingers, but now indicating a different man. Finally, he swept his hand around the remaining men and indicated himself. He slapped his open palm against his chest twice, made a sequence of hand shapes and stood to attention. He nodded slowly as he slid a column of around a dozen coins to each of the men.

"Good." General Eer Een, condescended to add a single word. Skabenga removed the privacy device and the men stood with military precision and left silently.

As his lieutenant rose, the General uttered one more word, "Stay." The two men and their female companions remained in silence as the privacy field was lifted from the booth and the curtains opened.

Ling Rong-Yu sat stoically throughout the brief given by her First Clerk. She admired the elder's green silk scarf emblazoned with her family device. Planning and execution were tasks fit only for underlings; hers had been the divine revelation of what needed to be done.

It was she, their Divine Goddess, that revealed the Australasian continent was their rightful home. It was she, the Guardian of their Future, that foresaw the destruction of human life in all its major towns and cities through the use of a genetic virus. It was she, the Wisest of Leaders, who gathered her followers to the luxury and security of a clean and fertile continent still unravaged by the abomination of the World Gov, and it was she, the Embodiment of Truth and Love, that had negotiated the current mutuality pact between the ancient Asian enemies ruling body.

Of all the criminal sponsors visiting their lunar prize, Ling Rong-Yu the many titled divinity, was accompanied by the most substantial retinue; a veritable army of devoted followers. There was no device on her table to enable privacy, but both she and her First Clerk had tiny flashing green lights visible within their wrists. If you looked closely at the men in her booth you may have noticed none ever opened their mouths to venture comment nor opinion. The instructions were given in code. Mandarin language was easily interpreted by the computers, but the words were simple parables accompanied by hand gestures that meant nothing after direct translation. Whatever they planned would remain secret.

Sarko had already sampled four types of vodka and had decided he no longer needed to play to the oligarch stereotype he had engendered most of his life.

"Let me try that Brandy stuff," he leaned from the edge of his booth seat, almost falling to the ground as he tried to grab a passing young blonde-haired waitress. "What are you called, little angel?" he gurgled in a patronising manner. Unlike the other booths no privacy screen was in place and the occupants were open to view.

As she'd been trained, the waitress turned to the customer and held her head high, crossing her hands in front of her, flat against her apron. In the one-piece red striped, white armour of the hospitality staff she stood silently, ignoring his personal enquiry, waiting to receive her instructions from this boor of a man.

Sarko squinted, "Brandy!" he demanded. He read her badge with some difficulty from his bent over position, but was soon pulled upright by a virile young man in bright green armour, with hair to match, accessorised with a huge diamond ear ring, "Angie 09," he managed. "What's the 09 for Angie." he gave a forced smile.

"Pay grade," lied Angie with a practised smile. As she'd been taught, her gaze was trained forward, slightly above her customer's head.

Sarko's strength was in taking advantage of situations. He was rich, but his prize possession was his life. Sarko was a survivor. He'd made deals and broken just as many, he'd promised a lot and given little, but he didn't have an enemy in the world. Once he'd crossed you, he made sure you weren't around to tell anyone. He was jaded and wanted out. Too many friends had died; too many opportunities would never come around again.

"I'm here, because," he put a finger to his lips and swayed a little, "because, him... they," he swept his arm to indicate the assembled bodies in the booth, most of whom were half his age and all of whom seemed to find other interesting things to look at as he talked, "...they said, I'm not me, I need a holi... howli," he coughed and wheezed a little, "...a break."

"Just bring him a bottle of brandy, Angie. Thank you." The handsome young man pulled the older man upright again and leant his boss's flaccid body against his own. He placed his arm around Sarko's shoulders, turning his head to face him, the drunk nodded and his head fell as he was kissed gently on the forehead. A glass was raised and everyone in the booth shouted, "Nostrovia."

Angie left to service the order, the ordeal over. Walking back to the bar, she was beckoned over to the roulette table by the senior croupier. "Everything alright, my love?" Concern was evident in her voice.

"Fine Belle," replied Angie with a weak smile. She noted her room-mate had changed her hair colour to brunette since arriving for work. "Open less than an hour and one of them is dead drunk already. It's going to be a long night."

The lights dimmed and the music rose in volume as, what appeared to be a scantily clad dancer slowly crawled onto the raised stage in the centre of the lounge. She wrapped her body suggestively around a tall golden pole, which slowly and evocatively rose in the middle of the podium. Her voice was soft and sensual and her body lithe. Her attraction though, lay in her enhancements, forbidden on Earth.

Aneksi had taken the form of a cat, genetically melding her own features with selected features of the feline race. Her visage was not offensive... it was stunning. At first glance most people didn't register the subtle changes. Her act brought the room crashing to silence as her mobility and strength were demonstrated by gymnastic gyrations held at impossible angles, designed to tease both men and women in the room, but no matter the pose, it never affected a single note of her hypnotic song. As she moved, portions of her nano-suit would become transparent, enough to tease, but not to show, before seductively increasing opacity once more.

Just before her final vocal crescendo, with her hands holding the front of the stage, her chin to the floor, her back arched, a naked leg held high, and her sultry eyes fixed on the mouse within her selected prey; with every spectator drawn to her allure, wishing they'd been chosen... all hell broke loose.

4: Power

"Guard that door! No-one in, no-one out." The barked orders were acknowledged silently, a curt nod and the immediate mobilisation of the two shadowing bodyguards. Like ancient biblical devils in their red one-piece armour suits, they obeyed without hesitation. A quick scan of the docking bay and the doors were sealed. The last of the day's shuttles had berthed, only staff remained in the area.

The alarms pierced the corridor and destroyed everyone's ability to think. Flashing strobes, pulsed at regular intervals, seared their tortuous message on every retina; this is not a place to be.

Trent, moved quickly to the wall and placed his hand at head height, in response the wall shimmered and produced a visual display. He selected the red flashing 'Status' button from the side of the new display. An imposing triangular warning icon flashed red indicating an approaching meteor shower.

Shouting above the din, he yelled his commands at the interface, "Lock down all transport bays. Seal the Domes. Mute alarm, West corridor, Sector 6G." and with a huge effort of will, he forced his demeanour to subside ten points, banishing the anger he felt for the universe. He straightened the paper-thin tuxedo suit cover he'd worn to de-militarise his appearance for the first commercial passenger liner and took a deep breath as he selected 'Broadcast'.

It took a second before the alarms were silenced by his command, enabling his next task. Closing his eyes, he calmed his mind and forced a smile.

"Would all patrons kindly move to the Khonsu Lounge. For your safety and comfort, please move quickly and calmly to the Khonsu Lounge." He pushed the 'Repeat' button and slid the delay bar to around fifteen seconds. He absently admonished himself, to everyone on staff the lounge was essentially the Casino; that was its purpose. It was only after the World-Gov propagandists complained about the overt negative image of the word that Trent had agreed to refer to it as the Lounge. Years of references to 'The Casino' as the central hub of the complex were never going to be brushed under the carpet overnight.

It had taken seven years to resurrect this abandoned marvel of engineering, billions of dollars and millions of man-hours to complete the project and after two days of flawless, lucrative business, Trent was not going to allow an unplanned meteor shower to take down his dream.

"Liza!" He called his senior security Captain. "What's the hold-up?"

He knew it would take only one fatality to have his complex confiscated by the World Gov, their greedy eyes fixed firmly on the prize, though their parsimonious hearts lacked the courage to take the leap of faith required to settle on the hostile moon. None of the council had ever left the comfort of their homes to even inspect the place.

"Reports of confused guests," she responded almost immediately. "One group refusing to leave their apartment."

"Well stun them and drag them out. You know the procedure."

Dubious deals and shady agreements with the worlds least desirable sponsors had been needed to complete the endeavour, but Trent had negotiated like a demon collecting souls. He'd deliberately sought successful members of the depraved underworld society, to convince his rulers of his 'pure' intentions. The iconic Moon Base, standing high above the earth, appealed to those who lusted after infamy for their own petty empires. But these same people were unused to following orders.

"It's okay, sir, they heard you. They're moving." Liza cut the comms while shouting further instructions to her team.

His ability to 'read' people was both a boon and a curse. Since moving to the lower gravity of the moon his 'gift' had unexpectedly evolved. He could usually read the auras of those around him, when he wanted to, but now he felt their emotional extremes thrust upon him, like needles behind the eyes. What had once been an unreliable uncontrolled affectation upon his vision, now demanded mental discipline to raise barriers between himself and others, lest their powerful feelings swamped him; something he'd never had to do on Earth.

In his mind's eye, he created colours, acting like filters that interfered with the powerful auras emanating from the passions and emotional angst of others. In a matter of hours, he had become adept at selecting his protection. Now, creating his mental shield had become second nature, as automatic as breathing and confidence in this gift from Khonsu, had risen once more.

"Let's move." He turned to his guards and was pleased with their control. There was definitely an element of fear from each, but rather than deeply colour each man's aura, they simply radiated a washed-out red tinge, showing their ability to control their emotion.

The main lunar complex could withstand the physical onslaught of the meteor shower. The three domes. The Bio Dome, Flight Dome and Main Casino were equipped with multiple shields and advanced alloys making them the safest places to be. However, the other outer buildings, standing proud of the surface were sacrificial by design; he hoped everyone understood this as well as he did.

Within the complex, advances in nano-technology experimented with for a hundred years in construction yet always abandoned, had been perfected by Trent, building upon his father's specialist research. The walls were alive with communities of microscopic single use mechanisms whose power could be harnessed to create self-repair and sensory systems to feed and display links to the central data systems. Usually inert to conserve power, the nano devices were commonly used to program unique textures, structural designs and colours, giving each customer a tailored living space during their stay.

The nature of the emergency had changed their role. Gathering all of the information needed by the Base Commander to enable his response; his location lit up. Charts, Video images and statistics flooded across the walls.

"Cancel display," he yelled, after absorbing the details of the threat. "Status only."

A long, illuminated banner across the top of the corridor wall flashed to amber from red. It followed him as he made his way to the lounge, entering sectors that were still hosting the debilitating sirens; their impact receded as safety approached. The wall messages went from a sporadic countdown in red of "At Risk" guests, to the amber 'ABAF' sign, "All Bodies Accounted For".

He cursed the protracted delay, but soon, the banner turned green; 'ABS', "All Bodies Safe". The sirens stopped, his ears rang and the corridors throbbed with the shriek of silence. Of course, the word 'bodies' just meant customers. His staff would still be busy all over the complex carrying out their assigned duties in the face of the oncoming danger.

"You two stay here." He stationed his red suited guards at the outer blast doors of the Casino Lounge, "I don't want to march in their like a general with a 'kill squad'." One of the men chortled at the prospect; Trent ignored him.

Alone, Trent stopped outside the last set of armoured doors leading into the lounge; closed but not locked. Through deft selection across the wall panel interface, the Base Commander accessed the live radar image, tracking the threat. Twelve minutes to impact.

He activated the wall comms and selected 'Station Defence', inwardly relaxing as he recognised Jan's voice acknowledge his call. Flicking the video on, she appeared busily monitoring and controlling the systems across a wide desk.

"More power from the Reactor. Balance Tom, balance!" Looking away from him she shouted orders to staff beyond his view.

She saw him and took a breath, but before she could begin any report, he issued his order.

"Let go the net!" he instructed calmly. She gravely nodded in reply. The screen vanished and he bowed his head and gave a sigh. The shot would take power, a lot of it.

Life on this rock was a continual bargain. There was no point in surviving the attack if there wasn't enough energy to warm the bodies of the guests or shield them from the incessant radiation of the sun.

He stepped back from the wall, stretched up to his full height and again straightened his thin tuxedo suit cover. He whistled his relief through itchy teeth, then, taking a deep breath and pushing out his chest, he strode purposefully into the lounge, his well-practised smile firmly in place.

The opulence of the Khonsu Lounge was second to none, the huge domed roof lit by a central crystal chandelier and supported by a plethora of stylised wall sconces provided the ambience, while the timbre was dictated by the throng of bodies insinuating themselves around the glowing gaming tables on the lower floor.

On the balconies above, a hundred guests bemoaned their rude evacuation. Below, waves of high emotions pulsed through the floor. This was the heart, the bankroll of the complex. Any great adventure needed to be self-sufficient to succeed and what his complex needed was a life-blood of currency.

Trent knew people, he knew their desires to escape the poisoned planet, he knew the suppressed guilt that often afflicted the unscrupulous wealthy and the yearning inside those with vision. His gift was that of broker, to cut through the prejudice and the emotional baggage they carried, to leave only what was comfortable in front of his stakeholders, making them feel honoured to be part of the complex, to make them feel at home.

He chided himself, 'Honour' he thought, what a strange word to apply here. The assembly comprised the pushers, the cut-throats, the gangs, and kingpins of their own constrained, violent worlds. Each aching for recognition, but only if well away from the World Gov authorities. Trent had levered their desires and pilfered their purses to build his dream, his sanctuary from the madness below.

He was now heavily involved in fulfilling the promises he could and eliminating the more inconvenient pacts, made through necessity.

As he entered the casino lounge gaming area, he was approached by Tom Massado, looking every inch the duke of some lost Bavarian fantasy castle in his custom white suit. His sash was resplendent with medals and honours he'd never earned and his face contorted to hold his ancient monocle in place.

"This is fine, Mr. Trent." He saluted, raising his glass of red wine high. "Has the danger passed?" His cowardice shone clearly through the question, a bright yellow sun emanating brilliantly from the blackened heart of a drug smuggler and unscrupulous arms facilitator serving terrorists all over the world.

"We'll see it eliminated soon," Trent gave a quick nod and a wink and moved on, reassuringly touching Massado's arm as he passed. The man's cowardice blazed for a brief moment as his hand reached out, but diminished greatly at his gentle touch.

Trent moved to a raised podium at the centre of the lounge, recently vacated by the gorgeous creature Aneksi. He walked to the rear of the bijou stage and gestured. One of many free liquor dispensaries rose to meet him, he withdrew a chrome handset from a hidden panel and spoke into it calmly.

"Ladies and Gentleman," he spied the few privileged families included in the guest list, "boys and girls!" He exuded charm, flashing his practised smile as his soothing voice pervaded the room through the cleverly designed sound system. "If I may, please, have your attention?" He took a deep breath and continued to smile as he surveyed the glittering mass assembled.

"I will relay the threat, that has unexpectedly come our way, upon the main screen. If you would move up to the gallery you will observe a much-improved view. I will be interrupting your gaming pleasure for only a few moments to facilitate the images. Thank you." A genial smile was offered to all in view. He nodded reassuringly as the last few die-hard gamblers walked past his perch to access the gallery stairs, shepherded by his dutiful, uniformed staff.

Trent selected another control on the handset and the blue-lit gaming tables dimmed, a moment later the wall sconces receded, seemingly folding into the wall, their glow reduced to a mere brown stain, while the crystal chandelier flickered out of existence, replaced by a fully three-dimensional holographic view of the approaching meteor storm.

There wasn't much to see, but occasionally the spinning surface of a rock reflected the sun and the twinkling arc of light flashed closer.

Trent double tapped the subcutaneous comms link behind his ear and heard Jan's voice acknowledge the call.

"Sir?" she snapped, obviously busy doing something else.

"Time to impact?" he queried.

"Fireworks in six seconds," she responded. He caught the exasperation in her voice. Balancing the load from the three power systems was always tricky.

Solar was the workhorse, while the Cold Fusion system was still in its infancy, more of an attraction to lure the technologists than a dependable supply. Deep below the surface, several miles to the north-east, the Nuclear system provided the meat of their defensive power. Rebuilt and refurbished the power plant was archaic, but well understood and historically the deadliest.

"Great job," his compliments were always well received and he imagined Jan's smile as he terminated contact.

He counted down under his breath and at 2 seconds announced in a stentorian voice, "Behold!"

On cue the focussed plasma barrage impacted the leading meteors and energy flares of various colours filled the holo-vid as the lights silently consumed the approaching threat.

Extroverted squeals of delight emanated from the audience as moments after the screen showed the colours of elemental particles being ripped apart, the now transparent dome above their heads flashed with a myriad of colours. The show ebbed and flowed in intensity until, after a full minute, the light show ceased. Trent tapped his personal comms link again.

"Report!" He was calm, but he knew the response, he'd been through too many simulations. With an impact at 5000 klicks and the net at a standard 60% efficiency, it would make a dent in the deadly storm, nothing more. The net, his main defensive system able to project a mesh-wall of plasma energy using a barrage of plasma cannons, would only have ripped apart the atomic structure of the leading edge of the approaching threat.

"38% reduction in mass, 22% dispersion; impact reduction 72%." Jan's tone in his ear, belied no opinion, no emotion; she paused while she absorbed further readouts. "Depletion of power reserves twelve percent. I estimate four hours to full recovery; all systems nominal."

Much better than he expected, a minimal targeted salvo from the secondary protection field would easily mop up the remaining dangerous missiles and the shields would vaporise the rest. For a moment he considered the risks of allowing the force fields to act as a final defence. Not much of a risk, but so early in the business operation, he didn't want any adverse reports affecting the lure of the complex, or worse, inviting closer scrutiny by some ambitious would-be commander on Earth.

He looked at his guests and detected the envy of his power. He knew there would be those amongst them that would covet his position. One more lesson he thought and his good humour returned.

He raised the control to his mouth and spoke with gravitas, "Send the Worm!" His face betrayed his contempt of his captivated audience, "...deflection priority." This would reveal his private party piece to any that doubted his control or had other less favourable intentions. The 'Worm' was overkill in this situation, but he couldn't pass up the opportunity provided for the demonstration. The loss of another 5% of power reserves would be worth it.

"Aye, Sir!" Jan affirmed his instruction in his ear then cut the private audio link.

Trent looked upon the masses in the gallery; the Net was always impressive. They congratulated each other on the powerful destruction they had witnessed, as if their observation of the event had contributed to its effectiveness.

He caught the eye of a svelte lady dressed in a shimmering red gown; holo-beads danced around the bodice. She raised her glass to him and winked in a salacious manner. Her violet flaring aura shouted her immediate feminine desire. He couldn't place her name, but he knew her as the trophy wife of Garvy. The gangster stood beside her, ignoring her, engrossed in conversation with his bodyguards, slapping their backs, congratulating them on his survival; 'Garvy, The Butcher'.

As he looked around the assembled entrepreneurs, similar themes of relief and jealousy tinged with hatred, coloured the gallery. He raised the comms unit to his mouth and began his public rhetoric once more.

"Of course, the fragments are just as dangerous as the boulders," he began quietly, milking the ripe audience for every ounce of emotion. Playing upon their insecurity, watching as their assuredness crumbled. He couldn't afford to allow this congregation of criminal potential to arm themselves with confidence.

"As we speak, several thousand tonnes of iron fused silicon-carbide destruction is hurtling towards us." He absorbed the genuine fear from the crowd, the red shone from within their glorious raiment, mingled with the yellow cowardice from surprising sources. The back of his eyes itched and he wondered if he'd gone too far.

"But fear not, after all folks, does not the Devil look after his own?" He laughed in good humour at the uncertain responses from the gallery above. They were uncomfortable now, as he cast himself in the role many of them aspired to. The croupiers and the floor attendants began a round of applause; smiling enthusiastically, they led the subdued revellers out of their personal qualms.

"I have a gift for all those who survived the initial barrage, please, continue viewing." He bowed in a somewhat mocking manner and selected a new control that switched the holo-projection view, out to a much further distance. The image angle, changed. The moon came into view and the whole complex was now visible. Forty-nine hours into a lunar-day cycle would alleviate some of his customers anxieties, but the sunlight clearly showed the base in the path of a thick fog of grey debris; the deadly meteoric remnants speeding towards them.

"Observe!" A bright point of deep blue light erupted far to the rear and high above the complex.

Gasps of doubt and dismay escaped the audience. Surely, the shot had missed, it was on the wrong side of the debris to intervene? Their auras betrayed their thought, but the orbiting camera belied the perspective of the attack. The light opened, becoming paler as it widened, rotating faster as it grew. Within its hollow structure, bursts of lightning could be seen and brilliant flashes emanated from within the darkening centre, expanding, leaving only a faint shimmering darkness as the rotating structure gently faded from view. An observant astronomer would notice that the stars revealed in the middle of the turmoil had changed.

"I summon Charybdis!" Trent demanded, revelling in his high drama. His arms flung wide to accentuate his power and his smile eclipsed the wonder in their eyes. A moment later, his voice returned to that of a simple narrator, informing his guests of the sight they were witnessing.

"The implosion has caused a wormhole, a gravitic dump if you will, and..." he raised his voice, unable to forsake all of the drama, "I command it, to swallow the threat that approaches."

On cue the fog altered its course, the massive momentum of the storm could not withstand the forces of gravity conjured and without complaint the approaching barrage of debris was silently sucked toward the gravity well. The storm of lethal particles coloured the forces and a grey twister became visible as the material was sucked into the abyss: the threat torn from the galaxy.

The gravitic whirlpool lasted only a few further seconds before disappearing completely, taking its repast with it.

An enthusiastic round of applause ensued and Trent made a mental note of those who were far from amused. This power was beyond their wildest dreams, yet its development had remained hidden. The gallery now contained hotspots of shock and anger bordering on murderous intent.

Aneksi slinked onto the podium behind Trent and began to fawn and caress him. He replaced the microphone and colouring with embarrassment, quickly withdrew from her stage.

The lighting returned, the music resumed and the show went on.

5: Business

"*Stay clear, work in pairs. No violence here.*" The recording of Garvy instructing his team was perfectly clear. "*We find out what's worth taking and we go. We can always come back later, for the rest.*"

Garvy could be excessively violent, but at heart he'd always been a petty thief. His admission of fact finding and taking what was available was expected and manageable. He'd find out what Garvy wanted and slip him a convincing fake. He sighed at the predictability of the man. He could easily deal with his petty avarice.

Trent examined the recordings from the booths in the privacy of his apartment, at what he referred to as his office desk. It seemed to him Garvy didn't understand the privacy devices were useless. After all the World Gov had invented them and sold them, no one could possibly imagine they wouldn't have some way to render them obsolete.

Both Ling and General Eer Een, were uncommonly clever. Trent appreciated their devious communications. He had specialists working on their techniques, but the human mind was a rare thing and no computer was going to understand their conversation without being privy to the code itself. He made a note on his pad to contact World Gov for regional communications assistance. They couldn't get upset about a request for a translator.

Sarko, really looked like he was ready to throw in the towel, but Trent was shrewd enough to realise the man had killed hundreds and was probably the most unscrupulous of the bunch. No, nothing he saw could be taken at face value.

He didn't recognise the waitress Angie and that irked him. He'd been present at all of the staff recruitment events and he prided himself on knowing everyone who worked for him. A man in his position couldn't allow unknowns into the operation. He made a mental note to meet and talk with her.

Scanning the room recording of the night before, his eye was caught by a pompous remonstration in one corner. He focussed the recording and raised the volume; he didn't like what he heard.

"*She's an abomination,*" cried the portly lady bedecked in diamonds.

"*She's an entertainer,*" her husband appealed for his partner to lower her voice. Senator Ahmed Wilson, old-style republican, outlawed terrorist until the Moscow incident; joined World Gov shortly after. Trent nodded. There was no harm in the old man, but it seemed his wife had taken offense at one of the dancers.

"*Genetic mutilation, that's illegal. I know my rights,*" cried his wife.

"*It's just make-up darling, she's an entertainer.*" Her husband tried to calm her down.

"*She's a harlot,*" announced the lady, actively being shushed by her husband, "*and I bet she's a prostitute too. I know about these 'entertainers', they'll destroy civilisation, mark my words.*"

Trent laughed at the futility of the lady's concerns. Aneksi was no problem, he knew her from the bad old days. But the lady was right, it wasn't make-up.

After perusing the recording for another twenty minutes nothing else seemed to be of interest. He called Jan on the monitor, "Anything to report?"

"Everything's fine, quiet night, all power levels 100%. One late arrival, commercial liner, forty guests no V.I.P.'s, delayed by the storm. Routine maintenance ongoing, no problems," she flashed him a smile. "So, am I going to see you today?" she laughed as though she'd just requested an audience with a unicorn.

"Actually, that's why I called. I have a shareholders meeting in twenty minutes, I'd like you to be there." He made it sound planned and organised, but really, he simply felt she would be useful as a second pair of eyes. He realised he was not being honest in his own mind and berated himself. 'She makes you feel comfortable,' an inner voice accused.

"Oh, okay, where are you?" she sounded flustered, obviously unprepared to leave her station. She was a little thrilled at seeing him as well. She'd made herself a promise that once the base went live, she was going to finally pin him down.

"Board Room 2, Casino Lounge, East." He regained his composure.

"I'll be there in ten," she confirmed.

The screen flickered and went dark. He sat for a moment wishing he could see her aura on the screen, but that's not how it worked, auras came from empathy with the soul not the image of the body. He wondered if she ever thought about him, other than as 'the boss'. He smiled at the memory of that night in Prague when he'd first spoken to her and ruined her dress. Since then, their paths had crossed several times, but he'd never had a chance to see her beyond her role of Senior Technician. He'd seconded her to the project, because she was the best, but as the project became operational his thoughts had evolved.

He made one more call, but there was no reply from Liza. "Security?" he called the station. It's Trent, where's the Duty Chief?" he asked firmly, but evenly, he wasn't used to his direct comms failing to connect. Nervous people were stupid people; he needed someone with a clear head.

"Ivor here, sir" a young sounding voice appeared and a square jawed man sat in front of the screen. "Liza's attending an incident with Martin at Docking Bay Four, sir. Can I help?"

Trent knew Ivor was security clearance '04'. He was the same rank as young Martin, but had eight years seniority; second only to Liza. He remembered talking to him about martial arts at the recruitment event in New Europa, in fact, Ivor was a familiar face around the base, he'd do. "Good man. I need you in Boardroom Two in ten minutes, do you know where that is?" Trent was pleased with the response.

"Casino Lounge, East, sir," replied Ivor.

"Full armour and weapons, Ivor, you're going to be the stick I hit them with. Remember, it's the Khonsu now, not the Casino." His face relaxed into a smile, dismissing the common mistake light heartedly.

Ivor grinned enthusiastically, "Yes, sir!" The irony of political niceties considering their current guests was not lost on either of them.

Trent cut the comms and considered Ivor's eager response. 'Everyone must know the lowlife we have here', he thought.

Trent stood beside a line of archaic computer gambling machines as Jan and Ivor arrived together in the Khonsu Lounge. He thanked them and gave an appreciative nod, acknowledging their presentation and timeliness. Ivor had additional armour pads, redundant but showy, and three brutal looking weapons attached to his suit. Jan held her communications pad, capable of accessing and projecting any schematic, anywhere. Strapped to her thigh was a well-equipped tool case, 'ever the engineer', he thought.

"Show of force, technical and security," he quickly briefed them. "Say nothing, respond to nothing, let me do the talking." They both nodded as if the mute order had already come into effect. "And if I ask you anything directly, don't think, only reply with a 'Yes, Sir', no matter what I say, okay?" Trent was having an inkling of a plan.

"Yes, Sir," replied Ivor.

"Well, okay," Jan was a bit more suspicious, but she trusted Trent's motives.

Twelve bodies were seated at the table, several others seated behind them and a few were stood, through choice.

"Good morning, ladies and gentleman," began Trent. Silence reigned and the meeting was called to order.

"First let me say, welcome, and may I express my deepest thanks for the trust you've placed in me so far."

Trent turned on the charm and talked about staffing, supplies, employment at the earth end and finally the expectations of profit. He presented the whole thing as boring and mundane, goading the criminal element with statistics and fears of logistical breakdowns. He knew it was not why they were here. Trent reached his final issue and was about to wrap up the meeting as a failure when a hand was raised.

"Where did the Wormhole thing come from?" Skabenga asked on behalf of his master. "We have no knowledge of this device, yet we are entitled to share in all of the technology you have used."

The room began to murmur. Everyone agreed, sharing new technology was a key part of the sponsorship deal.

"Yeah, it seems to me," supported Garvy, he stood up and glanced around the table, "...us, I mean us... that you been keeping secrets, Mr Trent." His lazy Chicago-esque accent was meant to intimidate, but from the assembled stakeholders he garnered looks of contempt.

Collectively, the auras were predominantly green with envy, but around the room shone beacons of blue hate. From the far end of the table, Trent noted pure pink curiosity from two distinct sources and made a mental note to pursue these later.

"I'm sorry, but that technology was fitted by the World Gov. Isn't that right Senior Technician Brennigan?"

Jan hesitated, she wasn't even aware Trent knew her surname, he'd certainly never used it before. "Oh, yes, Sir!" Jan felt the pressure of every eye in the room upon her, convinced they could see through her deception.

"I don't know how it works. I just know how to pull the trigger," Trent lied smoothly. "As it's not developed here as part of our project, I'm afraid I have no information to share."

Jan was finding it hard to keep a straight face. She'd developed the modification to the gravitic plate technology with Trent; just one of the 'special projects' he'd secretly worked on while managing the revitalisation of the lunar base. Together, the two of them had designed the focussing beams to control the effect.

It was a minor side effect they'd encountered as they repaired the original gravitic plate technology, when they first arrived at the abandoned base. The plates were necessary to replicate earth's gravity, reducing a raft of medical problems associated with long-term, low gravity living in space.

Trent had been fascinated by it. "If we can increase gravity," he'd realised, then can we reduce it?" That was the concept behind the Flight Dome. Set the plates to almost no gravity and you had the ability to fly. Typically, this was followed with the realisation that if gravity can be nullified, "...then why can't it be reversed?"

They'd started with two plates and lost the lab. Three plates gave full directional control, six plates added power; focussing twelve upon a single point created a stable, controlled 'Worm'.

Trent was surprised nobody had thought of it before. But then, when the planet began to die and the last war started, the Moon had been abandoned and Earth didn't need artificial gravity.

Jan had been impressed when Trent redesigned the system, improving the geometry of the antennae, increasing power and making the system almost portable, but she also harboured major concerns about the technology. Mainly, that the 'Worm's' opening location was unpredictable; they had no idea where the other end was appearing. Image analysis suggested it was different every time, but Trent argued it could simply be a change in orientation, as if looking through a rotating bent pipe. They were both aware, gravity could bend light and both agreed they were not creating a super dense mini black-hole, the mathematics proved that. Trent accepted the possibility of some tear in space, but was unconvinced the power they used could damage the fabric of their universe.

They'd agreed it was safe to operate this end, but if it was a door, as Jan suspected, where was the room on the other side and was anyone in it?

She surveyed the angry faces and realised that perhaps Trent was right. These people should not have access to such power.

"However," he continued in his patronising tone, "I will allow accompanied groups to view the technology and you can scan the system yourselves to learn whatever you can." This offer seemed to appease his audience.

Jan broke protocol and grabbed Trent by the arm twisting him toward her, placing her mouth close to his ear.

"You can't be serious," she hissed. "If you show them the gravitic plates and the amplifiers, they'll suss it out in a week! It's just tweaked old tech with your fancy maths."

"Shush!" He moved his lips to her ear breathing in the scent of her hair. "We'll take them to the sewage ionisers," he whispered, "gas pipes and pretty lights always look impressive, and we'll ban recording devices, maybe run some interference on their scans. They won't know what they're looking at." He gave her a cheerful smile as he was called back to the table by an irate voice.

"Yeah!" Garvy wasn't about to be set aside, he had the floor and he wanted more. "What about the Cold Fusion generator, you said it wasn't working, but my lads got told by your tech's it was up and running. Where's the plans for that then?" Garvy rousted another strong reaction from the seated members, Trent was ready for this... but he never got to deliver his speech.

As he appealed for calm a call came through on his emergency channel. He touched his ear to accept and noted Ivor did the same.

"Sorry to bother you, sir," he recognised the voice of Liza his Senior Security Chief, "Security Code One. We've got a body, Docking Bay Four. Doctor says it looks like murder."

6: Murder

"Ivor, could you please give the lecture marked "Safety", it's there, on the lectern, thanks." As he issued the order, he tapped a message and sent it directly to Ivor, 'Keep them here.' Ivor glanced at his arm and nodded, shouting for order above the din. Trent hooked Jan's arm and urgently indicated they should leave. She was a little resistant at the rough handling, but he quickly explained.

"Blackout all Earth communication, everything." They half-ran through the Casino, Jan issuing terse orders over her comms as they went. The plush surroundings ended abruptly as they exited through an unremarkable side door. Descending rough steps, they emerged at the central point of the staff transport system. A pod was waiting, probably sent by Liza thought Trent and made a mental note to increase her pay. His Security Chief seemed able to read his mind.

The door closed on the transit pod with a rudimentary hiss of air and the two sat facing each other as Trent typed in their destination.

"What's happening in Docking Bay Four?" she asked.

"It's started, first body has turned up. Look..." he felt uncomfortable, his feelings were bubbling just beneath the surface. His hands were steady, but his mind was trembling. He knew her presence was affecting him in some tangible way, he was struggling to control his thoughts. "...I need you to be safe."

He looked at the expression on her face a mixture of shock and horror at his announcement and the obvious expectation of more violence, but she felt a wave of warmth wash over her at his first open admission of his care for her.

"Satellite's down, all comms set to internal." she announced staring at her screen seeking safety in the technical data presented. "Laser Line... offline."

He tore his gaze away from her brilliant white aura.

"Murder," he announced as the confused Jan looked up from her pad. "Why did it have to be murder?"

Liza called and he listened intently to the report she gave from the scene. He nodded in response. "Be there in two minutes, seal off everything," he instructed.

"There could be damage to the air pumps..." he began to relay Liza's observations.

"I'll check it out," Jan's engineering mindset focussed her thoughts. Once again, she busied herself with her computer. The complex was a technical wonderland and she was its Alice. Jan knew every system and every connection; she'd been down every rabbit hole.

Casting a quick glance his way, she noted his look of concern, "I'm probably the best person to check out any interference with the systems, anyway."

"Can't you do it from your own office?" he tried to spare her what could be a grisly sight, after all the suits were very difficult to defeat to achieve murder, he could only imagine what they would find. "Your office at the power complex is a lot safer than the main base. They can't get to you without going outside and they're not equipped."

She looked at his concerned face and considered his fears for her. "I'll take a quick look," she sighed, his anxiety was plain to see, "if there are any problems, well..., you can look after me," she winked.

Trent didn't need his gift to see her affection and suddenly he felt self-conscious sat so close, being so open with his emotions. The trembling had subsided and he mentally reprimanded himself for what he considered a temporary loss of control. He coughed and straightened a little in his soft transit seat.

"I just meant, I...," he stammered as her smile grew at his discomfort. "I just thought, you're the last one I need being abducted or harmed. I need to keep you safe."

"Of course, I understand," the smile diminished, but it still played gently across her lips. She'd waited since Prague; she could wait a little longer.

With a sense of relief and a slight adjustment to his suit temperature, Trent stepped out of the pod into the transit hall. His two bodyguards had arrived before him. Alerted to the incident their first allegiance was to the World Gov and this situation had been relayed immediately. Trent saw them guarding his exit and scowled.

He walked to the gaggle of bodies by a solid plain white door in the corner of the hall and shouted to the bodyguards. "You two, secure the pod!" There was a moment of indecision; the two men looked at each other, as if deciding whether Trent was still in charge or not, before they silently acquiesced and walked away.

"Sir! It's this way." Liza, her badge showing 'Liza S. 02', the highest rank on the base shared only with his senior tech, parted the crowd.

Miss Shishaw, a stickler for discipline and routine, the middle-aged woman of Asian descent was the head of his security. Her diminutive height was incongruous to her appointment, but she was born to the task.

She strode quickly to keep up with Trent who seemed overly anxious to get to the scene. Jan and a few others from security and maintenance, created an entourage that followed through a controlled access door and down a flight of iron steps to an area of pipes and valves. High upon the wall a bulky louvered cupboard door was open and, on the floor, behind thick orange pipes, lay the body of a man face down.

"I found him in the ventilation feed," a short man dressed in grey and orange stepped forward. His badge declared him to be 'Cooper M. 08'. "Technical Maintenance team, sir!" he indicated his taller partner similarly attired. "We were sent to check a drop in airflow in Bay Four, sir." Cooper glanced at the body, "Found him, sir... in there," he indicated the open cupboard door.

Trent could see the door held fans and filters and the inside of the cupboard was lined with polished metal. There were no marks of blood or signs of a struggle, the man had been dead before being placed out of sight.

"What are those straps on his head?" asked Trent, now taking in the details of the victim, after internally confirming Cooper's identity.

"Packing tape." A new voice entered the conversation, deep, calm and confident. Trent turned to face the newcomer and his whole demeanour changed. The body was almost forgotten as he recognised his old friend Cole Harper.

"Doctor Harper I presume?" Trent was surprised by the presence of his old friend from the ministry. "When did you get here?"

"They sent me to assess you and your staff," he stated the task as if it were no more than a minor inconvenience and acknowledged Jan with a nod. "I came in on the public shuttle late last night." The men shook hands and Cole went as far as to place his hand on his friend's shoulder. "They kept us hanging out there for a while, something about a meteor storm." Trent could feel the genuine warmth from the man and felt relieved he had another ally.

"But why are you here, at this?" Trent was suspicious his old partner had appeared without warning, but more concerned that his old friend had been inconvenienced.

"I left one of my bags behind, last night. I just came down to get it and someone screamed for a medic, so..." he shrugged.

"That was me, sir!" admitted Cooper shyly. "Sorry sir! It was a bit of a shock when that... man... fell out."

"I've recorded the scene, sir. Would you like me to retrieve the victim?" interrupted Liza.

"I can take a look, while I'm here, if you want," offered his friend.

"Okay, just bring him out here." Trent indicated the open space at the foot of the stairs. Liza and the maintenance team manhandled the body's dead weight over the pipes while Trent and the security team received him and reverently laid him on his back.

Whoever hid the body was no weakling, thought Trent.

"Oh!" Jan was taken aback by the sight of the victim's bloated face, but recovered swiftly. "Anyone know who he is?"

"He's been suffocated," Doc Harper knelt down and withdrew a pen sized laser scalpel from his belt. Slicing the lower strap, he retrieved a piece of plastic wrapping from the contorted face. Everyone waited in silence for Doc Harper's analysis.

"Held in place by two packing straps," he leant further forward and examined the mouth. "Throat and mouth choked with expanding packing foam. Quick squirt, plastic on top and held together with packing tape. The tape expanded and hardened, as it is designed to do. When thickened it was impossible to remove without proper tools. The foam suffocated him." A cursory inspection of the body led to a startling conclusion. "No visible impacts, no blows, probably held by one or more men, while another did the deed."

"Why didn't his helmet prevent the attack, all he had to do was think it on?" asked Liza.

"I thought they automatically came on if you needed them," commented Cooper to his buddy, nodding sagely.

Trent considered the facts as his friend stood back from the body. This was impossible. He knew, more than most, the suits capabilities. The helmet would activate as soon as the man needed protection, he'd have his own oxygen supply and the helmet should remain in place for about fifteen minutes after it was no longer needed; until the suit concluded the wearer was dead.

"Let me through." Trent knelt by the body, beside Cole. He placed his palm on the suit of the dead man and ran a diagnostics check.

"Anything?" His old partner queried his actions.

"The suits power is at Seventy Three percent, inconclusive. If it had been closer to a hundred percent, we could be sure he'd struggled with an assailant. If it had been less than two percent, the suit looks old, it may have glitched."

"Not much help then?" summarised Cole.

Trent was aware he was expected to take control. He stood and addressed the crowd.

"If the body loses oxygen," Trent explained, "the helmet seals to supply its own." He looked at Jan. "If he'd consciously activated it, while alive, his helmet should still be up." He paused and looked at the concerned faces around him, "I've never heard of a suit failing before."

The crowd nodded, murmuring their agreement.

"Let's get the body to the infirmary, I'm sure you'll want to perform toxicology and other tests to get to the bottom of this." Doctor Harper issued the orders, but Liza obeyed without hesitation.

"Now Trent, where can you buy me a drink?" The medical man stepped back and seemed to mentally remove himself from the scene. He grinned broadly despite the situation. "It may be morning here, but it's evening where I've come from."

Trent was deep in thought, to those gathered it was as if he simply ignored Doc Harper. He was going over the suit schematics in his head trying to detect any weaknesses his father may have overlooked in the design.

"Trent?" another voice intruded on his thoughts and slowly he realised Jan was talking to him. "Trent!" He responded with a nod. "I'll check the equipment and draft a report within the hour, okay?" She asked permission to get on with what she'd come to do. Trent looked distracted which meant something other than the body in front of him was troubling his thoughts.

"Yes, fine... within the hour," Trent recovered himself. "Liza, when the medics get here, stay with them and observe the analysis of the body. Make sure no one gets close to it." Liza nodded and turned away; she activated her comms with a quick touch of her ear to check the progress of the medics.

Trent sighed, placing his hand on his friend's shoulder, "Follow me Cole, I have just the place."

The two men took a public buggy and stopped at the Khonsu Lounge, followed closely by Trent's 'honour guard'.

"So, this is your great idea?" Cole's eyes wandered around the plush lounge.

"No, this is the place we enjoy, while the great idea is facilitated around us." Trent corrected, but any trace of a rebuke was lost in his light tone. He waved to the nearest barman and held up two fingers. "We bring them here, we relieve them of their money, we listen to their secrets and for some we tease them, lead them on and record their sins for later."

"Later?" Doc Harper took the drink and emptied the glass in one swallow. Raising his empty glass, he challenged Trent to do the same.

"Well, ours is not to reason why, but today's henchman may be tomorrow's lieutenant and maybe even next week's leader." He swallowed the drink in one gulp and pulled a face, smacking his lips and contorting his features in disgust. "Sometimes, it's not about wiping the board..."

"No..." finished Doc Harper, "...sometimes, it's all about controlling the pieces." The mantra was Level 1, Basic Strategy, direct from their school days.

"Every word spoken here is recorded, filmed and relayed to World Gov on the planet below." Trent casually warned his friend while signalling the barman a second time.

"Every word?" queried the Doc, his face quizzical.

"Yup! No exceptions." The barman came over and refilled the drinks in front of the men. Trent's communicator beeped and he read the screen directly beamed onto his retina. He waved off the service, "Not for me I'm afraid, you have fun." He stood and slapped his friend on the shoulder.

"Not bad news I hope," Doc Harper sounded sincere.

"I'll catch up with you later, looks like we've found our victim's next of kin."

7: Kinship

"A ten thousand credit suit defeated by a dollar's worth of packing materials. Are you kidding me?" Garvy was angry. "One of my men, murdered and dumped in a cupboard and you can't tell me who did it?" Garvy played the role of victim well, but Trent could see his deep red anger edged with dark blue hate, as well as the flare of self-doubt as he reconsidered his plans. Some people broadcast their auras a lot more readily than others. Garvy was easy to read.

The faux wooden desk and art nouveau stylings of Garvy's quarters were reminiscent of the luxury aspired to by his historic mentors, but seemed to cramp his oversized quarters. There were no chairs for Trent or his security captain and the silver tray beside him held only one cut glass tumbler containing a pungent liquid.

"Can you tell me what your man was doing around the Docking Bay at that time of night?" Trent maintained a cool demeanour, refusing to become embroiled in Garvy's indignation. He nodded towards Martin who flipped open his hand-pad. The holographic screen illuminated and his captain read the movements of the victim prior to his body being found.

"System puts him at the bay, after walking around the internal perimeter of the Khonsu Lounge, at 2:30am station time, he visited the Bio Dome at 3am, then took a pod to Customs Bay One, but the duty guard had no recollection of seeing him." Martin stared at Garvy trying to gauge his response to the veiled accusation, but Garvy remained indignant. "There was an activation of a wall panel by the deceased inside Docking Bay Three, which was locked down and shouldn't have been accessible to the man in question. At which point the gentleman disappeared from our sensors." Martin flipped the pad, the screen died and he replaced it in his belt.

"Okay," Garvy took a swig from the tumbler and grimaced as the sharp-tasting liquid was swallowed. It seemed to calm him. "So, the man went for a walk and got lost."

"More than lost, sir! He was in completely the opposite side of the complex from his ship and his quarters, avoiding a duty officer and defeating at least three security points to get there," remarked Martin.

"Got lost..." asserted Garvy, aggressively replacing the now empty tumbler on the tray, "...and accidentally went somewhere off limits." Garvy stood to project his anger, feigned now as the hate swamped the last vestiges of his tolerance.

Trent watched as the dark blue aura coalesced around his body, but despite his words, Garvy didn't seem to be directing his hate at anyone. It was almost internal and Trent realised, Garvy didn't know about his man's venture.

"But that doesn't mean you can kill him and stuff him in a ventilation shaft." Garvy, punched the desk communicator, "Get out! I'm calling my lawyer."

"Will you be calling the man's family?" asked Trent "Or perhaps you feel that is my job... as Commander of this facility?" He didn't need any empathic ability to see the flash of pure jealousy from Garvy. Now Trent knew everything he needed to know about the criminal's intentions.

Garvy snarled in response.

Once clear of Garvy's quarters Trent's red-suited bodyguards fell in behind him. He stopped in the quiet corridor and turned to Martin, who'd walked silently beside him making no comment on what he'd witnessed.

"Martin, re-instate Comms, Security access only, everything recorded, analysed and stored." Trent figured World Gov would know everything by now, but this way he controlled routine communications forcing people to apply to security to make a call. That would reduce unnecessary chatter and make it a little easier to track anything untoward. He thanked Martin and apologised for the level of disruption his squad would have to handle.

"Don't deny anyone, just ask them if their call is important and remind them all calls are recorded for World Gov analysis." Martin nodded his understanding and left Trent to his thoughts.

On returning to his quarters, still dogged by his red-suited baby sitters, Trent locked his door leaving them to their corridor and checked for any new spy devices.

In the past, he'd defeated them all, once he'd detected them. Having determined their sensory capabilities and frequencies of operation he'd replaced their signals with his own box of tricks and destroyed the planted devices completely. The listeners would still receive signals from his room. They'd believe

Trent was healthy and quiet, given to nights of solitude and ancient music, before long bouts of restful sleep.

Now he kept the surveillance of his private apartment running full time as part of his routine. Despite his skills, there was always someone willing to earn a little extra who could potentially slip through. He processed the last Ultra Sound check and was about to shut down the monitor when he heard a disturbance outside his room.

There was a familiar caller at the door dressed in the standard red and white casino uniform, embellished with the black stripes of a croupier. The bodyguards stood back as she explained in very simple terms what she could do to them if they got in her way.

"Come in, Belle. Please, take a seat." The door opened at his words and he gestured her to sit. He moved to the wall dispenser. "Water!" he requested. Noting she still stood, a bulky parcel under her arm; she was obviously unsure, anxious about something. "Is that for me?" he asked,

"Security asked me to bring it up," she replied, handing it to him.

He thanked her and formally invited the vibrant red-head to take a seat on his couch while he remained standing. He remembered her from their time on Earth and considered her as beautiful as she was intelligent. Forthright and assertive, the two qualities that got her into so much trouble with the World Gov.

"That must be the only drinks machine on this rock that provides the pure stuff." Belle relaxed a little. She was unabashed and the comment was friendly. Whatever turmoil was raging in her thoughts, she was not scared of Trent; she'd known him for over ten years and she considered him intelligent and fair.

"Want one?" he offered, losing the modicum of authority he'd tried to engender.

"Thanks," she stared as he passed her his own drink and ordered again.

"Sir, if it..." she began, thinking she knew exactly what was going to happen.

He stood and placed a finger to his lips. He produced a small box from his desk and began tapping upon a screen. The device flashed twice as he setup his surveillance interruption device. He chose a set of false data transmission, adding a boring pre-set work appraisal interview to the signal and closing his eyes checked his internal security system to ensure it was working.

Cyber implants had been around for years, so Belle recognised his hesitant mannerisms. They were extremely expensive, very personal things and no-one would ever ask about someone else's implants, it just wasn't done.

"We're off grid now, Belle. No sir's, no lies, just you and me." Sitting on the edge of his desk he sought to put her at ease, but Belle didn't get nervous easily, especially around the few friends she had. You had to do a lot to prove you were in that category. "Who's Angie 09? I didn't hire her."

Belle sipped her water, wondering how to answer and almost immediately knew she could only tell him the truth.

"She's my... partner. I hired her. You said..." Belle began her defence.

"I said you could bring in anyone you knew, but I do the hiring not you." He wasn't angry, but the concern showed on his face and Belle knew she'd overstepped the mark.

"She was with me. I couldn't leave her." There was an edge of defiance to Belle's manner.

"You didn't hire her, because she's not on the payroll. She has no legitimate identity card, so how does she eat." Trent was intrigued, if Belle had done this, who else...? The thought trailed off.

"We share... everything. I was coming to see you, but you haven't been the easiest person to speak to recently," she accused.

"We've just gone live and I have every criminal and crooked politician on earth visiting. It's not easy to chew the fat with old friends." Trent refreshed his glass and offered Belle a top up.

"Do I need to send her back?" he asked quietly. Belle knew he owed her very little. He was doing her a favour, offering her an opportunity to make Angie's case, asking for a reason to let her stay.

"She'd be dead in a week if you did." Belle stared at the floor. Sipping the precious water, she sighed and seemed to sink into the couch, deflated. For the first time he saw her aura and perceived her sadness as it grew within. His talent seemed to be getting stronger and he no longer reacted to an aura's unbidden appearance.

"I rescued her from the pits." Belle began her tale and Trent noted how her sad aura began to colour; fear, shame, anger, "She and four other girls were taken from a backwater community in Urzon, the back end of nowhere; tied up, bundled for sale. Their town had been burned," she pulled a sarcastic face relaying an evil snarl, "...sorry, 'purified', the day before."

"How did you get involved?" Trent could see her fear and watched her anger building in the telling of the story. He guessed the tale would be close to their own. Oppression, death, pity, rescue, flight.

"I was hiding out after we..." but she didn't rehash their past. "I was working at a run-down diner, middle of nowhere... when a group of your World Gov soldiers turned up, got drunk and decided to kill everyone. I'd hidden, in case they were looking for me. When they left, I buried the bodies and inherited the place. I'd been there a few months, everyone knew me, but no-one knew who I was."

He imagined the place was probably a dive, somewhere off the beaten track. Prohibition had been law since Trent was born, at least, for those who weren't rich or in the higher echelons of the World Gov. There were hundreds of illegal bars across the world. Even the legal temperance places often brewed their own alcohol to supplement the state supplied substitute.

"The Traders, Belle, what happened?"

"They made a mistake!" She swallowed the clear water and tears filled her eyes. "...stopped at my place and tried to sell one of them to me for easy cash."

"Angie?" he asked, already empathising with the torment she was reliving.

"No, one of the older women. She was scarred from the fires and had a twisted arm. Very little value where they were heading." She finished her water and a tear fell. "I asked to view the rest of the merchandise. I knew they had more in the transport, I could hear them crying, their sobs, their pathetic pleas, but they wouldn't bring the others out. They said they were reserved! Like some prime meat for a butcher." Her angered flared.

"What did you do, Belle?" He moved to sit on the couch and held her hand, gazing fondly into her eyes, remembering the cost to his own soul when he'd liberated her, many years before.

"I agreed to their terms for the old woman, paid them, and served them a drugged whisky to seal the deal. The old guvnor made it special for his rowdy customers. They were asleep within seconds. I freed the women; most of them stayed a day or two then left, but Angie..." Belle give a sad little laugh. "...she was so pretty, so innocent, so broken."

"What did you do with the 'Traders' Belle?" He moved close beside her and stroked her hand.

The Traders were legitimate. The World Gov licensed them to enslave survivors of a 'purification' event. It was 'God's will' that those not killed had been divinely judged to be punished further. Slavery had always been lucrative.

Trent saw the guilt; the anguish was building inside her and instantly he knew. She'd always been a hard woman, her tongue was vicious, but he'd never known her to do anything out of malice. Nothing more than humiliate the occasional blowhard.

The knives behind his eyes pricked and tore, burning into his mind, he squeezed them tight to shut out the pain. Removing his hands from hers, he gripped his forehead, trying to massage his temples, to relieve the pressure.

Belle failed to notice; her head was bowed. She stared sullenly into the empty glass; tears fell as she relived her own torment.

He experienced a flash of pure pain and for a moment panicked as his eyes saw only an intense whiteness.

"Killed them all," she whispered. "All the Traders..., then later, the three idiot drunks that tried to rape her." Her anger rose, as did her voice. "She was in my protection; catatonic on her bed and the bastards tried to rape her." She looked at Trent, she needed his forgiveness, she needed him to understand. She had never told anyone that she'd done the killing, but they'd all seen the eight grisly heads stuck on the rails of the diner porch when she'd left with Angie a few days later.

He hugged her and she collapsed into him. His gift soothed her pent-up emotions, the colours paled, washed away by his brilliant white soothing empathy, as he brought balance to her mind.

"You did what needed to be done, Belle, as always." He remembered the men he'd killed to rescue Belle, three World Gov soldiers' intent on destruction, rape and murder. The 'divine' heroes of the day, butchering innocent unarmed civilians... and once they'd had their fun...

This was back in the early days, before the World Gov had modified the suits; he sniggered at the thought, 'Pathetic navvies, trying to perform brain surgery on his father's creation.' He breathed deeply and gently tapped her shoulder releasing her from his embrace.

"Well, I've already seen her at work, and I liked the way she handled Sarko," he enjoyed the way Angie had dealt with Sarko's boorishness and the humour in his mood was infectious. "I'll assign her a payroll number, post her to your staff and move the pair of you to double quarters, but I'll need a genetic sample for admin. Bring her in tomorrow morning, before your shift."

Belle was never one for thanks, but she felt so indebted to Trent that she did something she'd never done before, she kissed a man. Trent blushed and his hand went to his cheek.

Pulling herself together, feeling lighter, almost cleansed after reliving her destructive memories, Belle stood, took a deep breath and simply said, "Thank you."

He moved to the device on his desk and ended the fake interview. She left and his eyes followed her as she went. For a brief moment he wondered what his bodyguards would make of her visit. He didn't routinely bring staff to his cabin.

The door closed and the enormity of what he'd done for her hit him. For the first time ever, his gift had moved from passive to active. He'd reacted to her, quelled her violent emotions, influenced her.

"So, this is what they were afraid of," he whispered. Slowly his anger rose, he kicked over the table, scattering the glasses, "This is why my father had to die!"

Two mobile robotic devices emerged from the wall and gathered the glasses, stopping momentarily to dry spots of liquid. They manoeuvred to the table and extended new arms, latching quickly and silently to the table and righted it. Finally, one of them retrieved the fallen package and replaced it on the table, minutely adjusting it to ensure it was exactly as it had been before his outburst. He didn't see them exit the room, but the whole episode made him smile. The automated servitude and attention to unimportant detail seemed to parody his life, restoring his humour and refocusing his priorities. He retrieved the parcel.

Closing his eyes, he initiated his cybernetic implant and saw in his mind's eye his personal menu. By thought, he selected an ancient book title from his digital library, written by of one of his more obscure, yet favourite authors.

As he highlighted the title the presented cover glowed before his vision in pink. The selection of the second word was his passcode. The system accepted, access was granted, and in his room, the back wall shimmered as he stepped through into a brightly lit workshop. He laid the parcel down on the central worktop and unfolded the dead man's suit. After half an hour of analysis and digital interrogation of its system he called for assistance.

"Jan! I need you, where are you?" he sounded desperate.

"End of a long day, I was just about to turn in." She yawned to punctuate her reasoning.

"Never mind that, my quarters. Now!" His command was short sharp and to the point, undeniably a command.

8: Weapon

"It's a weapon, and it's deadly," he concluded.

Jan sat on the couch while Trent stood by his workbench in his hidden lab. She was the only other soul who knew about his secret facility, having helped construct it and worked many days inside to create the gravity plate enhancements. It was the only place on the moon that contained such high spec nano-engineering devices and probably rivalled, if not exceeded, the best the World Gov had. The removable wall was gone and the cabin took on the air of a secret lair. He passed her the suit and relayed his findings.

"Five punctures, here on the shoulder. Plasma Needles, but applied at the same time. Only twelve nano-meters apart; blasted the circuits in the neck piping, rendering the suit temporarily useless. The shots disabled the brain link, hence, no helmet. I estimate it would have taken up to fifteen seconds for the suit to repair itself. I'm not sure if the brain link would ever have been fully repaired. The damage is beyond anything I've ever seen."

"And that's what killed him?" Jan was fascinated. The revelation that there was circuitry in the suit went against common knowledge. Everyone knew, it was obvious, the protection was the living fabric. Part of the suit's success was the secret of its operation. By telling everyone the whole suit was a one-piece thinking organism no-one looked for any isolated control mechanism and the nano-tech was impossible to find, unless you knew where to look with the right equipment.

"The suit was rendered benign, no matter what it sensed it couldn't react. I don't think we have the medical equipment here, but a micro scan autopsy would probably reveal bleeding on the brain from a stun weapon. Stunned, it would be easy for one person to hold him while another used the packing materials. Even if the suit recovered before his brain stopped, it was too late, once that stuff was in his throat, he was already dead."

"But all weapons were scanned, we've seen the list. Nothing we detected could account for this damage." Jan was inspecting the suit, looking closely at the points marked by Trent, unable to see where the plasma damage had been inflicted.

Trent closed his eyes and ran a new search using his implant. He checked for any technical parts within each shuttle baggage consignment.

"Construct possible high power plasma delivery weapons from any detected items." He expected the query to take several hours to sift through the data. As he moved to sit on the couch the holographic projection that detailed his wall resumed, but without the nano-structure in place behind it, it had a ghostly appearance.

Within moments a list of frighteningly powerful weapons was presented on the holo-vid screen above the table, but nothing explained the marks on the suit. The list grew over time with more and more diverse weapons from antiquity being added to the deadly roll call. A two-man Battlefield Walker, a four-man P-4a Tank and a range of autonomous drone delivery systems were presented. The limits of his query had not been well defined.

"Maybe we're looking at this the wrong way!" It was half thought, half self-recrimination. Jan stared hard at the suit fabric as she spoke. She picked it up and ran it through her fingers as though trying to feel the damage. "Think of the instant power required to energize five plasma needles at the same time, that's not a portable power pack. Anything that powerful would be easily detected, surely."

"World Gov has hooked up weapons to additional suit power packs before. It looks like someone else must have figured out how to do it. But their weapons were integral, created as part of the suit, a single unit." Getting the energy to the weapon efficiently had always been a problem. Trent sighed, "Okay, let's just say we know how, now we need to know who." After a moment of reflection his face fell, he admitted something he'd feared, something he hoped would never happen in his lifetime. "We also know they're ahead of us in at least some technology."

"We can't rely on our suits to save us either." Jan was thinking fast. "You're going to have to train security in old defence techniques. All they do is stand there and quote regulations until there are enough of them to cage the bad guy."

"Mobile cages are still a good idea, don't forget they drain the suits power and render the nano-tech inert; besides, I don't think there will be many of these weapons around." Trent was worried. He knew how fast World Gov could mass produce new weapons. What if they were involved?

He moved to his desk and tapped the comms pad, "Security! Get me a list of all guests tied to World Gov, openly and otherwise, and their associated weapons; and get me a line to World Gov HQ on Earth."

Jan stood as he returned to her, reaching for the suit in her hand. She stepped toward him and frowned.

"You'll have to tell Liza how to defeat the suits."

"I think the secrets out anyway," Trent sighed at the inevitability.

"You know…. one day I'll get a visit here that'll involve less work and more wine."

"Oh, I'm sorry, I never thought…" Trent stumbled over his thoughts, his awkwardness increased by her smile. He hadn't even offered her a drink of water.

She pushed the suit onto him. "Well, I'm off to bed," she declared.

He stared dumbfounded as she left. Turning at the door she gave him a wink and smiled. The door opened and she devilishly whispered, "Bye, lover!" and the two guards outside looked on lasciviously, eyeing Trent with a new found respect.

Trent called for another glass of water and removed his suit. He replaced it with a silk dressing gown, stepped through the wall projection and seated himself at his workstation. He turned to a threadbare soft toy, out of place on the stark clean digital work space, a ragged floppy puppy with oversized eyes.

"Time for an upgrade," he announced to the empty room. He opened a shallow draw which seamlessly emerged from the table. Retrieving a thin square attachment, he slotted it onto the sensor arm of the material analysis machine he'd been using when Jan arrived. Reaching across the table he picked up his only possession from his childhood. He removed the left eye of the puppy and inserted it into a slot provided by the new attachment.

"It's all in the eyes," he whispered.

Before him, his beige suit appeared holographically enhanced. No other suit in the world would have looked this complicated if subjected to the same scan, but then, no other suit in the world had been tailored by its owner, whose knowledge came directly from its inventor.

There was a murderer on the loose and at least four guests were intent on causing him trouble. World Gov were itching to replace him with one of their own and there was at least one weapon on the base that could actually kill someone wearing armour.

"Okay computer," he addressed the diagnostic machine, "I need an edge."

***

"It's late Garvy! Let it go." Carney tried to appeal to her boss. In the corner of the suite Harvey was lying in a newly generated reclining seat, courtesy of the design control panel he'd been playing with since entering the apartment. He was half submerged in the soft fabric, snoring loudly.

"My man! They dared to kill, my man!" Garvy was pacing, wringing his hands and slightly foaming at the mouth. "Right, that's it, I'm taking it all," he declared. His bitterness seemed to swamp his reason.

"We don't know who did it," Carney's calm voice interrupted Garvy's anger. "I'll guarantee it wasn't Trent. He's too soft. I'll bet it was Gen'eer," Carney used General Een-Eer's contracted criminal name, the man hated people using it, but then he was a pompous idiot. "Rick probably got too close to his ship. Was he sent to bug it?"

The strange flicker in Garvy's countenance revealed more than it should.

"You didn't even know his name!" Carney accused her boss, raising her voice in disbelief. "Did you see that, Cutter? He didn't even know Rick's name." Cutter was perched awkwardly on a thin bench, folded down from the pseudo wood panelling of Garvy's wall. The room was not designed for visitor comfort.

"Well, he's only been with us four months," Cutter defended his boss. He'd seen Garvy angry before and understood where his nickname 'The Butcher' came from.

"That's not the point," Garvy was not in the mood to be ridiculed by an underling, no matter who she was. He stepped towards her shouting, "He was one of mine." Garvy's anger was born of indignation. He viewed the murder as a personal attack on his reputation, he didn't care about the man, he didn't care he was dead; he cared someone dared to question his power.

"Go buy another one," she mocked in a voice full of contempt.

As Garvy raised his hand to respond with sudden violence, he found himself staring into the barrel of an antique pistol. The blue protection field encased his head instantly.

"Heirloom," she noted his arrested motion and crowed over her power. "It's only a 50 calibre Desert Eagle, won't kill you, but I bet it'll hurt."

Garvy dropped his raised arm and stomped back to his desk, throwing himself into his chair in silence, his helmet disappeared. Carney un-cocked the ornate weapon and caressed the polished metal as if thanking it for its protection.

"Okay, we're all tired," Carney tried to defuse her boss, "but we're listening. We're one man down," she replaced the gun in its holster low down on her thigh and revelled in her allure as Garvy's eyes followed. Lifting her leg, holster forward, she sat on the corner of his desk.

He was mesmerised by her, enthralled by her sudden violence, excited by her smooth threats and lithe figure as she leant towards him. For a brief moment he compared her to his so-called wife... no contest.

"Now, how are we going to take over?" she whispered.

9: Belief

"Sorry to wake you, Sir!" Ivor's voice followed the cancelled alarm. "There's a Mr. Skabenga causing an issue."

"Okay, hold on. Tell him I'll be there shortly," Trent sat up and stretched, he felt absolutely washed out.

"He's not actually in Security, Sir!" Ivor was being cagey; he sounded a little too formal and slightly embarrassed.

"Just tell me. What's going on?" He glanced at the time and worked out he'd had four hours in bed.

"He's in his shuttle, sir. He's demanding to dock in Bay Twelve." Ivor felt wretched. Why had he dragged the boss out of bed for a parking issue? "It's just that, I know you were particular..." he began.

"You did the right thing," Trent yawned. "Why's he moving?" He couldn't remember the last time he'd slept in. He spotted his suit draped over the couch and remembered the work he'd done.

"Okay, now... this is what he said... his words, not mine. 'There's bad Ju-Ju in Bay Four'. Apparently General Een-Eer believes, and I quote again, 'The spirits are angry and will reward the violence with misfortune.' Are you still listening, sir?" Ivor couldn't believe the superstitious nonsense he was relaying, but the procedures didn't cover supernatural motivation, he'd looked.

"I'm here," Trent acknowledged, but was thinking hard about the real reason behind the move. "Who's in Bay Twelve?"

"V6 Commercial Passenger Liner only. There's room for him, but there's an issue with the neighbours, sir." Ivor sounded concerned, but the formality had receded.

"Who's in Bay Eleven?" but he knew the answer as soon as he'd asked the question.

"Ling Rong-Yu, sir."

Trent considered this development. Gen'eer always put on a show, but he doubted his motivation was spiritual. On the other hand, Bay Twelve was the furthest bay from Bay Four and there had been a murder, maybe he was acting the role for his men. If it was a power play, well... it would be easy to seal off both bays from the rest of the complex... if it got ugly... What would Rong-Yu think?

"Ivor, despatch a squad, fully armed. Don't allow any interaction between Bay's Eleven and Twelve. I'll speak to Gen'eer and Ling Rong-Yu myself. The shuttle bays will be placed out of bounds until they depart."

Oh well, I've started today's to-do list, he thought. Smiling to himself he entered the bathroom and spent an extra minute in the sonic shower before rinsing with real water.

There was a knock at the door as he finished suiting himself up. The vid screen showed two women in hospitality uniforms. "Come in," he yelled. The system unlocked his door at the invitation and admitted Belle and Angie.

"Morning, sir." Belle formally greeted Trent with a smile.

"And this must be Angie," he stepped forward and held out his hand to greet her, but Angie simply held her hands together flat against her uniform.

"I figured," Belle hurriedly spoke to prevent any awkwardness, but Trent could see the mistrust, the fear at the edge of her reason and the internal torment the girl was still experiencing. "It might be better if we took the sample here, instead of at the medical bay."

Trent noticed the deep bond Belle felt for Angie and the protective barrier she projected around her. He'd only ever seen that effect shared between mothers and their offspring. Trent reappraised his imagined relationship between the two women. He walked calmly to his office desk and withdrew a clear medical box from the top drawer. "Here," he offered it to Belle, "you do it." The women sat on his couch.

The box opened to reveal a cylindrical device which, when Belle pointed at Angie's eye, took a record of her iris, retina pattern and with a quick, intense prickle of air, dislodged and retrieved a sample of cells from the edge of her eyelid. Angie sat relaxed on the couch and flinched at the uncomfortable pressure as the sample was taken. There was no pain; it was just a little strange.

"All done," enthused Belle. "Thank your boss, please Angie."

Trent felt uncomfortable, rooted to the spot until Angie spoke. "That's okay," he blustered.

"No, it's not. She has to learn not everyone is the same. You're the safest guy I know, and if she can't respond to you..." Belle was getting upset.

Angie's core blazed the red of fear as she looked up at him. He wasn't observing her aura, he was looking into her soul, and it was in torment. He wished Belle would calm down; couldn't she see the girl was afraid to her core. Without thinking he extended a calming energy, washing away the intensity of Angie's unreasonable emotion.

"Thank you, Commander Trent." Her voice was quiet and gentle, her smile beguiling. She took a deep breath and shuddered. Belle reacted to Angie's four trivial words with the joy of a mother watching her daughter conquer the world. She hugged her tightly.

After a few self-indulgent moments of joy, Trent huffed artificially, "Sorry, ladies I've got to be somewhere else," he made gentle waving motions with his hands, unwilling to break the bond between the two soul mates sat on his couch.

Belle stood and hugged him, "I think I know who you are..." she whispered cryptically. She grabbed Angie's hand and the ladies left, laughing together, as they passed Trent's bemused red-suited babysitters in the hall.

There was a beep in his ear, "Squad in place, sir. Shall I let him in?" asked Ivor.

"No, let him hang out there while I speak to his boss. Where's Gen'eer now?"

"Suit tracker puts him in his quarters, sir."

"Are the base lasers on show?" Trent was having evil thoughts.

"No sir, retracted, they only surface when there's a collision threat identified." Ivor was confused; the laser weapons were for protection from external long-range threats to the complex.

"Lift two or three around Bay Twelve, point them at Skabenga. He should know better than to fly without clearance." Trent's smile contained no humour.

"Yes, Sir!" Ivor was beginning to see the plan. The criminals were pushing, testing; now they were going to push back. He shouted orders across the security floor and had to raise his voice before his men understood his intent. "They're up, sir," Ivor informed Trent as he stepped into the public transit pod.

"Put some lights on, and patch a vid feed through to channel three." Trent took his seat in the busy transit pod, laughing quite audibly. Several tourists politely acknowledged him, recognising his Commander's insignia, wondering what good news he'd received.

***

The stark white hotel corridor leading to Gen'eer's cabin was lined with six well-built henchmen. Trent realised Gen'eer wasn't blinkered in using members of his own tribe in his gang. Despite his spiritual claims of purity, he was protected by Asian and Caucasian guards in addition to African. They were all attired in suits that seemed incomplete, mimicking the ancient tribal dress Gen'eer favoured.

Two of the imposing men blocked Trent's bodyguards at the entrance to the corridor. The World Gov men squared up to their adversaries and Trent sensed the hostility.

"Stay there," he commanded, more for the look of the thing than any hope that his two red suited goons could push past the line of stationed guards.

Diminutive in comparison, but feeling huge in stature, Trent walked casually down his corridor. He didn't knock, he assumed Gen'eer would be watching and he was right.

The door swung open beckoning him forward. Coloured silks and cottons were strewn around the cabin, hanging from the ceiling and stretched across the walls. All were plain, but with a textured surface that played with the light from around thirty flickering candles, strategically placed to gently illuminate the room.

"Come in, my friend. You play host to me and now I return the favour."

Moving aside a long yellow hanging cloth, Trent revealed Gen'eer, lounging on a low couch covered in silk cushions. Sat either side of his head on short stools were the two identical women he kept beside him.

"Okay, Gen'eer, what's the game?" Trent was smiling as he seated himself at the foot of the couch on the only vacant stool. The self-styled warlord radiated an aura of white calm. There was no passion for revenge or indeed any fear or hatred displayed by the man.

"You use my friendship name, though I do not believe we have ever socialised. Maybe that is something we can remedy." He clapped his hands and called for tea, "Still, I am in your home, I will allow it." He performed a micro-bow, inclining his head a fraction to show his acceptance.

"What are you playing at Gen'eer, you know I could deprive you of your shuttle and your right-hand man in the blink of an eye. What's he doing out there?" Trent pretended to yawn, he knew that to play Gen'eer's games of fealty and pander to his self-aggrandising fantasy would complicate things, so he ignored the trappings and the man's act.

"I had a vision, Mr Trent," began Gen'eer. "My ancestors came to me and warned me of fire and death". He sat up, leaned forward and opened his arms to accentuate his tale.

Ever since the World Gov had claimed power by 'The Divine Hand of God', every two-bit hustler had credited their worthiness to their self-defined spiritual credentials. Gen'eer more so than most.

It was a cheap and easy way to pass the blame for inhumane acts. 'Your people have been punished by the gods for being unworthy' sounded better than 'I rounded up your village to sell into slavery because I needed the money' or, 'I burned you out because your land is better than mine, but you must still follow me'.

Trent hated those that used superstition and fear as a basis for power. It was as if they sacrificed their compassion to the lie.

"Too much cheese before bedtime," Trent's remark was designed to raise some anger, possibly to irk Gen'eer and get him to drop his holier-than-thou act, but it didn't work.

"You insult my religion?" observed Gen'eer calmly, "yet, I am supposed to believe yours." It was like watching a scientist study a worm, the statement was just there, a fact, just words to convey a thought. "Mine warns me, helps me to save lives. Yours, however, is used to take them."

The comment fell flat. Trent was about as far from indoctrinated into the World Gov cult than it was possible to be and remain alive, he simply dismissed Gen'eer's bluster.

"You think moving next door to Rong-Yu will help save lives?" For just a fraction of a second Trent detected the flash of fear. No! Not fear, more like concern, the guilt of being discovered red-handed. So, there is an ulterior motive. "Have you seen channel three?" Trent casually enquired.

"No, I do not..." his pious tone was starting to annoy Trent.

"Holo, Channel three!" commanded Trent. A cube of light appeared between them. It held a three-dimensional image of Gen'eer's shuttle hovering outside Docking Bay Twelve. The viewing angle gently moved to show the placement of four huge laser weapons pointing at the vehicle. "He didn't file a flight plan. Unauthorised, simply shouldn't be there." Trent studied the man closely, still no emotion. "I can make it not be there." His voice was calm, assured; Gen'eer knew he had no reason to bluff.

"I am a senior stakeholder...," there it was, the anger, the blue hatred seeping into the beige of self-doubt.

"And there are a dozen or so more!" interrupted Trent, "Shall we put your request to the vote?" A flash of fear stained the warlord's aura. "It might be interesting to see who supports you." The two female guardians stood as one, as if some unbidden command had been received. Trent was shocked, not by the synchronised motion, but by the realisation neither woman had an aura. Synthetics! Outlawed everywhere by humanity.

"Sit, sit!" Gen'eer's voice had an edge of panic. The women regained their seats.

Trent hoped his shock hadn't been seen by Gen'eer.

"I humbly request," Gen'eer began. His whole demeanour had changed, there was a real underlying fear motivating this request, "that my ship be allowed to dock, away from the cursed Bay Four."

Trent looked at the man, his head low, his shoulders turned in and the red of fear staining his aura. Maybe he really is scared of Bay Four, he thought. He's like Rong-Yu, he rarely gets his own hands dirty, so maybe he's freaked out by the murder. It's a rare enough event to be out of the ordinary.

He touched his ear, "Ivor, allow Skabenga to dock in Bay Twelve, then retract the guns. Maintain precautions." He looked down and detected relief in Gen'eer's aura as it returned to beige, fading to a white calm.

"Thank you, Mr Trent. You have the wisdom of Solomon." Gen'eer's insincere praise fell from Trent's ears without consideration.

Trent stood and turned to leave. He blew out three candles on a floor standing candelabra beside him, "You know candles are illegal here, don't you? There are holographic substitutes available," he informed the now fawning man.

"I need them for my religion," he complained, appealing for clemency.

"Very well." He witnessed the criminal overlord's smug grin return, "but each one uses the same amount of oxygen as one of your retinue, therefore, I shall have to charge you the price of thirty extra guests. After all, it's a rare commodity."

"Oh, come now," challenged Gen'eer.

"Or I could simply provide your cabins with only enough air for your human guests and you can share it any way you please. I'm sure your ladies won't mind." He blew out another candle and walked smartly toward the door. If he'd looked back, he'd have seen a blue aura of hate with an intensity to rival Garvy.

***

"Her divine countenance is indisposed, you may leave." The tall thin man, who was Rong-Yu's First clerk, sniffed the air and turned his back on Trent. They stood beside the apartment's armoured blast doors. Watching him slowly shuffle away down the accommodation passageway toward a generous ante chamber. Unlike Gen'eer, Ling Rong-Yu had the hotel corridor bedecked in tall red banners bearing archaic golden symbols from her own fabled part of the world.

"Stand still, you worm!" shouted Trent. The First clerk, conditioned to respond to authority, halted. "Your boss may think she is spawned from the divine ancestors, but in this place, I am God!" Trent had had enough of this man's feigned ignorance. He knew the clerk was only protecting his boss, that was his job, but Trent was not going to be treated like an inferior in his own home.

The man turned, but slowly, under protest. There was pure defiance in his manner.

Touching his ear, activating his subcutaneous comms and selecting the Power Complex from the listed contacts beamed onto his retina, he heard Jan acknowledge his call.

"On my count of three, cut all power to Rong-Yu apartments, radiation shields, heat and light. Leave them enough oxygen to last about thirty minutes; long enough for them to realise who rules this heavenly rock." Trent was still in there, so Jan wasn't about to comply, but the First clerk didn't know that.

"Very well, I will seek an audience with her divine majesty." The elderly clerk executed a military about turn and strode off.

"I see no reason to wait," shouted Trent. "You've got one minute." There was a muffled snigger from one of his red-suited body guards and Trent spun to face him with a look of thunder.

Around the spacious room, which Trent recognised as a dojo, an open training area, blue hatred discoloured the watching warriors stationed around the walls. Each stood to attention, unmoving, wearing their discipline with pride. Trent walked over the rough woven carpet to one of them. The young man was shaking, trembling with anger at the insults he'd just witnessed from this 'baizou'.

"Nice ribbon," he teased. All of the warriors were clothed in loose white cotton gowns, tied around the waist with a silk sash. A variety of sash colours were on display. The man slowly reached for the hilt of his ornamental sword threaded through the coloured silk.

A sharp shout came from behind as a senior figure entered the room and the warrior snapped back to attention.

"Mr Trent, kindly follow me." The man bowed quite low and without any further indication as to his intent, the white gowned newcomer sporting a black sash walked from the dojo.

Residential cabins in this sector were quite voluminous; Ling Rong-Yu travelled with an extremely substantial retinue. His guide took station by the door of a wood floored room, but did not enter. Ornate decorated panels lined the walls within. The hall was half the size of the dojo and Trent recognised it as an audience chamber.

In the centre of the room, stood by a short, padded stool, was the First clerk. He beckoned Trent forward to kneel. As Trent's bodyguards moved to flank him, the elder statesman signalled that they should halt at the doorway. Trent noted his protest and nodded his agreement, silently signalling his guards to remain at the door.

Trent understood the custom. Words spoken here were important, they held honour and metal that should not be sullied with menial commands to underlings. He took his place, though uncomfortable kneeling, he sat cross legged upon the stool. As he settled the First clerk clapped twice.

Carried into the room from the opposite doorway, Rong-Yu sat atop a highly decorated litter supported by four tall, well-developed men, their suits cut back radically to accentuate their physique. The transport flanked by two veiled women wearing ancient Geisha attire and gauze face masks, emphasizing their captivating dark eyes. The sound of a distant tiny bell being gently struck, warned those within earshot of the important person in their vicinity; though no-one could be seen holding the instrument. The litter sported a heavily embroidered silk canopy and a thin crystal encrusted veil hung down at the front and both sides, obscuring the occupant.

Switching to ultra-view, Trent's cybernetic implants negated the flimsy obstruction, revealing a nervous passenger and the details of a litter heavily laden with circuitry. He recognised several sensors and an advanced protection field, while the rear of the seat contained a bulky power pack. Experience told him it was too big for just a shield. He surmised the chair had to have some offensive capability.

The bearers placed the litter gently upon the floor in front of Trent. The rear guards, for that is what they had become, stood back, arms folded, looking directly ahead.

He waited for Rong-Yu to speak first, there were some niceties he was willing to offer; after all, she hadn't tried to insult him yet. The two masked women moved to the front flimsy veil and pulled it aside revealing an elder stateswoman with a white painted face. Her forward guards stepped aside as the two women moved forward to kneel either side of the Base Commander, upon the supplicant's stool.

Trent's scans identified the short knives each had attached to their wrists, and the snub-nosed blasters at their hips, concluding no threat to his suit or his person.

Ling Rong-Yu was revered by her cadre; she was impressive, her mind devious and sharp. Though credited with several daring raids and actions against the World Gov, her most significant feat was surviving for eight years as their leader.

Trent recounted her history, not the simple dogma force-fed by his trainers in the education camps. Ling Rong-Yu led the "Divine Quiangdu", an acculturation of the two organised criminal gangs that survived the last big war on the Asiatic continent. After the declining empires of the American's and the Russian's turned on their economic superiors, attempting a first strike nuclear annihilation, Asia was all but destroyed.

They failed, losing almost all of their own major cities to complete destruction and gaining five hundred years of lethal radiation in the automated retaliatory strikes. The whole world was plunged into its final days. Among the few Asian survivors, the old enmities were forgotten in the wholesale slaughter and a powerful organisation arose to replace the previous governments.

No-one believed the Tongs and the Yakuza would ever co-exist, but the threat of extinction makes for strange bed fellows. Their gangs were already established all over the world. Despite the destruction of their homeland, they were able to recover their cohesion quickly, if not their full power.

The world had been fighting a cold war ever since. Political parties were perceived to be the enemy of the people. Only the World Gov had been strong enough to break the stalemate, playing on the distrust and hatred of organised governments, garnering support with their claim to purify and heal the planet.

"To what do I owe the pleasure of your company, *mister* Trent," she graciously used his name, but made his honorific sound like an insult. She leered, like a hungry cat discovering an unguarded nest of baby rats.

"I simply bring a message, Madam." Trent could see her discomfort, but he surmised, that, as far as she was concerned, he was part of the World Gov, the only real threat to her power on earth. "There has been a re-organisation of shuttle bay assignments. I am here to advise you that Bay Twelve is now occupied by General Een-Eer's shuttle. You may retrieve what you desire from Bay Eleven within the next two hours." He noted her body relax; was she hiding something?

She remained outwardly calm, but Trent knew from reports that she indulged in long periods of meditation and he suspected she probably had gifts of her own to survive this long. "After that, your shuttle bay, and Bay Twelve will be sealed until your departure." Trent awaited the complaint, the outrage, the guarded emotional outburst, but she remained unmoved.

"Thank you, Mr Trent." She forced another smile; flicked a finger sign toward her hand maidens who returned to the chair replacing the veil once more. Without another word, the chair was raised by the bearers and the divine Ling Rong-Yu retired from the impromptu audience. The sound of the distant bell faded as the litter departed.

Trent was bemused. He thought hard about what he'd seen and heard.

"This way, Mr Trent," the smiling First clerk interrupted his reverie, escorting him out through the dojo and into the corridor beyond.

There was the sound of a sharp slap and a stifled grunt behind. One of his red suited bodyguards swung to protect his charge; the sudden movement causing Trent to turn. On the far side of the dojo, the warrior who had trembled at Trent's approach was on his knees, a long knife protruding from his shoulder. Blood stained his outer garments. Standing over him was a tall bald man in a dull black gown tied with a black sash. Unlike everyone else in the dojo he was wearing thick tasselled black gloves decorated with chrome studs. He glowered at Trent.

"No suits?" the bodyguard observed incredulously. But Trent had seen the victim up close, he was sure the warrior had been wearing a beige suit beneath his white gown. There was a signal in his ear, it was Jan, but before he could acknowledge her, he was interrupted by the clerk at his elbow.

"Lessons must be learned, Mr Trent. Is that not so?" The First clerk flashed his crocodile smile and ushered them to the end of the corridor. "Good day, Mr Trent," and they were waved through the outer hotel safety doors, away from the Rong-Yu apartments. He turned to watch the old man re-enter the dojo and watched the heavy blast doors close slowly behind him.

10: Apprehension

Trent waited until the blast doors were fully closed before answering Jan's signal.

"It may be nothing," she began. "I know you invited them to take a look around, but I've got unauthorised signatures at the old Reactor building."

"No-one should be out there. Contact security and get two Bugs out." Lengthening his stride, he headed back to his office. He could monitor everything from his desk. "How did they get out there?" He was concerned. There was no direct transit link to the reactor, they must have obtained surface vehicles, any unauthorised bay launch would have set off alarms; they'd caught Skabenga.

"All shuttles accounted for, hold on," the pause seemed to go on forever. "I've got two missing Rover's from the hire facility; signed out two hours ago and ninety-five minutes ago. First one was 'Rover 4', Senator Wilson and four guests. Second... 'Rover 2', General Een-Eer party of eight, though it seems he wasn't on board." She finished the report with a tone of expectation.

"No, half an hour ago he was with me. That could explain why he looked upset when I called. It could also explain Skabenga's little diversion." There was nothing wrong with guests using the Rover's, but there were no signs and no maps that could have led them to the Reactor. It wasn't easy to spot. Like most of the complex very little of it was visible on the surface. Someone planned a visit. "And he's not a General, he's just Gen'eer, he's a psychotic, genocidal scumbag with delusions of grandeur. I don't want to hear that title again."

Trent's bodyguards couldn't hear the whole conversation, but they understood something was going down and Trent was obviously in a hurry. As they entered the Khonsu lounge, despite it being early morning, the room was quite busy.

"Out of the way," one yelled at the mass of guests ambling around. He passed Trent and opened up a clear space, it wasn't difficult to work out where they were heading. It was no secret that Trent's cabin could also double as his command office. The bodyguard reached the lift and pushed the call button, but Trent ran through the emergency door to the side and leapt up the stairs two at a time.

"They're inside," Jan's voice raised a little in tone. Six males, looks like the General's men."

Trent cursed and started to run, "Get two more bugs up, and warn Liza; I've just seen someone stab through a suit." Bursting through his office door he shouted "Control Desk" and the room changed. The door bolted behind him barring the red-suited guardians from following him in. Three monitors appeared in thin air, hovering above his desk. Gone was the desk's smooth walnut veneer, seeming to melt away and soak into the surface revealing a crisp white desktop which lit up like mission control. "Focus, Nuclear Power Reactor; Internal: Find intruders. Vid-cam-1 external." He orientated the surveillance at the scene.

Two security Bugs had arrived, each carrying two security personnel. The sleek, fast short-range security vessels could hit tremendous speeds as they flew low across the surface. Housing the manoeuvring jets and the thrusters in the rear body gave the planes the appearance of spots across their back and the two narrow laser guns mounted at the front looked like the mandibles of an insect. Their advantage was the inclusion of gravitic plates on the lower fuselage that gave a tremendous push against anything with sufficient mass. Angling the plates produced gravitic acceleration in any direction, far beyond anything created on earth. Painting them bright red and giving them a black cockpit seemed the only way to go when Trent designed them.

"Two in custody," came an eager voice over the security channel. "Still in the Rover."

"Got them all, sir! Guest suits, all registered to General Een-Eer's party. They all claim they're just sightseeing." Trent was confused, but relieved there'd been no bloodshed.

"How did they get in?" Trent was sure they were guilty of more than sightseeing.

"Pass card, sir. Code seems legit, but there's no name on it, no image." The security guard was surprised at the obvious forgery.

"I want to know..." began Trent. "Hold on sir, two more just turned up; that makes ten, including the Rover crew" Trent was worried, two against two in the Rover was not an issue, he had faith in his men, but four against eight in the Reactor Plant was just not safe.

"Okay, restrain them, put them back in their Rover and deliver them to cells. I want to know what's really happening." He looked at the images floating above the desk. Addressing his listening room, angered by Gen'eer's games, he yelled. "Replay boarding, 'Rover 2', today." The centre screen flickered and became an overhead shot of the guests walking onto the boarding steps of the public surface transport vehicle. The video clearly showed the men enter the disc shaped body. Two moved to the left and descended into the cockpit, the others silently took their seats in the viewing cabin. Trent's view was unobstructed, after all it was a sightseeing vessel, the full circumference of the Rover's upper fuselage was transparent. If they'd spoken, he'd have been able to read their lips.

He counted eight, "Replay from 30 minutes before boarding, faster..." but no other bodies entered the Rover. He checked up to two hours before without any luck. On a whim he decided to check out another theory, "Locate 'Rover 4'." A mobile camera drone took a few seconds to locate and approach the vehicle, sending a live feed to Trent's main holo-screen, an external shot of Rover 4, parked on an angle upon the rim of a boulder strewn crater.

"No issues with power, all levels nominal. They didn't touch anything that I can see," reported Jan in his ear.

Designed as a tourist observation vehicle the Rovers were constructed with reinforced clear panels layered with nano-polarisation to protect the occupants from the unfiltered sunlight. The guests in Rover 4 could be seen raising champagne flutes and toasting each other as the sun rose over the far crater rim, the shadow of the Moon falling away, revealing the planet. "Earth rise on the Moon," he whispered and sighed at the pointless extravagance.

"Pardon," Jan asked for clarification.

"Sorry, just... never mind. I need the whole Power Plant swept for anything. I don't buy this sight-seeing nonsense. They were doing something; I need to know what."

"Already putting a team together, I'm taking twelve bodies, engineers and security in pairs, but it'll take a while."

"Double it, call in off-watch personnel if you need to and use anyone with a pair of eyes. I don't like this." Trent was starting to feel like he was herding cats, but short of locking his guests in their quarters, how was he supposed to keep tabs on all of their exploits.

"Duty Chief," he called security.

"Liza, Sir," the answer was brisk and attentive.

"I want the logs for the Rovers..."

"Both log's locked and downloaded as soon as the incident began, sir." Liza knew what her boss needed; her twenty years of earth-side law enforcement experience came to the fore. "No activation of airlock recorded for either Rover, until docked at the Reactor. Cabin air pressure remained constant throughout the journey. On-board camera records a passive journey. No-one spoke, no one moved around; it's like they were cargo. Nav control shows, direct point-to-point, straight line to the Reactor. They knew where they needed to be and didn't care how they got there. Crawled over two deep craters rather than going around, must have been uncomfortable."

"Just humour me, Liza. Isolate one of them and check he's human."

"Sir?" He could understand her query.

"Don't be alarmed, but let's just check they bleed. I don't want any Synthetics in here with us. Old style blood collection and analysis, don't trust any scanners. I want them caged and their suits removed."

"Synthetics? Aye, Sir." She cut the comms with the urgency that the request implied. The last word in artificial intelligence and robotics. The walking, slaughtering, death machines were responsible for so many atrocities against humanity. She corrected herself, you couldn't use the term 'Robot', that implied some sort of servitude. Once activated, these things were intelligent, self-motivated and almost indestructible.

When the final curses of defeated governments were heard it became common practice to unleash the Synths to exact revenge. More effective than explosive strikes these automatons could take their positions among the populace undetected. Interfacing with government databases they would systematically destroy a country, eradicating a people, their culture and finally emerging from the shadows they'd turn cities to dust. It took serious weaponry to defeat them.

No country wanted to outlaw them, after all, they each had their own; a proven doomsday weapon.

Then, fears grew when squads of Synthetics from various factions were discovered living together. They'd rebuilt facilities in uninhabitable regions, poisoned by the war. They'd developed their own power sources and were creating their own modifications. No one knew their agenda, but fear was a common instigator of violence and the so-called 'Nomad Synths' were attacked and destroyed at great human expense.

On Earth their very existence was now punishable by death for anyone associated with them. It was a long hard fight, but ten years ago the World Gov declared them extinct. Since then, only a few patched up lobotomised imitations had been discovered, held by faction leaders. The machines held as trophies rather than offensive weapons.

"No Luck, Trent." Jan's report was disappointing. "All equipment checks out. No interference, no resistance changes, all diagnostics one hundred percent. Scanners show nothing that shouldn't be here." There was a pause. Jan stretched out and slouched in the driver's seat of 'Tech Rover 1', sipping her water.

For hours Trent had looked over the Reactor schematics. The old, leather bound technical manuals had been stored in the archives and he had several of them open across his desk. Pages unfolded three times to show intricate cable runs and pipe intersections. Above him two holo-screens floated showing minute details of the updated sensing circuits. He was trying to find something that could warrant the intrusion into the old technology.

Everything they had was available just about anywhere on earth, if you knew where to look and these people knew exactly where to obtain anything. There were even old school books available that showed you how to build your own. Gen'eer had two modest automated reactors powering his own private island back home. Why would he pull this stunt?

"Do you want us to go over it all again," asked Jan. She was tired, it had been a long day and she didn't want to waste all of it in this old mobile tin can, but Jan had a personal stake in all of the equipment on the base; cut her in half and she'd have 'engineer' carved through her bones. This was simply another one of her wayward children that required constant care.

"Leave two teams and rotate for the next forty-eight hours. I need a presence out there. I want no-one else thinking we can't protect our site. Keep them looking, focus on circuit and wiring interventions. Whatever they did was secret, subtle, hidden..." he turned the page and saw the schematic of the nuclear pile cooling system, "and probably extremely dangerous." He was convinced it had to be sabotage. It was the only thing that made sense.

"Okay, I'll be checking in with the Fusion power gang to see if we can up their contribution, just in case." She yawned, "See you later," and signed off without waiting for a response.

"Garvy!" Trent exclaimed. He'd wanted to get his hands on the Cold Fusion system. Thoughts whirled around Trent's mind; destroy the reactor, force the use of Cold Fusion. If it was hooked up to the base, he'd demand the knowledge owed.

It didn't bear scrutiny. Gen'eer hated Garvy and the enmity was returned in spades; there was no way the two would work together. Maybe Gen'eer had the same motive, but a little more discretion. He mentally rebuked himself and pushed back, stretching in his chair to relieve this aching back. "More discretion than Garvy? You'd have trouble finding anyone with less."

"Liza, any news?" Trent contacted his Security Chief.

"Not yet, sir. They don't like the idea of powering their suits down. We've got two in cages, but they're fighting like demons. I'll have access to their fluids in about an hour." Liza was the ultimate professional, but for the first time, Trent heard stress in her voice and what sounded like, strain on her breathing.

"Are you in there with them?" Trent was concerned. Liza stood only five foot four, and had little bulk, those thugs were all at least six foot four and sported enhanced musculature, their purpose was to intimidate and maim.

"Shorthanded, sir," came the uncomplaining response. In the cell Liza stepped forward and ducked to her right avoiding a wild punch from the excessively strong, aggressive prisoner. Her men dazed from the initial berserk explosion of violence, she rolled behind her opponent and performed a perfect leg sweep. The huge uncooperative detainee collapsed landing hard on his back. The other guards, who'd been violently forced against the walls of the cell, saw their chance and leapt upon him, while a fourth laid the cage on its side, beside him. The uncooperative intruder, his arms now pinned behind him, was rolled unceremoniously into the device. Liza activated her internal security implant, securing the open side of the cage with a force field. She stepped back from the mini-prison and selected the power drain mode.

"Stand him up, put him with the others." Three guards struggled to lift the dead weight of the caged man, while a fourth slid a thin gravitic plate into position. Once on the plate the cage was manoeuvred through the cell block by one guard, all weight negated.

"Sounds like you're busy." Trent's voice reminded her she was still on live communications. "Get someone to push out patrols, at least two bugs. I want the area monitored. Shut down the Rover's for forty-eight hours, no-one on the surface. Can you manage a continual presence?"

"No problem, sir, in hand." Liza clicked off her comms as she considered the henchman in the cage being taken away; it was as though his aggression had been turned off. Maybe Trent was right, maybe they're not human.

"Ready for the next one, Captain?" asked one of her guards behind her. She recognised Largo's voice, one of the latest recruits. A keen lad, but a little on the willowy side for the more physical aspects of the job. His voice was a little muffled and the fight was evident in his voice, she assumed he still had his helmet powered up.

"Five minutes," she offered a pause in their schedule which they eagerly accepted. "Largo, bring in two bugs for recharging. Widen the patrol of the other two to include sectors one and two, pattern delta, four minutes apart; make then visible across the complex." She didn't like to tell the boss she knew her job, but the schedule of constant patrols for two days was a little longer than she'd already set up, but two bugs instead of four would give a bit more opportunity to keep the others fully serviceable and charged, prepared for anything. "Contact everyone, no Rovers on the surface unless explicitly authorised by us... or we shoot." She walked out of the cells into her office and called up a fruit juice to slake her thirst. Sitting at her desk she stared at the holographic crime wall she'd begun, each criminal overlord had their face hanging in front of the overlapping mug-shots of their retinue, in the middle were images from the murder scene and beside them, the Reactor. As she evaluated the details, animated lines grew and changed colour, linking across the points of interest. At each intersection a value of probability percentage was displayed, sadly most were below thirty at this early stage.

A spider's web of intrigue and dishonesty slowly growing as data was accumulated.

She'd cage one more, and then hand over to Martin. He could manage the rest.

"Permission to leave the Reactor," Jan called Security, "I'll be heading back to the Power Complex shortly. Waypoint input: Confirmed." It was past nine in the evening and Jan was over-tired. Unhappy with the results of the search, she'd decided to get back in there and try again and she'd found herself back in her old office. A new batch of inspectors had arrived and she was taking the opportunity to call it a day.

"Evening, Jan," Ivor always sounded happy over the comms. "Permission expected and granted." Although officially the night watch Captain, Ivor believed he was on the moon to work. He often turned up early and then much to Martin's annoyance would hang around for hours after his shift ended.

Jan was sat in the Reactor's monitoring station as she remotely programmed the Rover Nav. console. She was watching the two designated teams of the next shift perform their part of her intricately planned search. Comfortable at her old station, she observed as panels were removed, lights brought to bear within the hatches and after several minutes, a head would shake and the panel would be replaced and locked.

Time to go, she told herself. She was tired and a little unsteady as she rose to her feet. A little off balance she grabbed the desk, and accidentally activated the top drawer. It extended to show a few reports pinned to an old mechanical clipboard. She retrieved it out of curiosity, wondering how long it had been since someone wrote anything down about this place. It was an old test log. Noting the date she remembered fondly the frantic workload back in the day; two years ago, just before the mainframe came online and there at the bottom was her own signature. On a whim she decided to tuck the board under her arm and take it with her. As she pressed the drawer gently to close it, a shiny coin caught her eye. Automatically, her hand darted to retrieve it, the drawer halted and reopened. Her first thought was that it must be a gambling chip, but upon retrieving it she noted its smooth metal construction and studied it closely. Nobody had used metal coinage for at least forty years, an antique curio.

"Ready to depart!" a voice called in Jan's ear. Her team were waiting for her in the Rover. She slipped the coin into a pocket on her tool belt and tapped the drawer to close again. She'd show it to a couple of the newbies later. Some of them had never seen actual money.

***

Tom Massado was a self-aggrandising, slimy worm of a man. Given the option, Trent wouldn't spend enough time with him to slap him in the face, but he had his uses. As an arms dealer Massado was known too, and spent time with, all of the gang leaders. They all dealt with him and as far as these things went, trusted him. Luckily, so did Trent.

"So, you see Tom, I need a couple of extra big plasma cannons just to... you know, control the neighbour's cat." Massado gave a short, excited laugh in his strange high tone, as he felt a wave of bonuses heading his way. It never bothered Massado that Trent was essentially in the pocket of the World Gov, after all, as Trent kept saying, they were no longer part of that world below. "How soon, do you think?"

"Well," Massado was in business mode, he'd arrived in his white suit sporting a simple thick black belt; gone were the ridiculous monocle and sash with its multitude of fake honours. Trent could see the greed pulsing from within, his aura colouring all of his thoughts. "I reckon for an extra ten percent I can get them to you in a fortnight, weather permitting," he grinned to highlight his own witticism.

"No good, I need them in a week or forget it." Trent saw the look of consternation cross Massado's face as his fingers massaged the tablet and the profit margin, in front of him. "Fifteen percent extra," offered Trent, "and you can throw in a couple of those knives Rong-Yu has."

"Why? You want to hang them on your wall?" Massado's offhand remark showed no change in his manner, it was as if Trent had asked for a dozen spoons. So, Massado didn't supply the knife he'd seen pierce the suit. It was a long shot, but at least he knew now they weren't freely available... yet.

Massado was many things, but he wasn't ignorant of his own market. Tom Massado was successful because he got on board in the basement; it was too late in his line of work if you waited for the ground floor.

He still hadn't agreed to Trent's terms; it was the perfect opportunity to bait the trap. "Tonight, I was thinking about bringing the big players into a special game, would you be interested Tom?" Massaging the man's ego was the easiest way to manipulate him. "I thought, for those that could afford it," the challenge to the dealer's pride was implicit, "a night of poker, might be relaxing. No limit, off the books, in my executive suite."

"Who's coming?" Massado was hooked.

"No one yet, I figured I'd ask you first. What do you think? Around nine?" Massado sat up, his spine stretched as though the gravitic plate beneath his feet had been turned off. He wallowed in the compliment, and returned the sentiment in kind, as Trent predicted.

"Leave it to me, Trent. I know exactly who to invite," he crowed.

11: Games

"Drinking alone?" the friendly voice observed. "Sign of a troubled mind!" It freely offered its analysis.

"Hi Doc, take a seat," Trent recognised his old friend's voice and invited him to sit without turning around. "Sign of no friends," he sighed into his empty glass.

"I heard..." began the Doctor, but Trent sighed theatrically cutting him dead.

"It's a small moon, everyone knows everything. No secrets here. Terrorists in the Reactor, twenty dead men in the air vents, or is it the one about the orgies in my cabin?" Trent was not in the mood. People were complicating his plan by having their own and he wasn't used to being the one who had to sit back and wait to respond.

"I heard," repeated his friend, "there's a high stakes poker game about to start." Trent stared at his old partner and looked into a bemused face. Dressed in a neutral brown suit with no badges of affiliation or rank, Cole looked like any other down on his luck punter. He started to laugh.

"You don't want to be in there," suggested Trent. "Psychopaths, murderers and underhanded lying..." His voice was displaying too much anger and he stopped.

"You mean, another day at the office?" Cole tittered again.

"I don't get it, Cole. Of all the people I've ever met, you have to be the last one I'd have pegged as becoming a respectable quack. What happened?"

"Faced my own mortality... one too many times. Makes a guy think."

"Is there a Missus Cole Harper?" asked Trent.

"I haven't changed that much."

An aroma of fresh sweet flowers washed over the two men and an inquisitive voice interrupted their camaraderie. "Well, who do we have here? Two strapping, virile young men," teased a sultry voice.

"Hi Aneksi," Trent turned to drink in the beauty of his star performer. "This is Doc Harper, an old friend." He introduced the man beside him who seemed to be lost in the sight of the beauty that had spoken to him. "Turn it down, he's a Psychotherapist. He's seen pheromone manipulation before."

"Cole, Lady Aneksi, just Cole." Knowing the pheromone trick was at work could allow a strong-willed man to overcome their effects, if he really wanted to. "Never have I been so pleased to be so enchanted." He took her hand and kissed the soft blonde fur presented. Up close without her stage make-up, Aneksi's alterations were subtle, her pert nose was slightly wider at the top than the bottom, the eyes held a larger iris with stronger colouration, currently a vivid orange, and her cheeks were a little higher and sharper. She draped a loose brown jacket over a grey non-descript suit that played down any further enhancements and when she was relaxed, her pupils were almost indistinguishable from human.

"I heard you had special guests staying overnight." Though she brushed her cheek against Trent's face as she spoke and slid her hand up his back and on to caress his ear, Aneksi's whispered offer alluded to the prisoners from the Reactor incident. "I could talk to them, if you'd like."

"My lady," began Cole, gently reaching for her hand, "those neanderthal ruffians require a little more persuasion than your beauty and your delightful pheromone trick." Cole patted the back of her offered hand and gave a quick condescending grin to gift wrap the patronising comment.

Trent was surprised that Cole had recognised her intention. His partner of old would have purposefully jumped to the wrong conclusion. His friend's mindset was always tuned to lurid matters of the flesh. The way Aneksi was speaking and had been affectionately stroking Trent's hair was a neon sign to sexual intent and with the current gossip of Trent's numerous trysts circulating wildly, he'd already prepared arguments to defend accusations of his supposed 'womanising' from Cole. Aneksi's possessive jealousy over his other female visitors was the obvious conversation piece for his friend. Still…, Prague was a long time ago.

"That's fine Aneksi," Trent knew her special skills went far beyond smiles and smells, "Liza's handling it. There's no rush." He winked at her and nodded slightly to indicate the Doctor. "Perhaps you could…?"

Without looking away from her eyes, Cole interrupted. "Thanks, old friend, but tonight, I think I'd just like to play cards."

"No limit, Cole. Can you afford it?" Trent was concerned for his friend.

"Don't worry, World Gov has deep pockets and I'm on expenses."

At the invocation of the organisation, Aneksi withdrew her surrendered hand and stepped back involuntarily from Cole. Behind her back long claws emerged from her fingers.

"History," explained Trent. He could see Aneksi's aura flaring into the blue.

"Understandable," accepted Cole, nodding sagely.

"Aneksi, darling," he reassured her, "I need a croupier in the executive suite in about half an hour. Can you ask Jack to come over, please?"

"Of course," her composure quickly regained, her sultry voice assumed its earlier power and Trent was filled with admiration by the way the hatred was expertly willed away by the professional actress.

"Maybe you could bring in some fresh cards and some of the old bottled stuff, to settle our guests a little later." His face betrayed his true intent and he smirked knowing her appearance would do exactly the opposite.

"Okay, my darling," she purred at Trent. "Excuse me, while I go and make myself, presentable." She bent close to the Doctor, "Lovely to meet you," she huskily lied as she kissed him lightly on the cheek then took her leave.

The Executive suite was decorated in an old-fashioned style with dark wood panelling across the walls and a plush red carpet underfoot. The only light was a three bulb, elongated fitting bearing a gold tasselled, green glass shade above the centre of the circular green baize table. The whole ambience achieved by synthetic materials and holographic lighting effects.

As expected, the table was populated with all of the gang leaders. Tom Massado had performed as predicted. Gen'eer had left his Synthetic women behind, but was accompanied by Skabenga. Beside them moving clockwise around the gaming table, Ling Rong-Yu took her seat, though she did not acknowledge anyone's presence.

Jack stood by the table next and had Garvy on his left. He was accompanied by a svelte lady with short black hair, dressed all in black and sporting a silver dagger brooch; Trent recognised her as Garvy's pet assassin. She was introduced to the table as 'Miss Carney'.

"Not accompanied by your lovely wife tonight?" leered Sarko, who turned and shared an in-joke with his young green haired partner.

"A slight headache," responded Carney, to cut off her boss's less than convivial reply. "I like to take a hand, now and again," another false snigger followed, shared by her boss.

Sarko reappraised the witty girl and whispered something lewd to his partner who barely raised a sneer, but his green eyes beneath the green hair fixed upon Carney with death uppermost in his thoughts.

Squeezing a new seat between Green Hair and Trent, Doc Cole sat and made himself comfortable, re-arranging the chips in front of him, he seemed totally oblivious to the power plays and insults bandied around the table. To Trent's left was Massado who seemed eager to play.

"Jack. If you would..." Trent invited his croupier to be seated and motioned him to begin the ritual.

"Ladies, gentlemen and players," Jack began, manually shuffling the cards with great dexterity. "I see from the chips there are seven players and three observers at the table. House rules will be played. No talk from observers, the game is five card poker. Opening round, fixed raise of one thousand credits, after that... well, take a look outside, the sky is no longer the limit," he laughed at his own joke. "The game will finish in five hours should anyone still have funds to play. No Credit will be extended by the bank." Jack's smooth patter and easy manner focussed the players on their cards and the opening ante was declared by Garvy. Each player raised the ante by the maximum until the circle was complete.

Cards slammed to the table as the door opened to admit Rong-Yu's First clerk, who silently took his seat at her shoulder. Old habits die hard and the interruption, so early in the game, was a sign of what else was on the minds of the players. Several tensed and Green hair placed his hand upon his weapon beneath his thin jacket, though Sarko gently patted the youngster's arm to defuse him.

Trent relaxed and decided to lose the first hand. Massado folded first and the commentary started. Jack had been warned to let the talk continue unless it degenerated into slander. It was strictly speaking, against the rules of play, but Trent was there to socialise and winkle out information. Sarko and Gen'eer folded next, followed by Trent and Cole leaving Ling Rong-Yu and Garvy staring at each other, trying to read the others hands through their tiniest flickering features. Rong-Yu said nothing, awaiting Garvy's next move, he could simply call and then move on to the next hand, but Trent could see the underlying doubt, his hand was weak, it was a bluff.

Ling Rong-Yu seemed perfectly poised, but Trent knew she was a master of her own emotions, he needed to study her to identify her tells.

"I'll raise five hundred thousand," he counted his chips and threw them onto the pot.

"You do not call?" she asked gently.

"I don't, Miss Yu," he laughed at his own pathetic joke, barely conceiving the insult he'd just thrown. The single word translated to 'fish' and the First clerk made to stand in indignation, but Ling Rong-Yu flicked her little finger and the old man forced himself back to his chair. Without a word, Ling Rong-Yu moved a pile of gambling chips into place and Garvy began laughing. She held her hand high, palm out to silence him, indicating she was not finished.

"I do not see the entertainment for our fellow players," declared the Asian gang leader. "Not while this drags on, Mr Butcher." A few players giggled at the acculturated name she'd given Garvy. "...so, I will simply call you."

Garvy flipped his cards and laughed aloud, "Go on take it." He displayed his pair of tens, king high, for everyone to see.

"Nonsense," Ling Rong-Yu threw her cards face down onto the muck pile of discarded cards in the centre of the table. "You win," she declared.

Garvy was shocked and silenced for the first time during the game. He reached out to retrieve her cards, but Jack's hand beat him to it.

"Dead hand," Jack informed him with a smile, "but your pot, sir. Well done." Garvy stared hard at Jack, his dark eyes narrowed and a snarl grew upon his lips. He was not pleased.

"Fine game, sir," Cole distracted Garvy, who was receiving a vicious whispered remonstration directly in his ear from Carney. Garvy was not used to anyone telling him he couldn't have his own way. If he'd had been in his own club back in New Chicago, Jack would be dead by now.

Trent wished Garvy had revealed her cards, it would have helped him evaluate Rong-Yu a little quicker, but there was an air of betrayal in the room and Trent was distracted by the nagging thought that something was going down while he was confined to this gathering.

The game was even tempered and the chips rotated around the table, without any dominant player gaining too much money or enmity. Then, two hours into the session, the door opened once again, this time to admit Aneksi.

"Ah!" called out Cole dramatically, "my muse has descended from heaven. Come, sit with me, my angel." Trent was entertained by his friend's romantic outburst.

"I bring sustenance and nectar from the gods," Aneksi caught the vibe from Cole and emulated his flowery speech. "I have here," she held aloft a bottle, "four-hundred-year-old brandy, bottled by the emperor Napoleon himself. A gift from your host."

"Bravo," shouted Sarko, "is it the real stuff?"

"Absolutely authentic, I can assure you," Trent stretched in his seat. "Though, I apologise for my assistant's erroneous calculation." He winked at Aneksi, who was busy insinuating herself around all of those seated at the table, wafting her charged pheromones and batting her accentuated eyes at everyone. They each felt she was there to sate their own desires, just before she withdrew and turned her wiles on her next target. All eyes followed her as she sat on Cole's lap and caressed his hair. "It's closer to five hundred years," Trent concluded to deaf ears.

The pheromones acted as a kind of 'reset' for the emotional walls built by those practised in hiding their thoughts behind fabricated states of mind. Even Ling Rong-Yu was distracted and after about five seconds, she let her guard down.

Gen'eer fell hard and so did Sarko and Garvy, arrogant men convinced of their own superiority, while Massado became timid and mouldable as soft clay. Skabenga and Carney were also hypnotised by her act. Trent was amazed at the pure adoration shown by Skabenga a man indoctrinated by Gen'eer to believe his Godhood, but he was worried at the jealously growing within Carney. As long as Aneksi was in the room their minds were open, displaying every emotion for him to see and their motivations were becoming difficult to control. Trent was taken aback; he realised the heightened emotions were turning the room into a powder keg.

"Tone it down," he whispered forcefully.

The surprise Trent felt was not that her affect was so strong, but that as the criminals caught sight of each other their pure hatred and envy flared in equal measure; except between Gen'eer and Ling Rong-Yu, there was something else, something deeper between these two. They showed an understanding, an uneasy appreciation of each other, a begrudging respect.

"Enough!" yelled Rong-Yu. "Remove this harlot." A trained strong mind can recognise the effects of the chemicals in the pheromones and Rong-Yu had disciplined her mind everyday of her life. She rounded on Trent, anger uppermost in her mind.

"This thing is poison, remove it at once." Rong-Yu was beside herself. Her First clerk, however, was in possession of a pliable mind, made so by Rong-Yu's constant demands for instant obedience and enamoured as he was by Aneksi's presence, he made no move to support his mistress.

Trent beamed at her proud of the division she'd sown, as everyone else around the table chose to defend Aneksi, jeering at the mad jealous woman. Rong-Yu's hand automatically went to the dagger sheathed beneath her chiffon robe.

"Interesting weapon," Trent was beside the angry criminal in no time. Rong-Yu's eyes fixed him with every morsel of hate in her soul. For a woman who prided herself on the control of her mind, the last three minutes had been close to the greatest humiliation and degradation she'd ever felt.

"Tell me," he continued smoothly as he gripped her wrist, preventing her withdrawal of the blade, "is it ceremonial, or illegal?"

Rong-Yu was unused to being handled by anyone, the sense of his grip on her arm, restricting her movement, highlighted her current vulnerable position. The idiot clerk was besotted with the feline whore and the other fools were in thrall to her. She released the dagger and stared at Trent.

"You have made a mistake, Mr. Trent," she quipped and ceased her struggle against his hold. He gently guided her arm back in front of her and released it. "No mortal is allowed to touch me, under penalty of death," she sneered.

"Must make for an interesting sex-life," whispered Aneksi, who had silently crept up behind Rong-Yu, prepared to do what Trent may have hesitated over.

"It's okay Aneksi, thanks for the drinks, you may go now," he dismissed her with a wink. "Miss Rong-Yu is fully aware that here, in this place, I am God." He stared into the raw hate of Ling Rong-Yu, considering whether to quell its potency or turn it away, but she was too in touch with her mind to allow that to happen without realising, she was dangerous to him and his gift.

"I am tired. I will retire," she announced as she slapped her First clerk and walked quickly from the room. The clerk rubbed his face where the rebuke had landed, collected her chips in one scooping motion and leapt after her.

"So, the angry woman has gone, good riddance," slurred Sarko, refilling his brandy glass. As he put the bottle down, he slapped his associate who was trembling while staring after Aneksi like a lovelorn puppy.

Cole scrutinised Trent, impressed by his intervention with Rong-Yu, questions formed behind those intense eyes, but they'd keep until later. Despite his proximity to Aneksi, Cole had been prepared for her appearance this time and he had not succumbed to any revealing desires.

To Trent, Cole's mind had been strong enough to see past the fog of lust and he knew his old friend had clearly witnessed what had passed between Rong-Yu and himself.

A single thought circled Cole's mind. Why had Trent thought it important to stop Rong-Yu from drawing her dagger? Everyone was wearing a suit.

Aneksi left the room in turmoil, the players and observers calling platitudes and promising eternal favours for her mere presence. Surprisingly, it was Garvy who called for the next hand to be dealt. Beyond Sarko's observation, no-one seemed to care that Ling Rong-Yu had left.

"Powerful enemy, that one," whispered Cole, indicating the empty chair.

"Ha!" shouted Sarko contemptuously, "A man is honoured by the enemies he makes."

"She is careful and deadly," offered Gen'eer. Trent looked at the man and saw only earnest concern.

"Crossed swords with her before, General?" asked Cole, staring at his cards.

"Once was enough." Gen'eer would say no more, but Trent could see the man was deeply unsettled by the conversation.

"If I were you," contributed Garvy, "I wouldn't let her anywhere near any important systems in this place." Carney elbowed her boss.

"What do you mean, Mr Garvy," asked Massado. "You don't think she'd do anything rash do you?"

"Rash? Ha! If I was spitting blood like her I'd probably wreck the place. Start with the Power Complex, control the air to the main citadel and shutdown all essential systems...Ow!" Carney kicked her boss hard. He started to argue, but the look Carney gave him made him realise his error. Typically, he only made things worse by continuing. "Just saying, you know... if I ran the place."

"And is that your intention?" asked Trent. He watched as the shame was replaced by anger. Garvy was an open book. Carney was the one to watch, she seemed to have some hold over the gang leader.

"If I ran the place," added Sarko. His Russian accent tempered with alcohol made his voice deep and authoritarian, demanding silence and attention from the others. "I'd sell it. It seems like too much trouble, too much to go wrong. Okay, I admit, I love the Flying Dome and the Casino is very good. That whirly-gig worm thing was impressive too, but everything is rationed, controlled, everything is fragile, too much can go wrong." His green haired partner patted him on the shoulder nodding in agreement. Trent saw the beginnings of self-pity take over the calm beige of Sarko, lined with the ever present thin red glow of fear.

Trent realised Sarko didn't feel safe on the moon. The reason the man needed his distractions was the constant fear of the vacuum of space on the other side of the wall. He was a loner, used to being self-reliant, self-sufficient, a free spirit. He couldn't stand the idea of his total dependence on unknown technology, being controlled by unknown people, working behind the scenes to keep him alive. Sarko knew he had little control over his own survival and that seared his soul.

"We're all perfectly safe Mr Sarkovich." Trent tried to appease the man and decided it was time these ambitious men understood what they were up against. "We have a brand-new technology that no-one has ever seen, almost limitless power to run it and the skills to develop it. We already have shields integrated into every wall, floor and ceiling, and weapons to disarm any potential threats." Trent wanted to cast doubt into the minds of those who had the suit defeating knives. "We are self-reliant when it comes to food, water, power and air and it is all controlled through the cybernetic implants of specialists in their field." He didn't mention that he could usurp any cybernetic implant in moments and take full control of the base if necessary. "So, you would have to find these people, coerce each one to aid you and hope they didn't self-destruct their area of operation before you took over. You can't just hold a gun to someone's head and take over the control room. Those ideas belong back in the adventure books of years gone by."

Garvy looked severely downhearted by the revelations of Trent. "What would happen, Trent, if for example, you had a nasty accident, maybe a fatal one.

Would we all die?" He tried to make the question neutral, but came across as the greedy heir apparent. The mood around the table darkened.

"No, Mr Garvy, in the event of my untimely demise my cybernetic disconnect would simply fail to run certain systems. You would..." he thought a moment staring up at the ceiling to collect the events that would occur, "...lose gravity and then there would be no new air or water, but you would be able to survive a couple of hours, enough time for you to leave in your shuttles. World Gov would send a replacement and start it all up again in a few months' time." Trent could see the common emotive response was envy and dismay, obviously Trent's speech had thrown a spanner into whatever plans Garvy had. "But I assure you Mr Garvy, I am in good health and I'm a very careful man." The last part of Trent's assurance held an unmistakeable intonation of menace.

The current hand was won by Tom Massado and with it concluded, Garvy stood. "Thank you, Mister Trent, for a pleasant evening." Carney gathered his chips and without a further word he stalked from the room.

Sarko's youthful green haired partner gathered his boss, who was much the worse for wear through drink, and apologised for their inability to continue.

Massado seemed embarrassed and started to apologise to Trent because it seemed like the thing to do. "I'm sure Mr Garvy was simply concerned about..."

"Don't speak for Mr Garvy, Tom. He wouldn't appreciate it." Trent politely curtailed further comments from Massado.

"Oh well, it was fun while it lasted," Cole sighed as he scraped his few remaining chips from the table. "I'll have to win my fortune some other way." He winked at Trent and tapped him on the shoulder as he stood. "A drink, Mr Massado?" he offered.

"Very kind of you, sir." Massado felt in some way responsible for the evenings turn of events, after all he'd recruited the players, but this Doctor had given him a chance to escape, and he took it.

"Just Cole," he openly offered his friendship, "All my friends call me Cole. And you sir, must be my friend as you seem to be looking after all of my chips." He laughed innocently and Massado's anxiety reduced.

"Well, allow me to use them to buy you a drink, Cole." Confident his charisma had triumphed over this prospective new client, the two men walked out of the room as good friends.

"Thank you, Jack. Take a tip," Trent flipped him a thousand credit chip. "We'll clean up later."

Jack surveyed the room, empty now, but for Trent, the stoic Gen'eer and his first lieutenant Skabenga. "Thank you, sir." He responded as he slowly pushed his chair into place, reluctant to abandon his boss to the two criminals remaining.

Gen'eer said little, especially in front of his underlings, but Trent was not going to give him the satisfaction of opening the conversation. Skabenga sat quietly beside his boss, he was continually threading and unthreading his fingers yet Trent could see his calm aura, just like his boss.

Trent was confident he had the upper hand. The threat of monitoring sensors was real and these two obviously thought the room was bugged. They were right of course, but their practised mindful exercises were not robust enough to obscure the inner eye of Trent.

Within minutes, Gen'eer's anger bled through the calm facade and Skabenga's hate tinged the edges of his aura.

Trent sat quietly contemplating the neat replacement of Jack's chair.

"You have imprisoned many of my men." Gen'eer eventually broke the silence.

"Yes," agreed Trent. This simple acknowledgement infuriated Skabenga, who clenched his fists and brought them down heavily before him.

"Yet," Gen'eer continued calmly, "they have not been accused of any crime?" it was definitely a question; Trent had denied any visitors to the security section.

"Paperwork," responded Trent, deliberately goading the so-called spiritual warlord. "We'll get around to it."

"They have done nothing wrong," Gen'eer opened his hands to plead for his men, "you yourself invited us to look around your base. What harm have they done?"

There was an importance to this question. He detected a need, desperate enough to show the fear of discovery clearly to Trent.

"Were they doing something, General?" Trent focused on the uncertainty. "Everyone can look around Gen'eer, but no-one should be forging security passes, stealing restricted keys and misappropriating vehicles to do so."

On a whim Trent used his internal cybernetic implant to text a query to Liza asking for a status update on the prisoners. Ivor responded with a quick message. 'Not Synthetic, heavily modified genetic engineering; clones definitely, possibly designed drones. Two Humans, isolated', Trent tutted gently at the news. Gen'eer's followers were clones; that made sense. Cloning was illegal without license, but programmable drones were classed as dangerous machines.

"We seem to be having difficulty extracting a report from your men, General." Trent noticed Gen'eer relax, obviously this was something he had previously considered in his plan.

"My men are devout followers; they have had their voices removed to enforce their oath of silence. We do not teach the writings of other cultures. Your words are blasphemy to our ears: your writing profanity to our eyes." He grinned expansively, proud of his achievement, he displayed his self-satisfaction at the charade that excused so many idiosyncrasies in the men's behaviour.

"Not all of your men remained quiet. So far two have told us very interesting things." Trent was still playing poker, though to be honest it felt hollow, after all he'd seen Gen'eer's hand.

Skabenga thumped the table and Gen'eer, rebuked him with sharp guttural noises, a language Trent did not understand. The henchman stood and left the room.

"You know, Mr Trent," began Gen'eer. He sat up straight and proud, but spoke conversationally. "When we arrived, my close friend advised me that we would not be guests, but hostages while we were here. I had met you and I respected you and told him his fears were nonsense, for you are an honourable business man. Tell me, Mr Trent, what deal can we make that will restore our trust?" He relaxed back into his seat and awaited the proposal.

"First you can tell me who gave you your security key-card, then you can tell me what your men were really doing at the old Reactor and if I find your explanation satisfactory, I will return both of your men." Trent put his demands on the table and watched his opponent falter.

"But you have ten of my men in custody, Mr Trent." Gen'eer didn't like what he was hearing.

"No sir, it seems we found eight abandoned clones which have since, ceased to function. Are they yours, General?" Trent knew that clones had no rights. "These clones should be registered and declared as machinery. The clones in our cells have no ownership marks and no registration chips. I fail to see how they can be licensed if they cannot be identified." Trent guessed Gen'eer had no certification of ownership for his 'men'. "These are illegal and by law should be disposed of."

If Gen'eer claimed ownership he would be guilty of several genetic violations, by his own admission; recorded on a sanctioned World Gov base, witnessed by a World Gov officer. A mandatory ten-year sentence would be imposed on his return to Earth, his assets stripped and his empire dismantled. More importantly, what would his people think if his preference for using biological machines over his human followers was made public?

"You are mistaken sir," Gen'eer had another lie prepared. "My men share in the genetic pool of their righteous leader. Your instruments are simply misreading the level of piety within my followers."

Trent wasn't fooled by this weak excuse. It had been used many times before by egotistical owners basing their clones on their own genetic code. There were many ways to detect factory clones; he didn't appreciate being treated like a fool.

"I must admit," Trent decided to play with the fish on his line, "we do not continually link our security and medical databases to those of World Gov on Earth. The rotation of our insubstantial rock makes communication difficult at times. Perhaps we could delay further investigation until we are in contact once again." Trent smiled; everyone knew that despite the fact the moon rotated in relation to the Sun, the base continually faced Earth. Most would have understood the necessity for constant communication, but it was easy to forget that a lot of communication satellites had been replaced in the last fifty years by the World Gov. Communication was easily available across the globe.

Everyone knows the tale of the sparkling heavens and the falling stars that presaged the final war. Few understood the extent of the World Gov repairs that had been made. Effective logistical control required good communication.

The thing visitors were often unprepared for was the 28-day rotation of a single lunar day and night. The term 'dark side of the Moon' was a misnomer. Those not equipped with the basic knowledge of celestial mechanics often believed the side of the Moon facing the Earth was always exposed to sunlight.

Gen'eer showed his confusion, but nodded and grasped at the opening, interpreting the statement as an invitation for him to make a substantial offer for the return of his men and Trent's silence.

"What is it you desire, Mr Trent? A town, a city, maybe a whole country. A less important one of course, but it can be done." Gen'eer was oblivious to the crimes that were being discussed, he was simply negotiating the return of his men. In his world, land was a commodity and people were cheap.

"Brandy?" Trent proffered the bottle and filled two glasses. He did not intend to return the clones to their owner, but he was interested in knowing what Gen'eer would offer.

***

"I want Trent dead!" Garvy was staring at his drink in his adopted booth. The electronic privacy device was in place, it's green lights flashing and the curtains were closed.

"That's a bad idea," counselled Carney. "Come on let's get you to bed, it's been a long day." Garvy reacted violently, throwing his glass across the booth and impacting Harvey, his solid henchman.

"Don't tell me what's best!" he glared at Carney who was tensed, ready to defend herself. "I pay you for your special skills, use them." He scanned the booth and noticed Cutter cowering behind Harvey waiting for his boss to resume a modicum of control. "Tomorrow!" he pointed at Cutter, "you will get what we came for from the fusion labs." Cutter knew better than to reply and simply nodded.

Garvy turned to Carney and beamed an evil smile, "What the boy's need is a diversion. Maybe, loss of power, water and fresh air," he stared lustily at the woman he admired so much, "and you and I will give them what they need." He reached out to caress Carney's hair, but she slapped his hand away.

"It's still a bad idea," she stood her ground, daring him to hit her. Instead, he grabbed for the bottle on the table and took a deep drink.

He didn't see Angie enter the booth until too late.

"This time tomorrow I'll be king of the Moon," he laughed and nervous laughter trickled around the table.

"Any more drinks, sir?" she asked innocently.

"Sure!" Garvy seemed unconcerned by what she might have heard. "A fresh bottle and a couple of clean glasses my darling," he requested, with a genuine smile. Angie nodded and stepped back from the booth.

"She heard. You stupid oaf!" Carney slapped his arm.

"She's nothing," Garvy dismissed the serving girl as immaterial.

"There's no sound suppression field up you idiot." She picked up the flashing green device, "These are for electronic snoopers. She could have been out there listening to everything." Garvy rolled his eyes. "She's a danger," insisted Carney.

"Okay, well, see she doesn't tell anyone... whatever you think she might have heard. Cutter, Harvey the girl needs persuading, but wait until I get my fresh bottle."

Angie had heard the boast and the raised voices, but wasn't sure what it all meant. In times of confusion and uncertainty, whenever she needed clarity she always confided in Belle and that was what she did now.

Belle saw her approach and announced a two-minute break for new cards effectively pausing her table. She stepped away from her punters and greeted Angie with a smile. She could see the girl was wearing a troubled expression. Smiling weakly, Angie relayed what she'd heard at Garvy's booth.

"He said he was taking over?" Belle summarised the tale. Angie nodded.

"This time tomorrow, I'll be king of the Moon, he said." The girl repeated. Belle confirmed the other fragments Angie faithfully reported.

"He said they want confusion and diversion. Okay, I'll warn Trent. You... act as though nothing has happened, serve them their drinks then come straight back to me." She gently patted her arm to remove the worried expression from Angie's face. Reassuring Angie was second nature to Belle.

Belle spotted Jack sat at the wrong side of the bar enjoying a tall drink. She signalled him to join her and he complied.

"You shouldn't be drinking here, customers only." She scolded him, but there was no anger in her voice.

"I'm finished for the night and am enjoying my gratuity." He flashed her a wide carefree smile.

"Listen, I need to speak to Trent, urgently."

"Good luck," Jack's sarcasm was plain to see. "He's in there with Gen'eer and his crony Skabenga." He took a sip from his drink, "Gen'eer looks far from happy."

"Never mind, this is important. Garvy's planning something for tomorrow," Belle confided in Jack, he was someone she'd trusted before and he hadn't let her down yet. "Can you watch my table for five minutes?" Belle was earnest and secretly, Jack was eager to help. The scuttlebutt was that some of the criminals were out to make trouble and Jack had often imagined himself as some sort of sheriff in the frontier lands of space.

"Sure, no problem," Jack agreed with a genuine smile. He watched her step quickly toward the executive suite then slid into position at her table. "Okay folks! Who's ready to win big?" he gave a feral grin while deftly shuffling the cards, introducing and ingratiating himself to the punters he was about to fleece.

12: Blood

Belle knocked on the executive office door and stepped into the room without waiting for an answer. Skabenga was nowhere to be seen and Trent and Gen'eer were shouting good naturedly at each other across the card table.

"What!" shouted Gen'eer, "I cannot give you the whole of Kenya. It is the land of my ancestors."

"That's what you said about Angola," argued Trent.

"I have many ancestors and I am proud of them all." Gen'eer was as indignant as he could be, considering his lack of sobriety.

"But, what about the people?" Trent twisted the demand to focus on the other commodity promised rather than the land.

"People shmeeple," Gen'eer slurred. "There's people everywhere. Admittedly, not as many as there used to be, but plenty for you." There was no sign of the spiritual leader Gen'eer had cultivated as his persona. Trent was simply bargaining with a ruthless criminal.

"Enough for my own army?" teased Trent.

"Yes, but they're rubbish for soldiers. What you really need are clones." He looked bemused at his empty glass.

"Like yours," urged Trent, topping up Gen'eer's glass yet again.

"Yeah, they do as they're told and don't whine; cheap to feed and last longer than people. Never run away." Gen'eer was boasting in military mode. He always thought of himself as a great leader and in his mind, obviously that meant he was a great General too.

"So, then..." Trent seemed to slur his words, "do they blow up as well?" he laughed at his own suggestion.

"Nah! That'd be a waste, but it's safer for them to plant them than me," Gen'eer laughed and caught sight of Belle at the doorway. "Who's this?" he asked, an element of surprise and hope audible in his tone.

"This is my darling angel, Belle, come to tell me to go to bed," laughed Trent. He opened his arms expansively to welcome Belle into his embrace.

"Sorry to interrupt, sir." Belle remained by the door. She knew Trent rarely, if ever, got drunk. She guessed he was acting for the benefit of Gen'eer, who had slowly wobbled to an upright position.

"I take it we're done then?" Gen'eer tried to pull himself together, but half a bottle of brandy can rattle the wits of most men. "Did we agree?" he asked.

"I think so," agreed Trent, holding his glass in the air. "To you and your ancestors, Gen'eer," Trent saluted the retreating drunk.

Gen'eer half waved, half swatted his hand towards Trent and staggered past Belle out the door. Belle gently closed it behind him.

"To you my darling, I think I own half of Africa now," he laughed richly and slammed his empty glass on the table.

"Knock it off, Trent. This is serious." Belle cut to the chase and was in no mood for Trent's act.

"Okay, my angel, what is it?" Brushing his hair back with his hands he then proceeded to slap his face to assume a more sober role. He hadn't drunk that much, but it had been a tiring evening.

"Garvy's planning a take-over tomorrow." Belle stopped to allow Trent to digest the news. "Angie heard him declare that as of 'this time tomorrow' he would be, in his words, 'King of the Moon'."

"So, we have his schedule." Trent stood and paced the room. "Do we have any details?"

"Angie said they were fighting and she went to see what was going on. She made a point of asking permission to enter the booth from the bodyguards outside, so she heard the arguments before she went in to get the drinks order. That woman Carney and Garvy himself are going to create confusion with a diversion, for his '*boys*' to do whatever they plan to do. She thinks they were talking about you." Belle was concerned for him.

"Where's Angie now?" he asked.

"I told her to sort Garvy's drinks and then come straight back to me."

"You sent her back?" Trent knew Garvy wasn't the quickest to spot danger, but he was the most lethal to counter it. "Get her now!" he shouted.

The two of them exited the suite at a run. Neither of them had seen Garvy, and so they acted on previous knowledge of where he'd been sitting the night before. Trent recognised his guards, pushed one aside and ran into the booth. Garvy and Carney were alone, sat close, but were definitely not intimate. A look of horror crossed Garvy's face as he jumped to the conclusion he'd been rumbled.

Trent saw the tray prepared with fresh bottle of Brandy and four clean glasses in front of them and knew he was too late.

Running across the casino, Belle had called security and asked for a trace on Angie's badge, thanking all the god's that they'd registered her earlier that day as a member of staff.

"Bio-Dome," Ivor's voice replied, "Trouble?"

"Trent, she's this way!" She pulled him away from the now fully shielded booth and dragged him past the complaining bodyguards. She ran to the east exit of the casino lounge, into the long storage halls that acted as a buffer between the domes. Full of boxes and crates for immediate use by the restaurants and hospitality staff, the fortified areas allowed for a reinforced structure to protect the separate dome foundations. Trent ran alongside the frantic Belle. There was only one feasible destination through these halls.

"Security, cages and an armed squad to the Bio-Dome, now!" he yelled into his communicator.

The Bio Dome was a recreation of dense woodland, manicured meadows and flower gardens providing suitable conditions for a multitude of plants to thrive, from the planet below. The dome was constructed of nano-controlled gold filtered glass allowing harmless light in throughout the lunar day and providing insulation during the long lunar night. The problem was that it was huge.

On entering the dome, the darkness robbed them of their vision. It took a while for Belle to become accustomed to the change in light and her pace faltered. It was close to one in the morning, obviously there would be no light in here. The plants were from Earth; the normal daylight cycle had to be maintained.

Trent's vision was not interrupted. One of the personal gadgets fitted to his suit recognised the drop in light intensity, raised his helmet and activated the incorporated light sensitive viewing. He thought, 'thermal overlay' and footprints freshly trodden on the grass glowed white; three sets.

He moved deep into the greenery; behind him Belle shouted for Angie. A scream came from ahead and Trent doubled his speed, bringing online his augmented suit-legs. He felt lighter and the suit took over the movement of his muscles. He knew there'd be a price to pay later, but right now he didn't care.

Ahead, the mass of bodies appeared and the thermal vision reduced to resolve the detail. Angie was on her knees, her helmet was in place, but Cutter, the scar-faced lackey and professional hanger-on of Garvy, was holding what looked like a plasma needle gun to the suit control piping at her neck.

Speeding up, Trent fell back on his infantry training. He covered the distance to Cutter in just over a second, using his massive momentum as a weapon. The impact lifted the lighter man from the ground even in the simulated normal earth gravity, depositing him fifteen feet away from his intended target. Trent staggered two steps beyond the impact and turned to see Belle screaming, charging toward the bigger man. Harvey had reached out for Angie as his comrade was violently rammed and launched across the grass. Trent noticed that he too was holding a plasma needle gun.

Belle yelled her anger at the imposing muscular thug and ran.

Harvey heard the commotion and turned to see Belle bearing down on him. He raised his arms to protect himself, to ward her off, instantly forgetting Angie. Trent recovered and ran forward to grab the weapon, but he was too slow. Belle collided with the thug and a blue flash lit up, Belle's suit.

Trent could see there was no evil intent, Harvey was simply trying to save himself from the attacking woman, but the impact had discharged his weapon. She'll be fine he thought, as long as Harvey doesn't fire again through the damaged suit. As he studied the scene, everything seemed to slow down; she crumpled to the grass beside Angie and he knew he was wrong.

"I... I didn't," Harvey protested his innocence and dropped the weapon. Trent hit him as hard as he could with the strength of his augmented suit. He couldn't hurt Harvey, but he could vent his anger and knock him down.

Angie was cradling Belle's helmet. The suit was still trying to protect her and would do so for at least thirty minutes after death, a minor modification Trent had uploaded to all Lunar suits after the murder.

His macro-vision kicked in and Trent used his enhanced diagnostics to survey the area of damage. The suit was not badly damaged, but the proximity of the discharge meant the plasma needles went fully through the suit and by a quirk of fate, straight into Belle's heart. The muscle was pierced by three precise lacerations causing the pump to fail. To add insult to injury, the suit was already repairing itself.

Using his personal override, Trent remotely dropped Belle's protective helmet and allowed Angie to experience the dying warmth of Belle's fading vitality. Tears fell as she gently stroked her saviour's face. Belle was her best friend and mentor, the nearest thing she'd ever had to a mother. The only person she'd ever known who loved her for who she was and demanded nothing in return; now she was gone.

Trent knelt beside her and Angie could see the tears in his eyes, "You loved her too!"

Deeply, he thought, but could not voice the word.

She knew Belle had trusted him, she knew they had a history and those few tears bonded Angie to Trent in a way no amount of words ever could. Their shared grief united them.

Trent witnessed the change in Angie's aura as the internal loss and grief was turned outward seeking love and friendship. He'd only experience a change like this once before, when he'd rescued Belle from the hands of those soldiers. He gently nodded at Angie as she caught his eye and knew he had assumed responsibility for this sweet vulnerable child.

Ivor rushed into the Bio-Dome carrying a long cumbersome weapon and saw Cutter, still stunned, trying to crawl away into thick leafed bushes. He immediately assessed the scene, removing one of three long projectiles from his belt. He saw Harvey curled up crying on the grass. He saw the body of Belle and the grief shown by Angie. Without a second thought he loaded the weapon, took aim and shot the incapacitation net.

With a shrieking whistle the thin metallic net was dragged forward by a shaped weight, splitting into six projectiles as it approached its target, to wrap around

Cutter. On impact the net bound the target, like multi-armed bolas, fusing to itself wherever steel threads crossed. Tiny nodules on the wires used a micro plasma blast to drill through the surface of the suit and insert pins, and finally a massive blast of high current electricity rendered the suit protection useless.

It was a new weapon Trent had designed for crowd control. Ivor had taken it upon himself to upgrade it and now field test it. Cutter experienced its agony in full.

Two men ran forward to retrieve the screaming, bound murderer. "Leave him!" shouted Ivor. "He'll be live for a couple of minutes. Let the energy dissipate."

Trent witnessed the agony on Cutter's face and repressed his engineer's instinct to suggest reducing the exposure to the current. Cutter's screams were minor recompense for the damage he'd caused. 'Let him scream.' he thought.

"And him," ordered Angie, screaming at the top of her voice, "he killed her." The guards looked at Trent who, in turn had become distracted by the change in the girl. Angie had lost the innocence, the vulnerability that had defined her, now her gentle unsure aura was flooded with the blue of hate outlined with fear. She demanded retribution. A steel edge had been welded to her soul and she was determined to wield it.

Harvey looked at the fallen woman and sobbed. He'd never killed anyone, he just intimidated them. He was tall, big and strong and that's what they paid him for. Sometimes, he held people while Cutter hurt them, but he didn't do the hurting.

"I never hurt no-one," he sobbed. In his simple mind he too was a victim. Why did she blame him? The lady attacked him. He crawled upright and stood to apologise to the angry girl and as he stepped towards her a second net was fired.

Trent looked intently at Harvey and was confused. Whatever was going through his mind was not evil. The only colour in his aura was the pale blue of pity, there was no intent to harm, no hate, fear or greed and he too was suffering. Grabbing Angie by the wrist Trent pulled the girl to him to suffocate her anger and hate. He heard the whistle of the net and felt the anguish of Harvey as he fell.

The solid pathetic man did not scream, he simply cried, sobbing like a child.

Addressing Ivor, who was now kneeling beside an unconscious Cutter, Trent took command of the scene, "Clear this up!" With a nod, he indicated a female guard and motioned her to take Angie, she was fragile enough without being thrust into the arms of a strange man. "Thanks, Amy, " he sighed as Angie was gently led from the dome. "Cage these two and find me Garvy."

"Garvy and Carney are locked in their respective cabins. A guard stationed outside each door," responded Ivor immediately. "Their bodyguards were unhappy with our actions. They've been locked down too." He'd been briefed by Belle during the chase regarding Garvy's threats and the kidnap of the waitress. Ahead of the game, Ivor instantly put one of his new procedures into action.

Amongst the three security watch captains, plans had been drawn up to deal with each of the criminals should they step out of line. The first murder had really focussed their minds.

"It's late, clear the corridors of any of their party and lock them all in their cabins." Trent was tired, the price of his run was being extracted and he knew he needed to deal with this fresh tomorrow. "Anyone who argues, cage them. Put them in cells for obstruction," he looked at the peaceful body of his long-time friend, "and please," his voice fell, "find someone to look after Belle."

"Fenwick," called Ivor, a young guard standing over Harvey looked up. "Go with him." He indicated Trent walking slowly away.

Ivor started work gathering evidence and pulling the recordings of the crime from the mainframe as Trent, shoulders slumped, dragged himself from the dome.

Ivor knelt beside Belle. "Tomorrow," he promised the peaceful body, "Garvy will pay."

***

As Trent got into bed he was looking forward to the peaceful release into the arms of Morpheus. The face of Belle smiling was prevalent in his mind and flashes of the cries for retribution from Angie plagued him. Harvey's innocence irritated him and Cutter's screams did not feel like compensation for his loss.

"Sorry to bother you Sir," came a formal voice in his ear, "Communication Priority One, from World Gov, sir." There was no permission request, this was

Priority One. No-one was allowed to refuse a call of this importance.

"Hold for three seconds then put it on my desk." Trent fought his pains to climb out of his bed and dressed in his robe. He was too tired to be worried, nothing short of all-out war would prevent him returning to his bed as soon as this call was dealt with. A declaration of war would have been easier.

"Mother?" Trent was shocked at his mother's appearance. She was drawn and fatigue showed on her gaunt face. He checked himself, "What can I do for you Commander?" he asked in a formal tone.

"Listen, I know we don't see eye to eye," Trent huffed at the understatement, "but there's real trouble here." She sounded desperate. "That body you reported, he's one of ours... theirs." She looked off screen to her right, Trent could see the fear in her eyes. "There's a coup going down, the Two-Hundred are being exterminated. About thirty officers have decided it's time for a change. They poisoned at least a hundred and have slaughtered us in our beds, five of us are holed up on the eighteenth floor, but they know we're here." Her frantic movements scanning off screen were testament to her fear. "They have you in their sights, son. They'll be taking your place too." She looked uncomfortable, her lips dry, her wide eyes betrayed her fear and she sounded distressed, reluctant to bring forward her next words, "If you've got your father's gift, use it!" She disappeared from the screen, but Trent stared as flashes lit the wall behind her. Repetitive thuds from plasma pistols were being discharged. The room went silent for what seemed like an age.

"Mother, are you there?" Trent shouted, showing concern for her for the first time in over twenty years.

Her head re-appeared, there was damage to her control piping on her suit. "They'll be back, but listen... they're allied with civilians, well equipped, with weapons that can damage the suits. I think it's..." There was a huge explosion in the World Gov building and communication spluttered and was lost.

"Security, cut all channels to Earth. Lock down the base. Get everyone out of bed. I want all staff in the Khonsu Lounge now!"

He looked at the blank screen and considered the enormity of what had just been revealed. Trent had no love for the World Gov, but it was the only thing keeping the planet alive and out of the hands of the cut-throat gangs and despots.

"Thirty officers from within," he muttered, "...allied to a group of well-equipped civilians," he thought long and hard, "and we're a target."

Trent hated stimulants, but he knew he wouldn't survive the night without one. He called Jan, "Yes, yes!" she yawned and sounded weary, "I'm on my way." She'd already been roused by the staff call.

"Arms and full protection," he advised her.

"What's going on?" Her voice was muffled as she struggled with her suit.

"War!" He cut the comms and felt the stim's effect flood through his body.

Going to his wardrobe he selected a black suit with multiple lines of red piping patterned across the shoulders and arms. He'd never worn it before, he hoped he wouldn't have to; he still considered it a work in progress. Padded on the shoulders and shaped across the chest it made him into a caricature of himself. The integral feet also had thicker soles than normal and gave the impression of military boots. The suit had a mean look to it though the weapons it contained were not on display.

The dead man had been one of Garvy's, he thought. Could he be in league with the World Gov, surely not. He finally swung a black waistcoat over his suit, though thin it contained a supercharged repair net, another layer of protection from those unknown magical knives. He buckled a belt around his waist that contained two pistols, one was a standard issue plasma needle gun, the other longer and thicker. As a last thought he grabbed a spare waistcoat for Jan and reached out to open his cabin door.

The explosion pushed him back into the room and for a moment he was knocked senseless. His vision paled and a spectrum of colours washed over his sight as his helmet instantly raised, automatically saving him from the concussive blast. Multiple shields of energy danced in front of his eyes before settling to full transparency.

Shouting erupted from the corridor and more explosions followed as violence played out in the corridor, his fear spurring him to full awareness. He rolled to his knees and crouched over as he ran back to the side of the doorway. His cabin door had been blasted to splinters; whoever had fired the missile had been too eager. A second later and the missile would have impacted him.

Two suited bodies lay at the end of the corridor neither seemed to have an aura. Trent's upgraded suit diagnostics kicked in, but detected no sign of life. From his current position, he could see no damage to the suits they wore. His red suited guardians were absent and he wondered whose side they were on.

The shouting had moved away from his corridor and he slowly ventured out with his modified pistol in his hand. Reaching the bodies, he saw the unmistakable marks of the grenades he had been developing with Ivor and Martin, his eager security weapons experts.

The grenade was a double skinned spherical mechanism, first to plasma cut an entry point into the suit on impact, then to inject a powerful anaesthetic into the wearer. Someone had swapped out the anaesthetic replacing it with an explosive. The suit around the impact site seemed to be empty where the contained shock had liquefied the body within.

More shouting ahead brought Trent to his senses, 'This is a war zone, and weapons can now kill,' he told himself.

A tall shape appeared in front of him wearing the blue of security, his face obscured by a dark blue armoured faceplate. He recognised the gold trim on the suit insignia, it could only be Martin or Ivor.

The levelled gun was lowered as the guard recognised the black rank insignia on Trent's arm almost invisible, black on black with a flash of blue and gold. Trent was crouching over the bodies wearing a strange suit and he didn't look too steady. Then he saw the damage to the apartment at the end of the corridor and understood why.

"Martin, Sir," he introduced himself, "Came straight here to escort you. We disturbed this ambush." he explained. "Looks like two of Garvy's men." The helmet faceplate paled and Trent saw the worried features of his security Captain.

"No, this one is Gen'eer's, I recognise him, not sure if I've seen this one before." Trent was analysing the bodies, comparing them to the guest list presented through his cybernetic implant.

"Security communication only, Sir," Martin gently rebuked Trent's choice of a public communication channel. "It looks like the way is clear to the lounge," he reported. "The third one got away. I sent your bodyguards after him. Looks like they took a beating."

"The grenades?" asked Trent, indicating the bodies.

"Yes sir," Martin looked abashed, "You did say think outside the box, sir."

"How many have you got?" asked Trent, his mind moving into logistics mode.

"Only a dozen... well, ten now, sir." Martin didn't know whether to boast or apologise. "Ivor took the nets."

"Now listen, this is bigger than you know." Checking the man's aura for any sign of contempt or betrayal, Trent explained about the earth-side coup.

"Wow!" Martin was totally shocked and dismayed that anyone would have the audacity to attack the World Gov. His thoughts then went to the people below.

"Will there be another war?" There was no sign of betrayal and Trent was satisfied with the man's response. He stood and put away his gun.

"Let's get to the lounge." Trent cut off any further questions racing through Martin's thoughts.

The corridors had resumed their peaceful countenance, not a single person was seen and the base took on an abandoned air. They approached the Khonsu lounge and Trent wondered if it was all real. There was an edge to his vision, it looked like everything was lit from behind. He rubbed his eyes and noticed Martin was watching him.

"It must be the stimulants kicking in," he explained. Although his body felt re-energised, he could taste the metallic chemicals in his mouth and his eyes seemed so tired.

"Careful, sir", Martin held him back from the blast doors outside the lounge, "Let me go first."

The doors opened and a tangible wave of fear and anger swamped Trent's unprepared mind. The raw emotion staggered him, pushing him onto his knees, his hand stretched out holding to the wall to steady himself. He closed his mind and focussed on his own inner strength.

"I've got you, sir." The concerned voice of Martin pulled him back to the moment.

After a few seconds, he realised with embarrassment he was being supported upright. The sudden wash of emotion from the highly charged crowd had over-whelmed him and his legs had buckled.

"I'm okay," he sighed, "just... not good with stims." Martin cast his eye anxiously over his boss looking for any damage to the strange black suit.

Trent took a moment to gather his wits, he inhaled deeply and steadied himself for the coming ordeal. Standing tall he stretched his spine, broadening his shoulders and taking another deep breath, he prepared his mental shield for the approaching emotional onslaught.

13: Defence

The standard opulence of the Khonsu Lounge had been set aside for the staff meeting. The room lights were fully illuminated. Gone were the stylised projections and artificial shadows offering an illusion of clandestine safety within a decadent entertainment palace of a romantic age. The walls stark and featureless while the cold light revealed traces of fear across the concerned faces of his assembled staff, expectantly looking up from the lower floor.

On the podium stood Trent, Martin and Jan, sporting her new waistcoat. He glanced at his staff seeking to discern their feelings. Martin was angry, his mind working double-time scanning the crowd for potential danger. Jan was difficult to read, her raiment of pale colours twisting and turning, covering her deeper feelings, but he figured, if she wanted any of them dead, they'd all be sucking vacuum by now; she had the knowledge and the means. Besides, her aura was only difficult because it was masked by the pulsating rainbow he now associated with love. He didn't think it was possible to act in malice while feeling that way. He knew his gift wasn't perfect. 'Maybe,' he thought, 'that's why it's dangerous.'

Once the fear she had for his well-being had been removed by a gentle hug, Jan quickly returned to what had become, her default state around him. Trent's only regret regarding his gift was his inability to view his own aura, idly he wondered if he loved her as much as he hoped he did.

The crowd of staff became silent and Trent considered the best way to approach the subject of war and treason.

"You all know me," he began. He hadn't bothered retrieving the microphone, he didn't need it; the room became deathly silent as he stepped forward in his imposing black suit. "In the next few hours all our lives will change."

He had decided he didn't have time to process each individual to see where their loyalty lay. He knew some would have been be coerced by the riches promised by his guests and he knew he had to have a plan to counter usurped loyalty.

Speaking with Ivor privately he'd determined his Captain's current loyalty beyond reproach. Liza was easy to read and her ambition did not interfere with her morality. Trent had confided his fears. The two Security Captains were now stationed at the back of the room, one at either side of the throng, weapons drawn, but held casually.

"What's happening, I can't get through to my family back on Earth?" came a worried voice. The general hubbub rose, but was quickly silenced by the discipline and camaraderie of the team.

"I have been reliably informed that we are a target for a rebel cadre within World Gov. They seek to destroy this base and us along with it."

The murmurs rose and took longer to subside this time. Trent gently motioned for silence and the noise instantly abated.

"I have been warned by reliable sources on Earth, that rebels are already here among us and I have been given a few names by loyal World Gov agents." The general curiosity in the room flared to fear.

In three tight groups around the room, spikes of hatred coloured several individuals. It looked like the rebels already knew each other. Into his headset he spoke quietly to his captains identifying the highlighted interlopers, usually by name, occasionally he only knew nicknames and had to resort to descriptions of clothing and locations based on proximity to other people and reluctantly, the feedback from his cybernetic links. His concern was that the employee database was only as accurate as the people who had access to it. To cover his actions, he motioned Martin forward,

"I need a minute," he whispered.

"Listen!" Martin, unprepared, licked his suddenly dry lips and stepped forward to address the frightened crowd. "Common sense tells us the base is more valuable in one piece. If they wanted to blow us into space, they could have done so a hundred times over since arriving." People started looking around; suspicion of their neighbour foremost in their minds, but it was hard to step away in the crowded lounge.

"Keep calm. Most of you won't even register on their radar." Making it up as he went along Martin was frantically trying to reassure the staff, but each phrase seemed to make matters worse. "Their targets will be key systems, which they'll need... so probably won't destroy, and probably key personnel... like me!" The young pink faced captain stood exposed to the crowd looking less like an indispensable cog in a machine than anyone could imagine.

For a moment the silence was intense, then at the back of the room Ivor started to laugh and the nervous laughter rippled through the assembled staff.

"Oh brilliant, thanks mate!" shouted Martin acting the part of embarrassed victim. The time had been filled and Trent had completed his computer checks using his cybernetic implant. He ushered his red-faced captain back with a smile and a knowing wink.

"Thank you, Captain." Trent strode forward and the laughter died. "I have no idea as to the accuracy of the names in this report and so, I will have to conduct my own investigation. Time is short and there are too many people to individually process. I would ask you to bear with us as we call you through to the restaurant in random groups, to answer a few questions."

The rebels calmed down, their aura's returning to a pale beige edged with hate. They still stood out to Trent. They were the only ones who had no red of fear or pinks of curiosity, staining their aura's. With only unsubstantiated accusations they were fairly confident they would be able to bluff their way through the checks.

Trent's red suited bodyguards who'd arrived late and remained at the back, retired from the Khonsu Lounge to check out the Commander's information.

Names were called by Jan; she scanned the room for badges and compiled a register of those present. Trent monitored each person heading towards the restaurant, chatting with each, reading their emotions, using trigger words and phrases he'd learned long ago. He'd done quite well in interrogation techniques at school, even before his gift developed. The first group of employees exited the Khonsu Lounge guided by Martin, without incident.

No questions were asked. Once inside, the security officers, selected personally by their captains, scanned each worker's badge and passed them through. The first rebel was known by name, his badge was scanned and two security officers guided the man through the restaurant and out through a side door, into a fully stocked store room, where he was instantly restrained. One guard held his arms while the other pointed a bulky plasma gun at him. The store room contained thirty cages; they hoped it was enough.

When Trent detected a rebel, he used his internal comms to let Jan know and she highlighted the name on the register, before they were submitted to the badge scan. It was simple and it was smooth.

The charade took just under two hours to complete. Processing slightly less than four hundred staff and imprisoning seventeen identified rebels. Trent gathered his trusted senior staff in one of the Casino's private rooms, currently setup as a meeting room for a commercial delegation.

An executive, white digital table, fitted with twelve interface panels, dominated the centre of the stark white illuminated room. Eleven mushroom seats were in place with the far end of the table clear for the presenter to stand and address the meeting. Trent sat on the nearest seat to the door, exhausted.

"Well, I think we've got them all; seventeen rebels apprehended," announced Martin, tired, but relieved there'd been no further bloodshed.

"Nineteen foot-soldiers," corrected Trent, don't forget the two dead ones outside my room." Trent was considering the message from his mother.

"Nineteen's a funny number, you'd have thought they'd send a round twenty," mused Liza. "None of them struck me as officer material." Liza had a way of highlighting the obvious that everyone else seemed to consider unimportant.

"My informant included an incomplete warning regarding an alliance with a group of well equipped 'others', but the communication was ended abruptly." Trent passed on the full intelligence and awaited their response.

"Well equipped, could mean any of the gangs," observed Ivor.

"Don't forget," warned Trent, "the architects of the plan are members of the World Gov, some of the Two Hundred themselves. There could be a lot more. Not necessarily gang related."

"What do we do now? In two hours the first of the guests will want to know why their comms are down with Earth." Jan was thinking about the day to come.

"Micro-meteor strike," suggested Martin, "...took down the main antenna array."

"Okay, we'll go with that. Everyone knows space is a dangerous place." Trent scanned the tired faces of the staff around him. "Everyone to bed, except..."

"My watch," volunteered Ivor, "we've got another 4 hours to go."

"Good," Trent appreciated the support from his team. "Not a word to the guests. Please, brief your teams."

"What about Garvy's threats?" asked Ivor.

"Don't know, don't care," Trent yawned. "I need my bed."

Jan stepped forward and took the seat beside him. "What's this about Garvy?" Jan's concern was obvious.

"Oh, he's promised fireworks tomorrow," Trent dismissed his comment as nothing special to reassure her. He turned his head to avoid her stare. Suddenly, he felt eager to leave the room and stood. Jan could tell by Liza and Ivor's reaction there was a lot more to it.

"Explain!" she demanded, stepping into his path, blocking his exit.

"Garvy's plotting something..." began Trent.

"...and," Jan prompted.

"...and he wants to remove an obstacle to his plan, which we understand he will do tomorrow." Trent held Jan's shoulders. She could see how tired he was.

"The obstacle, being you?" she guessed.

"It's okay; I can probably get six hours sleep before he tries anything," he placed his hand on her shoulder and tried to step around her, but Jan wasn't happy and refused to move out of his way. "If you don't let me go, I'll be in no fit condition to do anything tomorrow except lie down. Besides, Martin's got some new toys."

"No problem, sir. I'll accompany you back to your quarters." Martin stated this as a fact not to be argued with.

"Listen Jan," Trent held her closer, "I need you safe. Please..." he appealed to her out of concern rather than authority.

"I know, put myself back in the Power Complex," she sighed, frustrated by the unknown danger he was facing. Unable to be part of the solution, she didn't want to cause him any more problems.

He embraced her gently but awkwardly and gave her a peck on the cheek. "Just," he smiled at her in his charming way, "keep the lights on. I'll see you later this morning."

She watched as the two men left the room. Her heart heavy and her thoughts racing. She slowly followed them out and made her way back to her crew, reluctantly returning to her Rover.

Liza was pacing at the head of the table, talking to herself.

"The question is which gang," she paused, "...or gangs are in league with the rebels?" She considered getting her head down for a couple of hours, but this situation would continue to vex her. Instead, she announced to the room in general, "I'll be in my office," Ivor nodded, he knew his boss couldn't rest until she'd got to the bottom of this, but she was tired and he wished she'd rest.

Ivor ushered the security teams and duty workers who'd floated into the room for any scraps of information, back into the lounge, listening to whispered conspiracy theories and promises of retribution. He knew there would be more difficulties ahead than simply murderous gangsters roaming the hallways.

"Take these!" Again, Martin was uncompromising. Trent looked in no condition to argue with a child let alone take on Garvy. He handed two rough spheres to his boss. "I'll post two men in full armour at the head of the corridor and lock down this section." Trent was studying the improved grenades. "No need to prime, they'll detect when they're thrown and activate when they hit any nano-material."

Trent examined the spheres and recognised his own textured design. Each raised bump contained a sensor.

"When they impact, they immediately calculate position and movement against the target, initiating three plasma blasts tearing apart atomic bonds and drilling a hole in the fabric." Martin was proud of his toys and though Trent understood their operation he let his captain continue.

"While this is happening, an injector moves into position and discharges a measured amount of sedative to disable the attacker, but I've changed that and swapped out the sedative for a liquid explosive that detonates one second after contact with the air."

Trent had solved the hardest problem. The bulk of the heavy sphere was the multi-layered power storage for the sequential plasma shots. This had been the real work. The grenades were neat, safe and deadly with no collateral damage.

"Just don't throw then at the walls," Martin joked. He stepped inside Trent's apartment and automatically checked for intruders or anything else that shouldn't be there.

"Thanks Martin, you did well tonight." Trent dismissed his security captain and made his way to his bed. He didn't even remove his bulky black suit before he succumbed to sleep.

His dreams were violent and highly emotional. He saw his mother shouting at his father, heard the door shatter as the armed squad crashed inside their cramped apartment. He felt the sting of tears as his mother rushed to him and screamed, "Your father's a monster!" Beaten and bloody his father caught his eye as he was dragged away, a smile and a wink, a final act of rebellion to impress his son. He didn't shout, he didn't struggle, he was resigned to his fate.

Then, the world spun and Trent was returned to the bleak darkness of his school, facing torture at the hands of the three older lads in his dorm. Kank and his cronies, Suggs and Kel. Emulating his father, he stood unmoving, as they tore at his shirt and ripped his notebook, they punched him, called him 'Traitor' and spat in his face. His anguish triggered his gift and he saw their hate bloom into a deep blue that turned them into caricatures of demons. Their vicious laughter scarred his memories.

The older students were supposedly in the dorm to support and mentor the younger boys, but their idea of mentorship involved humiliation, pain and subjugation, not surprising in the fascist World Gov environment.

He re-lived the shock as the blood erupted from the face of Kank as his new friend heroically intervened. Unlike the others in the dorm, who hid beneath their covers thanking the lord they weren't tonight's target, Cole had come to his aid. He picked up a heavy fire extinguisher and silently crept up behind the bawdy thugs. The water filled lump of metal pulverised the side of the leader's head, teeth and blood spewed from his mouth. He witnessed again the fall of the limp body. Cole viciously kicked the leg of the second taunter, Kel, catching him on the side of the knee; he watched him fall awkwardly. Suggs turned from his defenceless prize and was instantly arrested by Cole's intense gaze. The bully squirmed, seeking escape from the horror he'd instigated, as the blood dripped from the extinguisher and quailed as he saw his violent comrades bleeding and broken. His aura flared red in fear, his hatred forgotten, cowardice bloomed and he fled from the dorm.

In slow motion he lived again the moment Cole coolly stepped toward Kel, raised the extinguisher and broke the skull of the squealing attacker, curled up on the floor caressing his useless leg. Trent felt again the anguish of his assailant, and the sudden emptiness, as the skull shattered, guilt swamped him as he remembered how he stared after the discarded bloodied weapon slowly rolling away, unable to look upon the bodies.

Trent cried out, reliving the agony of the moment, his own fear, his own anguish, his own pain and loss. Throughout it all, the emotions of the bullies flared. He couldn't picture Cole's aura, he remembered he'd been calm and measured, his eyes lit by a flame of justice, but in his dream, he saw no aura and recalled no emotion. He only saw Cole's triumphant smile.

The flood of light-red fear from Cole's second victim had coloured the whole scene. 'Never leave a wounded enemy behind you', that had been their lesson that day, but it was cold blooded murder.

Trent remembered his own tears of frustration and anger, then the joy at the destruction of his enemy. Tears of betrayal. How could he relish the destruction of his own principles?

But dreams aren't memories and he knew something in this one had changed.

An alarm sounded, intruding upon his dream and he awoke. He could smell smoke. He panicked, but quickly scanned the room and realised his nightmare had triggered his new suit upgrade.

A plasma flame had been ejected from his glove, burning the pillow he held tightly. Putting out the smouldering fire he called security to explain the alarm.

"Just a stupid accident, no damage. Put it down to a long night." Feigning laughter, he joked with the officer who answered his call, "I'll get a couple more hours and then be up to see the prisoners," he informed the desk, subtly changing the subject.

Discarding the damaged pillow, he retrieved another from the storage beneath his bed. He removed his black suit and noticed the charge was low. Dropping his fake workshop wall, he set to charging and arming the suit. After twenty minutes he lay back, still disturbed by the dream. Silently he cursed the stimulant he'd taken earlier; he was never good with drugs. He lowered his head to his pillow and quickly reverted to a state of semi-comatose relaxation.

A final thought nagged at the back of his mind. Where was Cole's aura?

14: Showdown

After a quick brunch, Trent began his morning later than planned. He checked his black suit and saw that it was still charging. A little disappointed at being deprived of his most intimidating armour, he called Liza.

"I'm on my way. Put one of Gen'eer's humans in the interrogation room. I want to know what happened at the Reactor." He didn't wait for an answer, but as he picked up his belt to wrap around his recently updated light grey suit with bright red stripes, his comms signalled a reply.

"I've dispatched two guards to your room, Malone and Singh. Garvy and Carney are still locked down. You go nowhere alone today!" Her voice was authoritative and Trent imagined there would be a new procedure somewhere detailing precautions to take when the boss has an appointment to be assassinated.

"Anything else?" he tried to sound light and hearty, but his mood was dark and his words sounded surly.

"Yes, your 'other' guards have re-appeared." As the door opened, he saw the two red-suited figures blocking the corridor and the two exasperated blue-suited security guards, gesticulating wildly, angry at being prevented from executing their assigned duty.

"Gentlemen," Trent appealed. "You're all here for me and I didn't ask for any of you, so do me a favour and just get along." He walked through the squabbling men and they fell in to step; two of Trent's base security in front, two World Gov behind. "You know, if

I knew we were going to do this," observed Trent, "I'd have borrowed Ling Rong-Yu's chair." He gave a little laugh and his good humour returned.

Taking the public transit, the five men commandeered a pod. Trent was unhappy with the World Gov bodyguard removing other passengers from their seats under the pretence of his protection. Some guests saw the pod transit system as one of the moon base attractions.

Their pod headed north to the Security Station. The doors closed and almost met, when a slender hand inserted itself into the gap and forced the machine's portal to open again, revealing Aneksi.

"Nice day for a ride," she raised her eyebrows at the first red suited goon, as if surprised anyone would stop her getting where she wanted to be. She insinuated her lithe undeniably feminine body, past the security squad to sit beside Trent. As she stroked his hair she whispered in his ear and drew a finger across his neck, "They're a lot of good aren't they." She derided the guards who seemed to realise they'd been caught unawares, unsure as to how Aneksi was now sitting so close to the subject under their protection.

"Morning Aneksi." Trent relaxed, comfortable in her presence and because she was so close, gave her a peck on the cheek; he always felt at ease with his top performer. They had a long history of mutual trust and he knew she would never be a threat to him.

"Do you know who told me?" Aneksi feigned anger. "I should kill you myself, making me listen to that slimy creature, Massado."

"Told you what?" Trent dismissed the hurt feelings she so marvellously portrayed.

"That this is your last day." She put it succinctly, "Garvy is so angry, he's offering anyone five million credits to finish you." She moved in close, showed her teeth in a facsimile of a smile and drew an extended claw down his cheek.

Malone, unhappy with Aneksi's cloaked threat and unaware of Trent's deep friendship with the actress, reached out to intercept her arm. "Back off lady," he ordered.

Her head snapped around and a look of pure hatred contorted her catlike features into a vicious snarl. Her eyes glowed green, the slit pupils narrowed and her bared teeth looked far too sharp. Her free hand offered five deadly claws to the face of the security guard and his helmet shield appeared.

The deep primal response unnerved him and he stepped back shocked by the sudden ferocity from this slender beauty; not all felines were domestic. Trent saw the jealousy and the love, Aneksi was probably the best protection he had right now.

"Its fine, we've got a plan," he lied smoothly. Almost instantly the feline was gone and the woman returned. "Garvy's been weakened. He needs a distraction to carry out whatever his master caper is and this is his last desperate gambit. I've got his two sycophants in jail for murder. Once I neutralise his lady assassin he'll crumble." The plan was forming... slowly, and Trent was beginning to focus on details, a state of mind he found relaxing.

"I could always..." she licked her lips and displayed her feral grin, her pupils transformed once again to become vertical slits within yellow jewels, "...say hello to her ladyship." The offer was playful but sincere and he had little doubt she could handle Carney, but the fight was his. Aneksi had a troubled past and he'd spent a lot of time and effort removing her from the World Gov's most wanted list, though he thought the genetic meld was a bit too much, especially after he'd altered her original DNA sequence recorded on the central database. He didn't want her coming to light as a hero, or a villain.

Aneksi was cursed with intelligence and compassion. Of course, that wasn't her real name. When her father was removed from what little power he had, looking after a breakaway group of self-sufficient isolationists, the World Gov had made a ferocious enemy. At the tender age of sixteen, Aneksi had gathered a handful of volunteers loyal to her father and waged a war upon the World Gov that cost them greatly in resources, and reputation. For a few months, she became the prime target for all European squads. Appropriating food convoys from the French Farm Domes, almost starving the World Gov garrisons, she fed the people and asked for nothing in return.

Soon, squads were doubled in size to counter her elaborate traps. Aneksi did not seek to kill soldiers, simply temporarily imprison them and destroy their transportation. Her team developed drone counter measures that took three years for the fascist rulers to counter and in that time, Aneksi almost destroyed the myth of the World Gov's divine right to rule. It was after he'd lost Cole as a partner and was given his own squad, that their paths first crossed.

Eventually, after several set-backs, Trent had her cornered. She claimed to be alone; his squad had lost, literally 'misplaced', eighty percent of his men and while regrouping she invited him in to parley. In the ruins of the old factory, they sat to discuss terms. The heretic cult leader and the renegade pacifist.

Her people had been scattered, arrested, and executed, though her ideology and her passion remained intact.

Trent held no zeal for his task, in fact he supported her actions to feed the starving, but he was watched closely and his position, as squad leader, was fraught with competition who would think nothing of climbing the ranks over his still warm dead body.

When he exited the building, it was as though a veil had been lifted and he saw the world anew. Officially, the report concluded she was never there. Trent stated they'd argued, fought and he'd been rendered unconscious by an unknown chemical attack. He claimed he'd walked out of the building as soon as he'd come to, after shooting her and several of her gang. But the lack of bodies meant a creative report was submitted to the higher echelons.

Aneksi was never, officially, seen again. Her tactics changed, her DNA changed, yet the World Gov still suffered. It was as if direct access had been given to the World Gov logistics mainframe and now problems simply occurred due to their own incompetence. Above all, Aneksi loved life and had decided she would not lose any more friends. Trent was in no doubt who masterminded the change in sabotage from external to internal attacks.

She was still on the top ten fugitives list, though most believed she was now dead. The official line was, they suspected she was being shielded by someone within their own organisation.

They didn't know whether to execute Trent for failing to capture her or decorate him for ending her reign of terror.

Only Trent and Aneksi knew what had transpired in that building. What was said and what was promised to change both of their lives, would remain a secret.

"You're free and clear," he looked into her eyes with genuine warmth. "Do me a favour and keep it that way." She threw him an innocent look, and made herself look small and harmless, but he knew better and laughed at her posturing.

The pod drew to a halt and the doors opened onto a concourse populated with armed security. The five men left without a word and Aneksi watched them go.

"Morning, sir," Liza greeted him at the door as he entered the security reception. It was a clean white space with a couple of holograms populating the corners with potted plants. Supportive messages were arranged around the empty seating area reserved for those wishing to report or complain about someone or something on their mind.

Trent admired the artwork as a poster displaying an image of a safe, with the word's 'Keep it Locked', was replaced by another showing two smiling moon-base security personnel, happily playing volleyball with a family in typical propaganda style. It declared, 'Remember! We are not World Gov.' He particularly liked that one.

He nodded to two guards over by the back wall, playing the old chess game he'd presented to Liza as a joke.

"Don't tell me. You actually wrote it into the procedure?"

"Certainly." No judgement, no sarcasm, just a simple response.

Trent valued strategic thinking and tactical solutions and when he appointed Liza, he'd suggested she write a training procedure to include learning to play chess, as a joke.

Three weeks ago, they were discussing station procedures and he alluded to the chess set as a possible inclusion in the list of casino games, just to lighten the meeting. A day later the security training procedure had been sent to him with a note explaining why the set was unavailable to the casino. He felt lifted by the memory; he'd thought it was Liza, just carrying on the light hearted banter.

"He's in room three." His chief security officer led the way down the side corridor to the interview rooms.

"Definitely human?" he asked. She nodded in reply.

"Do you want 'full' recording compliance?" She carefully offered the alternative. Handing him her tablet, he read her report containing all the facts they'd elicited so far. Liza stared hard at him.

He knew she was asking if he wanted the whole thing officially recorded or the opportunity to use 'other methods', but this was part of the game and he saw no harm in demonstrating his skills to anyone willing to sit through the hours of banal interviews.

"No. I want standard procedures for this one," he nodded his thanks and turned to his bodyguards. "You can watch in there or you can go and get a coffee." He offered his protection squad a break.

Entering the interview room alone, Trent saw the aura of sadness, frustration and failure; occasionally, a flare of blue would ignite, but then be instantly absorbed into the introverted browns of dismay and sadness. The prisoner, handcuffed to the table, seemed to hate himself. He'd seen it before; it was common when someone knew they were guilty.

"It says here... you call yourself 'Melo', short for Tumelo," Trent began. The tablet provided suggestions regarding the criminal's behaviour, origin and history. It was supposed to assist in directing and misdirecting the conversation. "Says here, it means you have faith. Who do you have faith in, Melo?" Trent didn't expect a response and moved around the table staring at the information in his hands.

"Interesting!" He seated himself opposite the self-effacing Melo. "You're not the Rover pilot, so I assume you're the handler." Trent could see the confusion on the prisoner's face. "Someone had to keep an eye on all of those clones, maybe correct their behaviour, clarify their orders. Was that you, Melo?" Still no response, no shock at the revelation of the clones, or maybe his lack of response was due to his absolute faith in Gen'eer.

"My brothers and I were invited to see the Power Reactor. We hired the Rover and..." The defence had been learned by rote, spoken haltingly, as though read from a creased postcard in obscure handwriting.

"Your brothers are not brothers; they are machines made of meat and synthetic fibres. They are not alive..." Trent saw the man's face open in disbelief; he really didn't know they were clones. "...and handling clones is an offence punishable by death." Trent noted the quick change in Melo's aura, brown sadness gave way to red as the fear erupted.

"I didn't know! They are my brothers; we work and worship together." Melo's confusion and fear were increasing, his aura was slowly turning blue. "It is a lie!" he declared, turning his anger upon Trent.

Trent dropped the tablet on the table in front of Tumelo, showing the scans of his comrades, for all the good it did. Melo didn't comprehend the medical jargon, but understood the word 'clone' emblazoned across the images of his brothers.

"Purpose?" shouted Trent, rising quickly from his seat. "Why were you there?"

"My lord... suggested we go sightseeing." Melo, once again sounded as though he was reciting his lines. He bowed his head and whispered, "My Lord will save me. I have faith." Melo closed down.

"Your 'lord' offered to buy my silence," Trent was quiet, but assertive. "Your lord offered me the whole of Kenya as a price worth paying." Trent retrieved the tablet and vigorously jabbed the screen. A holographic projection appeared in front of Melo, as Trent replayed their drunken bargaining the night before.

"No, it is a trick!" declared Melo.

"No, it is a recording," Trent replied calmly.

Reluctantly, Melo listened to the conversation, watching the two men drink together. He heard Trent refer to his Lord as Gen'eer, his friendship name forbidden to his followers, yet the Lord did not complain. Finally, he heard the words that destroyed his faith, *"People shmeeple,"* he heard his Lord discount his followers as merely a tradable commodity; *"There's people everywhere. Admittedly, not as many as there used to be, but plenty for you."*

"Enough for my own army?" Trent asked.

"Yeah, but they're rubbish for soldiers. What you really need are clones..." Trent froze the image.

"And now you are expected to die for your lord, to keep his dirty secret." An overtone of ridicule was clear in Trent's voice. He picked up the tablet, casting an enlarged holographic image of Gen'eer in front of Melo and studied the broken man. "Tell me Tumelo, where is your faith now?"

Trent vacated the room leaving Melo staring in dismay and disgust at his lord's visage floating just above the table. He tossed the tablet to Liza.

"You've torn away his anchor," she observed.

"Let him think for a while then hit him with a meal, whatever he wants. Then approach him gently." Trent felt emotionally drained. He'd dismantled the man's belief system; he'd exposed his lord for the conniving scum he really was. Then he'd declared a whole country of his brothers was not enough to corrupt his own honour. Tumelo would be re-evaluating his principles and Trent was hoping that rather than destroying his faith, he had offered him a way to redirect his allegiance, giving him a chance to find someone else, someone 'worthy' with whom to pledge his honour.

Liza made some notes on her tablet and looked up, trying to read her boss. "What next?" she asked.

Trent knew what he had to do, "Garvy," he said. "Do you mind if I use your office?" He turned to enter the room and stepped forward. A sudden blow impacted his head and he fell heavily to his right knocking over a chair. He heard Liza scream a warning and felt a weight impact his lower legs. She saw him recoil from the blow and reacted immediately.

Liza launched herself towards him, calling on the enhanced strength of her suit. Her shoulder collided with his hips as he folded, pushing him from further danger and drawing her gun as she moved. Diving into the room, she discharged her needle gun into the leg of the assassin hiding just inside the doorway. Not knowing who else could be in there, she'd thrown herself at Trent to force him beyond the immediate danger, pushing him closer to her desk for cover.

The assassin was down on one knee, one leg immobilised by Liza's well aimed shot. The assailant's force shield helmet was in place and coloured a deep blue, making it impossible to identify the attacker, but Liza's anger grew as she recognised the blue security armour. She didn't care about an identity; it was one of her own. Her anger turned to fear as she noticed the shining sphere in the attacker's hand, one of Martin's new grenades.

She raised her gun for a second shot, but her momentum and the collision with Trent had forced her away from the perpetrator and the shot, though on target, was ineffective at range against the rogue security guard's standard issue armour.

Now was the time to answer that question that had plagued her since she joined Security; could she willingly sacrifice her life for someone else? Time seemed to slow as the assassin's hand drew back to launch the grenade. She pulled her legs beneath her and coiled ready to spring into the path of the deadly object.

A red-suited blur appeared, charging through the doorway, bearing down upon the assassin. His high velocity, pushing their combined mass violently to the floor and knocking loose the grenade to roll harmlessly across the floor.

Another blue-suited guard appeared in the doorway, deep blue helmet raised and gun in hand. Liza saw the threat and brought her gun to bear, though at this range her plasma needle gun would be next to useless. The new arrival assessed Trent's condition and saw her intention immediately. He stepped into the room, knelt down and calmly placed his gun against the piping of the struggling assassin's armour, firing once into the shoulder piping of the pinned would-be murderer. Instantly, as the control circuits were damaged the helmet retracted, revealing the snarling face of young Largo.

Standing over the would-be murderer, the new arrival retracted his helmet and Liza relaxed, recognising officer Singh. The red-suited World Gov bodyguard rolled off his prey, reassured by Singh's needle gun hovering above Largo's unprotected face.

"You fools!" Largo yelled. "Someone's going to kill him. We could've been rich!" His words were cut short as Martin appeared in the office doorway and motioned Singh to stand back. The gun was withdrawn from the young guard's face and the captain discharged his net. Largo screamed as the inserted needles designed to pierce and disable an active suit, penetrated both his unresisting inactive armour and in some places his exposed face, before delivering a disruptive electric shock.

Liza looked at her fellow captain disapprovingly. The defeated inept assassin lay still.

"Whoops?" he grinned childishly.

Trent retracted his helmet, picked himself up off the floor and held out his hand to Liza. Helping her to her feet, he nodded his thanks.

"I daresay there'll be a few more of those." He moved to the desk and sat down in Liza's padded chair.

"Are you hurt?" Liza ran through the incident procedure in her head.

"I'm fine. Luckily, I got my helmet in place before he shot me," he grinned sheepishly and rubbed his head for emphasis. "Figured I'd need a bit more defence today." He tapped his grey suit.

Martin and the red-suited bodyguard lifted the now immobile Largo and took him from the office. They dropped him in the security hall with a thud and kicked the assailant with contempt. Other officers had run forward on hearing the commotion and looked on with expressions of disgust and anger at Largo's betrayal. His limp body was dragged unceremoniously through the security reception to his cell and caged.

"Put him in isolation. He was one of us." Martin spat the words in disgust.

Singh retrieved the grenade and placed it gently in front of Trent who stared at the lethal device.

"Wrong hands already!" the guard observed casually and walked from the office.

"Close the door Liza," requested Trent. The other bodyguards who'd rushed to the scene too late to be of use, hovered around the doorway. "You lot stay there, and thank you Officer Singh," he shouted as the door closed. Liza righted the upturned chair and sat in front of the desk.

"Largo was..." Liza began to apologise.

"...young and inexperienced. You can't instil loyalty overnight. How long has he been with us?"

"Two weeks." She seemed to want to take the blame for his actions, but Trent was not having any of it.

"The lad thought he could turn a quick profit. He hasn't worked anywhere else before coming here; he's spent his life fighting to survive below. Sadly, he's a pack animal; he thought you'd all jump at the chance to share in the spoils; it's the nature of those accustomed to deprivation." Trent lent back in the chair. "I hired him; I took the chance. The lad had nothing but good intentions when he came to my attention. You can't blame anyone for wanting to survive. We'll ship him back when all this is over."

Trent sat motionless with his eyes closed, he was silently running a diagnostic on his suit. The figures flashed onto his retina; power use, response time, angle of attack, distance and speed of approaching weapon.

Part of his recent tinkering had included an automatic trigger to raise his helmet on the approach of any weapon beyond a certain speed and size. He'd limited the scan to the 180 degrees behind his head, figuring his own senses would detect anything coming from the front, which meant the detector worked twice as fast. The helmet shield had raised twelve milliseconds prior to impact, too close for comfort. He made a quick mental note to calculate the power drain if he increased the scan distance to raise the helmet sooner.

Satisfied with the defensive performance of his suit he opened his eyes and refocused his attention on Liza.

"We stop Garvy, now!" he declared. He sounded determined, "But first..." his tone became even, "...any chance of a coffee?"

Liza used her comms and ordered a coffee while Trent began accessing her desk computer. He cleared an open space and typed like a demon upon his personal custom keyboard he'd called up as a hologram and overlayed on her desk. Occasionally, he closed his eyes to access his inbuilt cybernetic connections to his personal database. As the coffee began to grow cold, he stopped and exclaimed, "There!" with a huge smile.

"Would you like to listen in?" Trent felt it only right to include the patient Security Chief in his plan.

Once more, using his cybernetic control, he patched Liza into his call and selected Garvy's personal comms, voice only. Touching his ear out of habit, he activated his comms and contacted his enemy.

"Mister Garvy, I understand you wish to see me," Trent opened the conversation lightly.

"I've got nothing to say to you, Trent." He spat the name. "You've victimised me and my men since we arrived." Garvy sounded angry, but Trent knew the man was simply scheming.

"I understand you have employed the services of certain trades-people, Mr Garvy. I have one such soul here, right now. Would you like to speak to him?" Trent maintained his cool composure.

"I don't know what you mean, Trent. I want my men released, now!" Garvy had a leer on his face and it was plain to hear in his voice.

"Sadly, I have witnesses and confessions. Both of your men are being prepared for return to Earth on charges of murder." Trent fleetingly saw the body of Belle in his mind and his self-control almost deserted him. "No doubt they will die... honourably," he laughed at the jibe.

"You're dead, Trent!" cursed Garvy. "I have specialists..."

"I too have specialists, Garvy," the anger was clear in Trent's voice. "Tell me, how will you pay the bounty Garvy? I've already closed down access to your funds. On Earth, World Gov have frozen your assets. You are wanted for conspiracy to commit murder and are accused of complicity in the murder of an innocent croupier. You've been named as the architect of the crime by the person who confessed to pulling the trigger. You've literally got nowhere to go, and nothing to spend Garvy." Trent waited silently.

"What do you want, Trent?" Garvy asked, but he was not defeated, only interested in the deal he could be offered.

"We meet, you and me, face to face... for a chat. After all, these comms are so easy to intercept; anyone could hear what we say."

"And if I don't agree?" Garvy was almost laughing; he'd secured his distraction. He'd be wearing his suit, so he'd be fine and he'd have Carney close by. He could be running the show by tonight. Even if it all went wrong, they'd only take him back to Earth for trial and he had friends in very high places.

"Well, one good threat deserves another, Garvy." Trent's voice was far from threatening, almost jolly. "Within an hour your specialist companion, Carney, will be dead. Ten minutes after that, you'll join her." He actually chuckled.

"Very well Trent, somewhere I can see you coming. I'll meet you in the Flight Dome in one hour. Alone!" That'll give a few more would-be assassins time for a crack at him, he thought. Who knows, they might get lucky.

"Agreed." Trent cut comms and looked at Liza's reaction. She was remarkably calm. "Not too much?" he asked.

"No, you dealt with him on his level. Good work, Sir. Only..." she looked pensive.

"What?" he was eager to know what he'd overlooked.

"It's just that you now have an hour to kill, or rather be killed," she tilted her head and looked like she was reading his mind.

"No, I've thought of that, listen." Trent closed his eyes and using his cybernetic connection he edited sections of the call to Garvy. Over the full complex an edited version of the call was broadcast.

"I want my men released, now!" Garvy's voice arrogantly demanded.

"I have witnesses and confessions. Both of your men are being prepared for return to Earth on charges of murder. No doubt they will die honourably."

"You're dead, Trent!" cursed Garvy. *"I have specialists..."*

"I too have specialists. Tell me, how will you pay the bounty, Garvy? I've already frozen your assets, closed down access to your funds. You're wanted for conspiracy to commit murder and are accused of complicity in the murder of an innocent croupier. You've been named by the person who confessed to pulling the trigger. You've literally got nowhere to go, and nothing to spend, Garvy."

The call was broadcast as an information media piece over all of the channels in the complex, available in all languages.

"What do you think?" Trent enjoyed the response as Liza's face broke into a rare smile.

"Nice," she nodded in appreciation. "No-one's going to risk their lives if they can't guarantee a payday."

"Repeat it every ten minutes," instructed Trent, "but don't relax. There's always some idiot out there who thinks they can get rich quick."

The next call was expected and as hard as he thought it would be. Jan called and expressed her concern in terms that were a little too personal and made him blush.

"...and you know it's a trap, yet you're still going alone?" she calmed down enough to challenge his choice of action.

"Logic dictates he'll know, I'll know, it's a trap. He'll have Carney somewhere, stashed en-route, hoping she'll find her mark before I turn up. Liza's got squads everywhere and I've got two huge babysitters who make excellent shields." He didn't mention the few additional tricks recently added to his suit. He didn't want her to think he was boasting.

"It's not a good idea. Why not just send Liza in with a squad and arrest him?" she appealed for common sense.

"I know him. He'll have somewhere wired to blow, as a token of his chaotic intent, if I don't show up. He's an egotist. He's more likely to commit an atrocity if he feels insulted, than if he's attacked man to man."

"And is that you're plan?" she sounded worried.

"Maybe, but less said the better." The conversation was starting to feel morose and Trent needed to keep sharp. "I need you to be at your best in the next hour." he derided his own comment, laughing at the concept; Jan was always at her best, "We think this charade is a distraction for something Garvy's planning, so I need all eyes and ears on access points to every area of the base. The Casino vaults have accrued a fair bit of wealth, but I don't think that data bank will be his target. He's after something he can sell, preferably to multiple bidders. He mentioned the Fusion project and he lit up when we discussed the 'Worm'." Trent remembered the greed which blazed through Garvy's aura as the items had been mentioned, these would both be prime targets.

"I'll shutdown surface traffic and raise all weapons," she offered.

"Good, but keep everything normal within view of the Flight Dome. I don't want him spooked by a dozen laser canons rising from the ground." Trent knew it was time to go, but felt reluctant to end his call with Jan. "How's the power level?" he asked inanely.

"All topped up," she sighed, relaxing at their return to familiar procedural-talk, "everything nominal. Storage fully charged; despite all those cages you've got running." She gave him a mock telling off.

"Have you ever tried removing a suit from a six-and-a-half-foot angry clone, enhanced for strength?" he defended his security staff and trivialised her concern. Out of a sense of longing, and maybe a foreboding of the trial to come, he finished, "Watch those dials. Take care!" and ended the call.

"Love you too, you hopeless...," she quietly replied to the empty comms line.

15: Attack

Carney took another swig from her shot glass and pushed it away across the bar. Her guard had followed her from her apartment, sitting at the back of the room. She knew all eyes were on her, but she'd committed no crime and was confident in her ability to handle anyone who arrived to detain her. She had a job to do and as far as she was concerned, it was about time.

"Good afternoon," a smooth voice interrupted her mental preparation. "May I buy you one for the road?" Carney was angry at the interruption, but try as she might, she couldn't bring her full anger to bear upon the well-mannered confident voice beside her. "My name's Cole, lovely to meet you, miss...?"

"You know who I am or you wouldn't be sat there," she countered.

"Ah well, as a lonely man I try to meet all the attractive people I can," he laughed with genuine warmth. Carney turned to face him, looking over this strange man, brimming with confidence. In turn Cole turned to the bar and ordered two brandies.

"Not for me," Carney overruled the order. "Sorry," she apologised sarcastically, "I'm working."

"I understood you were unemployed," Cole pushed the wrong button and Carney moved like lightning, twisting his outstretched hand up behind his shoulder.

"Some of us, Doctor," she spat his title, "are self-employed. We value customer loyalty," she gave his wrist a vicious twist and released him.

"A shame," he sipped his drink, gently shaking the abused hand. "I thought I could persuade you to take a contract from myself." She studied his eyes noticing the intensity of his manner as he addressed her. It was as if he was trying to cast a spell on her. This strange man piqued her interest.

"I can't see our goals aligning," she began quietly, regaining her stool at the bar.

"I assure you; payment is both lucrative and guaranteed," he sipped his brandy.

"Sometimes, what's important is the service, not the reward."

"Very altruistic, I'm impressed, but I assure you Miss Carney, our interests definitely align... today." He looked deeply into his glass, "How about a soft fruit drink?"

***

Garvy positioned himself at the apex of the dome on the Upper Flight platform. Suspended from the five-hundred-meter-high structure, the Upper Flight platform was the main launching position for Zero-G acrobatics performed by the demonstrators and aerial performers throughout the evening shows. During public access sessions, it was the place amateur flyers aspired to reach under their own power.

Halfway down the sides of the dome, several viewing platforms were mounted close to the plentiful windows, allowing groups to meet up and enjoy the lunar views outside; both ladders and elevators were available to access these from the Lower Parade. The majority of visitors remained close to the wide circular platform housing bars and restaurants, raised a mere four metres above the gravitic plates that comprised the structure's floor.

Garvy knew the complete elimination of gravity by the adjustment of the redesigned plates had been Trent's main contribution to the design of the complex; after all, the basic structure had been in place for over a hundred years. Someone had told him that Trent also had a hand in the nano-shield technology, though Garvy found it difficult to ratify that level of engineering ability with the politically immature poseur he'd played cards with.

He hugged his uniquely powerful gun close to his body as he scoured the Flight Dome for signs of his men. Ineffective at long range, his gun was custom built and best described as a plasma needle blunderbuss, effectively a single shot weapon due to the power needed to charge it. Garvy had smuggled it in, piecemeal and assembled it himself; he liked it; close up, it made a mess.

His men had made a good job of clearing out the few holidaymakers and were now taking cover behind upturned chairs and tables on the Lower Parade either side of the dome entrance from the main complex. He didn't want any mistakes, or witnesses.

"Carney, where are you?" he called frantically.

"Nearly there, relax." She noted the edge to her boss's voice, but knew it wouldn't affect his efficiency. Trent was just another obstacle he was determined to destroy. "Sorry about that..." She apologised to her new employer for the interruption.

***

"You'll be exposed in the airlock," Liza warned.

"I'll take down the video and interrupt the comms from outside." Trent thought for a moment, "I can shut down the warning sirens, but the internal lights will activate as I open the inner pressure door. I'll set the interruption to reset after five minutes. Within six you'll have your eyes and ears back." It sounded like a good plan, or at least part of a good plan. He could disrupt any signals that would warn Garvy of his approach from the lunar surface and possibly get into the dome unchallenged, but he still didn't know what Garvy had prepared for him once he got into the Flight Dome.

"Here, take these," Liza passed him armour plates for his suit. He accepted the blue leg plates and clipped them on, but his waistcoat was several times more effective than what she'd offered and he refused the upper body armour, "I need to be mobile," he explained, refusing the chest armour.

Liza watched in dismay as he discarded the upper armour. He twisted and patted his limbs and body checking he had everything fixed in place and she shook her head disparagingly at the ungainly figure, "Quite a fashion statement! Come on."

She led the way to the airlock and used her key to open the inner door.

"I'll cycle it from inside," he told her. If this went wrong, he didn't want Aneksi blaming Liza for sending him outside.

He knew that Carney would probably be lying in wait, to take her shot as he approached the dome and between them Liza and he could think of no fool proof way to avoid her. If she missed her mark, her shot could compromise the safety of the complex, putting hundreds of lives at risk. His final desperate solution was to remove that possibility by entering the Flight Dome from outside. Once inside, the dome could be isolated from the rest of the base.

Jan was watching the Flight Dome interior through the security cameras. The screens floated silently above her desk in the Power Complex. She saw Garvy and his men settle into their ambush positions and called Trent to warn him.

The images flickered and turned to black. The comms went dead.

Beneath the black empty sky, Trent closed the airlock hatch and took his bearings. The sudden change to one sixth gravity took a little getting used to, but he'd spent a lot of time on the surface and his experience quickly came to the fore. He skipped effortlessly across the lunar dust and headed toward a pylon close to the Flight Dome. On the external junction box mounted at its base, he opened the hatch and fed in the serial numbers sent by Liza, which automatically appeared on his head-up-display. The override of the audio-video surveillance within the dome was completed without a hitch. Finally, he accessed the sensors and using his cybernetics he instructed the main system to place all non-emergency signals into 'Test mode' for five minutes.

***

"Mike, take two and get to the Flight Dome, Trent's being ambushed." Jan called on her friend and long-suffering lieutenant.

"It'll take us fifteen minutes to get there," Mike argued. "Can't you call Security?" he suggested. He was sat at his desk busy planning the next month's maintenance schedule for the three power systems, not an easy job.

"Comms are down." Jan knew her men would never get there in time. "Go anyway, please." She rarely pleaded and Mike could see the concern on her face. "Once the Rover's outside, try all comm channels to warn him."

Mike nodded to two of the men in the office, who'd been listening to their conversation and they all ran out.

"Keep trying," Jan shouted as they left.

It seemed only the audio-video surveillance around the Flight Dome was affected, the rest of the complex was okay. Surely someone will notice the comms are down, she told herself.

***

Aneksi and Jack were talking quietly at the end of the bar, watching Cole and Carney getting cosy.

"He's hiring her," announced Aneksi, who's hearing was acute.

"I didn't think she did that," commented Jack with a lascivious grin.

"Not that," Aneksi slapped him. "He wants an assassin."

"Who for?" asked Jack intrigued.

"It's got to be Trent. I never trusted that smarmy, gentleman act." She grabbed Jack's arm, "Come on let's follow her."

They acted nonchalantly, as Cole and Carney rose and parted ways. Over her shoulder Carney carried a shaped pack which blended into her suit, but Aneksi could distinguish its presence and make an intelligent guess as to its contents.

Garvy's pet assassin walked to the west Khonsu exit, past a group of irate guests who'd been 'so rudely' moved on from the Flight Dome by Garvy's men. Cole took a seat at the roulette table and began talking to the other punters and placing bets, one of whom was a blue suited security guard; Carney's shadow.

As Aneksi and Jack reached the gathering of offended guests, one of them tapped Jack on the arm and began to rant.

"I've never been so rudely treated," complained a corpulent woman.

"My wife and I have been ejected from our reserved lesson in the Flight Dome," explained her partner.

"Young Man! I demand you sort this out," the lady wanted no excuses and had grabbed onto Jack's wrist preventing him from moving away. Aneksi sidestepped and continued her pursuit of Carney. Jack watched her turn the corner into the storage halls between the Casino and the Flight Dome.

"I'm sorry," Jack had to yell above the four other voices that had joined the mass complaint, "I don't work here. There's the desk," he pointed to a sign which read 'Khonsu Reception'. "Tell them!" he shouted into the face of the woman who held him, but she didn't let go, instead she yelled at him in earnest.

"I've seen you, you dealt me blackjack last night, you're Jack." She defended her right to be his superior, unaware Jack had much more pressing concerns. Her grip tightened and she began shaking his wrist to emphasise her words. She would be heard.

He grabbed her hand from his pained wrist and roughly forced her vice-like grip open.

"I quit!" he shouted, as the lady screamed dramatically at the effrontery. How dare he overpower her hand. She shouted for security, screaming she'd been attacked, though none of the guests with her offered to help. Jack pushed past her embarrassed partner, and ran to the storage halls.

Carney had ascended a tall column of crates and settled herself into position. The mutated bitch had followed her, but she was ready. With a swift flick of her right leg the heavy crate beside her, stored in the gravity reduced column, moved easily and toppled. The upper crate left the boundary of the gravitic storage plate beneath as it tilted sideways. Its full weight impacted upon Aneksi as it silently fell.

"Carney, where are you?" Garvy called. He sounded panicked, but Carney knew him, he was just excited. Like a boy in a candy store, he was expecting to be given a treat.

"I'm waiting... patiently. I suggest you do the same. He'll be here soon," she responded, while climbing down the crates. She noted Aneksi's motionless body. It would be prudent to finish this one off now, she thought.

Jack ran into the storage hall, shocked at the sight that greeted him. Aneksi was beneath a deformed crate, easily as tall as he was and Carney was stood beside her, needle gun in hand, pointing at her unprotected head. Jack ran as fast as he could and made the emotional mistake of yelling, "Aneksi!" alerting Carney to his approach.

The assassin stepped smartly to the side, away from the crate, into the middle of the wide storage hall, gymnastically twisting she fell to one knee, lining up her shot to take out Jack's leg when he ran into range. "Come on, hero," she taunted.

Carney's world exploded. The crate which had been crushing Aneksi, impacted her side with such force it shattered. Her gun discharged harmlessly while bottles of water skittered all over the floor free from their containment. The heavy crate, chosen for its incapacitating momentum by Carney, had been launched across three metres of intervening space by an angry Aneksi.

Before the last splinters of the crate had hit the floor Aneksi was on her prey, the needle gun swatted from Carney's hand. The assassin's helmet had raised, too late to prevent her skin being grazed by the initial impact of the shattered synthetic shards.

The impact from the crate stunned the assassin, knocking her to the floor. She was dazed and confused by the sharp pain from her face and the pounding weight on her body.

Aneksi stopped punching, realising the suit was absorbing her anger and grabbed the suit piping across Carney's neckline, somersaulting from her victim. There was a loud crack as the alloy reinforced control piping split under the tremendous force of Aneksi's move. Carney flinched as her helmet disappeared and rolled to her feet in one quick motion. Her damaged suit could not enhance her speed, but she was still fast and agile without it.

"Poor little assassin," Aneksi, crouched a few metres from Carney. Her eyes green narrow slits, betraying her hatred; she taunted her opponent.

"I hate doing freebies," Carney cursed, distracted by Jack sobbing painfully, "but I've been paid well for you, bitch." She stepped back from Aneksi and glanced over at Jack.

He was bleeding, caught by shrapnel from the crate. He'd staggered and then stood on a liberated bottle as it rolled towards him, hitting the ground awkwardly. He was sat across the hall, twelve metres away, nursing a painful disjointed knee.

Assessing him as no threat, Carney pulled on her integrated backpack strap, sliding the pack to the front of her suit. The backpack settled into position. Garvy's hired-gun cart-wheeled into a well-practised gymnastic move, to dodge and simultaneously withdraw her favourite customised gun.

The assassin's hand entered her pack mid-rotation and Aneksi leapt, twisting in mid-air. She impacted Carney lightly, but her additional momentum caused the smooth cart-wheel to collapse. Aneksi impacted with her right hand on Carney's shoulder, the claws from her fingers extended. Passing easily through the damaged suit fabric and unyielding flesh, the other gripping the hand, now struggling to withdraw the holstered weapon.

Carney screamed in agony, no longer able to move her right arm as the shoulder shattered and the muscles were shredded.

When it came to bullish strength Aneksi was in a league of her own. Her modified bones and muscles throughout her body gave her excessive flexibility and compressive strength.

Carney screamed a second time as the bones in her hand were crushed against her own gun. The assassin's bones splintered under Aneksi's grip.

The two entwined women came to rest with Carney on her back, lying on the cold floor. Aneksi released her hold and adjusted her position, comfortably crouching on top of her prey. She grinned showing her sharp teeth and moved her head forward, nose to nose with Carney. The pained defiant assassin now unable to outstare the wide slit green eyes.

"Mutant Bitch!" she spat.

Aneksi responded by revealing her final gift. She placed her hand upon Carney's left shoulder, and slowly five sharp claws extended from her fingers, piercing the ruined suit like wet paper, proceeding slowly into the assassin's flesh.

Carney tried to prevent a third scream, but failed.

"Shush! Little one," Aneksi began stroking Carney's hair, playing with her immobile captive. "I prefer

'Marvellous Molly' or maybe even 'Devilish Dam'," she crooned, quoting from some of her publicity posters.

***

The yellow lights spun, illuminating the interior of the Flight Dome as the internal airlock door was opened. Trent stepped through; his helmet raised. Steadily he walked across the gravity reducing plates, to the centre of the dome.

"I'm here Garvy!" His suit thermal detectors highlighted the two hidden thugs as they twisted to face the threat approaching from the wrong side of their prepared positions.

"Up here, Trent. Why not come and join me?" Garvy teased. He was in no hurry to cut down Trent, he needed the distraction. Right now, a group of his men were ransacking the Cold Fusion labs, making him a very rich man. More importantly, he desired Trent's suffering. He patted the long instrument at his thigh, his favourite laser blade. Today, he'd remind everyone why he was called 'The Butcher'.

From across the dome there was a loud crash and the sound of a shot being fired. Two of Garvy's men stationed outside the Flight Dome entrance, sealed the main airlock doors and ran to investigate, leaving Trent locked in the dome with the three gangsters.

"Shall we await their return?" asked Garvy. "They'll be unhappy if we start without them." He laughed, convinced he had everything under control with the odds in his favour.

"Where's the action, Garvy?" Trent yelled as he walked slowly to the centre of the circular floor. Though his soles were magnetised, it was prudent to maintain as much contact with the plates as possible when he moved.

"Which innocents die next to satisfy your greed?" Trent engaged Garvy with the aim of eliciting any information he could. "We have everywhere covered, Garvy. Give up now!"

"Gentlemen," Garvy addressed his men. "Would you care to begin."

The two henchmen raised themselves above their barricades and began shooting. Trent had walked across the dome floor to less than a hundred metres from the thugs, but as the gangsters opened fire he simply stood still, allowing the old slug chuckers to impact and charge his suit. The trek across the lunar surface had diminished his power a little more than he'd anticipated and he was smiling as the crass actions of the henchman helped him regain his strength. Despite not moving, not every bullet hit him and he ignored those that did, looking up, keeping his eyes firmly on Garvy.

The problem with Zero-G was the inability to change direction once you launched yourself, until of course, you impacted something else. Once you'd set off you were a predictable target until you landed.

The loser in any Zero-G conflict was usually the person who moved first. Of course, the use of wing-suits and artificial air currents would allow slow alteration of direction, but they couldn't provide the agility needed to avoid a speeding attacker.

Garvy stood up on the platform in full view, "No weapons, Mr Trent?" he laughed. "Gentleman, would you be so kind as to use the other weapon I gave you."

Trent observed as the two henchmen discarded their old ballistic rifles and raised what looked like highly polished tubes. Trent recognised them as plasma grenade launchers. "Don't be a fool Garvy!" he called.

"Scared, Trent?" The Butcher sneered.

"They'll go through the walls, you idiot. Sudden decompression of the dome will collapse it." The men stepped in front of their barricades closing their distance by a few metres, as if that would help their accuracy. They joined their boss in jeering at the hapless Trent.

"Time for Plan B then," Garvy announced. "Helmets, gentleman!" Garvy activated a pocket-sized hand-held device and red and yellow lights flashed around the structure. No sirens sounded as Trent's hack had yet to reset, but it was obvious to Trent, Garvy was pumping the air out of the Flight Dome back into the base oxygen tanks. At least he'd had the sense not to lose it to space.

"A valuable commodity, Mr Trent, I wouldn't want to waste it," announced Garvy, as if reading his mind.

"What do you hope to achieve, Garvy?" Trent slowly turned to watch each of the men and then looked up to Garvy again. Each step took him closer to the Main Complex entrance doors. He knew they wouldn't risk puncturing the bulkhead between the Flight Dome and the Main Complex. Trent's currently magnetised soles kept him firmly in contact with the gravity plates as he twisted, making overt moves as though he was nervously watching both henchmen.

"Stop right there, Trent." Garvy now held a launcher too. "I see your pathetic plan. If you get too close to that door my men will enter and blast you from the airlock."

Trent couldn't see any men through the thick observation ports of the main airlock door, but he could see blue plasma flashes illuminating the storage hall beyond.

***

"Watch out!" the warning from Jack was sudden, and Aneksi's current state of excitement lent urgency to her response. Leaping from the recumbent Carney, she snatched the pistol from the assassin's useless hand and bounded to the top of the crates on her left.

One of Garvy's men had rounded the corner and identified the boss's favourite being pinned to the floor. He aimed his slug-chucker and opened fire. Aneksi cleared the space above Carney with a whisker to spare while Carney's damaged suit failed to stop two of the slugs painfully penetrating her leg. She felt the blood pooling in her armour and screamed in agony, swearing at the man who'd fired.

"Idiot! Her, not me! Shoot the cat bitch," she yelled and cursed the man's inept aim.

Aneksi leapt to the column of crates gracefully, but as she reached the low gravity storage area, she shot up into the roof space of the building in a flash.

The jumble of ventilators, cooling boxes, support beams and lighting provided a wealth of cover for her, prowling above the heads of Garvy's henchmen.

A second mobster ran into the hall from the Flight Dome airlock. He saw Jack and withdrew his needle gun. Despite Jack's pathetic cry as his suit was damaged and his helmet dropped, the gangster began pummelling what he perceived to be the enemy. Jack tried to hold his hands in front of his face, but the beating was brutal.

The mobster who'd accidentally shot Carney, ran forward to check on his injured comrade, receiving a swift kick from her good leg and an earful of obscenities for his concern. Falling to her left the man never moved again.

Carney spat the spray from her mouth as the man's brains erupted.

Aneksi had aimed and shot Carney's weapon expecting a stun bolt or an electro pellet to incapacitate the suit of the man attending his fallen compatriot below, but this was Carney's favoured weapon. What was launched was a unique shell which, upon firing, was programmed by intricate sighting circuitry. The overlarge shell dispensed a focussed plasma pulse within a finger's width of reaching its target. Aneksi had aimed for the man's head and her aim was true. The raised helmet remained in place long enough to retain most of the liquefied contents of the man's exploded skull, until his corrupted body seeped out, flowing slowly across the floor.

Carney had witnessed the carnage through her sights many times before, but never up close. The destruction fascinated her. Her weapon was a vicious hybrid of lethal technologies and as far as she knew, it was the only one of its kind.

Aneksi was shocked by the destructive power of the weapon, surprised by the man collapsing from a single shot, but she was already moving, seeking cover from the second guard who'd finished clubbing Jack into insensibility for daring to shout a warning. He had raised his helmet and now held a long plasma launcher in his hands, seeking his target in the roof space.

"Don't be stupid," Carney yelled, but her voice was little more than an angry whisper. "Shoot that and we'll all die."

It took a moment for the confused henchman to get the message, and seconds later he dropped the plasma launcher and hefted his oversized slug-chucker back into his hands.

Carney lay back, her head on the floor, feeling more pain than she'd ever experienced in her life. She whimpered in agony as she tried to move. Tired now by her exertions, blood loss and pain; she gave up.

"You need help?" shouted the henchmen, eager to help a woman he'd admired for years.

Carney didn't respond. Looking around and especially watching the roof space above, the henchman slowly, nervously approached the downed assassin.

"Above you!" Carney weakly informed the man where the threat was. His immediate response was to turn and empty a clip of bullets into the rafters. The gun clicked; the ammunition gone. Discarding the slug chucker, he withdrew his only other weapon, the close-range plasma needle gun he'd used on Jack's suit.

"You'll never get... near enough," whispered Carney, as she lost her fight for consciousness.

A bottle bounced to his right and the thug shot blindly. Another exploded next to him as Aneksi manoeuvred for position. Two more shots followed in quick succession, from the panicked gangster.

Without a sound, Aneksi dropped silently behind him. He felt her shadow brush against his and responded instinctively by turning into her waiting arms. One hand swatted the gun from his hand, the other was a blur as claws extended, she ripped apart the control piping of the moon-base issued suit and viewed his surprise as the blue helmet visor evaporated. The hand that disarmed him now held him by the neck. Blood oozed from her grip as her extended claws penetrated deep. The petite entertainer slowly raised the huge mobster from the floor. In response he kicked and yelled at her, grabbing her arm and struggling for a full minute before he lost consciousness.

Casting aside his limp unconscious body and engaging the assisted speed of her now fully charged armour, she ran to Jack's side. Beaten and bloody, his face swollen she feared the worse; he was pale and barely conscious. Leaning close she heard him breathing evenly, feeling for a pulse, his heartbeat was strong; he'd recover. Aneksi looked at the long plasma weapon discarded by the henchman and on a whim, retrieved it as she ran to the airlock. Her only thought now, to save Trent.

***

"One more step, Trent, and I end you here." Garvy was worried. His men hadn't appeared from the airlock to box in their prey. If Trent made it to the inner door he'd have to be dragged back to the outer skin of the dome. Garvy doubted the accuracy of his men and even imagined Trent could possibly survive the plasma grenade, but he knew if his quarry was exploded out through the walls of the dome, they'd never find his body. It wouldn't matter how good his suit was. He'd hoped to cut him first, but he'd forego that luxury if need be.

Trent took one more step, he was still about ninety meters from the airlock of the main complex when the amber lights on the door lit to indicate the airlock was cycling. They were coming back!

Spurred on by his men arriving at last and angered by Trent's defiance, Garvy shot his plasma bolt. Trent heard the whine of the weapon as it energised its charge and dived to his right. Caught squarely in the grenade blast at a range of a meter from the impact zone any standard suit would have been ripped apart, but Trent had armour which was far from standard.

"Shields one and two ruptured," reported his suit diagnostics, "Shield three at thirty-four percent, armour intact." There was a slight pause as Trent twisted to a halt, getting his magnetised feet back under him. He saw the damage and estimated at least six gravity plates had been destroyed. "Twelve seconds to shield recharge."

"No!" He instructed. "Recharge shield two only." Trent needed his power for speed; he couldn't waste it on a redundant shield.

The henchmen had been shocked and disturbed by the sudden violence of the grenade attack from their boss, the glare and the concussive wave had forced them both to turn away. Trent pressed home his advantage and utilising the hidden propulsion in his suit accelerated across the Zero-G plates towards the attacker to his right. Employing all of his skill he skated inches above the gravitic plates using the built-in jets, resisting the urge to rise. Coiling into a tight ball, at the last moment he sprang into his target on the four-meter walkway above him. With a mighty swing of his right arm Trent dislodged the launcher from his assailant's grip and catching it with his modified left glove, he crushed the weapon beyond use. The gangster wasn't comfortable in the low gravity environment and flailed around trying to stand. Trent gave him a suit-enhanced punch and sent him flying to the outer wall of the dome. One left.

"Blast him! Blast him, now!" Garvy was yelling at his final henchmen. Trent noticed his arrested motion now outlined him against the bulkhead. He was exposed to the dome wall destruction Garvy considered acceptable, that would result in his violent expulsion into space.

The mobster responded to Garvy's excitement by edging closer to his target, making sure of the killing shot.

In the delay, Trent dropped himself down from the Lower Parade, back onto the floor plates. He was still in danger, but the further away he moved from the dome wall, the less likely he would go through it.

His best plan would be to use his magnetic jet assisted soles to leap away from the grenade as it was fired. He stood facing the weapon, about to play chicken with a plasma grenade when he was grabbed from behind by the gangster he'd just disarmed and thought he'd defeated. The suit proximity alarm warned him, but it was too late, he was focussed on the tube pointing directly at him.

Reluctant to shoot his own compatriot, the armed henchman impotently stared as the men wrestled.

"Kill him! Kill them! Kill them both!" yelled Garvy with glee, at the sight of Trent wrestling with the guard.

One lower arm was pinned by the gangster, unable to be moved and Trent's other upper arm was held tight against his own body. The gangster had a suit enhanced for strength while Trent's was designed for energy weapon defence, but he was still equipped with a basic tool pack. He reached his free lower left arm around behind him and grabbed onto the gangster. His hand became a vice and he issued the command to the suit to close fully. The gangster holding him screamed and adjusted his hold, now holding Trent's hand clamped to his leg. The vice closed tighter, but the gangster manoeuvred his hand into the grip and using his suits enhanced strength sought to prise the hand open.

Trent was stuck and Garvy was screaming for blood.

Relaxing his mind was a simple thing for Trent to achieve. Making choices under pressure was second nature to him. He felt the vice like grip on his assailants' leg weaking and knew he had to do something else to free himself. He activated the plasma welding torch on the back of his glove and imagined the hole appearing in the hand of the bellowing gangster, no longer restraining him.

Dropping to his knee he grabbed his needle gun from his thigh and blindly put two shots into the gangster's chest. As the man released his tenuous hold, a third, carefully aimed shot ruptured his assailant's control piping and his helmet disappeared. The explosive decompression of the exposed body, sucked into the airless low gravity vacuum, twisted the macabre cadaver and a slowly falling ribbon of blood, away from Trent.

Garvy saw the tussle between his man and Trent. He screamed for the other man to shoot them both, his anger and his excitement had peaked; he was ready. When the airlock door opened, he would leap from the flight platform to join his men in the melee. He would use his laser blade and show them why he was their leader. With a quiet escape of residual gases, the airlock opened.

Trent stared at the hesitant gangster holding the plasma launcher. He watched, his anger rising, his hate building. A second launcher appeared at the airlock, he was torn, which way to jump, who would fire first?

An explosion impacted Garvy's last armed henchman, as Trent struggled to maintain one eye on each lethal weapon. The gangster was blown across the dome, the gravitic plate beneath his feet buckled and his tubular weapon shattered. He wouldn't be dead, but he was definitely no longer an immediate threat.

"Garvy, you scum!" shouted Aneksi. She emerged from the airlock holding the discharged plasma launcher in her hands.

Trent was still struggling with understanding what had happened when static burst into his comms and the Flight Dome system rebooted. A siren wailed, detecting people in the evacuated airless dome.

Jan's voice yelled warnings at him about Garvy's ambush, while Mike, her maintenance manager, was trying desperately to contact him. Liza's voice interrupted with news of an attack on the Cold Fusion Labs and Martin was screaming about another unauthorised break-in at the Reactor Plant. In the last five minutes the moon had become a very interesting place.

Trent blinked; halfway up the Flight Dome, Aneksi was now crouching on the balustrade encompassing the viewing platform; on the other side of the same platform stood a nervous Garvy.

An angry roar over his comms signalled the speeding approach, of the henchman who'd taken the plasma hit from Aneksi. He'd decided his fight wasn't over. His aura was black; the man had lost control. Trent stood impassively, awaiting the berserker's attack. Struggling to run in the almost zero gravity, the man launched himself at Trent, armed with his needle gun pointing toward Trent's head; he flew toward his stationary target. Trent waited, then stepped smartly to the left to avoid the gravity free attack.

The henchman flailed, unaccustomed to the lack of purchase and control. A victim of his own inertia, he passed his target shooting wide.

Trent dropped slowly to his knee and shot a thumb-nail sized disc at the man's armour from a tube which emerged from his suit on the side of his right wrist.

The attacker's armour encased body came to attention; legs straight, arms pinned to the side of the body and the helmet faceplate turned black allowing no light to pass through. Trent's device took control.

The henchman drifted across the floor and bounced off the far wall.

Seven years ago, Trent had been alone guarding caged prisoners wearing stolen suits, out in the Badlands of what used to be France. Paris had been destroyed in the atomic onslaught years before, but the huge farmlands of the country could not be abandoned. There'd been resistance to the protective domes being erected over the country, in order to clean the soil and safeguard food production from the nuclear winter and even now, hundreds of years later there were still small-minded people willing to sabotage the domes that fed most of the world. Guarding them was a boring duty, one that gave Trent time to think.

One night, alone in the dark, Trent had been struck with inspiration. The security cages were effective, but bulky, he reasoned. Instead of bleeding all of their power why not just re-purpose it. The control discs had taken Trent eight years of painful creation, failure, trial and error. Eventually, he had chanced upon a meteorological chaos pattern technique to resolve the simultaneous interrupt and control of the thousands of AI nodes within the nano-suit, allowing them all to be usurped together. Simple progressive control hacking from node-to-node was always detected as an attack, and the suit would repair the subjugated nodes before the takeover was complete, so no-one had ever been able to take control of someone else's suit. Though he'd never actually used this device before, the maths seemed sound; it felt satisfying to successfully test it.

High in the Flight Dome, two deep blue auras full of hate faced each other.

"I see from your expression, you recognise this toy," teased Aneksi.

Garvy panicked at the sight of Carney's gun. He'd seen it many times and knew the damage it was capable of inflicting.

"I see you recognise your assassin's weapon. Sorry, she's indisposed."

The gang leader stood facing Aneksi on the viewing platform, frantically trying to formulate an escape. He held his needle gun in one hand and his laser blade in the other, fully aware that in a tit for tat energy exchange he would lose. He lowered the needle gun.

"Please, drop all of your weapons, Mr Garvy." Aneksi poured the syrup into her voice and exuded the charm for which she was so famous. Garvy did as he was told.

"Send him down in one piece please Aneksi," requested Trent. He walked to the airlock panel and answered the frantic calls across the public channels.

"Jan, yes I'm fine, Aneksi's here."

"Mike, thanks, yes, I've spoken to Jan. Please return to the Power Complex." He dismissed the personal concerns first.

"Liza, what happened at the Fusion labs?"

"No fatalities. We had evacuated the Labs just in case. I've got two wounded and seven of Garvy's men were netted and caged." There was no follow up asking him how he was, she knew his plan and he'd assured her he would be alright. He was talking to her after the showdown; he must have won. What more was there to say?

Finally, he contacted Martin, "Martin, what's this about another break-in at the Reactor." There was only dead space in reply. "Martin!" With no answer Trent called the General Security frequency and heard screaming and explosions.

"What the ...! I can't see." Mike panicked.

"The base has blown." Cooper ran to the front of the Rover. "No! Look there's a shuttle."

"I was looking straight at it. Damn, plasma flare." He tried to blink away the retina after-image obscuring his vision.

"Gunfire! Look at the impact sparks. He's raking it with heavy fire. What building is that?"

"Security." Mike's voice dropped.

"It's moving off! Look... and there... the Bugs'll get it." Two sleek red craft flew toward the scene. A third came down from above.

"Come on, they're going to need help." Mike set the new waypoint for the damaged building and engaged the Rover Nav system. "Coop, check we have everything on-board."

"Security! Station under attack. All hands respond." Trent looked up as Garvy floated down from his perch with Aneksi behind him. "Sorry Aneksi, got to go. Can you watch him?" He activated the airlock as he spoke.

"Sure, what's the rush?" she asked.

"There's a war going on at Security. Martin's not answering."

Garvy impacted the floor awkwardly, misjudging the slow fall, trying to watch Aneksi and Trent at the same time. Trent shot a control disc at the back of his suit. The criminal's body went rigid and he yelled at the irresistible force used to restrict him. The device blackened Garvy's visor and muted his comms cutting off Garvy's curses, making him a prisoner in his own suit.

"Oh! Jack needs help," Aneksi suddenly remembered the beaten croupier in the corridor."

"Okay, I'll alert medical. Garvy had some control pad with him on the Flight Platform. He used it to drain the air, any chance you can sort it?" He smiled at his long-time friend and marvelled at how they always seemed to survive when the odds were stacked against them.

"No problem," she replied. As he stepped into the airlock, she wished him, "Good luck!"

"Liza, what's the situation at the security block?" He requested an update, as he initiated an emergency call for medics to attend Jack, and security to pick up Carney, helpless to do anything else until the airlock completely re-pressurised.

"It's worse than we thought," she sounded angry. "Outside attack from an armed shuttle, the cell block is destroyed, all prisoner's dead. Fenwick reports twelve officer's dead."

"Get the bug's up," Trent was dismayed by the news.

"In one now; two wingmen. Target in sight... guns locked. Firing." The voice went quiet.

Three security Bugs pursued the shuttle, racing across the brightly lit ground. Using craters for cover seemed to be the only strategy of the fleeing shuttle. Dip into the craters vanish in the shadows, hug the rising lip, up and over to shake off pursuit. In this type of chase, the security Bugs gained the advantage of gravitic speed. Flying close to the ground, the plates pushed against the solid mass below adding to the engine acceleration; they closed in quickly.

"Target damaged... one engine down, port thrusters destroyed. He's heading for..." her calm narrative played through Trent's raised helmet as he ran through the Casino Lounge.

Fully re-instated gaming tables and decoration had kept the customers ignorant of the war that was brewing around them. Oblivious gamblers glanced up to see the strange semi-armoured grey apparition with bright blue shin protectors and put it down to some promotional stunt, before shrugging and returning to their games.

Two medics ran past him heading in the opposite direction, followed closely by two Security officers, who sealed the west doors to the storage halls behind them. Nobody gave them a second glance.

"Ship I.D... it's Gen'eer." Liza's voice raised a little before correcting herself. "No, it's his lieutenant, Skabenga." There was a small pause as Liza checked the Security system. "Gen'eer's tracker puts him in his cabin. Ship is heading straight to the Reactor."

"What is it with that place?" Trent was getting frustrated, what was he missing? "Who authorised Skabenga to leave the dock?"

"Hold on!" Liza was abrupt, the sound of repeating heavy guns reloading clicked over the comms. "He's down, outside the Reactor." Liza cut Trent off the comms as she instructed her wingmen to apprehend Skabenga.

"Records show Skabenga's shuttle never left the dock. Video confirms Gen'eer's shuttle is still in place, Bay Twelve. It looks like they brought in a spare." Liza's logical view of reality did not cater for redundant phrases, but Trent decided to voice one anyway.

"But that's impossible," he announced. "I'm in the transit pod moving North to Security."

"Skabenga is trying to run across the surface, heading for the Reactor. Security following." Liza relayed the chase taking place across the lunar surface. "Door is sealed, he's stuck. Looks like his access card doesn't work." There was a short delay and the silence tormented Trent, he didn't want to say anything in case he missed her next update.

"Netted and caged," she reported. "His ship is immobilised, guard in place. Coming home!" Liza's final communication needed no embellishment.

"Jan!" Trent called her from inside the transit pod. It had halted mid-tunnel, half a minute before the Security Station and was busy relaying automatic information which apologised for the lack of progress in the journey. "I need assessors and emergency crew at the Security Station now."

"Mike's there! He witnessed the whole thing from his Rover." she answered. "Are you okay?" she was worried.

"No problems my end, I'm just stuck in the transit pod, too much damage to move on to Security. Can you send me back to the first maintenance access port? I'll carry on outside." The pod instantly stopped apologising and slowly reversed back the way it had come. "We've got Skabenga which means we'll get Gen'eer. I think he was trying to clean house; destroy the clones, remove the evidence."

"What about the rest of the people in there?" Jan showed concern and Trent guessed she was more interested in the security officers than Garvy's henchmen.

"I'm surprised at Fenwick's tally," Trent admitted. "The suits would have taken most of the damage. People could be pinned or more likely stunned. I'm hoping Fenwick's inexperience has clouded his judgement."

Like everyone else's interview, Trent had been present at Fenwick's and he recollected the young lad as keen and sensible, but untried.

"Are you armed?" Jan was thinking about other issues which Trent had already dismissed as dealt with.

"Garvy's down, Carney's in traction and his henchman are caged back in the Flight Dome."

"There was more than one!" Jan sounded anxious.

"Don't worry about that, Garvy's empire is over." Trent had endured a busy morning and he knew the day was going to get worse, but he believed they both needed cheering up so, off the cuff he asked, "Would you, er, like to share a bottle of wine and some, er, Stroganoff in my cabin, around um... seven-ish tonight?" He wasn't prepared for the noise that erupted from his comms.

"Interesting," Jan exploded with laughter, her fear for the executive trouble-shooter's life being instantly eclipsed by the absurdity of the proposal from the inexperienced naive romanticist, "Maybe, but you have to tell me what Stroganoff is before I decide."

Trent relaxed at her acceptance, "Meat and vegetables in a savoury cream sauce, ancient family recipe," he boasted. "I like it with rice." He rose from his seat and defeated the public lock with his override, exiting the pod onto a basic plascrete bay. He checked his suit pressure and air supply. Plascrete had no nano-technology or shielding attributes.

Passing through a simple locked door he was presented with an ancient airlock.

"The food of gods and kings, my father used to say."

"Well, how can I turn down such a gracious offer." At last, she thought, her anxieties momentarily forgotten. Opening a drawer in her desk, she retrieved the shiny silver coin she'd found in the Reactor and flipped it in the air. "Heads or tails," she asked cruelly.

"Heads," he guessed. "Why?"

The coin landed on her palm, highly polished both sides, she examined it, but once again found no markings. "You win," she laughed gently. "See you at seven."

It didn't take Trent long to cross the distance from the maintenance airlock to the remains of the security station. He saw the parked maintenance Rover being used to illuminate the wreckage of the building, its lights searing into the destruction. Shadows gouged holes out of the structure and Trent felt a strong sense of loss. The feeling grew, antagonising and oppressing him, as he moved slowly toward the macabre scene.

A couple of workers in orange maintenance suits were plasma cutting and piling debris a few metres away from what used to be the offices. They'd set up a mechanical winch and one of their number was removing heavy uncooperative chunks of twisted metal from within the structure, being guided by an officer within the ruined building.

Several blue suited guards were milling around on the lunar surface. One was sat on a chunk of painted rubble, another crouching beside him. Trent skipped to the side of the building and went to speak to them. He switched to the security channel and heard them discussing the events with some passion.

"Quiet!" A leader rose from among them and demanded order.

"Fenwick, you were here, what happened?" the leader demanded.

"Big, huge explosion, blew everything apart." The voice was shaking, hesitant; Fenwick was in shock.

"One explosion... just one?" The leader was calm and understood the condition of his witness. His tone mollified to ease the stress of the situation. Considering the carnage and the dead prisoners around them, Trent was impressed with the leader's demeanour. "And before that?" he pressed gently. "What was everyone doing?"

"I was in the kitchen clearing up. I'd just done all the lunches for the prisoners. Brad and Jules were playing chess while they had theirs, Vic and Amy were feeding the prisoners." He stopped and seemed to get angry, "That Cutter was in the interview room swearing at everyone, he said we were killing him, but we weren't," his tone subsided and he went quiet. "We all complained," he sobbed, "we all wanted to be where the action was."

"Who was in with Cutter?" asked the leader gently.

"Er, no-one, Amy said we should leave him to wear himself out, she cuffed him to the table to cool off," he remembered his friend Amy and sobbed. "She went to help Vic." His voice trailed off. The leader indicated one of the other guards and without speaking the guard helped young Fenwick off the debris, to his feet.

The leader stood up, turned and recognised Trent. "Did you hear that, Sir?" asked Ivor.

"I did. What are you doing here? I thought you did the night shift. Have you seen Martin?" Trent interrogated his senior officer.

"I heard the news, got here as soon as I could," he responded, "about two minutes ago. Haven't heard from him yet, Sir."

"What do we know?"

"We have two fatalities, looks like they were caught in the initial blast," he sighed and moved to the edge of a damaged wall. "One shot plasma canon, took out the side of the building."

Trent knew that's where the chess board had been set up, there would have been no warning and no chance to raise their helmets, especially if they were concentrating on their game. Jules and Brad stood no chance.

"Only two?" He saw the damaged suits, chunks of material seemed to be cut away, no helmets were visible and no occupants obvious. From the lay of the material there was very little matter occupying what was left of the blue armour.

"The Cell-Block has been destroyed, that seems to have been the target. All of the prisoners in there are dead." There was a loud thud over their comms and they turned to see the cause. Mike had attached an emergency repair bulkhead to the building and had illuminated the area with red light to speed up the nano repair bonding cycle.

"I think we should move inside." Trent motioned the guards forward. They stepped over the debris of the remaining walls and entered the incomplete shell of the Security Office.

"What about Vic and Amy?" Trent was more interested in the officers than the prisoners. "Fenwick said..."

"They'll be fine. Half a wall fell on them before they were raked with explosive rounds, not the best warning to stick your helmet on, but it worked," reported Ivor. "They were scrambling out of the wreckage when I turned up. I sent them to medical. Fenwick was in the kitchen, buried under dust and crockery by the explosion. I found him sat in the Cell-Block shaking like a leaf and was just about to pack him off, once I got his story." Ivor beckoned to one of the medics.

"He reported twelve officers down." Trent let the statement hang.

"No, he was a bit incoherent," Fenwick was badly shaken, but his story had been consistent, "I think he actually claimed twelve bodies down." Ivor felt sorry for the lad. "Which was a pretty accurate estimate considering what happened to him."

Trent accepted Ivor's judgement and focussed on the building. He could see the way the spherical plasma ball had carved through everything it touched. Blasting atoms apart in an area five metres wide, eliminating the floor and ceiling to create a violent decompression that tore down both the building support frame and the inner wall between the station office and the cells. The rear wall of the interrogation room had been ripped down and the tables, bolted to the floor, had been torn apart and blackened by the immense heat at the edge of the plasma explosion.

They walked across the littered floor to view the remains of the cells. The vertical bars were still in place and behind them lined up like a gruesome freak show, were the prisoners. The cadavers, grey and distorted by the implosive effect of air in their lungs as they were exposed instantly to the lunar environment; their skin sucked dry by the vacuum of space. Each body had been pierced several times by bullet holes wide enough to fit his thumb in. Each gruesome cadaver supported upright by the cages that denied them their shields and helmets that would have rendered the attack ineffective. It was an eerie sight and the two men understood why Fenwick had lost his reason.

Trent recognised the deformed body of Harvey, the big innocent oaf who'd killed Belle. An accident, he was certain. He'd already written the report to exonerate him and reduce the charges, placing the full blame at the feet of Cutter and Garvy, but now, poor Harvey had paid the ultimate price.

Was it my fault? Was it the right thing to do, take away the protection of the suits as a punishment? Trent felt the up-swell of sorrow and regret and tried to focus on something else, but his mind tormented him.

He wasn't someone who accepted death easily. His developments to improve his father's suit design were all about continuing the challenge to foil the ever-growing power of death. Yet here, the victims faced him, accused him and he had no answer.

"You okay sir?" Ivor noted the change in Trent's demeanour, as he turned white with the erroneous realisation he was to blame for this tragedy.

Nascent emotions, helplessness, abandonment, fear and pain lingered in the room and seemed to coalesce around him. His gift was tearing inward, punishing him. He felt as though his soul was being ripped apart as he absorbed the anguish of the dead.

"If they'd had power in their suits..." he began weakly.

"...then they'd have ripped the place apart from the inside." Ivor was angry. He was not going to allow anyone to shift the blame for this atrocity.

"Those suits were enhanced for physical strength to the exclusion of all else. They're not ours, they're from Gen'eer's stock." He saw Trent begin to wilt. "Come on sir, let's get you back into the air." Ivor assisted his boss, who seemed to have become a shadow of the buoyant leader who'd turned up a few minutes ago.

Ivor had seen it all before, he knew people didn't react well under these circumstances, but he never had Trent pegged as squeamish.

Another thud and a yell from one of the maintenance crew alerted them to the final panel being secured in place, completing the temporary seal over the breach.

"Good to go, boss," shouted Mike to Trent, but it was Ivor who acknowledged the report over the comms.

"How long before the air comes back?" he queried.

"Should be back in thirty seconds, but give it a couple of minutes. Let it warm up, make it easier to breathe," Mike responded with valuable advice. He gave a wave as his team dismantled their equipment and returned to their Rover.

Trent was wrestling with his demons, sinking deeper into mental anguish as the voice in his head told him their deaths were all his fault. He'd seen atrocities before, even blamed himself for following immoral orders, but he'd never felt so affected by death.

As Ivor held Trent in the outer office, he noticed the glazed look on his boss's face. It was as though he wasn't conscious of the world around him, but had retreated into a place of torment within. The seasoned Security Captain had witnessed drug induced catatonic states many times and wondered if Trent had taken something. He up-righted a bench seat in the waiting area and sat his Commander down.

"Quarantine's untouched and it's lucky the rebels were still down in the Khonsu storage, otherwise..." Ivor tried to console his boss, but Trent failed to respond.

It took a further twenty minutes before the transit pod arrived. Mike had placed a second team working from the security station platform, back along the track to check for any residual damage caused by the explosive decompression. The line was stable and the seals fine, but it took time to replace the lost air in the tunnel.

"Come on, sir. That's it one more step." Ivor's reassuring voice permeated his fugue. "Nearly there!"

Trent's wits returned while he was being half carried through the main complex. He was aware of his disconnection with the real world, travelling as a passenger within his own body. He understood the blue suited guard was supporting his weight. He'd felt Ivor take his arm and burden himself, escorting his boss to safety, returning him to his cabin.

Trent understood his gift of empathy had reacted to the excess emotion in the security building. The violence, pain and hate had permeated the very structure, suffocating his emotions, blanketing his mind; he also knew he was now somehow, different. Glancing at Ivor his mind could see lines of gold flowing through his captain's body. Each line carried colours; it was as if Ivor was glowing from within. Trent shook his head and the vision faded, returning to the simple colouration of a concerned aura.

"Thanks, Ivor." Trent tapped his blue armoured crutch on the shoulder as though nothing had happened. Ivor looked him over with a practised eye, checking for signs of concussion or drug misuse.

"You took a bit of a turn there, sir." Ivor's voice showed his concern. "You were in a bad way, sir. Maybe, you should call medical."

"It's okay, now. I'll be fine." Trent regained his composure and declared his recovery complete. Ivor bathed in the calm peace his boss emanated; he too felt fine, reinvigorated. "See to Fenwick, give the lad support and tell Liza to use the Flight Dome as a new home for security until we record the crime scene and sort out the Security Station. I'll see to the gravity shift and the couple of damaged plates, courtesy of Garvy."

They'd reached Trent's cabin and Ivor was reluctant to simply drop-off his patient. "She'll need cages, if we've got no cells." Trent continued; his thoughts crystal clear.

"We should have some in stores and raid the Rovers, they carry a few each." Trent looked fine and sounded as competent as ever and Ivor couldn't remember the depth of his original concerns. Trent just moved to his desk and activated a holo-viewer. "Thanks, Ivor. Oh, find Martin and get some rest." he shouted, as Ivor closed the newly replaced door behind him.

"Where's the bosses guards?" demanded Ivor, activating his comms as the door closed. "He's back in his cabin and this ain't over yet!"

16: Discovery

The episode with Garvy and the destruction of the cells had worn Trent out. To recover, he'd taken a rare long hot shower, using real water, which always helped him to unwind. The therapeutic affect seemed to relax his mind and he was able to replay and scrutinise the day's events. It occurred to him that there were still questions to answer.

Sat at his desk in his quarters, sipping a cool glass of water, he selected some gentle music and closed his eyes to help him think. He considered Gen'eer's next move and the conundrum of the Reactor. Trent wasn't convinced Ling Rong-Yu would remain quiet for long and Sarko had yet to show his hand.

He activated his daily work schedule and tried to pretend he had a normal routine to follow. Looking over the station reports he noted several requests to leave the station, people cutting their vacation short. A knee-jerk reaction to Garvy's power-play; there would be a lot more when news of the attack on the security station got around. He wondered if they'd still be so eager to leave, once he told them of the events on the planet below.

Massado seemed to be in a hurry, he'd placed two requests to leave, while his pilot had also made a case for early departure. Neither mentioned the events perpetrated by Garvy or Gen'eer.

He moved to his couch and surrounded himself with holographic screens showing information about station diagnostics, customer complaints, and current supplies. Air was okay, but reserves were low, power was full, food production was running smoothly and water reclamation was ticking over... yet Trent felt uneasy.

"Sir!" Liza's voice interrupted his train of thought. "Sorry to bother you, but..." everyone was pussy-footing around their boss, obviously seeing him carried away from the carnage of the security building had led some to draw their own conclusions and on a communal base like this one, those colourful embers of half-truth would spread and grow like wildfire.

"I'm fine, just looking over logistics. I see a few rats are trying to leave... are we sinking?" He cut through Liza's concerns with his typical banter.

"Sorry Sir," and that was it, Liza returned to her normal professional self. "Skabenga's in a cage. Got him isolated in a box, but there's little privacy here in the Flight Dome; not that he's saying anything coherent." In the background Trent could hear a weird wailing sound at Liza's end.

"His ship is identical to the one they arrived in, data and serial numbers match. Everything's the same, except the mining drill fitted beneath the nose. Massive power, slow recharge. It was designed for hollowing out asteroids. I've seen the plans, but I didn't think anyone had actually made one yet."

Her remark caused a ripple of concern to run through Trent's mind. Someone was beyond simply planning the next phase; they'd started producing the tools. Once the base was established and fully self-sufficient, Phase two involved gathering resources from anywhere except Earth. Trent had several ideas, but nothing had been built beyond basic prototypes.

"Thanks for the heads-up!" Trent wanted to get back to his planning, he needed to challenge Gen'eer and was eager to add this detail to his itinerary.

"Just one more thing, sir." Liza's voice took on that, tell me to shut up if you don't want to hear this tone. "I took a statement from Aneksi, Sir... and Jack. Did you know...?"

"I've worked with her in the past," Trent was about to say remove her from the enquiry list, keep her name out of this, but Liza continued.

"It's not that, Sir. She thinks Dr. Harper hired Carney to kill her. She claims she heard them discussing details of employment and says Carney boasted about the amount he'd offered for the contract to kill her." Liza didn't ask a question, but Trent felt she was waiting for a reply.

"Okay, leave it with me." Trent was thrust deep in thought. Aneksi doesn't lie, but he'd known Cole since he was a kid. Could he know who Aneksi was, if so, how? He thought Cole had come to assess his staff, but he'd done no work with anyone. He'd just turned up, at the murder scene and sampled the brandy. What game was he playing?

"Do you want me to question Doc Harper?" asked Liza.

"No, use digital surveillance, keep tabs on who he sees, where he goes. Be careful, he'll spot anyone paying attention to him. I'll speak to him later."

Another piece on the board, thought Trent. He pictured his mental chess board. An unregimented group of dark opposition pieces stood around his crystal king. A single line of glass pawns stood between them. At the edge of the board, two glass pieces lay shattered and across the other side a heap of dark slate dust, but now a new piece of indeterminate shape and colour sat behind the opposition. 'Why there?' he thought.

The call Trent received later that afternoon was a surprise. He'd placed his grey defensive suit on charge and dressed in his typical unmodified beige and orange striped suit, his appearance slightly nearer standard than his other suits, in a bid to force some normality into his routine. The station still needed to run and he had admin to oversee and customers to mingle with. Until he knew more about the threats he was facing, it was business as usual. So far, there was no news from Earth and no sign of anything leaving the planet.

There was also no knock on the door or comms request as Trent busied himself with daily tasks at his desk, but his cabin door opened.

"Hi Trent," Cole greeted him cordially, "been through the mill I hear." Doc Harper entered without any formality and headed across the room, directly to his friends drinks dispenser.

"Help yourself," offered the Commander from behind his desk, studying Cole as he poured himself a drink.

"Ivor called, he said you were a bit 'out of it'," he laughed at the imperfect medical diagnosis. "He said he thought you might need someone to talk to."

Trent sat and studied his friend; something was not quite right with Cole. "How are you feeling, Doctor?" he asked smiling gently.

"Me? There's nothing wrong with me that a couple of shots of your excellent brandy won't cure." He raised his drink ostentatiously and to punctuate the statement he emptied his glass and dispensed a second.

"Please, take a seat," requested Trent.

"You sound very calm. Are you on something?" Cole Harper sat down on his friend's couch and seemed to relax.

"I was wondering if you'd had a chance to talk to any of the staff yet?" Trent was calm and tried to be conversational, but the problem with Cole had hit home. Doc Harper had no aura, but why hadn't he noticed before. An insistent irritation, like an itch in his mind made him uncomfortable. He tried to ignore it.

Cole shook his head and grunted in dismissal. "I'm on holiday," he said, "I'm sure you'd tell me if there was anything I needed to worry about." He sipped his drink and began reading a screen floating above the table by the couch. The images extolled the virtues of a walk through the Bio-Dome and boasted of 'over five thousand species of flora,' available to see.

The itch got worse. Automatically Trent rubbed the back of his head, "Any news from home?" he said, changing the subject and shutting down the regimented screens of figures and charts he'd been studying.

"How?" Cole laughed, "Meteor took out the array, no communication with Earth." He sipped his drink and stared at Trent.

"Are you telling me you don't have your own comms," he sneered. "Not the Cole I remember." Trent stood and poured himself a glass of water from a half full crystal decanter cooling on top of the dispenser. "You always had a way out, an ace up your sleeve. You never relied on anyone, not even me." He took a seat next to Cole, sitting forward he waved the last illuminated screen away and returned the stare of his comrade.

"Do you remember when we got blown up in Prague?" Trent closed his eyes and thought back to that night. He sipped from his glass. "You ejected me, and drove into that building, straight through the wall. Next thing I know I'm in a ditch, the cars ablaze and you're sniping from the top of the building."

"That was the night of the ball," Cole nodded.

"We'd been attending the ambassador's gala; we weren't even armed." The itch increased and now Trent brought his cybernetics into play. Instantly they reported the presence of a subliminal message, 'I'm your friend. I'm calm; Do as I say.' Eight times a second, the message burrowed into the subconscious.

Cole was not Cole, not the boy he'd grown up with, the friend he'd respected more than anyone else in the world, the only person he'd ever trusted. This thing had replaced him.

"Get me another brandy, will you?" Cole offered the empty glass and Trent stood to refill it, without a moment's hesitation. He noticed the smile appear on his visitor's face.

"I'm sorry, I'm just tired. Garvy tried to assassinate me earlier, and have you heard about the attack on the Cell-Block?" Trent made small-talk. He had replaced his upgraded suit with his normal, only slightly-enhanced suit; he was essentially unarmed. He couldn't stand against this thing pretending to be his friend, whatever it was.

The hardest thing was to resist the urge to scan. The most advanced Synthetics, even twenty years ago could detect when they were scanned and the results were usually quick and violent.

He handed the simulacrum of his friend a drink and through a huge effort of will began to complain about his day. He used words like 'mortality' and 'fear' a lot, he talked about his 'hopelessness' and his 'dark thoughts' and for a psychologist, Cole seemed quite bored with the whole discussion, adding very little to their conversation, but the itch had changed slightly to 'I'm your friend. I'm calm; tell me everything.'

Eventually, Cole sat forward, "Interesting, but not unexpected," he declared. "I have to go. You take it easy and get some rest; Doctor's orders." He passed Trent his glass and made his way to the door. "I must say, you're very calm for someone who's been through what you've experienced. Let's hope it doesn't hit you hard tomorrow."

"Good company and good memories do that for a person," Trent responded honestly, broadcasting an aura awash with pure white calm. There was no visible effect on the thing claiming to be his friend other than an almost imperceptible flow of twinkling gold within its head. The spark was gone in an instant and Trent dismissed it as nothing but a jaded reflection of the peaceful appeal he'd offered.

Sadness descended as the door close and he mourned his old partner. He'd always had his doubts about the events relayed by Cole at the Prague debrief. Surviving the crash, his friend would seek cover and call-in help, not ascend an ancient ruin, take out a lone sniper on the roof with his bare hands then use his gun to protect the burning wreck from a squad of resistance fighters.

But Trent himself had been dazed and confused by the sudden turn of events, he didn't know if he'd been in that ditch for ten seconds or ten minutes. The car still burned when he awoke covered in poisoned dirt and he'd surmised the charred body inside was his partner, while a squad of enemy soldiers lay dead around it. When Cole turned up brandishing the high-power rifle, he'd been so filled with relief it never occurred to him to question who the burnt corpse in the car had been. Now, he understood why.

"Liza," he called his trusted senior captain and switched to a high security channel. "Cole's a Synthetic; highly advanced with mind altering capabilities; simple subconscious brainwashing techniques, but effective. I think he was probably one of the last Synth's produced, that makes him doubly dangerous. We've got nothing here that will hold him, keep him under surveillance and keep him sweet."

"Will do," Liza knew the dangers of Synth's, but there was no point in agonising over something beyond her control.

"Any news on Skabenga?" he asked, more to lighten the mood.

"He started to make a racket as soon as we caged him. It sounds like he's praying to Gen'eer, for all the good that'll do him." There was an edge of frustration to her voice.

"Okay, I'm about to drop in on Gen'eer for another chat."

"Do you need back-up," she asked, ready to volunteer herself for anything, to get away from Skabenga's wailing.

"No, I'll be fine." He turned off his false wall, entered his workshop and bent over the diagnostic tool focussed on his black suit lying on the brilliantly illuminated worktable. He selected a report tab on the machine's holo-projected screen and an image of the suit glowed red, the words 'Power 100%' appeared followed by the notification, 'All weapons fully charged.'

His four-man entourage were waiting outside and fell into step behind him as he left his cabin. Trent was surprised at the re-appearance of the World Gov guards without any explanation, but then where else could they go.

He was now dressed in his outlandish black suit. Red stripes offered a pretence of fashionable design while the strange armoured plates enhancing his physique looked old fashioned and comical, drawing humorous remarks from guests as he passed through the Khonsu Lounge. They headed toward Gen'eer's apartments.

The African warlord's corridor contained only two guards stationed outside their master's door. They challenged the approach of Trent and his men, silently standing forward with hands raised.

Trent's red suited World Gov bodyguards stepped forward and without a word physically pinned them to the wall. Trent witnessed for the first time, the strength enhancements of the World Gov red suits. Gen'eer's men struggled, as he re-appraised the work of the state engineers. The strong defenders were rendered inert, unable to free themselves and execute their duty.

The remaining two blue suited station security guards entered Gen'eer's apartment with Trent, but this time there was no cordial seating and the hanging silks looked sparse and flaccid. Gen'eer was positioned on his 'throne' between his two feminine bodyguards. Trent took a chance and performed a quick diagnostic discovering they were only Mark-3's, early subservient Synth models with little independent thought and more importantly, no integral weapons. Still, their strength was prodigious and their speed well beyond that of humans. There was nowhere for Trent to sit and Gen'eer was obviously in no mood to talk.

"You murdered my men and drove my servant mad," he announced, spitting his vitriolic bile at Trent and his men. Two of Gen'eer's henchmen, humans in enhanced armour, moved into view from behind the hanging silks. "And now you have come to murder me!" Undoubtedly, Gen'eer was recording the conversation for later use in his defence.

"Calm down, Gen'eer." Trent appealed to the man, speaking gently. "We only need to talk." He could see the warlord's fear and even a stroke of cowardice, something he hadn't expected. The criminal leader rose from his throne, a snarl contorted his features, hatred bloomed and the order to attack was given with a swift gesture of his hand.

"Down!" ordered Trent, as the two henchmen moved to attack. Crouching behind newly upturned tables, Gen'eer's men fired their needle-guns at Trent's security guards. The range was over two meters and the chance of damage was slight, but the recent surprises Trent had received from newly developed technology had left him wary.

Gen'eer leapt away from his seat and his Synthetic bodyguards rose to create a barrier for him to hide behind. "You got nothing on me Trent!" shouted Gen'eer.

Trent's upgraded diagnostics scanned the female figures in depth, searching for a way to incapacitate them. His men ran forward, tackling the two human aggressors unleashed by Gen'eer. Hanging silks were ripped down as they tussled, seeking to incapacitate each other with effective holds and discharge control damaging shots into their opponent's suits.

Despite having no built-in weapons, the old Mark-3 Synthetics were armed, each carried a powerful slug-chucker and a laser knife. Trent knew the knives could eventually cause harm to the suits, but it would need accurate repetitive blows, however, the Synthetics were unlikely to miss.

Charging his weapons for the first time in anger, he sighted the power conduits behind the sternum of the Synthetic women, just above their power storage system. He didn't want to cause any explosions in the complex, only neutralise the threat. Using his cybernetic link, he selected a shaped plasma shell, twice as long as normal, capable of burrowing through the internal alloy skeleton and blasting apart the power distribution network within.

It took a high proportion of his stored energy, but Trent reasoned it was a risk he had to take. The Synthetics, commanded to defend their master, were too late to respond to his unexpected attack and folded as the intense blue projectiles erupted from his forearms, blasting through the metallic skeleton of the inhuman creatures. Falling to their knees and collapsing without grace, the toppled barrier revealed a cowering Gen'eer.

The criminal leader was not unprepared; he threw a palm-sized red disc which landed beside Trent discharging a concussive force that created a two second window for his escape. Trent crouched over it to minimise the explosion he thought was coming. Turning his chest armour to the device, hoping to absorb the energy, he took the audio-visual blast squarely in the face. His disorientation shook him and prevented him calling out a warning, as Gen'eer ran towards the open doorway. A second concussive force then a third was discharged in the corridor, obviously to dissuade the World Gov guards from pursuit.

Beyond the doorway, alarms sounded and warnings flashed. Information warning triangles indicating bulkhead damage from the stun grenades, projected their details upon the walls, recommending 'Human Avoidance', as repairs automatically ensued; so powerful was their explosive force.

In the moments of confusion, Gen'eer had escaped. Trent activated his comms, "Liza! Track Gen'eer! Where's he gone?" The delay that followed was interminable, but only lasted a handful of seconds.

"Tracker says he's still in his cabin," Liza sounded disappointed, she knew Gen'eer must have had a work around for the badges after the extra men were discovered hiding in the Reactor. I've asked central to track him visually, but not everything's working since the altercation with Garvy and Carney."

Trent stared at the immobile Synthetics, machines of hate and fear. Only fifty years ago they'd been undefeatable, responsible for hundreds of thousands of deaths on the planet below, now nothing more than oozing scrap. He checked the health of his men, each with their armour deprived, bound captives, then left the cabin. The red-suited guards still had their prisoners pinned against the wall. He faced one of Gen'eer's men, now too exhausted to struggle, matching the anger in his eyes.

"Your so-called 'god' has fled." He didn't smile, he wanted the man to understand the contempt with which he held his leader. "Hiding behind Synthetics, while using a clone army. Some leader of men," he spat on the floor indicating his disgust.

"Our Saviour..." began the pinned man,

"...has committed murder and planned to steal technology to make himself richer and more powerful; not stopping to rescue you I notice." Trent smirked and stood back. "Release him," he shouted.

"As expected, the brainwashed follower launched an immediate attack on Trent, but as he moved a control disc was already heading towards the suit he wore. The angry attacker screamed as his raised arms were forcibly pinned by his side in the rigid suit, his legs straightened and the incapacitated man fell to the floor in pain.

"Stand up straight and the pain will be reduced," Trent offered the second of Gen'eer's guards, but the man was pinned by his neck with one arm held away from his body, his back against the wall. The disc snapped his arms into position so quickly the Red suited guard had little time to respond, he was up close to the man and heard the bones in his quarry's arm snap as the suit immediately assumed its rigid position and fell to the floor.

"Forget me," ordered Trent angrily, "I want Gen'eer found." The World Gov guards nodded and left, following Trent's security men in pursuit of Gen'eer without hesitation. Trent was no longer their assignment. After the assault on World Gov and his commensurate actions, he had become their Commander.

"Liza," he contacted security again, "cancel all door passes for any keys and codes issued to Gen'eer's party. Report any attempted use. I want them rounded up and made safe."

"Sir!" acknowledged Liza, "Last code used was to enter... Ling Rong-Yu's apartments." No offer of action followed, no judgement, this was Trent's call.

Why would Gen'eer go there? The two were mortal enemies, competitors in the world of corruption and control.

"Understood," Trent replied.

What was going on? How could World Gov intelligence be so out of date? He answered his own question. How long had the coup been planned? If the underworld was the sleeping partner in the new World Gov regime... maybe Ling Rong-Yu and Gen'eer had signed up... he let the thought hang, the consequences were frightening.

Trent took a deep breath and collected his thoughts, he realised that the adrenaline rush in Gen'eer's cabin had angered him and his treatment of Gen'eer's henchmen had been harsh, but then an inner voice told him, 'they got what they deserved'. Trent thought about this errant idea, there was more to it than that, he'd simply allowed the emotions of the henchmen to be released. It was as if they'd judged themselves using him as a mirror.

Was his gift becoming a curse?

"Liza," he called his captain calmly. "Can you speak to Skabenga, please."

"No problem, Sir." The comms remained open as she walked through the Dome to the hastily erected panels providing the illusion of privacy. At least he'd stopped caterwauling.

"I want you to tell him about the destruction of the Synths, Gen'eer fleeing and the arrest of his compatriots. Use my suit record. Let's see if he's more willing to co-operate when he learns his boss has abandoned him and is on the run." Trent explained the plan. He doubted Skabenga would give anything away, but there was always a chance.

"Sorry, Sir, he's dead." Liza's matter of fact report was made with no emotion, just a tired resignation and maybe a sense of aural relief. "I'll look into it."

***

Jan called Trent as he walked back into the complex. "Security just informed me of an unknown cavern, excavated recently, about five klicks from the Reactor."

"Why did they call you?" Trent was angry with the disappearance of Gen'eer into Ling Rong-Yu's apartments and he instantly regretted the tone in his voice. He was busy trying to build a cohesive strategy, but he knew the numbers were against him and frustration was getting the better of him.

"I'm back checking the Reactor again and I think Liza nominated me while you were talking to Gen'eer. How did that go?" The question was innocent and Trent almost laughed when he tried to describe it succinctly.

"It was, interesting," he sighed. "It didn't end well for him, so he ran away."

"But how?" she began

"Just... don't ask." He arrived at the Casino complex. "Tell me about their cave."

"Airtight, poorly lit, big enough for maybe two ships with a simple two stage airlock hangar door. I've tracked the power feed. They've hacked into the Reactor quite well, adjusting the readouts so we didn't notice their drain. They've been here at least a couple of months. The good news is we have slightly more energy in storage than we thought."

"How did they get in and out?" asked Trent curious about the level of work that had been performed without his knowledge.

"Narrow passageway, spray lined plascrete, almost airtight; temporary at best, no lighting. A good quake would bring it down." Jan had walked the route twice with her team; it wasn't a relaxing experience. "We found a few more of those coins scattered around the place. We've collected a couple for forensics to check them out."

"What coins?" Trent was concerned.

"I found one in my old drawer. I think its old money. Hard to say, it's polished on both sides."

"Not that many collector's left, let me know if they're worth anything. Be careful, I'll see you later." Trent made to cancel the comms.

"Just one more thing," Jan interrupted the disconnect. "They had their own Rover, parked in there. It's been modified," she reported.

"Modified how?" Trent stopped at the Casino door.

"Guns fitted, just slug chuckers, enhanced power storage and..." she paused for a moment unwilling to deliver more bad news, "...another huge plasma mining drill." The line was silent for almost half a minute before she heard his exasperation.

"You're saying," he couldn't believe what he was hearing "...we could have a whole underground tunnel complex on our doorstep that we know nothing about."

"No, we've done some calculations. We reckon the power drain would only charge these drills enough to maybe excavate one more cave, about half the size of the first one." She knew it sounded bad so hurried to tell him her solution. "Mike is leading a seismic team to map the area around the complex. If it's close, we'll know in a day or so."

"Okay, thanks," he sounded despondent.

"I'm sorry," she finished.

"What for?" She'd done everything she could, discovered more of the plot against them and seemed to be taking the blame.

"Everything we do seems to be going wrong," she explained.

"Don't worry, I think we've sorted the main problems for now." He spoke to reassure himself as well as her, knowing he was tempting fate, inviting more disaster. "I'll try not to burn the Stroganov." He broke contact and stepped through the blast doors into the Khonsu Casino.

"Get down!" screamed Ivor. Trent's helmet automatically raised as the roulette table before him exploded.

17: Raid

Trent lay on his back, liberally sprinkled with pieces of the gaming table, his shoulders against an ornate pillar to the left of the doors. He could hear screaming from all directions. Lights flashed to indicate plasma fire and bulkhead damage vibrated through the floor as walls and galleries were hit, but there was no alarm.

"Are you okay, sir?" the insistent voice of Ivor was yelling in his comms.

"Fine, what the..." Trent had walked into a fire fight and had no idea who the enemy was.

"Your mad cat lady called me in, about a minute ago, she said there was a robbery in progress." Ivor sounded harassed. Explosions ignited columns of air around the casino lounge. People screamed and ran for cover, but obstacles were being eviscerated quickly. "They've got plasma grenade launchers and hi-explosive rounds. There are casualties everywhere." Trent rolled over and peeked around the column, immediately feeling the impact of a hi-explosive round as it contacted his helmet. A normal suit would be damaged and the wearer concussed, but most of his customers were in fashion suits, their armour weakened to allow material effects to utilise the limited power available. He had no doubt there would be death in this room.

"Liza," he yelled into his comms.

"On my way!" she replied.

"No! I need you at Central Control, keep the squad outside till we know what's happening. Seal all doors." He bit off the final order.

"What about civilians? Can we get them out?" Liza had already started to run back to her desk where temporary control had been patched into the new Flight Dome office.

"It's a warzone, Liza. No civilians, no witnesses, if we're lucky maybe a few survivors. I need trajectory input, open the room's data feed to me." Liza's hand punched a myriad of buttons and a red banner briefly flashed a security warning. She dismissed it with her own twelve-digit code and the feed was re-routed. It would have been easy for him to do, but after the run in with Gen'eer's Synths he needed all the power he had left.

"Okay, you've got everything they've left intact."

"Thanks, get Med-bay ready, evacuation teams and triage outside these doors." Trent sounded grim. His past was coming back to haunt him. Back in the Badlands skirmish wars, it was duffel coats and bullet proof vests against his new suit, now it was their standard armoured suits against his latest modified design. Back then he'd marched down the street of collapsed rubble taking any hit and returning fire with deadly force. As he stood up with his back to the column, he reminded himself of the unknown tech he could be facing and decided to change his tactics; hit and run.

There were six shooters around the north side of the lounge. They had improvised plasma shielding panels, but all were stood upright, exposing their chests and heads, shooting indiscriminately at any movement, showing their over confidence. So far, no-one had sent a single shot in their direction.

The data feed showed bodies everywhere, badges relayed life-signs where appropriate, but these were a fraction of the number of corpses littering the burning palace of iniquity.

Trent reset his plasma guns and programmed the locations of the terrorists. He was just about to step into their line of sight and return fire when a commotion occurred to the left of the assailants. A black blur descended at speed and a terrorist ceased to be, the other five turned to witness the event. Trent knew it could only be Aneksi.

He stepped out from behind the column his arms extended, "Stay left, Aneksi." He ordered as loud as he could. The first two shooters were dead before they could react to his shout, the second two saw the plasma shells burst from his arms; their final sight in this existence, while the fifth shot found it's mark as the target's grenade launcher was ineffectually raised. For a brief moment he panicked as the sixth shot exploded against the plasma shielding of the programmed sixth shooter's position, he doubted whether his warning to Aneksi had been enough, but his thermal scanning revealed her safely on the gallery to his left, unhurt.

"Four more she yelled, waving her hand, four fingers extended. She pointed to the door at the far side, behind which lay the vault. Four suits came rushing out, two fired their grenades toward him and two cloaked in white cotton gowns kept running at him waving... swords.

"Ling Rong-Yu!" he shouted as he shot at the heavily armed warriors taking aim. One took a hit to his shoulder. Trent's plasma shell kept going creating a perfect hole and a useless arm. The second shot went wide, dissipating as it hit the bulkhead, leaving a round charred hole in the internal wall, but the shooter ducked, delaying his lethal plasma grenade response. Out of the corner of his eye he saw Ivor aim a plasma pistol and fire towards the threat.

With a split second to spare Trent rolled away from the first sword as it arced through the air, crackling and hissing a fingers breadth from his head. The thick black studded gloves caught his eye as he ignited his boot jets and clumsily darted backward, away from a second swift slash of the sword. The tassels seem to have been woven into the suit forearms and Trent realised they were the power conduit for the fearsome weapon. Avoiding the sword left him crumpled in a heap against a hard column, one of the few remaining upright in the devastated lounge.

The two swordsmen stopped to circle their prey. Trent could see the shooter he'd hit in the shoulder was now restrained and disarmed by Ivor, the aggressor's suit damaged, probably by Ivor's needle gun. There was no-sign of the second shooter and Aneksi was missing too.

"What do you hope to gain," Trent sneered at the sword wielding criminal, "a few trinkets for your mistress," he goaded the man. The swordsman was ultra-calm, his aura was a pristine white outlined by the faintest pale blue of pity for his enemy. He was confident of his skill and firm in the belief of his victory. The second swordsman displayed hate and a little jealousy, a strange mix in the midst of a battle. Trent deduced the jealous man was subordinate to the other and turned to face the master.

Gracefully stepping toward Trent, the master swordsman feigned a chop to Trent's head; the student took a step back allowing his leader the honour of the kill.

As the sword tip held steady in front of Trent's face, he noticed the strange straight head of the weapon and the plasma flame erupting from tiny holes replacing the usual pointed tip. They were a perfect match for the murder victim's injury. A quick analysis told Trent his suit could probably stand up to the sword, but he wouldn't want to bet his life on it. Trent raised his arm, his weapon charge was low, but he figured he had maybe one weak shot left.

Suddenly, a movement in one of the video feeds to his helmet distracted him as he saw Aneksi struggle with the last armed man inside the vault. Choosing that moment to attack, the sword-master rained a series of slashing blows upon Trent, which he barely managed to ward off using his armoured forearms. He felt the impacts grow stronger as the attacker's ferocity increased. A warning showed him the structural integrity of his left arm had reduced by twenty three percent, but try as he might he couldn't make headway toward his enemy. Finally, as the sword was drawn back to lunge forward and stab him with the plasma tip, he used both body and leg mounted jets to blast away from his assailant.

The uneven ground, strewn with rubble and bodies caused him to stumble as he landed. Turning the ungainly landing into a shoulder role, he guided himself to the base of another column. He detected the laboured breathing and raised body temperature of his foe and knew the vicious attack had been physically demanding.

Trent remained crouched, monitoring the meagre gain of energy from the thin contact edge of the sword blade. He heard the scream of the second swordsman's war-cry and turned to see the man run towards him, then stared fascinated, as the assailant's chest exploded. The blast was so intense it knocked Trent back, while the energy release offered him a modicum of power, lifting his weapon charge enough for one powerful plasma round. A killing shot.

The remaining swordsman stopped and scowled as Sarko stood up from a pile of bodies holding a customised plasma rifle.

"Do you need a hand, Mr Trent?" he asked politely.

Trent stepped towards the sword-master.

"Lower your weapon," he requested calmly. The swordsman twitched between Sarko and his quarry not knowing who would attack first. "There is no honour in death here." Trent tried to appeal to the sword-master, but failed to understand the ancient code he followed.

The sword lifted above the sword masters head and the helmet dropped. Trent recognised the Dojo master who'd disciplined the nervous trainee. His face contorted into a snarl full of rage.

"Stand back, Mr. Trent," urged Sarko, but Trent stood his ground. He studied the man's aura as the calm brilliant white aura flared with an inner flame of beige self-doubt, a core of deep red anger and as his loathing erupted, the aura turned black. The master accepted his fate and gave in to a complete loss of control. The berserker charge was halted by a single shot from Trent's wrist mounted gun. The honourable master crumpled to the ground.

For the benefit of Sarko, Trent activated his comms overtly, he dropped his helmet and called loudly for Liza and the medical team to enter. "All enemies restrained. Keep weapons holstered."

The doors burst open seconds later, but there was a pause as the newcomers tried to take in the scene of utter carnage. Liza saw the black suited figure, and then Sarko with the plasma rifle and instantly drew her weapon. "Get down!" she commanded him.

Trent raised his hands in supplication and turned to reassure her. Sarko dropped his weapon and stepped over his fallen comrades.

"Drink, Mr Trent?" offered Sarko, walking through a gap in the damaged bar and retrieving an intact bottle of spirit from the floor.

"On the house, Mr Sarko." Trent moved to the bar slowly picking up a stool from the rubble, he sat with the criminal overlord and shared a moment of silence. Sarko poured two drinks of what proved to be an inferior whisky.

"Diya Mertvym," yelled Sarko.

"For the dead," translated Trent, showing his limited knowledge of Sarko's language. The two men swallowed their drinks and, despite the foul after taste of the cheap whiskey, Sarko refilled their glasses.

"To the living," called Trent. In the back of his mind, he remembered his old commander warning him that toasts should always be balanced.

"No, No," warned Sarko, "Zhalko zhivykh", he mouthed the words slowly and together they pronounced "Zalky shifik", "Close enough," yelled Sarko.

"What does that mean?" Trent asked as Sarko filled the glasses again.

"It is truth! It means, pity the living."

Trent watched as the bodies were covered and shifted onto the floating gurneys. A handful of walking wounded followed, most weeping for their loved ones, unable to comprehend the sudden violence they'd experienced. For these elite it was the first taste of the war that they'd encouraged and profited from all of their lives. Trent was moved by the sadness permeating the room.

"Again!" demanded Sarko, and the drink helped.

A hand rested on Trent's shoulder and Aneksi's perfume filled his mind. "They wanted this," she handed him a compact black box. "Martin's back there with Ivor." She indicated the vault. "He's pretty badly beaten, but he'll survive. Med staff are treating him."

"Ling Rong-Yu had him?" That made sense, they'd have needed someone of his clearance to get into the vault room.

"Looks like they beat him and drugged him, but the Medics say he'll be fine."

"Where did you get this," Trent waved the data safe she'd handed him.

"Took it off one of their black-sash lad's."

"Can he talk?" asked Trent, already knowing the answer.

"Not without a Ouija board," she smiled and walked off to help the wounded. Trent's eyes followed her. The green haired youth, always by Sarko's side, was standing up, leaning against a medic.

Trent watched as Aneksi took a blanket and placed it around the shoulders of a grieving widow, the same woman who'd cursed her during her performance that first night. It seemed like a lifetime ago. The old woman had lost her airs and graces and was crying on Aneksi's shoulder. Her hatred forgotten, her emotions reserved for herself and her pitiful dead husband.

"Your young man survived," commented Trent.

"My son, yes, he's tough. Not as tough as me, but he'll get there!" Sarko showed his pride in his offspring.

The two men sat in silence drinking slowly. Ivor, then Liza came over and gave status reports on the people, the damage and the predicted recovery times. Trent nodded politely then shooed them away. He sat in silence next to the big Russian. His suit slowly recharged and healed, and his self-absorption and melancholy lifted as the people left.

He idly watched the three-man maintenance crew attach innocuous devices to damaged walls and furniture and select the appropriate program, instructing the nano-filaments to re-grow.

Occasionally, they scooped a mound of gloopy gel from a bucket and slopped it onto a scene of ruination, close to a crack or hole and he watched as it melded with the destruction, rebuilding, reforming, eliminating all evidence of the recent violence.

"Why did you help me, Sarko?" asked Trent. There were few people left in the lounge, and his head felt clearer as he nurtured his harsh drink.

"I think..." Sarko paused and poured himself the last dregs from the bottle. "I think you are like your father, Mr. Trent, a good man. I see with my heart..." he pounded his chest, "...not my eyes." Taking a final drink, he emptied his glass, rolling the empty bottle away along the newly repaired bar.

"You knew him?" Trent was shocked that anyone would mention his father let alone claim any association. His whole life he'd experienced derision and pain for even discussing his existence.

He was an anathema to the World Gov. They owed him everything, yet abused his work and murdered him, publicly honouring those that betrayed him.

"He made me this," Sarko indicated his suit. "He told me I should settle down and tame the world. I liked him." This revelation stunned Trent.

"But my father was just a tailor..."

"A very good tailor, but sadly, it's a bit tight now." Sarko lifted his arms to demonstrate the tight fit beneath the arms.

"Did you... settle?"

"Of course, but then the World Gov would come along and we would move."

"In Russia?" It was a natural assumption and Trent wanted to know more about this stranger who claimed friendship of his father.

"No, too much poison. We did well in Budapest, but the World Gov came, then we set down roots in Prague, and you and the dead man took our Power."

"The 'dead man'?" The reference was lost on Trent.

"Your friend, the Doctor."

"Why do you call him the dead man." Trent wondered if it was something lost in translation.

"Because I killed him, Mr Trent. I remember all the men I kill; it would be rude not to."

"You caused the accident; you shot the driver." Surprisingly, Trent felt no anger. It seemed all the pieces were fitting together.

"I am sorry you were involved, but you destroyed many years work, Mr Trent."

The big man furtively scanned the room and a serious countenance straightened his features as his eyes narrowed; he lent forward conspiratorially, and whispered "I think you just got mixed up with wrong crowd."

Trent laughed derisively at the big Russian's words. "Are you afraid of the new World Gov? Did you know it was coming? Is that why you want to retire?" He watched Sarko and saw the sobriety crawl over the criminal warlord's face.

"There is no World Gov, Mr. Trent, not anymore. Idiots make deal which will kill them. I did not. They think they can dance with Chort." Sarko stood up and gently placed his hands upon Trent's shoulders. He stared intently into the younger mans tired eyes.

"I am Sarko, I am afraid of no man. I would suckle at the teat of Baba Yaga to survive, but, Mr Trent... I fear what is coming this way."

Trent could see the honesty in the man's eyes. His aura was outlined with the light red of fear, but his inner core was at peace. Sarko tapped his shoulder, almost affectionately, and gave a sigh of resignation; he turned and left the lounge without another word.

A personal alarm rang in his head interrupting his reverie as he watched the Russian walk away. It was six o'clock; Trent felt tired and woozy from the afternoon's adrenalin and alcohol. His screen told him it was time to put the Stroganov in the oven. "Damn!" Clambering off his stool he hastily headed towards his cabin, hardly noticing the almost complete reparation of the Khonsu Lounge.

Jan arrived just after seven, dressed in a chiffon gown of red over her white suit, every inch a goddess in his eyes. Bumbling like an idiot he was taken by surprise by the effect she had on his reason. The table had been set for two, without ornament or candles, but his idea to bake fresh bread filled the room with olfactory temptation. His purple velvet jacket over his usual beige armour looked comical to her, but he'd tried and she appreciated the effort.

"Not too spicy for you?" he asked, worrying about the meal he'd promised, desperate for it to live up to his expectations. He'd researched complementary wine for the meal and stood to pour her a glass.

"It's lovely." She licked her lips and nodded her appreciation and he saw for the first time the true flickering rainbow at the edge of her aura and relaxed.

He'd found love was such a difficult thing to nurture outside the bonds of family. His father had warned him of its fragile nature and intemperate structure and had told him on many occasions of its beauty, but Trent had only ever seen it washed with jealousy or wanton lust, staining the purity of the emotion... until now.

A silence bloomed that Jan found she needed to fill and so, casually, she asked him about the events in the lounge.

"It was Ling Rong-Yu's men. They were after the data records in the vault. Somehow, they knew the technical backups were in there with the account information and deposits of the guests. They kidnapped Martin to use his access, drugged him and wrecked his suit, but he's doing well in medical. In the end it was just an old-fashioned bank robbery."

"Liza said there was a lot of death and destruction." She watched her fork as she gathered another mouthful of her meal.

"Seventeen dead." He responded with a faraway look in his eye, contemplating the damage to the bodies, guests more interested in their appearance than basic protection, here on this hostile rock.

"She said, you and Sarko... had a thing." There was a slight tease in her voice that brought a smile to his face.

"He saved my life."

"I heard he blew you up," she countered.

"And here I am in bits," he laughed. "Do you know what a 'Chort' is?" he asked.

She shook her head having taken another mouthful of the spicy food.

"I looked it up. Sarko believes Gen'eer and Ling Rong-Yu have made a deal with a demon. A deal they can't hope to survive. He believes the World Gov is gone and we are about to be visited by this demon."

"Typical superstitious Russian," she dismissed Sarko's warning. "They see spectres of death everywhere."

"No... not this time. I believe whatever is coming has him truly frightened."

Jan stared off into the distance for a moment and he knew she was accessing her cybernetic comms. They weren't common, but he'd insisted both she and Liza had been fitted, as senior staff, just in case anything happened to him.

"There have been no launches from Earth in the last forty-eight hours. Radar sweep reports clear space in every direction for two hundred thousand klicks." She reassured him, "We're floating all alone up here." She saw the frown appear on his brow. "What have you done with Ling Rong-Yu?" she asked in a clumsy attempt at lightening the mood.

"What can I do?" he sipped his wine and smiled.

"I locked her in her apartments with Gen'eer, 'accidentally' reduced her gravity to moon norm and tonight she will experience at least three fire drills." He snorted at the childish inconveniences. "She wasn't there. I can't charge her with anything and her men won't talk. Hopefully, tomorrow, I'll find out what I need to know." He topped up her drink as she finished her meal, congratulating his cooking skills. Together, they took their drinks from the table and made themselves comfortable on the couch.

18: Succession

Trent rose early, refreshed and eager to face the day ahead. He was confident the main players had each shown their hand and he felt he was at last up to date with their agenda's.

Garvy and Carney were locked in cages in the Flight Dome along with their remaining henchmen. Largo and the rebels had been moved in there too.

Gen'eer and Ling Rong-Yu were locked in her apartments and Sarko was still in bed. The Synthetic that was Cole had been acting as it had throughout its stay, gambling, drinking and flirting. It had left its room an hour ago and had somehow eluded observation. He was a little perturbed, but was sure the sensors would find it soon. At least it wasn't anywhere public.

His mood was improved as he checked the production schedule, he'd initiated two days earlier in his workshop.

Yesterday's gunfight in the casino had highlighted the weakness of his offense and he vowed he would improve it. Working with Martin's grenade design, he'd reduced the weapon to a smaller size, seeking to incapacitate rather than eviscerate opponents through their suits.

He felt the overkill of his plasma guns had been a strong solution to a difficult problem, but the concept of automatic death was abhorrent to him. He designed and saved smaller projectiles giving himself a range of options. The reduction of size meant a corresponding reduction in energy use and the incapacitation rather than the automatic termination of his enemies.

He'd also made a change to his suit control disks. Instead of setting the suit rigid and isolating the wearer, he'd incorporated a facility to override the control of the suit. The new discs were short lived, allowing maybe two or three instructions to be sent, before the suit would purge the hack, but they were no less effective at restraining an enemy.

Dressing in his fully charged black armour, in preparation for his meeting with Ling Rong-Yu, he left his workshop and ordered a relaxing coffee. As the frothy drink dispensed, his cabin door opened. Immediately, the unauthorised intrusion caused an alarm to sound and his helmet to appear. He rolled behind the desk and slowly raised his head to view the intruder. Cole stood in the doorway. He looked pale and bruised, as if he'd been in a fight. In the corridor behind him lay the red suited guards.

"They're... not dead!" he gasped. He staggered to the couch and fell into a sitting position. "Coffee? That would be nice." He sounded as though he was in pain.

"Cole! What happened?" Trent performed an analysis using his suit diagnostics and discovered the true nature of Cole's Synthetic structure for the first time. "You're breaking down!" The thin holo-screen floating above his arm flashed yellow and red; bars registered zero across the spectrum while a single spike of power grew and fell as Cole's compromised body tried to grasp energy from the environment.

"Coffee... please." Trent recovered his composure and retrieved a coffee from the dispenser. He slowly walked around the couch to Cole, aware that at any moment this thing could attack. He placed the cup on the glass table in front of his 'guest'.

"You knew?"

"I suspected," Trent gave nothing away.

"We thought," he began, "we could do a better job if we had more time."

"Who?" Trent tried to get more details.

"No, just listen. You think you know what I am, but you're wrong. I'm also me, Cole, your friend." He reached for the coffee unsteadily spilling it as it lifted from the table. He started to ramble, "Prague... was the death of me. I should have stayed dead."

Trent moved forward, steadied the cup and helped his friend drink. A spike of energy registered on the screen then the line went dead. As the energy source was held, the line trembled, but internally Trent's diagnostics could see the charging system within Cole was damaged. It was as if his own nano-repair system was eating away his vital systems.

"We found a way to copy our minds and tried to put them in here," he banged his head with his fist. "It was fine for a while, but it wasn't... right." He lifted the coffee to his lips and drank, no energy spike registered. "No taste! No joy, no pain... no emotion; only shadows of a life remembered. It drove us mad... some worse than others. Just discipline, procedure... survival."

Every word was an effort. Cole's arms sagged and the cup fell. "We're prisoners. They wanted me... to kill you. I couldn't..." he managed a gentle smile, "...you always needed protecting." Trent realised then that his friend really was speaking to him and he felt a wave of sadness, his eyes stung. "They want the Moon... plan to sterilise Earth... with radiation, start again... new future... time is nothing." The eyes closed and watching the levels drop, Trent thought this thing, the last remnants of his friend, had gone.

"Who did this?" he demanded, suddenly angry. The diagnostics flared once more as Cole jolted at the sound.

"I failed... expendable," the voice fell to a whisper and his eyes closed.

"Cole!" Trent shouted his concern, his frustration mounting, too much loss, too much death. "Cole?" The eyes opened slowly revealing a glassy stare, the mouth opened and a sad sigh gave form to his last words, "...they're coming." The head bowed, too heavy to lift and a whisper escaped unmoving lips, "I'm sorry." The barely trembling power scan values, flat-lined.

Trent choked back his unbidden tears and activated his comms.

"Jan, Liza, we are about to be attacked by a superior force. Scan for approaching ships. Liza arm all Bugs and Rovers. Get them out on the surface in case they're carrying Electro-mag and Thermal cloaking. Ready all defences: Priority One! Lock the base down. Jan get back here to the main complex with your crew. Citadel protocol, all guests to safety."

He thought for a moment then added, "Gen'eer and Ling Rong-Yu are in league with the attackers. If they or their crew leave their quarters, they must be considered hostile. Jan, cut their light and limit their heat."

Trent lifted the thing that had been his friend. The Synthetic body was heavier than a similar sized human would be, but his enhanced suit allowed him to manage easily. The worktable was cleared and the analysis began in earnest. An hour later the dismembered artificial life had given up its secrets.

Trent was angry. They'd ordered his body to self-destruct, ended his friend's life at the push of a button. The final act was evil and pointless, but they'd done it anyway. After the body was internally destroyed, they'd wiped his mental data record. Cole was truly gone.

"No sign of approaching ships; no launches from Earth detected," reported Jan.

"All crew assigned. Bugs up and Rovers out," reported Liza. "Martin's in the Lounge with Aneksi enforcing Citadel Protocol."

"Good," He was genuinely relieved Martin was back at work. " Get every drone up! Keep watching, they're coming." Trent stared out of his window at the lunar surface.

"They're Synths, they don't need air or water or comfort; fast and hard to kill. If they're in suits they'll be even harder to knock out." As an afterthought he added, "Cole was a renegade Synth, on our side. He came to warn us. They've just killed him."

Ling Rong-Yu and Gen'eer are the key, he thought. If he could get through to either one, he might find out when they'll arrive and the size of their force.

"I'm off for a chat with Ling Rong-Yu. Liza, my guards are..." He checked the corridor and saw the red-suited bodyguards were still unconscious, "...currently resting. If you could send a couple to meet me at Ling's apartments it would help."

"Things must be bad," joked Liza. "That's the first time I've ever known you ask for backup."

"Anyone of their crew could be Synths," added Jan. "Our measures won't affect them. Take care."

On the way to Ling's apartments Trent crossed the floor of the Khonsu Lounge. Not a mark could be seen, not a single hint of any violence from the day before.

People were circulating quickly, bustling with purpose. Gravity sleds were moving crates, boxes and barrels were being manually shifted. Teams were being dispatched to areas within the hotel structure. In the eye of the storm stood Aneksi and beside her, Jack.

"Nice to see you up, Jack," called Trent. "You might want to fold down some of the tables," he suggested.

"No problem, sir," the smile said it all. Happy to be at work, happy to be with Aneksi; Trent nodded.

"I heard Martin was with you."

Aneksi, glanced up from her tablet, "Inside," she indicated the hotel elevator, "auditing essentials," she winked, but was immediately harangued by a short lady rolling a hefty grey barrel.

"I don't mind helping," she haughtily complained, " but do we really need to have this much processed fish. It's ghastly and..." Aneksi put her arms around the lady who been conscripted to help and walked her to the elevator.

Aneksi was sure to survive, she was born to it, he thought, and if she had any say in the matter, she'd do it in style. He left, reassured the Citadel would be ready in time to offer some refuge.

***

Two security guards flanked the outer blast doors to Ling Rong-Yu's apartments. Trent recognised Singh and Fenwick; both held plasma grenade launchers.

"Okay, so this is how it's going down," instructed Trent. "I'm here to talk, to do that I need to be in one piece. Someone points a weapon at me, you shoot them. Got it?" The guards nodded in unison. "And try not to kill Ling Rong-Yu or Gen'eer, ...unless you really have to."

Using his cybernetics, he input his own override code, opening the outer blast door and then cycled the airlock. He restored light, heat and gravity to comfortable levels within the corridor and dojo beyond. The amber lights flashed and the warning siren blared its alarm three times before the inner doors opened. No one was there to greet them.

"Follow me, stay close." Trent led his men forward and headed for the dojo. In the middle of the empty wooden floor, meditating on his knees upon a short red cushioned stool, was the First Clerk.

"Get up old man," shouted Trent, but the man remained motionless. A quick analysis showed he was alive and Trent could see his aura fading through brown, red and beige; sadness, fear and self-doubt. He wasn't wearing a suit, just his formal robes of office.

As Trent stepped toward him, the old man's eyes opened and he began his flowery rhetoric. "Halt! Your audience with her ladyship, the wise and beneficent Ling Rong-Yu has been considered and her response is due. Please be patient."

Trent took another step toward the man and his aura flared in fear. "I will not hurt you, Sir." The words were meant to be comforting, but they only elicited a new flare of pale blue. The man pitied Trent. It was a trap.

"Back off" he ordered his men. The old man relaxed, regaining his composure.

"I am a man of peace, Sir. I thank you for not dying at my hand." The old man was sincere. "I was sent to delay and if possible, destroy you. I had to obey, though I feel inclined to avoid any death."

"Has she gone?" asked Trent gently.

"Yes Sir, though I fear I shall not rejoin her." His voice was respectful but sad, his aura lost its fear, replaced by a creeping tide of pity.

"Will you help me save lives?" asked Trent. He was nervous. He had no idea what the power of the explosive was, but Ling Rong-Yu had a reputation for thoroughness. Any evidence she'd been here would probably be eliminated.

"Of course, Sir," compliance was automatic. The honourable servant had evaluated his existence and found it wanting. He had no desire to harm anyone.

Trent tentatively scanned the device located beneath the stool, attached to the old man. Powerful, but it wouldn't breach the blast-doors.

"You are the trigger?"

"I am."

There was nothing Trent could do to disarm the biological trigger. Wires led to a complicated sensor implanted in the old man's chest.

"If you move it all goes up?"

"It does, Sir... and if I die, Sir." The old man took a slow deep breath to calm himself. "I believe the explosives are also linked to my brain and respiratory system."

"Will you assist me in making your last moments safe for the guests of this hotel?" Trent saw no hope of saving the old man. A bomb this intricate would also have a fail-safe on a timer and probably even a remote detonation circuit. At any moment Ling could push the button.

"I will, Sir. I wish to harm no-one." The man's eyes closed and a tear fell down his cheek.

"Singh, get back to the airlock fetch me a breathing kit." Singh ran off down the corridor. "Fenwick, I need you to help Aneksi in the casino. Do whatever she asks of you to aid the evacuation."

"But sir?" Fenwick was unhappy about leaving his boss alone.

"It's fine, go now, no arguments." Trent was soft spoken, but insistent. Fenwick hesitated and then slowly walked from the dojo, back to the Khonsu Lounge, all the while watching his boss, looking for any signal that could demand his return.

Singh returned moments later with the breathing kit and without asking permission, moved to fit it on the First clerk. The full-face helmet allowed Trent to witness the old man's sorrow.

"Go!" the old man offered his final counsel, "Live well." He tried to smile, but his guilt and his predicament produced only thin tight lips. Singh retreated from the room, followed closely by his boss.

In silence, Trent re-engaged the airlock blast doors and closed his eyes, activating his cyberlink.

"Jan," he called gently. "I have to depressurise Ling Rong-Yu's apartments. She's gone... but she's left us a surprise, an obstacle." No matter how he phrased the old man's presence it seemed an insult to his honour and devotion.

"I can do it from here..." the offer was instant.

"No, I'll do it. I made a promise." He didn't explain the remark; she didn't ask him to. "There will be an explosion. Please monitor and reinforce all necessary bulkheads around the affected breaches. Priority is to save air, it's the one thing we don't have in abundance." He and Singh stood facing the outer blast door looking through the window, in the direction of the old man; out of sight, but foremost in their minds. The red lights whirled and muffled sirens sounded within the apartments as the air was reclaimed and in no time, decompression was complete, the alarms fell silent.

The notification came through his cyberlink connection that the apartments were now at full vacuum, temperature minus twenty-three degrees and falling. It took a further thirty-four seconds for the old man to fall, triggering the explosion.

Trent's eyes stung as tears appeared, precious inadequate gifts offered in return for their lives. He realised he didn't even know the name of the man, whose lifetime of servitude, abused and discarded by a pretentious coward, was over. He swore Ling would pay.

"Internal walls ruptured," Jan's report pierced his anger. "External walls at 72%. Repairs underway, estimate two hours to full strength." She paused. Watching the report flow as the power was taken to rebuild the apartments. "System is rebuilding internal walls," she declared. "Is that power drain a good idea."

"No. Leave it in vacuum, shut down the internal build systems. Seal the apartments." He promised himself that when all this was over the brave old man's final act would be honoured.

Singh stood passively, while his boss considered the next steps of the complex's upheaval. He too had a code which honoured the old man's sacrifice, but he believed in balance. As he had not met the First Clerk before, but understanding his role to be that of First Lieutenant to one of the most vicious gang leaders in the world, he found it difficult to feel saddened by his demise. The old man must have been culpable in hundreds of deaths before his own.

"Scan Gen'eer's apartments and Garvy's place; check for explosives matching the residue in there." He needed to know if there were any other traps being set around the place. "Then get the Bugs to sweep the surface outside." Ling Rong-Yu had gone and she didn't get out through the main complex.

"No problem." Jan contacted Liza and passed on Trent's request. She completed the analysis of the explosive residue adhering to the walls and reset the internal sensors to sweep for the additional chemical signature.

"For crying-out loud!" Mike covered his ears to ward off the pain from the emergency alarm system directly above his head. On his back, recumbent on the raised platform tracing cable feeds, his position was precarious at best. The alarm was close to his head and derailing his thought. "Turn it down," he yelled. "What's happening?"

"Explosive's detected, here... this office," yelled Jan. Her fingers danced in the air selecting focus and calibration checks from the projected screen.

"Where? How? No one's been here but us."

"Just get out!" she yelled, but Mike was already down from his perch and crawling under desks and chairs searching for anything that didn't belong.

"Can't see anything!" he shouted, after checking the power control modules.

"My desk," shouted Jan in reply. She cancelled the alarm as Mike ran in toward the source of danger. On the desk lay Jan's silver coin. She scanned it with a hand-held probe and analysed the readings as they jumped on the projected screen. "Well, we know it's not set off by noise or movement," she picked up the coin as she'd done a hundred time before and flipped it in the air. "Liza," she called on her comms, "I have a small bomb that needs disposal."

Within a few minutes two heavily armoured blue suits arrived in their Bug's. One was struggling to carry a sizeable box. She watched as the box was opened revealing a silver liquid that emitted a pungent vapour. She flipped the coin into the liquid and observed carefully, as the guards sealed the lid.

The Power Complex had been the brain of the base since the rebuild. Strong and heavily defensible when held by an armed force, but not by half a dozen techs, and certainly not currently equipped for a long siege. When Trent initiated Citadel Procedures, Jan and Mike decided to set-up control in the Hotel Bunker. Sadly, it was just a working theory, now they were executing the plan, they found they needed to cannibalise a few units. At least they would be able to watch what was happening as they were invaded.

Jan's sensor sweep ran through the full Khonsu casino and hotel and into the storage halls. The Flight Dome was deemed a priority as the new home of Security and the Power Complex had been checked. She looked at the lower apartments chosen as the Citadel Shelter and was about to begin moving her equipment to the Rover when she was interrupted.

"Here grab this," Mike had recruited Cooper, one of their junior technicians to help with the cases. On the holo-screen Jan had a 3d image of the coin explosive slowly rotating.

"They're all over the Docking Bays," Cooper announced.

"I was just telling the lad's what happened," Mike explained and Cooper got quite upset.

"Those disc things, Mike said they explode, they were all over Bay Four, in the vents." Cooper explained.

"When did you see them?" asked Jan.

"When I got sent in for that murdered guy." he shuddered at the memory of dragging the corpse out of the air filtration cupboard. "I noticed them in the shaft, but they looked quite innocent; my scan didn't pick anything up. I thought they were new sensors, or something."

Jan typed instructions into the control desk and red flashing lines appeared on a complex map all over the Docking Bays.

"Good grief!" Mike exclaimed, "they're everywhere."

Trent walked across the lounge floor and stood silently beside Aneksi. Singh followed his boss and was immediately given curt orders by the glamorous cat woman, to make himself useful in the west storage halls. He looked at Trent, who nodded compliance and the guard jogged away to join the throng of labourers.

"We'll have everything we need in there with us," Aneksi updated Trent. No alcohol, no entertainment, but lots of everything else. "We're confiscating weapons; nothing lethal in the Citadel."

"You may have to fight your way out," Trent looked at his dishevelled customers, worn out from shifting a few boxes.

"I don't think that's a viable option," replied Aneksi. An elderly man collapsed, dropping his box marked 'Ration pack B'. Close by another put down his carton and went to aid his friend. "They've never had to do anything for themselves before." She spat, full of vehemence, deriding the people she was protecting. "Privileged elite, don't you just love them?" She considered Trent's face as he took in the enormity of the task. Protection and survival was hard enough with a trained army, Aneksi had worked wonders, her special skills cutting through the arrogance and egomania of the diva's, reminding them of what it means to be merely human.

"Do you know Angie? Have you seen her?" Trent was concerned that the innocent girl would be lost without Belle. He hadn't followed up on his offer to take care of her and it suddenly hit him he'd neglected that promise.

"No problem. I've got her down below working with Ivor, assigning bunks."

"Who brought her in?" He wondered who he had to thank for taking his responsibility.

"Who looks after all the strays?" she winked and he relaxed. Aneksi had stepped in and Angie couldn't have asked for a better guardian.

"So, what's this 'superior force' I'm hearing so much about." He noticed the change in her eyes and saw her playful teasing, "Another battalion of World Gov?" she asked.

"No, much worse. World Gov's been overrun by Synths. We've got a ship full heading our way." Her demeanour didn't change. Her playful smile across her beautiful face betrayed her inner thoughts, she relished the challenge, but she could see Trent's concern.

"So, we close up shop and they pass us by," she laughed. "Are you serious?" She questioned him and for the first time her glib smile faltered.

"I thought you were getting these out of the way so we could sort out the gangs." She sounded betrayed, her voice a harsh whispered accusation of exclusion, as if knowing earlier would have changed her plans, given her other options; maybe she could have done more.

"Minimum collateral damage, you said." She sighed; she knew the words were empty.

"Sorry, but the gangs are only part of the problem."

"Synths? But they're extinct!" Hopeful denial appeared.

"No, not quite alive, but definitely kicking. They plan to move in, and they don't want to share." He stared at her, watching her aura, but at no point did he detect fear.

"Okay, 'Superior Force' it is." She tapped her comms and called for Martin. "Hi, darling, remember what I said about those plasma launchers, scratch it, we may need them after all." She turned back to Trent, "Any other surprises?"

A signal in his ear and a message from Jan interrupted his conversation. "Trent, they've mined the bays!" She blurted out. "I've cleared all personnel from the local area." Her voice sounded almost hysterical.

"Who?" was his first response, but he knew the answer already.

"Residual scans show similar explosives in every Docking Bay except..."

"Bay Eleven?" he completed her statement.

"Bay's Eleven and Twelve." She finished in agreement.

"Ling, and Gen'eer." He cursed their stupidity.

"Priorities, get the air out of those bays now. We can't lose it." Trent was frantically thinking on his feet. "Shutdown all power to all Bays, Eleven and Twelve included. Seal them off. No one in or out." What else, he cursed himself. "Tell Liza what's happening. Get everyone into the Citadel now."

"What's happened?" asked Aneksi. In response, the world around them shook as explosions rocked the whole complex. A dull roar, like thunder, was heard across the base. The lights flickered and resumed basic emergency status, no longer showing images of chandeliers and period sconces, only projected light spots around the walls, creating an uneven illumination throughout the lounge.

A general cry of despair arose from those carrying supplies into the Citadel.

"Dammit, the Bays! They've blown the Docking Bays," he cursed, then saw the angry look on Aneksi's face and remembered her aversion to being trapped. The idea that she had no way off the moon would play on her mind, even though she had no intention to leave. He could tell her there were other ways they could escape, but he'd rather keep his secrets hidden, for now.

Her wild eyes and dark blue aura lined with red disturbed him, while she struggled to control her hatred and sudden fear.

For just under a minute the comms went down and the information panels remained blank. She needed something to occupy her frantic mind.

"Aneksi, get down to the Citadel and take control, wait for stragglers, don't seal it yet. Audit all essentials including weapons and send Martin up to me." If she was busy and in command, she would be less likely to feel the need to run.

Without a word Aneksi obeyed, helping two elderly ladies by relieving them of their back-breaking loads of dehydrated food as she went.

The Citadel was an iron encased portion of the north west hotel block, on floors sixteen to thirty, deep below the surface. The hotel building was surrounded by four layers of shaped iron alloy walls, six feet thick, capable of stopping a hundred megaton missile at ten thousand klicks per second.

Originally intended as a meteor bunker for the early moon pioneers, it was massively improved by the military, before becoming an irrelevant footnote on the Holiday Resort Safety Pamphlet, as the complex evolved.

Trent had incorporated the idea into the lower portions of all four hotel buildings, but the north west was equipped with a secondary comms system and deeper storage bays below. The protection was designed to keep the inhabitants alive after a destructive meteor strike until help could arrive. In a time when spaceflight was not a routine activity, the bunker was a long-term survival shelter, catering for both safety and privacy.

"Martin," Aneksi called as she exited the elevator. Martin was stood at the reinforced door to the hotel corridor, searching guests as they arrived, before admitting them into the Citadel. He was dealing with an uncooperative gentleman at the head of the line who stood at least a head higher than himself.

"Trent wants you upstairs!" She passed the message, while appraising the troublemaker.

Martin acknowledged her with a look of exasperation on his face. He shrugged as the arrogant man batted away his detector, foiling his attempts to scan his body.

"Problems?" she grinned at the uncooperative man, placing her two boxes on the floor. The self-righteous thug sneered at her with a look of contempt. He compounded this mistake with a casual sweep of his arm to push Aneksi away from him, treating her like an irritating wasp. She grabbed his outstretched arm and twisting it, leapt upon his shoulders catching his second arm as it moved upward to grab her. Pushing back upon his spine she jumped back; gymnastically arcing away. She pulled back on both of his arms and dropped, jabbing her toes directly behind his knees. The tall man fell backward; mid-fall he felt his knees unexpectedly collapse and painfully crash to the ground; involuntarily, he emitted an agonised scream.

The claws that pierced his neck silenced him and allowed her time to whisper a warning that rendered the man fully compliant for Martin's security scan; two heavy blaster weapons were detected and confiscated. A murmur of appreciation travelled along the queue of refugees

"What did you say?" asked Martin, smiling at his agile helper as the contrite man limped away rubbing his shoulders.

"I reminded him we were going to be roomies for the next month," she laughed, her good humour restored, her joy infectious. "I'll take over," she took the scanning wand from his hand and shooed him away.

"What was the ruckus?" he asked, referring to the thundering roar they'd all heard on the lower floors. Aneksi glanced at the grim faces of the people waiting in line to gain their safety. Discussing explosions in the Docking Bays was not going to be helpful.

"I'm not sure," she tactfully lied, "probably just another light show; ask Trent." She immediately turned to smile at a young child waiting to enter the Citadel, offering the orange fur of her hand to be stroked. He turned to leave, but became enchanted, as the child's fear of the strange lady was replaced by laughter. She was a goddess, he thought.

Martin crossed the lounge at a fast pace against the flow of refugees. Approaching his boss, he noticed Trent's enthusiastic activity slow and stop. His Commander pulled a chair toward himself and flopped down, dejected.

"What's up boss?" asked Martin more out of interest than concern.

Trent looked up at Martin seeing the new scar above his eye and a little facial bruising, but detecting no other signs of his recent ordeal. He looked deeper using his inner eye; Martin's steady orange sense of peace became pierced by the flicker of pink curiosity, turning to the red of fear as Trent explained.

"There's a Synth gunship on its way."

"A gunship?" Martin was aghast.

"Two hundred thousand klicks and closing," Trent used his cyberlink to create a projected image on the main screen in the lounge. The remaining few staff and customers stopped to stare at the behemoth on the screen.

It looked to Martin as though three octagonal liners had been glued together and stretched lengthways, then someone had built a luxury yacht on top. The whole of the outer surface bristled with pipes that could only be weapons. Huge glowing blue engines were dotted around the structure. Martin counted to twenty then gave up.

"I didn't know anybody had built anything like that," whispered Martin in awe. His hobbyist knowledge of space vehicles told him he'd been studying moths while eagles soared overhead.

"Nobody did, they're Synths." He stared at the screen with the others for a few moments then shut down the image. "It looks as if the new landlord is determined to evict us."

19: Ultimatum

"We've located the Rovers Ling Rong-Yu used to leave her apartments. They're outside Bay Twelve, Sir!" Liza made her report. "Three of them, they look empty."

"Blow them apart," Trent replied. "I want no escape for this lot." He looked at the collection of guards and maintenance staff who had coalesced around his position. Now that the refugees had thinned-out, he decided his staff deserved to hear something positive.

"On the record," his voice assumed a formal tone as it blared through the speakers around the base. "The persons known as General Een-Eer and Ling Rong-Yu, along with their associates and accomplices, have been found guilty of murder, attempted murder, wilful destruction of government property with the intent to cause murder and illegal possession of lethal weapons, including, but not limited to Synthetic automatons, clones and plasma launchers." He thought for a moment about adding minor charges then realised he didn't need to. Quoting the offensive World Gov laws he despised, he continued confidently.

"As Commander of Moon Base Complex WG-1, I judge them guilty based on the evidence in my possession and sentence them, according to rank and privilege afforded me by my position and authority, to death." He felt conflicted. His mind told him it was the right thing to do, while his heart accused him of being as evil as the World Gov.

"Very decisive, sir! And very official." Liza's voice came across his comms. There was a crackle from the sound system within the base as she switched her channel within the Bug she piloted and once again a voice was broadcast for all to hear.

"In accordance with World Gov Protocol, as Senior Security Officer, I attest to the validation of your evidence and I witness your pronouncement." Liza took two shots and destroyed a Rover, her wing men each did the same. The shots were heard across the base and finally she reported, "Targets destroyed," before shutting down her public broadcast.

"What do you want us to do now?" she requested further orders on Trent's personal link.

"Jan's detected a huge gunship heading our way. Ling and Gen'eer are working together with the Synth's approaching." The line went quiet as Trent sent the images of the gunship to Liza. "I'm open to suggestions."

"Hit them with the net," suggested Liza. "See how they handle a mass missile attack."

"Agreed!" he called Jan. "What's the power level? Can we use the net?"

"Affirmative, we're pretty topped up. Give me a second."

"Good evening, Mr Trent" The sound of Gen'eer's voice rung out across the complex. "I understand you are aware our comrades in arms are approaching." He laughed emitting a taunting guffaw of glee, confident in his superiority.

"Let go the net, Jan." He whispered through clenched teeth. Stood in the Casino, Trent felt a minor tremor.

"I can't." Jan's frantic voice came over his comms. "They've blown the Reactor interlink. I can't get any power from it."

"Repairable?" he asked, desperate for some power, to exact his revenge on somebody.

"Not from this end," she confirmed his worst fears.

"You see, Mr Trent, we have left nothing to chance," gloated Gen'eer. "Our partners will arrive and finish you and your supporters. We will return to Earth with all the knowledge of your research and become richer and more powerful as fully fledged members of the World Gov."

"You're an idiot Gen'eer, there is no World Gov anymore. The Synths destroyed it and now they plan to destroy the earth. They're going to irradiate it, and simply wait for a couple of million years before starting all over again. Time is nothing to them."

"Desperate tales will not save you, Mr Trent." Gen'eer admonished him as a school teacher may reprimand an unruly child.

"Trent," Jan sounded scared. "The Reactor cooling system has been compromised; the whole thing is going into meltdown."

"How long have we got?" he asked, his mind racing.

"Maybe two hours, then 'whumpf', a big bang." Jan expressed herself freely, but got the message across.

"What's the safe zone," he needed the Citadel to be protected.

"Blast radius, two miles, but there'll be massive quakes and unpredictable collateral damage." She monitored her calculations and ran the simulations as she talked. "Most of the complex will escape the explosion, but the quakes..." she went quiet.

"The Citadel was designed for that. They'll be safe. What's the power situation?"

"With the Interlink down, we can't access the energy stored at the Reactor site. We have thirty percent power available to us, I estimate we'll lose a further eighteen percent, stored in range of the blast. I'm shunting everything to the far side, but I don't know..."

"I know, I know," he empathised with her dilemma. "How long will they survive with only twelve percent power?" he asked, desperately trying to assess his resources for the coming battle.

"Twelve percent gives them about two year's power for basic food recycling, lighting and heating, in the Citadel." The figure seemed to be a long time, but Trent knew the ship approaching could probably finish them in two minutes.

"That power, we're going to lose anyway," he felt a moment of outrage, "Let's do something useful with it. Charge the net from storage and let fly at that ship, minimum spread."

"Okay!" The idea of taking storage energy meant for survival and feeding the weapons was against everything Jan had ever believed, but the expected loss of energy from the Reactor explosion meant it wouldn't be retained anyway, so Jan's logical processes resumed control, pushing back the affective domain that briefly interfered with her reason. "Ready!"

"Let go the net," he sang musically. It was a hope and nothing more. The Synths would have known about the net and factored in the chance of an attack, but there was always a possibility some damage could be done.

"Impact at one hundred and seventy thousand klicks, in fourteen seconds." Jan updated the defensive salvo's progress.

"Due to the fact," began Gen'eer's mocking voice across the public address system, "...our glorious leader Mr Trent, interrupted our endeavours, I am willing to offer safe passage from your lunar tin can back to Earth."

In the Citadel the loud murmuring stopped, as everyone listened to Gen'eer's offer.

"Ignore him," shouted Aneksi, "He can guarantee nothing."

"I have fifteen seats available to the highest bidders, on my commercial liner here in Bay Twelve." Gen'eer sounded like a fairground barker as he teased and cajoled his audience. "Anyone who wishes to bid has ten minutes to see my representative at the Docking Bay doors. I can take cash or bio-credit transfer." His demonic laughter should have warned each of them of the devil they were dealing with, but still, uproar ensued as people of wealth, but little worth headed out of the Citadel. The doors were still open and Aneksi had little reason to prevent the exodus of the hopeful elite pursuing a glimmer of a chance to escape their fate.

"You too?" she asked quietly as Sarko, his wife and green haired son walked slowly past her, back into the main complex elevator.

"I save my family," he shrugged, unconvinced by his own words.

"Ladies and Gentlemen," Trent had taken position upon the lounge podium and retrieved a broadcast microphone from the dispenser. He stood upon it as the first would-be evacuees ran across the lounge floor to take the transit pod to Bay Twelve.

He appealed to the deaf ears of the panicked crowd, as more and more people emerged from the elevators, abandoning the safety of the Citadel below.

"The shuttle you are racing to board, is occupied by condemned criminals, sentenced to death. You are advised that, in accordance with World Gov protocol, the craft will be destroyed as it exits the bay. You are warned that your act of enriching this criminal makes you an accessory after the fact and you will be considered reasonable collateral damage if you are killed."

The warning was real and delivered in accordance with his laid down World Gov procedures, but Trent would never destroy a craft full of innocent civilians, no matter how tarnished their honour may be.

"Well done, Mr Trent." Sarko yelled up to the podium as he and his family walked across the lounge. "You play the part well," he nodded almost pridefully toward the Base Commander.

"He won't save you; he just wants to laugh at you and take your money," advised Trent. He watched as Sarko's orange and brown aura showed the man's resignation to his fate, the dark red of barely controlled anger coloured his son's aura, while his wife bathed in yellow and light red, each swelling in turn as her fear and her hysterical cowardice vied for supremacy.

"He also wants a shield, Mr Trent, he's seen your guns." Sarko waved. "Next time, Mr Trent." There was hope in his eyes, but Trent was unconvinced.

"Mr Trent," Gen'eer's self-satisfied voice entered his head through his comms. "Would you be so kind as to reinstate air for the evacuees, you seem to be impeding their rescue," he smirked again. He knew Trent had a duty to allow the rescue of those that requested it, by any means.

"All of your crew have been sentenced to death, Gen'eer. If my men see anyone, they have orders to shoot." Laugh that off thought Trent. There was no response.

"Jan," he activated his comms. "Put air back in the corridors to Bay Twelve,"

"Martin, take an armed squad," he considered giving the order to shoot no matter what, but then reprimanded himself. "Take out Gen'eer, Ling or their men, only if you have a clear shot. No heroics, no mistakes."

The crush outside Bay Twelve resolved itself as the outer doors opened to admit the evacuees. Martin stood back as the crowd of two hundred desperate refugees reformed at the foot of the Commercial Liner boarding ramp. Huge sums were offered in a cacophony of cries and appeals to two men dressed in the Commercial shuttle livery.

Stood upon the ramp the two men held powerful pistols looking uncomfortable and afraid while behind them others prodded and pushed, selecting the 'lucky' ones. The first to board was Tom Massado.

As the frantic bidding continued, Sarko took his place. He surveyed the desperation clearly displayed by the crowd in front of him and looked up into the face of Gen'eer. The criminal leader was stood behind the two uniformed liner crew, basking in the glory of the fear he'd induced. The role of the divine, arbiter of life and death, sat well in his mind.

"My wife, my son and myself," Sarko shouted, "and I offer four times the price of Massado." His stentorian voice carried easily across the crowd, silencing all but the few who'd almost lost their reason.

"I have only two seats left, my friend," crowed Gen'eer.

"Then eject one of your men," responded Sarko, as he pushed through the crowd, trailed by his fearful wife and snarling son.

"I will take your wife," Gen'eer laughed at his crude pronouncement, "But I have no room for children." Sarko's green haired boy pushed past his mother and grabbed his father's shoulder.

"This is wrong!" he demanded his father to reconsider. "We all stay!" He shook his father anxiously, frantically needing him to listen. "He'll kill us as soon as we pay him. There is no value for him in keeping us alive."

Sarko looked at his son, sadness in his eyes. "I know. You stay, you help Trent. I will help your mother." He leaned past his son's disbelieving expression and held out his hand for his wife. Together they broke free of the chaotic tide of pleading bidders and holding her close they stepped onto the ramp.

A henchman ran forward and took Sarko's thumb print, scanning the network of pumping blood flowing through his hand. He raised his hand to confirm payment and stepped back to allow the Russian couple to board.

It was quick and violent. Gen'eer pushed the blaster past his henchman at waist height and shot Sarko point blank, in the chest. There was no time for surprise as his face was torn and bloodied by the blast, his body folded to his knees and rolled off the ramp; his helmet activating too late as it thudded to the cold bay floor. A moment later, almost an echo of the same shot, Ling Rong-Yu appeared behind Gen'eer and silenced the screaming widow, blasting through her glittering fashion suit and tearing her neck apart with an explosive plasma round. The spray of blood drenched the crowd who roared in delight as, once again the two seats became vacant.

"I hated that prim whore," Ling laughed.

"Two seats left!" shouted Gen'eer, he laughed at the ease of destroying Sarko. His pride swelled as he thought of the stories he would tell about his great conquest of the Russian overlord.

Sarko's son had witnessed the death of both of his parents almost simultaneously; his anger was real, born of pure hatred and total loss of reason. He screamed his defiance... and fell.

"Get him back to the Citadel, now!" ordered Martin, as he struggled to pin the flailing green-haired youth he'd just stunned. The two criminal overlords stepped forward emboldened by the guard's struggle to contain the anger of one young man. The enhanced suit of Sarkovich's son was powerful, but no match for two trained guards.

The spectacle was amusing, the crowd were restless and the enthusiastically screamed bids for the last two seats were rising in volume. Gen'eer and Ling walked a few steps down the ramp bathing in the glory of their chaos.

Fights broke out amongst the crowd as realisation dawned of their saviour's true characters. The shock lancing through a portion of the hopeful evacuees. Martin gave the order to withdraw as the gathering turned into a melee.

Dragging their prisoner away, the guards trailed behind them a weeping crowd, caught between the devil and the deep black sky. Choosing to hide, rather than trust their escape to the whims of murderous madmen.

No-one paid their respects to Sarko or his wife, the cadavers had fallen from view, simply cold dead meat. If they had, they've have seen the damaged corpse of his beautiful wife lying bloody and alone beneath the craft.

"Sarko's dead!" reported Martin, "Gen'eer killed him and Ling killed his wife." Trent acknowledged the message and halted his progress to the storage halls. Leaning against a column, he made to reply, but could think of no words.

"I've got his son. I'm bringing him back to the Citadel, but he's angry." Martin's voice evidenced the struggle that had only intensified since leaving the docking area.

"I'll talk to him in the lounge," Trent resigned himself to the exposure of such powerful emotions. He hoped he would be able to calm the lad down, rather than be affected by his passion.

"Direct hit, sir." Liza's voice relayed the results of the base attack on the Synth ship.

"Where's Jan," was his ungrateful response.

"She fired and left, sir. Took her team and headed your way. Power Complex is sealed and empty. All functions relayed to Citadel Control."

"I didn't know we had a Citadel Control," admitted Trent.

"We don't yet, Jan will set it up when she gets there. I think she's routed it through the security desks in the Flight Dome."

"Any damage to the Synth ship?" he asked eventually. He moved to a booth and took a seat, watching the few remaining souls scurrying back across the lounge, now carrying their personal bags toward the Citadel.

"Not much," replied Liza, "I'm five hundred klicks out... got a drone feed... here. He closed his eyes to concentrate on the images beamed directly from the camera drones to his cyberlink. The huge ship had taken numerous hits.

"Four of the larger engines destroyed," Liza's voice held a modicum of hope, but even Trent could see a further twelve engines on the ship on just the side he was viewing. There were two rips in the side of the lower cylinder and the main yacht construct had a buckled front-end, but as he watched he saw the healing ability of the ships metal reduce the tears and reform the blackened hull.

"Any thoughts?" he asked his Chief of Security for a tactical appraisal.

"The hull is not bleeding air," she observed. "The ship is healing, but the engines are not."

"They'll fit spares when they need them," surmised Trent. On the table in front of him lay a pack of cards, he picked them up and idly shuffled them.

"Schematic shows sixty-four engines, four dead, plus eight huge ion beasts for main propulsion, they're hot, but not active." She paused allowing the scale of the ship to sink in. "At least two hundred plasma canon and fifty substantial barrels visible. I presume them to be weapons of unknown purpose." She murmured in his headset and he didn't hear her clearly.

"Any thoughts at all?" he prompted. He laid out the cards in a pyramid shape and began to play patience. Slowly, he peeled away cards from the lower layers.

"Just thinking... they couldn't generate enough power for all of those plasma weapons. I suggest they probably rout power to the most effective unit. Quicker and easier than relying on a mobile turret mount." She murmured some more incomplete ideas before clearing her throat. "Okay... if my hypothesis is correct, continued concentrated firepower at one section of the ship will produce a blind spot for a safe approach. We get in close and take out their engines. Ignore the ion beasts, if they want to run let them.

"But," the deep voice of the enemy interrupted Trent's conversation. "...you are not taking into account our ability to spin the ship as we approach. Your tactics are for linear thought and limited minds. This is why you will fail."

"Who are you?" asked Trent, "and why do you seek to destroy us?" He didn't question their ability to interrupt the comms line, he could do it and they had proved their technology superior to his. His analysis of his friend Cole had revealed many of their secrets.

"We seek only the healing of our planet..."

"And you consider us the disease," finished Trent sarcastically. The rhetoric was old and worn. "Go and find your own planet. We'll look after our own without destroying it."

"Sadly, you have proven incapable of the task. Now, we will resolve the matter." There was no emotion in the words; a simple statement of what was to follow.

"Liza! Come Back." Trent closed down his comms. He'd had the words of Cole confirmed. There could be no co-existence, no negotiation. What was approaching was death accompanied by the new rulers of the Moon; the scourge of men and the destruction of Planet Earth.

20: Alliances

Leaning back against the cushioned bench in the booth, Trent closed his eyes and tried to balance his own feelings. The Net barrage had only confirmed his suspicions.

He felt unsettled. Images of the old man in Ling's apartments plagued him. The death of the First Clerk had hit him harder than he thought possible, the old man's devotion, a powerful source of emotion and now... Sarko knew Gen'eer would never tolerate his presence on the ship, he just hoped his wife and son would be safe. He'd sacrificed himself in the hope of safe passage for his family, and it had all been in vain.

A wave of despondent people were returning from the Docking Bay, a tide of misery; they were lost, sad and destitute. Their desperation was tangible to him, their emotions raw. Several guards began guiding the stragglers back to the Citadel elevators and he tasted their brief flares of hope.

He threw the remaining cards down upon the booth table and nodded to himself. The half-removed solitaire pyramid unable to be completed triggered his dad's advice.

"Sometimes son, there isn't a solution. Then you're in trouble."

"Do we have to lose?" he'd asked.

"Oh no, we can change the game."

"What do you mean, cheat?" young Trent was horrified.

"Not really. If a big bully wants to hurt you and you're all alone, you can run away and hide, you can make friends, you can fight and hope to survive or..." his dad posed the teaser.

"There's nothing else I can do..." he began to get frustrated.

"Logically there is one other thing you can do, but it is the hardest to bear and probably the most difficult to achieve." His dad didn't give him the answer and it was many years after his mother sent his father to his death, that Trent realised what the last option was.

Reaching over he scooped the cards up and absent mindedly began shuffling.

With the numbers of refugees dwindling, he rose to follow them. Walking through the lounge he stopped and stood silently among the thin stream of refugees. He leant against a tall unadorned column; his eyes closed, he watched their fears and hopes pass him by. He tried to add comfort to the skittering grey shapes in his mind, but slowly they faded from view, pushed aside by a warmth of flickering peace.

He lost himself in the approaching comfort, wishing it would envelop him, surround him, and keep him safe. He felt a peck on his cheek.

"Hello sleepy-head," whispered Jan. She saw the cards he was idly shuffling. "Looking for a game?" Trent opened his eyes and smiled at Jan. Becoming aware of the cards in his hand he slipped them into a pocket on his belt. He saw her team behind her, pulling a gravity-sled piled with equipment.

"Not sleeping, just thinking." He revelled in the joy he sensed in her. "What have you got there?" he asked, examining the mound of electronic boxes and cables.

"Remote system for the base, similar to the one I had in my office," she gave a mock bow; "You shall still have control of your world, Oh Great Master," she teased him.

The lounge door was flung open and a chair thrown at a guard, smashed against the wall. Russian insults were hurled with passion at three security guards. Trent and Jan turned to view the screaming, angry disturbance as it entered the lounge. Martin was being abused as he guided Sarko's son back to the Citadel.

Trent could see the anger and loss in the lad's aura, a dark red flamed within a deep blue core of hatred and Trent noticed the tiny glint of sadness at the very centre. He concentrated on the slight sliver of brown in the aura and pictured it swelling.

The youth fell to his knees as Martin gently shoved him forward, but he no longer railed at his escort, he simply sobbed. The enormity of his loss was laid bare before him and he wept. Trent walked slowly over to the kneeling youth and crouched beside him.

"Your father was a wise man. I'm Trent..." he paused, inviting the youth to give his name, but there was no coherent reply.

"In the end he was my friend." Trent took a breath and pictured the release of hate and anger, then concentrated on the flame of sadness. His words came unbidden, without conscious thought, they just seemed right. "I know I cannot imagine your feelings of loss, but his actions were his own. He knew their consequences, but hoped for the salvation of his family. What he did, he did out of love." Trent pictured a beautiful white sheet and watched it wrap around the boy. The sobbing ceased and the boy recovered his composure. Trent stood and offered his hand to the new leader of the Russian crime gang. "Your father and my father were friends. I would like to think I could be your friend," offered Trent, "...though our enemies are still close and very powerful."

The boy took his hand. He gave a shrug and a smile, reminiscent of Sarko.

"Thank you," he whispered. The young man, head down in thought, walked silently toward the elevators. He stopped after a few paces and drew himself upright. Turning to face Martin and Trent he proudly announced, "I am Sacha Sarkovich, son of Mischa and Alexei Sarkovich. I thank you for your kind words, and I will help you as your father helped mine." Sacha inclined his head in respect then turned and walked to the Citadel to help out any way he could.

Trent was pleased with the boy's ability to control his anger and was intrigued by the possibility there was more to discover about his own father. But time was pressing and he'd had an idea.

"Martin!" Trent greeted his guard captain as if he was a long lost relative. "Tell me, have you ever heard of a thing called a catapult?"

"How did he do that?" asked Mike, as Jan watched Trent's performance in awe.

"He understands people," she said simply. "That's his gift," she beamed with pride at Mike, his face agog. "Come on, we need to get this lot set up."

"Wait!" Trent stopped Jan and her team as they headed towards the elevator. "This doesn't have to actually be on the base to work, does it?"

"No, I suppose not," answered Jan, cagily. "As long as it has enough power and can connect to the Security mainframe." Trent had a wily look in his eye.

"That's what I thought. Follow me." Trent winked at Martin and tapped him on the shoulder. "Go help Aneksi. Don't wait for us." Martin watched them leave and surveyed the now empty lounge.

***

The transit pod system was still working, though the air warning sirens blared and lights blinked all the way. Before they entered the pod Trent made them all check and replenish their suit air-supply. They would have to rely on their own resources, sealed within their suits to survive the journey he had in mind.

Trent shutdown the pod in the middle of a transit tunnel using his override code. With hardly a grumble Jan, Mike and the two techs followed Trent through a maze of dark tunnels; the natural moon rock darkened by thin coats of sprayed plascrete. There were no lights except what they carried on their suits and the journey, pulling the loaded grav-sled, was eery and disturbing. No one felt like talking.

Trent led Jan and her team silently through vacuum filled corridors heading south. He recognised Cooper from the murder scene. It seemed like a year ago. Had it all come to this in just a few days?

On reaching a thick door Trent activated the outer airlock sliding open a simple hidden panel. There was no keypad code required, a simple red button cycled the automated lock.

"Old," explained Trent. "Never put on the system."

They entered the frail construction, unaware that hidden eyes were watching, following.

Eventually they exited the rudimentary air-lock and stood outside a dark grey twenty-metre-tall cylindrical bin. In large white letters the words "Refuse Storage 'B'." had been stencilled. Either side stood bins 'A' and 'C'.

"Here we are," he announced with genuine pride. They were in the huge central hall of the refuse energy generating plant. The hall, an original feature from the earliest days of Moonbase construction, was roughly hewn from the rock and thinly sprayed with plascrete. This was not a place designed for people. Yet, it was still full of air to facilitate the furnace systems and Trent dropped his helmet.

"What's this, camouflage?" asked Mike in disgust. "You can't get this equipment covered in sh..." he started to complain, but Trent shushed him.

The last stage in the recycling process was where unrecoverable materials were combusted to reclaim their final meagre energy. It wasn't used often due to the inefficient use of air, but they could all feel the heat on their faces and see the glowing flames reflected upon the ceiling. Enormous access doors to the furnace units were present on three sides. There were thermal barriers everywhere they looked, covered in toxic safety warnings and access limitations. The furnaces beyond these doors were deadly.

"This, ladies and Gentleman is not what it seems, behold..." Trent moved to the giant doors and activated a small digital panel. He typed in his personal code and opened the tall blast doors of Cylinder B, revealing... a garbage furnace. A wash of hot air flooded over them, making those who'd dropped their helmets flinch as they passed the doorway.

"Follow!" he ordered, then marched into the open flame and disappeared.

Behind the team, a fleeting dark shadow darted across the open space from the ancient airlock and slipped into the great furnace hall, melding with the deep shadows around the crude wall.

Jan made to follow her boss, trusting him implicitly, but Mike reached out and grabbed her arm. "These suits won't take that punishment... they're not like his." Jan heard Mike's fear and understood his concern, but her trust in Trent was complete.

"Trent, do we need anything special for these flames?" she asked. In response, the furnace flickered and disappeared, revealing a huge white space cruiser.

Mike was flabbergasted, "What the...? Where did you...? How...?", but his questions were redundant.

The holo-graphic flames and furnace shut off to reveal a huge three storey high, tear drop shaped cruiser parked in front of them; sleek and beautiful with no external fins or engines. The team were equally shocked, but Jan took it in her stride and ran to Trent, stood at the foot of the extending forward ramp he'd just activated.

"Come on, let's get that kit set up." called Trent. "Welcome to my baby, the 'Queen-B'. Every Captain must have his yacht, it's tradition. Come on!" he raised his voice. "How long until the reactor blows?" he asked Jan.

"Thirty-seven minutes," she replied, "but that gunship will be here in less than thirty-five."

"Good, let's see if we can get them into the wrong place at the wrong time." He ascended the ramp and Jan thought she understood his plan.

The team worked efficiently, each engineer knew their role and Trent assisted by unpacking equipment on demand.

He'd built the ship himself and quickly identified every system and outlet they asked for. Within fifteen minutes the new control desk was up and running beside the ship's main communications console.

"Cyberlink connection is good, Jan check yours." There was no response, "Jan, Jan?"

"Trent!" Mike shouted, "We've got company."

At the lower end of the ramp stood Jan. At her throat was held a laser knife. The charged weapon prevented her helmet from raising. Jan stood quaking in terror. Behind her, holding the knife was a deeply scarred Cutter.

"I thought you were dead?" began Trent, conversationally. He moved down the ramp and Cutter pulled Jan towards him, tightening his grip on her, letting the knife burn into her neck. He could see the deep red anger of Cutter flaring to black as the man's reason threatened to snap.

Trent witnessed the hope flash through Jan as he appeared at the head of the ramp, and was shocked when the hope instantly fled, replaced by terror as Cutter's knife sliced into her neck. His anger burned.

"You tried to kill me!" The deranged mobster started shouting, spitting angrily. "But I've got a good one too," he indicated his suit. Twenty minutes in that room gave me enough charge to survive your explosion, just. He turned his head to show Trent the burnt tissue, cracked and weeping, covering the side of his face.

"It was Gen'eer, not us." Trent tried to imagine a peaceful wrap to defuse Cutter, to bring him back to sanity, but as the peaceful calming projection impacted the black aura of Cutter's madness, the mobster screamed.

'Fire and Ice,' thought Trent. 'Twist it, turn it to hate, focus on something he knows, something he can relate to.'

"We took you away from death, we saved you Cutter. It was Skabenga at the controls... he said you were just collateral." Cutter's aura faded to the deep blue of hatred, so strong he could taste it, but the reason was not the one Trent intended.

"You were there, you watched as I burned, as I was tortured. I saw you looking down on me. The pain... you have no idea." Cutter was reliving the pain of the incapacitation net that brought him down after Belle's murder. He pulled Jan's arm down behind her back and the knife moved towards her neck again, this time she screamed as the burning blade sliced into her flesh. Trent could see the agony Cutter was inflicting on her and something inside him erupted.

"You were stung because you planned to rape and murder an innocent child," he yelled at the madman. He wanted to make himself the focus of Cutter's anger. "You escaped death because my guards took pity on you." He spat the contempt he felt for the coward. "Your actions have condemned you to death and only I can stop that happening," His anger took over, he stepped toward the hate filled psychopath closing the distance to barely two paces.

"Then watch her burn, Trent." Cutter moved his head, craning forward to watch his blade slice deep. He seemed to struggle. His hand holding the laser knife, peeled away from Jan's throat and a loud crack of bone was followed by Cutter's agonising curse. He screamed again as his other arm, restraining Jan, released its hold, his arm snapped behind him.

Trent's fear for Jan and despair at his inability to save her had triggered something deep within him. He saw the body of Cutter no longer as a man, but a black shadow filled with twisting golden threads, sparkling with the colours of hatred and anger. With a thought, he held the lines of gold, gripped them tightly and moved Cutter's weapon away from Jan.

Detecting the removal of the weapon, Jan's helmet immediately raised. As Cutter's hold relinquished, she ducked and ran forward to Trent, but she seemed to hit a wall, something pushed her and she tumbled to the side, falling off the ramp. Mike jumped down from the ship to help her, Trent looked like he was in a trance.

Screams erupted from the insane murderer as he collapsed and writhed on the ground.

Trent's eyes opened revealing unholy orbs. The whites stained yellow, moving to gold as he stared at the murderer, his iris and pupil blazed with a brilliant light, as Garvy's man cursed him with every fibre of his being.

Trent watched as the blue-black aura was ripped from Cutter's chest and squeezed tightly around his head, "Take it..." shouted Trent. His trembling voice forced its way through the thick ether, commanding the coalescing glowing fibres to penetrate his unrepenting victim's head. He forced it in through bleeding ears, eyes, mouth and nose. Trent ripped the man's violent emotions from his body and force-fed them to his brain.

So intensive was the power of Cutter's hatred that every cell in his skull ruptured. The murderer lay still and Trent collapsed; his world turned black.

He awoke with the cool hand of Jan stroking his forehead. Without opening his eyes, he saw the aura of fear emanating from the technical crew. He was lying down just inside the ship and his love was kneeling beside him.

"Cutter must have been in the transit tunnels all this time. His suit power was low and he had little air left, lucky he saw us." Mike was ruminating on the mobster's escape.

"Not that lucky," offered Cooper. "Not meeting... him."

Trent groaned as he realised Jan's aura was washed with fear and her normal pristine white calm was filled with the beige of self-doubt. He remembered the punishment he'd served to Cutter and a tear ran down his cheek.

"He's waking up," called Jan.

"Is he crying?" asked Mike and his fear and doubt changed to pity. Cooper's fear altered to pink curiosity as he moved closer to see Trent's tears.

"I'm sorry," Trent opened his eyes, no longer discoloured. He discovered he was lying on the deck of the 'Queen-B', at the top of the ramp. "It's never happened before," he explained and excused himself at the same time expecting them to voice their fear and challenge him, but their responses were all supportive.

"Bastard deserved it," observed Mike, there were murmurs of agreement.

"Did you see Jan's neck," said Cooper. Trent immediately cut short his self-pity and struggled to sit up to inspect her throat. Someone had placed a sticking plaster over the wound.

"That's the good thing about laser burns," Jan bravely sought the positive side, "...self-cauterizing."

He looked into her eyes and she fell for him all over again, leaning forward she kissed him gently on the lips. Her aura resumed the flickering colours of her love and he felt renewed.

"Cor, he is magic," yelled Cooper, "look at that. If I tried to kiss her..." There was a yelp followed by laughter from the small crew as Mike slapped the misguided joker.

"Reactor Core goes up in sixteen minutes, we're set." Jan ignored Cooper's remark. "What do you want us to do?"

"Let's take her up," Trent stood up and moved up into the ship. The floors were simple open plan layouts and anyone who'd been in a ship would recognise the demarcation between the pilot's console and the navigation console. In the middle of the cabin was a long holo table showing images of the base. Trent moved to the navigation station on the port side.

"Jan, would you?" he indicated the front seat and she made herself comfortable at the pilot's position. Mike took the third seat which he recognised as comms and the other two crewmen sat themselves around the new equipment they'd installed, ready to activate the new base complex control centre.

"Do we need to warm the engines up?" asked Mike.

"What engines?" countered Trent.

Trent selected some settings from his panel and the red air-pressure warning lights flashed outside. He recycled the air in the fake furnace hall back into the moon-base storage tanks. The hall began to glow as the roof slid open revealing the blinding direct sunlight and the multitude of reflections from the outer surface. A moment later the windows around the cabin, undetectable from outside, tinted to allow a much-reduced level of light inside the craft.

Without a sound or any vibration, the 'Queen-B' rose out of its home and hovered above the south side of the Lunar Complex.

"All Lunar Bugs and Rovers," called Trent across his public comms. "The big white teardrop rising from the recycling centre is my personal yacht and for the next hour or so it is our flagship. Please be so kind as not to open fire on me." He flashed an impudent grin at Jan.

She had deciphered most of the controls and had set a timer to the reactor core explosion. The polished black banner above the windows displayed bright green numbers as the timer ticked down. Six bugs flew towards the yacht and took up station beside it. They looked like ladybugs beside a corpulent white snail.

"Nice to have you with us, sir!" Liza welcomed him to the squadron.

"Switch to secure comms, channel 'D', frequency agility, phase two," Mike announced over the public frequency. He hoped the rapid switching of frequencies would hamper the ability of the Synths to intercept their comms.

As he dictated the comms information, Jan found the weapons controls and set them all to armed and charging.

"Okay, began Trent, our only concern right now is the big hostile ship heading our way. It's full of Synthetics who think they are people. Their plan is to annihilate everyone on the Moon and then sterilize the Earth with a nuclear bombardment. If you have any concerns about any of that then please listen closely."

Trent outlined his plan, the bugs would buzz and swarm, lay magnetic pulse mines and take pot-shots at the engines on the beast as it approached.

"You run interference and I'll lure it over the Reactor core. If we time it right maybe we can do some serious damage."

As he finished speaking a sequence of brief flashes caught his attention from a launch, exiting the

Docking Bays to the north east. "That's Gen'eer and Ling's Shuttles followed by the Liner with the evacuees," he casually commented.

"We have a few minutes," observed Liza, "I could disable their engines," she offered.

"If we survive this, so will they," Trent needed to focus. "Then, I think we'll all have a long chat later." He watched as the Liner led the way, followed by Ling's shuttle moving off from Bay Twelve. A few moments later Gen'eer's shuttle left Bay Eleven. The three ships from the undamaged Docking Bays were heading back to Earth.

"Head north two klicks, stay on me," and with that the diminutive squad of defenders moved to take up position against the huge gunship heading their way. "Mike, contact the Khonsu, public broadcast, tell them all blast doors will seal in two minutes."

On the main holo-table the view shifted to behind the approaching enemy. Their approach to the complex was outlined in startling clarity.

"Cooper and…?" Trent addressed the technician he hadn't had time to get to know.

"Webb, Sir!" The tech sounded younger than Cooper.

"Can you check the blast doors are secure down there?" The crew did as they were asked and reported in the affirmative.

"Aye, sir. Blast doors secure."

The Synth ship halted its progress fifty klicks from the Reactor and opened fire on the base. Streams of destructive energy poured into the shields protecting the hotel buildings around the casino.

"Okay, they're not coming closer without a shove." He stood up and moved to Jan's position. "Can you take tactical, and watch for patterns."

She stood, relieved she wasn't going to have to avoid a barrage of missiles from the gunship.

"Attack! Attack!" Trent gave the order to move in and harass the Synth ship.

He smoothly moved his ship to stare face to face with the bow of the Synth's upper yacht-like structure and received a blast from a plasma cannon for his audacity. The forty-klick range allowed him over a second to manoeuvre out of the way, easy in his yacht. He skipped up, then down, then left and up again, each time returning to the same point in space.

Mike watched the ship move on the holo-projector. He saw the flickering red dots as the Bugs attacked and lay magnetic pulse mines around the enemy hull, but he was drawn repeatedly to the 'Queen-B's movement.

"What is driving us?" he asked, "I've never seen a ship this responsive, and yet we can't feel a thing. We're not moving!"

Jan answered for Trent, who was busy avoiding incoming fire from multiple canons.

"He developed a toy to show how gravitic repulsion and attraction would work as motive impulse." She'd worked through the idea with him, but her pride was evident in his final achievement. "They wouldn't fund him, they said it wouldn't work on a big ship, ...he built it anyway."

"The really hard bit," explained Trent without taking his eyes off the battle, "was hiding the material usage from the World Gov auditors."

"Blast doors compromised in north east hotel complex. I've started repairs, but another couple of hits and there'll be nothing to repair." Cooper reported the damage and shrugged at the inevitability of his losing battle. Mike saw his consternation and offered to swap seats.

An explosion of yellow and blue flashed brightly across Jan's eye line, as bright as a nova, "Someone's engine and power pack has gone up." she observed.

"Who did we lose?" he yelled, praying Liza would answer.

"Not one of ours," called Liza, for the first time ever Trent detected stress in her voice as she fought to avoid the Synth weapons. She darted forward, releasing a magnetic mine and pulled out, twisting to avoid the rotating Synth ships protruding weapons.

"It's Ling's ship, engine blown, she's crippled," reported Jan.

"Synths?" asked Trent deftly making the 'Queen-B' dance.

"Don't think they're interested in anything except the base," Jan analysed the Synths targeting. "I've got a contact... no it's gone."

Mike looked up from his screen and scanned the space outside through the starboard window. A second intense flash caused him to avert his eyes as he blinked away the residual retinal flare from the space beyond. Light blue energy erupted and the shape of the commercial liner flared into silhouette. The glowing engines died and a moment later, another explosion erupted as Gen'eer's shuttle lost its main propulsion. The three escaping craft now devoid of power, tumbled and drifted in unplanned directions away from the moon.

"Who else is up here?" asked Mike, but there was no answer.

"Whoever they are, I wish them all the luck in the world," Trent wondered if everyone had been safely secured inside the Citadel. Maybe Ivor or Martin were using the base defence system.

"Can they use the Base lasers?" Trent asked.

"All power is routed to the shields," answered Jan. "It must be a ship."

"But all of the other bays were destroyed," Mike was perplexed. "Could they be from Earth?"

"Too far away, and there's no-one down there who could help us anyway," replied Jan.

Trent stared at the core countdown, two more minutes, time to make his move.

"Jan, you have weapons now, with tactical." He shared his weapons access with her, leaving himself to concentrate fully on his piloting controls. "Shields are good, but please try not to take too many hits, those canons are big and the shields won't last. Buckle up, we're going for a ride."

The 'Queen-B' accelerated toward the bridge of the upper part of the Synth gunship, on instinct Jan lined up the ship's forward blasters and took a point-blank shot.

At this extreme close range, the enemy ship took a hit that would have destroyed any human crew of a regular ship, puncturing the gunship's hull and ripping through multiple levels of the inner floors. Her shot must have hit them hard as the heavy barrage of the complex ceased. Trent hopped vertically over the ship and pulled a hard turn ninety degrees to port, accelerating in a planned sweeping curve to regain his former position above the lunar reactor core.

The massive reduction in offensive weapons fire was seized upon by Liza and her Bugs. They swooped in a ring formation from behind unchallenged and surrounded the Synth ship. As they accelerated along its length on all sides almost skimming the hull, they discharged their magnetic mines. Only as the Bugs pulled away did the Synth defensive guns erupt in fire. But it was too late. The gravitic acceleration pushing against the huge mass of the gunship gave them a velocity in excess of the erupting plasma charges. The squadron escaped unscathed.

"One minute, fifteen" Mike tried to be helpful and read aloud the countdown they could all see.

"They're moving towards us, but slowly. They'll be late..." Jan's voice trailed off in despair.

"Standby," called Trent, his fingers flickering over his panel in a blur.

"Mr Trent," the alien voice addressed him across the ship's speakers. "We heard your plan and have detected the imminent explosion of your reactor core. We have nothing to fear from the energy that will recharge our ship and energise our repairs. We are positioning now to maximise our energy collection from the core explosion." The Synthetic didn't laugh, but they all heard the mocking tone of the message.

"Your actions are inconsequential."

Trent threw a dozen switches and Mike's console lit up. "What's the Base power at now Mike?" he asked.

"Er, Base power storage, twenty eight percent," he answered, perplexed at the activity on his panel.

"Let's trim it shall we, maybe by five or six percent." Trent looked at Jan, an understanding passed between them, she smiled and nodded in unspoken agreement.

"Liza," he issued her one final order. "Priority, pull all bugs back to base, I'm going after the big one."

"What can we do?" Mike was anxious, he was coming to the realisation they'd lost and had nowhere to go.

"My father used to say change the game." Trent moved his fingers in a blur across his panels as he spoke. "You can run away and hide, but they'll find you. You can make friends, but you can never trust them. You can fight and hope to survive, but there are no guarantees, or... you can do the hardest thing, you can remove their power from the board. A lesson my old friend Cole taught me at school."

Trent withdrew from his perch above the reactor allowing the Synth ship to approach. Deftly he calculated a point above the huge gunship, extending a line between the reactor core and the Synths; a bright dot appeared. Gravitic beams emerged from three antennae around the complex.

"It's too low," screamed Jan.

"All part of the plan, my dear." Using his Cybernetic connection to the base he fed the weapon more and more power from the Base storage and finally the gravity vortex formed.

"Let's see if we can remove them. I give you... Charybdis," he quoted quietly from his earlier show. They all watched the holo-image above the table. The enemy ship tilted as it rose into the maelstrom.

"It's taking avoiding action, pointing its main ion drive into the vortex," observed Cooper.

"They're holding," shouted Jan.

"Those ion beasts take an hour to get up to full power," offered Mike, hopefully.

"Then let's give a little more shall we." The lights on the 'Queen-B' dimmed as a fourth gravitic beam was generated by the captain's yacht. Focussed on the same nano-metre target as the gravitational beams from the moon, the added energy created a lightning storm within the vortex that reached out and struck the gunship.

"They're moving... inward, but they're fighting it, they're slowing," reported Jan from her tactical screen.

Without a single observer the countdown clicked to zero and a few seconds later the core of the reactor violently exploded. A sudden pulse of energy accompanied by the blast wave erupting from the ground, struck the enemy gunship, for a few seconds the massive ship lost traction and began to move into the vortex, taking hit after hit, from a barrage of material liberated by the atomic meltdown.

"Inverse catapult grapeshot." explained Trent. "Pulling not pushing."

But the impacts were small in relation to the mass of the gunship and the benefit of the additional kinetic energy conversion was quickly directed to their engines. The Synth ship slowly moved out of the eye of the swirling beast.

"Mines, automatic detonation." Trent's program was immediately executed by Jan. A rhythmic chain of explosions erupted from the gunship.

The mines laid by the bugs had sat upon the hull and now every device that could add a directional push toward the gravitic whirlpool was detonated. As the ship rotated more mines detonated to push the ship back into the abyss.

"What's that?" yelled Jan, pointing to a flashing streak of light. It could only be a ship. A thousand rocks and structural pieces of debris were being sucked past the enemy gunship into the vortex, but they all saw the tiny ship dart across the flow of jetsam.

"It's not a Bug, it looks like Gen'eer's ship," she observed. Her tactical panel was receiving incomplete information from her sensors, the electro-magnetic pulse generated by the core explosion had disrupted her data feed; she couldn't be certain.

"Hello my friend, Mr Trent." A crackling message came across the comms, but Trent recognised the owner immediately. "I hope you do not mind; I find your ship from Security. I help you with your justice."

"Hi Sarko, I thought you were dead," Trent admired the perseverance of the Russian.

"I hard man to frighten, even harder to kill, my friend. Thank your man for saving my son, please." Sarko was cracking up, his words faded, then static swamped the comms. Finally, the shuttle appeared at the side of the gunship. "This is the bad ship?" he asked innocently.

"It is," replied Trent.

"Then I take into big hole." Sarko cut his comms.

"You don't have to Sarko, she's being pulled in..." he desperately wanted to see his friend again, he didn't need him to risk himself. No matter how tenuous, Sarko was a link to his father.

"Trent," Jan spoke quietly, checking her figures, "The worm is decaying and the Synthetic's ship is pulling away."

"Push more power into the vortex," commanded Trent, but he knew the vortex had a limited life once it formed, no amount of additional energy would make it survive any longer.

A single shot flashed from the Synth gunship and destroyed one of the Lunar Base's gravitic antennae, the power feed to the vortex was now dependant on the third beam from the 'Queen-B'. To maintain the beam and the wormhole, Trent's ability to move had been severely curtailed. They watched as the scarred gunship slowly rotated, aligning its forward guns to point at the insignificant white yacht. Lumbering on its side the gunship twisted to line up a serviceable weapon.

"Shields at fourteen percent, not sure about this one Trent," offered Jan.

There came a blinding white flash from the rear of the Gunship, the few nav lights on the hull flickered and went off and the huge ship continued to rotate, then twisted as it began accelerating toward the vortex. The wild lurch and twist disconnected one of the lower octagonal tubes and it crumpled. A violent explosion from a magnetic mine, ripped the tube to pieces, most of which headed into the vortex, but a section about the fifth of its length spun toward the 'Queen-B'

Trent calmly executed a short horizontal manoeuvre, side stepping the deadly chunk and allowed it to pass.

"Will that hit?" Trent shouted urgently, knowing there was nothing he could do.

"Trajectory puts impact... thirty klicks east of the base." Mike was relieved at the positive report.

"Liza! Wreckage heading thirty klicks east. Possible threat, get some Bugs out there."

"On it!"

As the colossal lumbering gunship rotated, the engine array came into view. They could see a massive circle of damage, as if some huge ravenous monster had taken a bite out of the main engines. Beside the rim of the damage floated Sarko's ship, powerless to escape, caught in the gravity of the massive gunship.

"This big red button... very powerful weapon, Mr Trent." Inside the small cockpit Sarko, gazed at his handiwork. His chest covered in blood, his face showing the pain of his life.

"It's a plasma mining drill, Sarko," he commiserated with his friend. They both knew Sarko's ship had little power left and a quick check showed them he was now drifting along with the gunship into the diminishing vortex.

A plan formed in Trent's head, but it was risky and he had no way of knowing if it would work.

"Does anyone mind if I try and rescue my friend?" he asked his team as his fingers flew across his console.

"He saved us," observed Mike, "We should try..." A round of murmurs came from the relieved crew.

"It would be rude not to," offered Jan.

"We might die," offered Trent, but he'd already plotted his course.

"Thirty-nine, seconds to vortex collapse," announced Jan. "If we're anywhere close it'll take us too."

The 'Queen-B' flew into the fringe of the swirling vortex maintaining the beam as long as it dared. Deeper and deeper until it was behind Sarko's commandeered ship. With an instant direction change, Trent accelerated toward the stricken ship that had saved them. The Beam failed and the Wormhole began to collapse.

Skirting past the huge gunship with inches to spare, to gain as much gravitic acceleration as possible from its large mass. Trent headed directly for Sarko.

The escape from the closing vortex took every ounce of power Trent could scrounge, removing life support, lighting, automated diagnostics and repair, he diverted all power to gravitic acceleration achieving an approach speed which was reckless. Eighteen milliseconds before collision, Trent's ship reversed the gravitic shift in the forward plates and punched Sarko from the vortex's grasp, within half a second, he angled the gravitic plates, thrusting against the mass of the stricken gunship and regaining his original speed, executing his escape from the deadly anomaly he'd instigated.

The huge ship vanished as the visible maelstrom of debris violently compressed to the point of eruption. There was no noise and no physical turbulence, but an energy disruption that large had to leave a mark on the universe. A bubble of electro-magnetic energy burst from the emptiness seeming to suck out the last of the ships energy as it impacted the 'Queen-B'.

Systems slowly came online and the red-lit bridge faded to white. Outside, Sarko's ship drifted, to all indications lifeless in front of the 'Queen-B'.

21: Survival

The punch from the gravitic plate had supplied Sarko's ship with enough energy to reinstate his life-support, but the gravitic shock had knocked the injured heroic occupant senseless for several minutes. Luckily the drained ship had been spared any physical damage from the final burst of electro-magnetic radiation emitted by the wormhole. The energy wave was huge, but its decay rate extremely fast as the forces expanded spherically in two areas of the universe.

The crew of the 'Queen-B' listened to the faint static, barely breathing in case they missed any signs of life. It could have been an air leak, a barely perceptible sigh, or possibly even a yawn, emitting gently from the speaker.

"Once again, my friend, I am not dead," Sarko gave a throaty laugh, but there was the definite sound of pain in his voice.

The faces within the 'Queen-B' relaxed and Trent breathed again.

"I was told you took Gen'eer's blaster point-blank. You should be dead!"

"Ahh my friend, did I not tell you. Your father... very good tailor."

"I'll give you a push, and stay with you until your thrusters re-energise." Trent didn't ask. He wasn't going to let Sarko out of his sight until they were back at base.

"Hey, Mr Trent?" Sarko's voice was weaker, but his spirits were high. "I too, dance with the devil, no?"

Together they headed slowly back to the battered moon-base. Beside Sarko the 'Queen-B' already looked as pristine as ever and had power reserves to spare.

"Liza," Trent issued his instructions, "Leave a couple watching the wreckage and get the rest of the Bug crews into Bay's Eleven and Twelve, we'll be home in a few hours."

"No problem, sir." Her voice had assumed its typically neutral tone.

"Not like that!" Jan admonished Mike and pushed him from his chair, stealthily assuming his role at the base control console. "Reinforce the bulkheads, then bring in the air and finally the gravity," she lectured him in basic space engineering.

"Hey!" Sarko shouted across the comms.

"What is it my friend?" asked Trent.

"My dispenser works! I have brandy!" he chortled with surprise.

"Cheers!" Trent couldn't help, but smile.

"Tell me, Mr Trent, why would you risk yourself for this old Russian smut 'yan?" Sarko sipped his brandy noisily.

"Well, Mr Sarkovich," Trent's inner cybernetics translated 'smut 'yan' as 'troublemaker' and he smiled at the understatement. "You see, I plan to retire soon and I can't do that until you pay your bar tab." Trent adopted a tone of authority, dismissing any revealing emotions he may have developed for the oligarch. "Call your son Sarko, tell him you are a hero... again."

"E.T.A. one hour and forty-two minutes, Sir. Although, I have no idea how we survived that thing."

Mike assumed the formality of his role, he reckoned it was a good idea, now they were all going to survive.

"Well, the odds were against us." Trent sounded introspective. "Maybe you were right Jan," suggested Trent. "Khonsu likes a gambler." She nodded and checked her control board.

"Base repair protocols in place, nothing else I can do from up here," stated Jan with a sigh. "What are we going to do to pass the time?"

Technician Webb had located the galley and served everyone coffee as they all sat around the central table staring at the 3D images of the base. Trent leaned across his panel and flicked a switch, killing the data feed to the holo-table, re-purposing the central control hub to a simple block of white plastic. From his belt he produced a pack of cards.

"Texas hold 'em, two's and one-eyed jacks' float. Minimum opening bid two credits, house rules apply. Who's in?"

***

Four hours later, Trent eventually got to take a shower and get some much-needed sleep. The threat to the station seemed to have abated.

Strangely, Aneksi had pleaded with him over a private channel as he landed.

"Please, please. Just for me. Can we keep them in here just for a couple of days?"

"Why? It's probably safe to come out," he was perplexed.

"We got them in here. Let them see how the other half live. It'll do them good." He relinquished, agreeing to one night only.

"But the Citadel will be opened promptly at eight in the morning," he promised. "Be gentle with them Aneksi," he warned her.

After satisfying himself that the habitable portions of the complex were safe and secure, Trent called Liza.

"Set a meeting for ten o'clock in the morning. I need station reports on everything, and we should have a plan of action for guest control, comms and station security, not forgetting a run down on medical needs and supplies. It'll be weeks before power storage is returned to comfortable levels." He took a breath and checked his tablet.

"Jan says, the Cold Fusion generator has been brought online, full time, to boost the Solar supply, and we need to plan energy distribution and planned outages, to facilitate the demand from the automatic repair systems. We need Bug patrols set up and all Rovers serviced and on the surface. Keep an eye out for any more material that came from that ship, and watch that debris that fell to the east. There may be a little spare power to generate additional food and water, just in case, can you organise that?" He stretched and yawned.

"Yes, Sir!" answered Liza. She called Ivor and Martin on the holo-vid floating above her desk. Aneksi was sat with them in the Citadel. "Meeting, ten o'clock guys." They nodded.

***

"Morning," Jan's aura was broadcasting her happiness as she came to meet him and walk the few minutes to the executive office together.

He wanted desperately to thank her for everything, to tell her how she'd changed his life, how the last ten years had been bearable because she was there. He wanted her to be with him, always. He stood facing her smiling face, unable to utter a word.

She kissed him and he responded in kind. She held his hand, bathing him in her brilliant, sparkling aura of love. It was the best conversation he'd ever had.

Liza greeted them at the door of the office and Martin and Ivor were sat inside talking to Aneksi and Jack. In the corner, away from the table sat Rhet from Docking Bay control, alone and uncomfortable. Martin waved the nervous man over to sit beside him.

The reports were standard and no-one talked about the elephant in the room. What had happened to the World Gov?

"Luckily, there is very little residual radiation from the reactor meltdown," Jan explained. "The Synth Gunship told us it was harvesting the energy; it probably took most of it into the vortex with it. And so far, there has been little secondary damage from the actual destruction of the reactor. Two minor quakes, no further damage to the base."

"Customers are happy and resettled," reported Aneksi. "The Khonsu is open and people are flowing back to the amenities. Two restaurants are already open and all Citadel supplies returned and audited. We're stocked for six months full occupation, two years at current complement, but we could cut back." She seemed eager to implement rationing.

All eyes turned to Rhet, "Bays Four and Five were only slightly damaged and are now operational." he began, reading off his tablet. "Er, we need to know if we're charging for the repairs to the ships, not all of them have full repair systems fitted." Rhet was out of his depth being included in the executive meeting, but Trent needed someone who understood the technical and logistics side of the business. There was an awful lot of work to do in the docking bays and Trent needed someone with the right knowledge in a key position, who understood the needs of the ships and Martin had recommended him highly.

"Thanks, Rhet," Trent calmed the nervous man with a few words.

"Oh and..." Rhet had something else to say, but wasn't comfortable voicing it. "People are asking when they can go home." An uncomfortable silence fell upon the room.

Trent's priority for access to and escape from, the moon-base had never been higher. He nodded to Rhet acknowledging his contribution.

"No one leaves. We'll get the ships put right to the best of our ability and if anyone asks, I've commandeered them all until further notice. Do the repairs, Rhet, but don't demand any payment yet. Prioritise those you can get working quickest. I'd rather have a working two-seater scow than an almost fixed liner. Let me know if anyone gives you any grief." Trent tapped the desk thoughtfully, "I need you promoted Rhet, any problems with that?" he asked.

"No sir." Rhet swelled with pride.

"Liza. Captain Rhet needs an '04' clearance." Liza nodded pulling out her tablet. Martin smiled at his friends' embarrassment.

"Okay, we have a couple of other problems," began Trent. "First, thanks to our Russian friend, there are three crippled ships of unknown complement that need to be recovered. We have to consider them hostile."

"Bring them back." suggested Liza, "Show them lunar justice. Bring them back to the Khonsu and ascertain the guilt of any survivors and any threat they posed due to their allegiance. Carry out sentences passed."

A general plan was hastily put together, with everyone contributing ideas. Trent agreed, proud of the way his team worked together.

Liza half-mumbled, half lectured for a few minutes and worked out a plan on her tablet to increase her secure holding capacity on the fly. Jan agreed with her power figures.

"Then there's that huge chunk of Synth gunship containing 'God only knows' what." Trent wondered how many of them had even considered it as a threat. The room muttered loudly and angrily.

"Bugs patrolling the area and drones are watching it," reported Liza. "No movement recorded, inside or out." Her tone was ominous.

"Finally," Trent stared at each member of his team in turn. He was confident in their professionalism and reassured by their calm auras. He knew what he was about to say would affect them all deeply.

"Earlier, we reconnected communications to Earth. It seems... there's no one there."

As the silence fell a commotion at the door heralded the arrival of Fenwick, red faced and out of breath.

"Sir!" panted the guard, "...the Synth crash site... two observation drones have been destroyed."

Other Books by this author;

Molly and Corry Series

Boot Up!
Satellite Sleuths
Smash 'n' Grab
Digital D-Day

Micro Fiction and Rhyme

Supernatural and Science Sparks

chris@chris-hart.org